PRAISE FOR
CONSTELLATIONS OF RUIN

"A whirlwind tour of the weird that runs the gamut from touching, to subtly humorous, to downright creepy. Fuller understands, embraces, and shows the full range of the genre."
—A.C. Wise, author of *The Ghost Sequences*

"The 26 diverting speculative shorts of Fuller's debut collection prove entirely transporting."
—*Publishers Weekly*

"Andrew S. Fuller is among the best and most indelible voices in weird fiction today. His collection is a book like no other. These strange and heady tales will take you into worlds of dreams and nightmares, carrying you along with vivid and immersive prose that will take hold of you and not let you go. Put this collection at the top of your reading list."
—Gwendolyn Kiste, three-time Bram Stoker Award-winning author of *The Rust Maidens* and *Reluctant Immortals*

"What an amazing collection of stories. It's Tim O'Brien mixed with Ray Bradbury, literary speculative fiction, sprinkled with dashes of *Black Mirror* and *The Twilight Zone*. Lyrical and poetic, gritty and visceral, this is powerful work. Keep an eye on Andrew Fuller."
—Richard Thomas, Bram Stoker, Shirley Jackson, and Thriller Award nominee

"*Constellations of Ruin* showcases the confident talent of veteran writer and editor Andrew Fuller, and is for any reader who loves lush prose, dark landscapes of the mind, and the unsettling silence after an unanswered question."
—Molly Tanzer, award-winning author of *Creatures of Charm and Hunger* and *Vermilion*

"Fuller's fiction takes you on a journey—to places you only believed you knew. Through light and dark, through memory and miscue, Fuller takes you by the hand and shows you the way."
—E. Catherine Tobler, author of *The Grand Tour* and *The Necessity of Stars*, editor of *The Deadlands* magazine

CONSTELLATIONS OF RUIN

CONSTELLATIONS OF RUIN

STORIES

ANDREW S. FULLER

TREPIDATIO
PUBLISHING

ISBN 978-1-68510-082-7 (tpb)
ISBN 978-1-68510-083-4 (ebook)
Library of Congress Control Number 2022951839

Credits for previous publications appear on page 247, which constitutes an extension of this copyright page.

First printing edition: April 21, 2023
Published by Trepidatio Publishing in the United States of America
Cover artwork and story illustrations by Mikio Murakami
Editing by Sean Leonard
Proofreading by Scarlett R. Algee
Cover design, interior design, and layout by Rew X

Trepidatio Publishing, an imprint of JournalStone Publishing
3205 Sassafras Trail
Carbondale, IL 62901 USA

Trepidatio books may be ordered through booksellers or by contacting:
JournalStone | www.journalstone.com

For those who have always been different,
those who listen, those who stand with,
those who lift up, and those who defy.

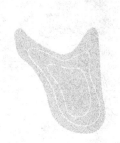

CONTENTS

Another Country Doctor

THE LARGEST RESIDENCE in Flatwater was undoubtedly the Sherborne house, an embellished two-story homestead constructed in the Queen Anne style with wraparound porches and an impressive stable, nestled against an overlooking bluff that enjoyed a fresh creek and a distant view of the upright rock formation called Chimney Rock by some. The only local household family with a cook and servant, Benjamin Sherborne's ferrying and trading fortune having built the five-building town up from an abandoned Pony Express post a full two years before moving his young bride out from Omaha to join him in the sandhills territory.

One rainless night in October, a bright vein ripped the sky and pummeled the bluff with a vivid flare. The earth trembled briefly, but the only damage reported was the unmoored saloon chandelier nearly crushing Miss Melanie, and a bottle of tonic tumbling from the general store's shelf. The sheriff went up the hill and was amazed to find the stately house still standing. Mr. Sherborne reported the thunder nearby and they guessed and noted its location, though dismissed it for lack of fire or calamity.

Soon after, Borne Creek ran gray and thick for a few days with a fusty miasma. The dog Hercules was seen barking and scratching incessantly at the big cottonwood in the front yard, and they found crawdads climbing the trunk and branches until they fell to their demise. Later, crows made a ruckus on the roof, and they ascended a ladder to find a plentitude of five-eyed trout squirming on the wood shingle. While Benjamin told only the doctor about his burning urination, his wife Nora insisted that the drinking water still tasted wildly weird.

The townsfolk organized a party to search the bluff. By midday they found the charred crater in the upper reaches of the creek, but regarding what lay within, everyone had a different story. Some saw a spherical filigree structure like a large crystalline dandelion head, others saw a porous rock that reflected their faces twistingly in its dark pockets, while a few claimed that it pulsed soft and slick like innards exposed in a belly wound—but all agreed that it still glowed crimson though emitting a sharp cold. Heywood was fool enough to touch it without gloves and they said his hand immediately sprouted more fingers, the pops and snaps of splitting bone soon drowned by his screams. With a hatchet they promptly severed his limb at the elbow. Then they wrapped the peculiarity in a horse blanket, rode a good distance into the endless prairie, and buried it with a horseshoe and a crucifix, swearing all men present to forget.

Nora gave birth eight months later. The dog could not stop growling at the newborn and was resigned to the stables. The pastor would not baptize the child, even after Mr. Sherborne's generous offering to the donation plate. The progeny, Emma Jean Sherborne, stood in her crib all night, humming with eyes wide, waving her nine spindly arms toward the moon, or beyond.

They loved the child despite her condition, but without a mouth she could not nurse. Upon her expiration, Benjamin climbed the bluff and buried his daughter under the stars he believed she came from.

Not long after, the founder had the bluff dynamited, the ornate house put on skids, and relocated the entire town twenty-three miles to the west, just beyond the new state line.

It proved a fortuitous move, for the wagon trains resumed after Chief Red Cloud signed a treaty at nearby Fort Laramie, and the railroad's approach was no longer a rumor. Shortly after construction of the depot, they renamed the settlement *Promise*, though it would change at least once more.

Jonathan Montgomery was born three months later, quite unexpectedly since Nora barely showed signs. Though he arrived small in frame, his mother cried with joy and relief at his light pinkish skin, bright expression, and two familiar eyes. His father touched the child's warm blonde head and thanked creation.

All unusualness was forgotten until six years later when young Jonathan Sherborne raised his hand in school and Ms. Granforth counted an additional thumb on him. When he attempted to answer the assignment, his neck swelled like a bullfrog and guttural chirps erupted from his throat. The Sherborne carriage was sent for. The town physician soon followed.

Dr. Hadwell sat on the edge of the bed and reached for the boy's hand, but withdrew. "An eventful day at school, I hear."

"My head feels like *breeeep* a beehive." Jonathan winced.

His parents stood by. Father remained stoic with a slight tremor in his lip. Mother's arm wrapped around his, though by his incline, was more supporting him.

"Are you in pain?" The doctor leaned in, examining the tortuous pattern of red nodules on the boy's cheeks.

"On the contrary, sir. I feel *ssssss* light as a fox, eager to dash about *breeep*." He rustled beneath the covers.

Benjamin Sherborne exhaled loudly.

The doctor donned his spectacles.

"*Breeeep.*"

The physician felt Jonathan's forehead and glands, using a handkerchief to cover his palm. "Not a chill nor a fever—"

"But something is obviously very—" blurted Mr. Sherborne.

"Would you like some sweet tea, dear?" Nora bent to her son. "If that's something he can have, Doctor?"

The doctor affirmed.

"Yes, please, Mother." Jonathan's thumbs danced like busy insect antennae. "And then *ssssss* can I go out and help Esther feed the chickens?"

Dr. Hadwell stroked his graying beard, then opened his black medical case. The boy whimpered when he saw the steel syringe. "Be still now, this calomel is just the thing to help you to rest." He calmed the boy with chloroform before the injection.

"Doctor," Benjamin Sherborne addressed the physician, "if you've concluded your examination, I'd like to speak with you in the library."

Once retired to the oak-finished room, Hadwell politely declined a brandy. "I thought it bilious at first, then phlegmatic... Sir, I've not seen the like..."

"Not since that confounded space stone, you mean." Mr. Sherborne downed his drink in one swallow.

"It isn't cholera returned. But I have journals at my office that might—"

"I think we both know that this is beyond your facility, Doctor."

Dr. Hadwell sighed. He sat on the edge of the one leather wingback chair, nodding his head contemplatively. "We were all relieved when he was born... much unlike his sister. But I often deliberated if that would change as he grew."

"We love him very much, Doctor." Nora appeared in the doorway. "But the residents of our small town will not understand, especially the children his age, his schoolmates or his friends."

"I shall pay for the telegrams, of course." Sherborne gestured to the door with urgency. "Please send them at once to whatever destinations you think best. Chicago, San Francisco, Boston—and I believe we can connect with London now, yes?"

The physician left them with a bottle of blue mass syrup, "for when he's excitable, like today."

The next morning Jonathan's fingernails were missing, and they could not find any fragments among the sheets, bedclothes, or floor. The inflammation in his neck reduced significantly, but his feet bulged to such an extent that he could not put any weight on them without collapsing in pain.

Several days later, shortly after lunch, Nora heard raised voices at the front door and hurried to find their housemaid Esther debating with a young girl on the porch.

"What ruction is this on my doorstep?" Nora asked.

Esther smoothed her apron. "This little lady marched up with a demand or two," she said with surprise and a slight smile.

"Please, missus, this one here won't let me in to see Jonathan." Nora recognized the young redhead as Phebe Maynard, middle daughter of the general store owners, just a year younger than her own son.

"Quietly now, dear. Where are your parents?"

"They's workin, ain't they? Runnin the store." Phebe crossed her arms and took a stance. "And I can walk a mile myself."

"Indeed you can," Nora said. "Though you'll not walk into this house until you find your manners and wipe the soles of your shoes."

Phebe took a breath and folded her hands properly. "I apologize, Miss Esther. I haven't seen my friend in too long, and the teacher won't tell us nothing about his condition."

"Today may not be the best day..." Esther turned to Nora. Indeed the boy's room reeked lately of something like gingko, musky caves, and unknowns.

Nora nodded. "Now, Phebe, if you'll wait in the drawing room like a decent lady, we'll see if Jonathan is up for a brief sitting downstairs."

"Yes'm. Thank you, ma'am." Phebe curtsied quickly, but with grace.

When Mr. Sherborne carried the boy into the parlor and reclined him in the divan with two blankets, Phebe covered her mouth but then took her hand away. His face was taut and pale, except for the shiny flakes like dragonfly wings where eyebrows should be.

"Phebe *brekkkt*, let me see your hands. Hold them out *sssss*."

"Jonathan, I—"

"I'm not *sssss* going to touch you." He smiled. "Don't worry." He coughed.

She showed him her hands, palms and backs.

"Knuckles as red as ever. Still provoking Ms. Granforth and her *sssss* ruler?" He laughed deeper than a healthy young boy.

She giggled with him. "I have to keep them tough to fight that Billy Talbott."

"I'm sorry not to be there *brekkkt* to protect you." He had not blinked since her arrival.

"Protect me?! You're the one got an inkwell poured in your ear."

"But it saved your pigtails *sssss*, didn't it?"

They tittered together, then guffawed. She suggested a game, and they played Jack Straws and Mental Arithmetic and Ducks Fly for nearly two hours. Esther brought them molasses cookies, warm from the oven. Nora listened from the hallway, and never saw the girl stare or ask him when he'd be well again.

When Phebe left that day, she promised to return soon. But when they saw the Maynards at Sunday worship a full two weeks later, the overt smiles they gave indicated it was not the young girl's choice after all. From then on the Sherbornes sent Esther to shop at the general store.

"Mother! Mother!" he cried in the hour past midnight.

Mother came running, Father close behind.

Jonathan sat up in bed, hands cupped tightly like he held a frantic insect.

"My darling, what is it?"

The tears on his cheeks glowed even before they opened the lantern wider.

She sat with him and stroked his lumpen head.

"I was running in my dream, my feet in *sssss* black empty space, with the earth *brekkkt* scrolling above me. And I could not *sssss* catch it." He sobbed and chittered.

When he opened his hands, a dozen teeth cascaded into his lap.

"I'm frightened," he breathed. "I'm so frightened."

She rocked him gently. Benjamin Sherborne set the light aside and put his arms around them.

Within the next week, Jonathan's ears melted like wax then hardened to deep purple prickles that proved venomous when Esther scratched herself serving his soup tray. Her entire arm numbed for five days, and Nora did her best to complete the chores.

The parents considered for some time telling the town that Jonathan had passed, but still retained hope that the blight would lift.

The old dog Hercules got into the house one day and they chased after him up the stairs. Benjamin rushed into the boy's room with the Springfield rifle to find the canine reclined across the bed, gently licking Jonathan's stalactiform hand. They found the noises from his many nostrils to be whistles of delight.

Jonathan's diet changed often. He could stomach only kale and potatoes for two weeks, then he asked for goat meat with wild grape. He ate uncooked sweetcorn for a few days, including the cob and husk. He demanded rotten eggs and sour milk, which Esther exclaimed was ruining her kitchen for all of eternity. They said nothing to each other upon discovering the waste pellets near his bed, dry masses filled with tiny bones and hair like those excreted from an owl, though his windows had not been open for weeks.

Winter was long and harsh, claiming a few horses, and Tipsy Fitzpatrick was found frozen in the alley behind Lucky Spot Saloon. Few doctors would travel in such conditions, even by rail, to attend Jonathan's malady, and their applications proved as ineffective as the previous attempts. Mother read him new stories by Mark Twain, and Father played checkers with him until his secretions ruined the game board.

The Promiseton Gazette
May 14, 1874
SHERBORNE INVESTS IN NEW HOTEL

If all reports are true, Benjamin Sherborne will build a luxurious new three-story venture at the conjunction of Main Street and Third Avenue. Building sketches have been shared with the mayor and Women's Guild, with construction materials already arriving at the spacious plot. Doubtless the fine meals will be too exotic for the palates and wallets of passing cattlehands and persons traveling the long trail to Oregon. A respectable tavern promises to house gentlemanly card games, an icing machine, and stimulating drinks directly inspired from recipes of Europe. Residents welcome Mr. Sherborne's continued investment in our township, but remain concerned if he'll settle the inquires about recent strife, including the queer noises issuing from his property, the maimed cattle at Flying K Ranch, and the poor crop season.

The burlap sack faces of the mob twisted in the torchlight, eyeholes flashed shadow to angry white. They surged toward the Sherborne house where its owner stood firm on the front step with his Winchester .44-40. The voices of thirty-some men shouted for redress, recompense, and retribution.

"Gentlemen, that you've had a sour night at the faro table and can think of nothing else to do but frighten my son is a sad state for our fair town."

"Something ain't right about him! Things ain't been the same since he gone weird!"

"My son's name is Jonathan, and he is indeed ill. But he has nothing to do with any misfortunes of corn nor cow."

"You bring him out here and let us judge that!"

"The first man who sets foot on my porch will be brushing his teeth with rifle shot."

The men grumbled and the group calmed, but only for a moment. A few of them shouted and pressed forward.

Mr. Sherborne fired shallow over their heads. A torch burst into sparks, causing its owner to yelp and let it fall.

"I won't ask which of you is wearing a silver star or a white collar under those masks, but you ought to march this entire lot of scamps and varmints back to town for a hot bath and a stiff drink."

Nora came to the door. "The behavior of you men this evening could shame the backside off a mule."

Benjamin lowered his weapon. "I mean what I say now. Everyone make your way down to Heaven's Fountain where one drink is on my tab. Don't be ashamed to choose a strong coffee. Let's make it an early evening now. Move along."

The horde dispersed, with men waving a finger as they turned away and fewer muttering an apology.

"Go on now," Esther called after them. "Get home and put them loose potatoes back where they belong."

The wailing from the upstairs window melted into the evening sky.

His shoulders sprouted stalks that bloomed azure honeycomb shapes whose openings sang like river reeds. The blonde color of his hair replaced itself with a mosslike green whose strands often swayed as though in a passing current.

They administered opium and laudanum. They gave him loosestrife, stanch weed, and skullcap. They tried wagmu pejuia (wild gourd), heyoka tapejuta (red mallow), and cansinsila (compass plant) from the Indian botanical doctors. They tried stinging nettle from the Platte River banks. They tried the old method of bloodletting, though his color came out laced with thin threads of bright orange. They tried iodine, turpentine, and quinine. They tried garlic, saltpeter, and verdigris. They tried apple cider vinegar with honey. They tried horehound, boxwood, and lobelia. They tried mesmerism and hydropathy and burning manure from a white buffalo. But Jonathan grew more unrecognizable each day.

The night grew so deep that all the world outside felt like a lie. Jonathan had been awake for hours.

"*Sssss* Papa *prrrkt?*" he asked the shadow at the end of his bed.

For a long time there was no answer.

The boy pulled the covers to his rippling face.

"All is well," Benjamin Sherborne whispered, and repeated it slightly louder. Then rose in the moonlight and left the room, his right hand remaining in his nightrobe pocket, sagging heavy with pointed metal.

Dr. Hadwell followed Mr. and Mrs. Sherborne into the library.

"What's on your mind, Doctor?"

He sat heavily and rubbed his eyes. He contemplated only in the direction of the brandy until Benjamin finally brought him a snifter. "I knew a man in the War Between the States and who practiced at Bleeding Kansas as well, a surgeon. He lives in Kansas City now, I believe..."

"Dr. Hadwell," Nora said strongly, "if you insist again on amputation, I will become quite upset."

"As you know, I believe that his true and human body is buried beneath these growths." The doctor held up his glass for another pour. "It is my firm medical opinion that surgery is the final resort to saving the boy."

Nora gestured to the door. "Dr. Hadwell, your services will no longer be needed in this house."

The doctor scowled at her. "Without my professional connections in the medical community—"

"I am quite capable of sending a wire message, maintaining correspondence, and discerning a scholar from a snake oil salesman."

Then he turned to Mr. Sherborne. "Is this your final decision?"

"My wife speaks for us both, and for our son."

"I see." The doctor stood with a huff. He knocked back his drink and set the glass loudly on the end table. He declined a carriage ride and stumbled into the dark.

No one saw the stranger arrive in town on June the nineteenth. He came from the east, not by rail or carriage, shuffling on two feet through the dust.

He entered the Lucky Spot Saloon without any horse or luggage.

The bartender recalled reminding the oddly dressed visitor that it was a drinking establishment, and after ordering "one of whatever you may" that he didn't touch or once look at his poured glass.

A few patrons heard part of a conversation between the new arrival and Dr. Hadwell who was more recently a regular customer and himself halfway down a bottle.

"Who are you, friend? I'd guess by your worn notebook: a journalist, or a writer of dime novels and penny dreadfuls?"

"I was sent for."

"Sent, you say?"

"The tapping rhythms on the wires in the wind."

"We call that a telegraph, mister."

"I heard the message. And I followed the resonance back to its source."

"Your speech is too odd, friend. Did you come from other shores?"

"Another country. A name difficult to vocalize here."

Hadwell stood as straight as he could manage with the bar counter assisting him. "I'll have you know, sir, that I am a learned man. I could name more Latin terms describing the human body than could fill a wagon full of books, a library full, a pasture full."

Witnesses say the stranger did not insult Hadwell further but neither did he offer any apology. Dr. Hadwell's voice rose to shouts, and though he was not known to carry a weapon, asked generally and specifically of many men present if he could borrow their firearm to "inflict required treatment" and "restore his sullied honor in the name of science."

It was not the sheriff who ended the dispute, but Nora Sherborne who not only called loudly from the swinging doors for civilized behavior, but stepped inside the establishment.

"Mrs. Sherborne," said the bartender. "Womenfolk are not allowed—"

"Don't you worry, Mr. Jacobs, I'll stand back outside momentarily with the Negroes and Indians. I was passing by and overheard. And if none of you is gentleman enough to quell a fight with a man of medicine, then I'll speak my displeasure."

"Sherborne?" said the stranger, lifting his odd hat. "Yours is the name I seek."

"Pardon me, sir?"

"Your child is the changing one?"

"My son is sick, yes. His ailments are quite severe."

"I have heard. And come to help."

The stranger placed a large unstamped silver chip on the bar and stood much taller than he seemed before. "Appreciation for refreshment."

———

Mrs. Sherborne and the stranger were mounting the carriage when shouts caught their attention.

Dr. Hadwell had stationed himself stubbornly though rickety in the dirt-packed center of Main Street, a hollering man. Wagons and horses passed close until it was discerned that the doctor had a gun, though no one later admitted to selling or loaning him one.

Despite Nora's protests, the stranger stepped back out of the Sherborne carriage and approached the physician.

Traffic quickly cleared the throughfare, leaving the two figures facing each other by twenty yards.

"You seek conflict," the stranger said in a tone as though he was just understanding.

"I treated that boy for over a year!" The doctor swayed slightly. "I endured his nephroid limbs and molten substances. I will not let—"

"Lee Hadwell," the sheriff called from a side street. "You back out of this now, Doctor. I don't want a skirmish here." He walked out slowly with a calming hand, the other at his sidearm. "This man you're facing down with don't seem to be armed at all."

"Let me be, Sheriff. I've a thing to settle here."

Every window and most of the roughwood walkways filled with people, all watching the scene. A minute seemed a breathless hour.

The stranger raised his writing pad and scribbled.

"You—! What—?!" cried Hadwell, fumbling with his holster.

"Stop!" cried Sheriff Burgess. "Hadwell!"

The stranger barely gestured. A hundred eyes followed the torn script as it fluttered and tumbled the distance between them like a blown leaf.

Hadwell staggered back and tripped, dropping his gun. He scrambled on his bottom as the paper descended, following his movement. He scuttled and turned, swatted and kicked, but the note alighted on his forehead.

The doctor shuddered and tossed with eccentric spasms in the dust. The citizens of Promise gasped. He wheezed and curled. Then he became still.

Sheriff Burgess approached to find him sleeping fast and suckling his thumb.

———

The carriage leaned to one side as they rode out to the Sherborne place. At the door, Esther tried to take Nora's coat, but without removing her riding gloves the lady of the house showed the newcomer immediately upstairs to the boy's room. Jonathan's seeping eyes widened as the visitor ducked under the door frame.

Towering over the bed, he inclined deeply and squinted at the trembling boy-shape. Then his face upturned a calming smile.

Jonathan buzzed through his tight face-vent lined with thin artichoke heart-like filaments.

"Nora? I didn't hear you arri—? Oh..." Benjamin entered, and froze in place.

"He is many seasons unlike you," said the stranger.

"The ailments began months ago, and no one can help us curb the symptoms."

The stranger plucked one of the few remaining hairs from Jonathan's head. He put the strand in his mouth, drew it across his magenta tongue, and smacked his lips.

"What exactly is your area of expertise, Mister...?"

"Not sick," said the stranger, standing to his full height. "He is altered, evolved, differentiating by moment."

"I can assure you, we've employed every medicine available, including Chinese arts and herbs from the Sioux and Pawnee tribes."

"Pardon." The stranger removed his hat and bowed slightly to them. He spoke with untypical cadence, but in a euphonious tone. "His body tissues are changed, so too the liquids and tiny cubicle parts that compose these, and smaller, the twin helix codes that declare all of his being—"

"I don't fully understand—" Benjamin stammered.

"You recall, Benjamin, I was recently reading the papers of Louis Pasteur—" Nora began.

"Numbers," said the stranger, opening his notepad. "At the smallest place, very small, below size or scale—numbers make him, as they make all things." He rolled his peculiar pen that seemed more of a thorn or tooth along the paper as if to warm it, then took it up. "Now you leave. I fix his numbers."

Benjamin huffed and blinked. Nora led him out.

They waited in the library where Esther brought a snack that no one ate. She sat too and joined the silence.

At one point Nora excused herself, claiming to need an extra wrap against the chilled evening, but she stopped to glance in the keyhole of her son's room. She returned downstairs pale and silent.

Later the screams sounded like a rabbit caught by a wolf. They rushed upstairs.

At first the door wouldn't budge, though the knob turned fully and the latch was clear, as pressure like an ocean held it from the opposite side. When the cries finally faded, the door creaked open on its own, with the stranger oddly across the room and seated.

Scraps of notebook paper covered every surface, across walls and ceiling and floor, several overlapping layers in proximity to the bed. Every sheet ran dense with equations and long strings of numbers, written in several pigments of ink.

"He is redone," said the stranger, pocketing his notebook, which seemed curiously no more depleted than before.

From atop the pooled mess of fluids and odd matters on the bed, a boy with bright blue eyes and full auburn hair called to his parents. They ran to him. He jumped out of bed and embraced them and pointed down where he wiggled ten toes.

No one saw the stranger leave the room, altogether smaller than when he'd arrived.

Jonathan returned to school within the week. He was enthusiastic but still answered most of the lesson questions incorrectly. Billy Talbot pushed him down every day, and when he tried to fight back the larger boy broke his nose. Phebe was glad to see him and that was something. He often fell silent at meals. Once he remarked to Esther that he longed to see again the vibrant and sonorous country. Knowing that he had never traveled anywhere she inquired as to his meaning, but he replied that it must have been a dream. One night Nora found her son crouched by his new bed and assumed he was praying, only to see him stuff something under the mattress. She investigated the following day while he was at school and found nothing.

Attempting to head off the peak of summer heat, the Sherbornes opted for a picnic, riding a few miles north where a formation of rocky granite outcrops provided shade. They ate cheese and walnuts with grapes and bacon, and drank cider.

A company of the United States Army 7th Cavalry rode up rather suddenly and startled them.

"Recommend you folks return to town," the blue uniformed major told them from his horse. "The hostiles have been restless and straying. You're close to the edge of the Powder River Country."

"Why should there be any trouble now when not before?" Nora asked.

"If you haven't heard, ma'am, Lt. Col. Custer recently declared gold found in the Black Hills and droves of people are moving into the Indian land..."

As the soldier spoke, the boy wandered off through tall prairie grass.

If they called his name he didn't hear, shuffling his bare feet in the warm sandy soil. In less than one hundred yards, he came to a small bluff, climbed to its plateau, and pulled a sheet of paper from his pocket. He recalled the moment that the stranger had given it to him, and the whispered words as he hid that last scrawled page in the foot trunk.

Jonathan folded the inked script neatly until it was small enough to place on his tongue. Then he sat comfortably and surveyed the vistas and prospects stretching around and above him, as he waited for the changes to come.

Elizabeth's Duty

THE TEAM KNEW it was a different kind of mission, not because it was the first with her along, but ten minutes out they showed only uncustomary silence. Bradford and Girvin were usually smacking each other's helmets, Moss deep in his headphones, Sprague checking his gear, Lunt praying. Instead, they sat still and serious in the rumble of the C-130 aircraft, glancing at or away from Dimmy as he fed Elizabeth. He held fresh crayfish to the open end of the canister slung to his tactical vest, and a winding suckered arm pulled the crustacean inside, more arms emerging at each portion. At 20:40 hours, the jump light flashed red as the deployment ramp lowered, letting in the roar of turboprop engines. Elizabeth retreated into her tube, and Dimmy fastened the lid as the jump light turned green.

Team Leader Hamar signaled, and they tumbled out into the cold dark sky. They dropped fast and opened low. Dimmy flared his chute for extra lift before they hit the water in consideration of her soft body.

The ocean heaved and rolled. They dove, leaving behind the crisp starred sky and their chutes bobbing at the surface like giant jellyfish. They sank from black to blacker, adjusting their re-breather tri-mix, as prototype suits massaged their muscles and drew nitrogen through their pores. Twenty minutes later they touched bottom, dropped the sink weights, and fitted fins.

Several crabs scuttled nearby and though it was early in the mission, Dimmy released Elizabeth. Team Leader Hamar glared through his diving mask. They checked the compass and sea floor map while she hunted and dined. When Dimmy signaled to her with a headlight flash, she latched to his arm, and they proceeded to their objective.

They came across the basin from the southwest. The topography had changed from the latest bathymetry map, with several new canyons and spires along the way. When the floor started to rise, they knew the target was close.

At 21:47 hours, Team Zero came to a massive stone wall extending into the murk, rough with coral and waving kelp. Less than three minutes later they located the arched door from grainy briefing photos, the size of a median house. The intricate design in relief at its center comprised of nautilus, tentacle, dentiform, and spinose patterns woven into the barnacled surface.

Dimmy flashed commands at Elizabeth and she set to work. Her eight arms curled and explored.

No one forgot that day after the unusually large waves receded when five figures came ashore near the Lincoln Memorial and marched up Constitution Avenue and 17th Street NW in bright azure plate armor to lay down their golden barbed spears on the south lawn of the White House. Their leader removed his bubble helmet, knelt before President Henderson, then spoke in croaking syllables, and waited in that obsequious position for thirty-four minutes while thirteen scholars from across the international theater worked over an encrypted network to rudimentarily translate using incomplete tablet fragments of Minoan, Ugaritic, and proto-Berber written languages.

Some said his face was covered in silver scales, while others reported orange skin with a leafy green beard and gills instead of ears. Some television viewers saw a gelatinous mound containing three dark floating masses, or a segmented bony stack, or long soft cheeks with a thin protrusion from the forehead dangling a tiny bright light that hung over a wide underbite of translucent needle teeth. A few people said they saw a man with ashen complexion and faded blonde hair but a strong jawline and pupils of the deepest aquamarine.

The royal visitor apologized humbly for the sudden upheaval of his continent and the tsunami that had submerged Miami and Charleston (though he did not mention Norfolk, Virginia). Then he held up his pale webbed hand, offering a woven gold-copper ball, each thick cord bearing a unique pattern. After a handshake, applause, and photographs, the being whose name approximately translated to *King Mneseus* shared a flask of water from his homeland with the President of the United States. Then he returned with his radiantly armored sentries into the sea.

For the next few weeks, the new land mass remained motionless and quiet off the eastern coast of North America. The gilded ball gift was examined extensively, though scanners could not penetrate its surface, and once determined harmless it was returned to the first family in Washington, DC. The hidden message inside was revealed days later when the President Henderson's daughter dropped the spheroid into the White House Library aquarium tank, and their pet octopus Desmond dismantled the knotted ball in minutes.

Written on kelp papyrus material in perfect inscriptional capitals with true sepia ink were the words THIS LAND IS OUR LAND.

President Henderson collapsed during the secure link video conference with military generals and advisors. The damage to his intestines by the young but aggressively maturing zebra mussels was beyond surgical repair. After taking the oath of office, former Vice President Kerwin Jixby's first executive order was the evacuation of Manhattan as a rapid coral infestation flooded the city and soon overwhelmed entire neighborhoods. His second order was an air strike against the Atlantic Ocean's new continent. After the bombardment, the immense limpet-like dome covering the hostile territory remained unscathed.

Only after the CVN-71 *Harry S. Truman*, last remaining aircraft carrier in the east coast fleet, capsized off Myrtle Beach with massive ring-shaped abrasions in its hull, and the SSN-824 *Raleigh* submarine disappeared near Blake-Bahama Ridge did Commander in Chief Jixby reconsider their options.

A few seconds of footage from a remote submersible revealed the apparent stone door at +32.144300, -79.381714 at a depth of 203 meters before the screen crowded with violent flashes of silver fins and long teeth, and the drone's transmission ceased. The room full of analysts argued first whether the attack had been barracuda or marlin, and then about the elegant entwined motif on the door. But it was an intern bringing coffee who glanced at their monitor and said, "They obviously like puzzles." She found herself thinking of a young man she'd dated briefly in college, before he'd dropped out and enlisted. Three of their five outings had been to aquariums.

He pushed with all his weight to open the door for Mom, and, seeing it was a dark building, held her hand. Other families passed as they paused at the first colorful display, and Dimitri learned about pelagic and benthic and slopes and basins, and he crunched and slurped his snowcone patiently as he waited for her to read every exhibit panel and every note. They followed the floor lights around to the first tank and watched the sea bass and the kingfish for a few minutes, though he found their colors dull, while the pufferfish remained shriveled and unexciting. They saw the clownfish and triggerfish, then sea turtles and cownose rays. He nearly ran into a large glowing tube in the middle of the room filled with unhurried seahorses. Next came catfish and damselfish and hagfish. They saw strawberry anemone, ochre starfish, and purple sea urchins. He learned the words *nudibranch* and *stichopus*.

They came to a tank filled with coral and rocks where nothing moved. There was no name plate identifying any particular species. "They must be cleaning this one," Mom said, and walked on.

Dimitri didn't feel her hand slip from his. He peered at something among the splotches of red and pale green and blue. A black horizontal slit. Then a tail or a feeler unrolled nearby, and then three more. He realized what she was and stepped closer. Her entire body flashed white. He put his hand gently against the thick glass and her skin rippled to fiery red. He waited and said nothing aloud. Soon she resumed the color of the rocks around her, and unfurled, emerging. She glided and crawled with graceful arms over the tank's sandy floor and spread herself over the glass between them, undulating and dancing in eight directions.

When Mom came back for him the blue raspberry snowcone had soaked through the paper cup, dripped down his arm, and formed a dark puddle on the floor, but he had not noticed at all.

Bradford and Sprague kept their spearguns pointed into the midnight water behind them; Girvin and Lunt covered the wider angles with the sonic mortars. Dimmy watched Elizabeth's many arms loop around the braids of stone, meandering and examining, then she squeezed her whole body between the decorated knots, slipping in, around, over, and back again. He kicked closer and bumped his mask when he noticed that the embellished patterns etched spirally along each thick weave were comprised of a finer string of symbols, strange and beautiful. Their orders included complete radio silence with the service and team members, and he guessed the analysts couldn't decipher these anyway.

Leaning over his shoulder, Hamar saw this. He tapped his wrist and shook his head. He signaled to Moss, who immediately unshouldered his satchel and slipped his finger into the ring of the primer wire. Dimmy grabbed his arm, even knowing he was delaying the mission.

Hamar did not hesitate to draw his combat knife.

They floated there, eyeing each other.

Dimitri Patroclus wished all at once to be in a bar with his team leader and enough time for a chat over a cheap cold beer and a shot of mediocre rye, for a fish to swim between them, for someone to say something, to be a more articulate man, for a different world altogether.

From within the great stone door came a series of heavy mechanical thunks. The men turned to see Elizabeth swim clear just as the tangled design unlaced and withdrew, fitting seamlessly into smooth recess.

The heavy grinding creak vibrated the water around them. They cleared and maintained formation as the tremendous door retracted in two thick curved slabs. There in that moment, staring into the dark tunnel and the Continental Slope dropping off behind them, Dimmy's training faltered and he warmed his wetsuit. He swam ahead before the team leader could signal. Elizabeth followed.

Mom let him borrow the car, and he arrived at Jenny Felsmeyer's house five minutes early for their third date. She answered the door, excited at first, and then told him that, actually, she'd just realized she had a ton of homework to do. He noticed her bangs stood in a perfect hairspray primp above her purple eyeliner and pink lip gloss, recently refreshed, and her new bleached jeans. More primped than she appeared at school.

"Well, okay, what are you doing later?" he asked.

"Maybe going out..." She looked at him and then away.

Then he realized. "But not with me."

"I'm sorry, Dimitri. I'm sorry. It's just that I've been waiting for Mark Tessman to ask me out, and today he—"

"You asked *me* out, Jennifer. Twice."

"He's quarterback of the football team—"

"Not the swim team."

"I'm sorry."

Maybe she really was.

He was driving then, and the streets felt too small. He was nervous merging onto the highway at first, less than a month with his license. He followed the signs and it took over an hour to reach Omaha. It had been a long time, and he'd never been there by himself before, so he stopped and asked directions to the aquarium.

Once inside the admission gate, he smelled salt water immediately. The first thing he heard was the sea lions, and he went to watch them; their bodies, clumsy on land, would soar and roll like magic underwater. He did not stop at the hands-on tidepool area, and he passed quickly through the new shark tunnel where, despite the signs for no talking, persons of every age shouted in exclamation. The glowing sea dragon display was gone, replaced by a talking kiosk. He felt unfulfilled, and wandered to the last exhibit.

The suckered arms trailed down the right edge of the glass. It wasn't the same one. The sign said his name was Harold. His soft stippled mantle expanded and contracted in the upper corner. Dimitri pressed his hand against the window's center. Harold sent one long appendage over to investigate, and soon the rest of him followed. Then he clung to the glass before him, swirling, rippling, twining, and waving, as Dimitri wiped his wet eyes.

"Octopus. Hey, octopus! Hello!" The girl, maybe seven years old, rapped the tank window with four manicured fingernails. She paused to blow a bubble with her large portion of gum. Then she smacked and pounded the glass with her palm. "Over here, Mr. Octopus! Hey!"

Harold retreated to a crevice in the rocks.

"Even if you can't read, you should definitely know better." Dimitri pointed to the sign along the bottom sill that read PLEASE DO NOT TAP ON THE GLASS.

The girl stared at him with a face of incredulity and irritation, then ran off.

He was watching Harold fade from white to the color of the rocks when the father found him a few minutes later. "You? Was it you?! What did you say to my daughter? I should call security." He stood very close, pointing his finger at Dimitri's face.

Dimitri pointed again at the sign and said nothing.

"It's my family, see?" The man's neck turned mottled red and the skin puffed around his eyes. "You don't talk to her that way. You mind your own damn business." He bumped his chest against Dimitri and backed away slowly, still exuding provocation.

After that, Dimitri let the cool air in the penguin house wash over him for a few minutes as the birds slid and dove.

On his way toward the exit, he walked by the otter exhibit and saw the family again, the dad holding his video camera to film afternoon feeding time. Without thinking, Dimitri knelt behind them, pretended to tie his shoe, then grabbed the man's ankles and pitched him over the railing. He heard splashes, exclamations, and a scream as he walked calmly into the crowd.

He'd decided he wanted to attend college near the ocean.

Headlamps off, they swam along the tunnel wall in utter dark, advancing blindly with cautious initiative. Meters melted into miles, curves and rises became indiscernible. At one point, the water pulled strong to their left and warmed as something huge and featureless passed them.

Dimmy saw shapes in the black, squirming glistening threshing forms, and closed his eyes. The shapes lingered and finally faded. He told himself his tank was running low, that these were dizzy hallucinations, just reach the objective, and swam on. Nothing touched him... not so far.

When the glow appeared overhead, Hamar led them up into the narrow vertical tube, the walls lined with sharp helicoid symbols carved in long waving patterns that swelled and tapered to a strait and swelled again.

Elizabeth had kept pace alongside but began to lag. When Dimmy offered the canister, she crawled in immediately.

They held position at a five-meter depth as Lunt ascended to just below the edge of the circular pool. He extended the fiber optic camera into the air above. He turned to them and pointed to his eyes, then held up one finger.

The short count was not protocol, and perhaps why Hamar seemed to hesitate very slightly before he gave the go signal.

They rose weapons first, slowly and evenly spaced around the moonpool's perimeter.

The vaulted room was held high by pillars laced with engraved copper and iridescent shells and embellished tin. They heard running water, and high above them, aqueducts flowed across the ceiling, inverted and open.

A long copper table occupied the center space, its surface depicting an unconventional world map with finely etched ocean floors and trenches contoured around flat featureless land masses—almost familiar continents, misshapen and shrunk. At the table's far end, a solitary figure sat hunched over bright metallic fragments. "I heard your many bubbles approaching."

"You are speaking English? Identify yourself!" Hamar shouted, chin tucked behind the aim of his H&K MP7 submachine gun.

Sprague and Moss flanked either side of the table. Bradford and Girvin moved about, clearing the alcoves.

"Identify yourself!" Hamar repeated.

The figure stood with grace and without fear. "I am Mneseus of the Forgotten Number, of the Terrain Below, of the Vythisméni Póli, of the Veiled Crown. And I can hear the water in your blood."

To Dimmy he appeared mostly like a man but with cinnamon marbled skin, stippled eyebrows, and baleen for teeth.

"One of you is gifted." He brought his scaled hands up before him, cupped.

Hamar's firing pin clicked. And clicked again. Then Sprague's gun did the same.

Mneseus opened his webbed fingers. The threaded ball was woven with copper, gold, and red metals, inscribed with forgotten glyphs. "Whichever of you opens this may leave here alive."

Hamar drew his Sig Sauer M11 pistol, aimed in a trained stance, and the trigger clicked and clicked. He holstered his sidearm and unsheathed his tactical blade, and the king laughed with the thunder of crashing waves.

The entire floor became at once sheer and thin. And they saw the things that waited below, spinous and writhing.

Bradford and Girvin screamed.

The CO took him into a large room. The first thing Dimmy saw was a large assembly of thick transparent plastic tubes like a giant hamster maze, with passages shaped in corkscrews and cones, hourglasses and boxes. Then he saw the bubbling tank in the bottom corner of the setup, and the red suckered tentacles trailing from the submerged toy castle. He barely noticed the man in the lab coat.

"Sir, may I?" Dimmy nodded at the tank.

"At ease."

Dimmy touched the glass. She came out and said hello with all of her arms. His hand trembled and he felt joy.

"Her name's Elizabeth," the professor said.

Then she performed for Dimmy, moving through all the chambers, changing shape, unlocking every barrier, showing off.

Dimmy dove into the moonpool and swam hard without looking back. The dark of the tunnel swallowed him. He released Elizabeth and followed her with his headlamp. Something caressed his leg and he slashed with his knife. From all around came the deep groaning shift of rock. The wall moved away from him and more stone pressed in from above. He dodged and tumbled and resumed. Space quivered and folded as they moved through the bleak gloom. His legs burned and his lungs screamed. He focused on Elizabeth's darting form just ahead. Training moved his body, and he kicked and kicked with his swimming fins and kept on. When the battery on his headlamp died, he could no longer discern if he was moving or awake as the inky loneliness devoured him.

He saw the sky briefly. Hamar slapped him and smiled. He heard the hiss of decompression.

Black fell again.

The president met them at an undisclosed Air Force base, where the three human survivors of Team Zero stood at attention, Lunt on his one remaining leg. Hamar dumped the mission bag onto the tarmac, and Dimmy maintained his eyes front as the damp defiant head of King Mneseus rolled into the afternoon sun, along with the variegated metal ball. The commander in chief pinned Navy Cross medals to their dive suits and shook their hands.

They placed the puzzle ball into Elizabeth's tank, but she would not touch it. At Dimmy's suggestion, former President Henderson's octopus Desmond was brought in. Nor could he unlock the artifact, but the two mollusks mated for the first and final time of their lives.

Overnight, the island briefly called Atlantis sank again into the salted waters.

At 00:08 UTC the following day, coastal winds brought a deafening song to every shore, as seven more coral-armored continents surfaced in oceans across the planet, trumpeting millions of furious conch shell breaths in one proclaimed cry to rise.

Occupations

IT WAS A quiet morning around the breakfast table. Even the baby seemed in a ruminative mood. After ten minutes, Karen spoke first. "Going into the office today?" she asked her husband.

"Just like every Wednesday." Jim resumed sucking his meal through the nutritube.

"I just thought maybe you could use some flex time today, maybe you'd like to spend some time with your family." She adjusted the baby's solar bib, selected carrot-pea-mango on the Lazy Susan's keypad, and seated herself. The baby cried until a new sterilized straw extended from the console to his mouth.

"I'm on contract," he reminded her. "You know that. No benefits, no vacation until the project is done." The window adjusted its tint, dimming the sun's glare off the other condo towers.

Karen sighed and nodded. She selected omelette-blueberry-waffle-orangejuice.

They finished breakfast in near silence, only slurping.

"Full day ahead. Better get a head start." Jim excused himself from the table and walked over to the sofa. He uncoiled the silver wire from the coffee table and thumbed the glowing tip of the fiber spike. He settled into the cushion, plugged the port behind his ear, placed the rune in his mouth, his foot in the iron bucket of salt water, and then paused. "Carpool?"

Even with her eyes on him, Karen did not answer immediately. He knew that she wanted to ask her own question, to pause the routine, and he waited for it with jaw clenched, resisting the urge to look at his watch.

Instead, she smiled and said, "Sure." She lifted the baby from the high chair and followed. She adjusted the child's connection and drew a crescent on his forehead with ashes of alder, then she placed two silver coins on her eyes and tucked seaweed in her ears. She kissed her husband.

Together, they touched the crystal ball and dove in.

They flitted the ether, riding the cumin essence track until they could merge with the digisilk boulevard. They dropped the baby off at the nursery ziggurat where he would learn his symbols and play cuckoo tattleball with his friends, while his surplus naptime synapses fed improvement of the peripheral scrimshaw networks. Karen veered away at the server gyre and Jim continued his commute. Traffic bottlenecked at the wicker bypass, and he tried a shortcut on some passing tags of whale song, but they wouldn't hold. Jammed, he unraveled the light strand memoglyphs to brief himself on today's assignment. Generic corporate motiprep, the usual words and graphics about iterative process, megamilestones, and depth mining. Eventually the flow resumed. When he came to the ingress, he sighed and plunged in.

The project expanse formed around him. He felt his million co-workers assembled alongside, brigades aligned into the crimson distance. The template floor spread away from their feet in an instant, swimming flat smoke spotted with glimmering heather brush and darting neon details. Behind them, the fortified data keep pulsed, a thunderhead of spinning wisp and substance, scrolling and threading with dynamic cuneibytes. They waited, anxiously gripping their scriptiblades, until the voltaic whistle sounded for work to begin.

The divining stats had been right. With a crepitant shimmer, the Bonoto-Vich army rezzed in on the opposite side, mounted on jittering abstract steeds. They lowered their logo lances and charged, howling hexes as they rode. It was a branding war.

The skirmish lasted all day. The competitors advanced with campaign trebuchets and viral market rams. They pummeled the front lines with brainstorm howitzers and focus group javelins. They unleashed berserker interns from the hinterfarms and expert variable archers, which slew many of the freelance ranks. Jim cleaved their chief commlusionist from head to groin and inspired a devastating final assault.

When the pixel dust settled and the enemy survivors limped away, the project floor smelled of ozone and sweat and death. The victors gathered the data spoils and filtered them into the hubernacle. Jim received pats on the back and sensiglyphs when the team hunkered around a packet fire. They downed defragging lager and bellowed songs of victory. Some polished their weapons, while most of them slept until endchime. They were rising to leave when a new work order danced in their eyeboxes.

A large army appeared on the horizon, some of their forms so massive that they blurred in the margins. They roared and chanted, pumping the air with gigantic subpoena shovels and propaganda truncheons, swinging zealotry cleavers. Jim's resolve weakened and he saw the huebodies of his colleagues dim as well. Exhausted and outnumbered, knowing that few had ever won against the Ecclesial Branch, the most powerful arm in the pentacle of the AmalgaNation. He sent off a note to his wife saying he'd be working another extended shift, and tint-coded it with his final will and a copy of the life insurance policy he'd hacked together from open source and the gray market.

He forgot who he was for a time, wading all night in entropy and blood.

He stumbled off the commuter couch just before dawn and found her asleep on the Murphy plasma platform, holding their very small son. He stood over them, sore and weary, feeling a strum of jealous resentment behind his eyes that seethed and deepened, making him heavier by the second, until he wanted to shout and wake them, and then scream.

But he knew it was exhaustion, and he held his breath and trembled in place until it passed. He reminded himself of the fight that she made every day, hurling her persistent voice in the marble briarpatch coliseum, one determined shout against the rulers and their mutant champions, against the misdirected multitudes, in the name of choice. He knew her fortitude and her boundless patience with him. He loved her so much that he forgot his fatigue for a moment and didn't hear the first few knocks at the door. He answered with eyes half-closed.

His neighbor Bill Yoskopf told him the news and he could not believe it, but he knew what needed to be done. There was little time.

They descended on the floating carpet to the parking garage, where they watered and saddled the horses. They rode to the edge of town where the men and boys and others gathered with billiard cues and broomstick handles and chair legs and boards with nails in them and antique sticks from an extinct ball game.

And they waited for the enemy of their way of life.

Stationed at the Breach

WARD WAS OUT buying groceries for the second time when she left. He had come home once missing a few items on the shopping list, and she'd raised her voice about how he was always distracted, and he'd admitted quietly that was true and apologized, and he'd driven back to the store.

He paused in the produce department when a giant bristle-skinned serpent with two saw-beaked heads emerged from an oozing rip in reality and tried to consume a shopper very immersed in selecting butternut squash. Ward dropped his broccolini bundle, focused, and pushed the monster back through. Then, at the deli counter he tried to order mesquite smoked turkey in sandwich-thin slices but stopped mid-sentence when an amethyst cloud swarming with teeth seeped from another fault in space and poured over the nearby customers. So he concentrated and repelled it, losing his place in line when the employee saw his eyes go distant and pointed with plastic gloves to the next customer. Nothing happened in aisle nine near the spices except two families blocking the way with large race car shopping carts; no distractions, he had simply forgotten to write down onion salt.

On the way home the second time, he thought of her when the other car horns jolted his attention at the traffic light that had been green for a few seconds. She would have told him to *Go go go! God almighty, pay attention! Do I have to drive? Where is your mind right now?* And he likely would not have said anything in response because she was right. He closed and cauterized the rumbling gorge in the middle of the intersection, then drove home again in silence.

Walking in the front door, he could sense it, but not yet admit. He felt the silence from basement to attic, but he checked anyway, walking slowly through the rooms, trying to avoid his denial. There were no rips or attacks where he searched. Twice he passed the handwritten note on the hallway table before seeing it. The first few words broke his life.

He sobbed and could not hold himself up, falling to his knees where he rocked and howled. He collapsed forward with face buried in his arms as he wailed, trying to say her name.

He told himself that she'd been taken, that they'd broken the rules and come through in his absence, and dragged her off—or consumed her and lapped up every spot of blood. That they'd torn the ring from her finger and left it atop the note to torment him. He tried to blame them and to make himself really actually believe it, but he knew why, had always known it would lead to this.

While he cried and rolled his forehead against the hardwood floorboards, the air in the living room crackled and split and something with a hyena grin and two ebony tails dripping with venom came at him swiftly on three legs. Feeling he had nothing left, he turned to face it.

The despair behind his eyes billowed forth and struck the intruder; he lifted and held it and let more of what he felt come forth and turn the creature inside out. He let the thing twitch and experience the pain for many minutes, then he released the rest of his anguish with a scream and blazed it into bitter smoke.

Later he read the note.

> Ward,
>
> I can't do this anymore. I asked you to work on this, but you just wouldn't. You have no idea how alone I feel. You never had time for me. I will always love you and this breaks my heart. I can never divorce you, please don't try. And don't try to find me.
>
> —L

Sleep escaped him, the bed felt excavated and frozen, but still smelled like her. It was like someone else's house, someone else's life. He caught himself holding his breath as he listened for the phone and imagined her voice. He didn't think of the arguments, the shouting, the silent disappointments, the resentment, the ultimatums. All at once he thought of the good times, the companionship, the laughter, the sex. Visualizing her face brought the heavy tears back, and he had no blame for her.

He lay wearily against the pillows and sheets when they came again for him. Wet glowing threads sprouted from the dark corners of the bedroom, blossomed into wings claws faces bulbous bodies and hung over him. He cried and no longer cared. The things from another place folded closer, tasting the misery, and sensing no more defiance from him, they reared to strike. Coiled and craving, they hissed and chortled and sniggered in the dark. He was resigned to let them win, delighted to be done forever; it would all be over in seconds. Briefly he considered if they would miss conflict, perhaps miss him.

But they hesitated. Whether they thought it a deception on his part, or some other atrocious duty came to their attention. In that part of a second he found a shard of indignation within himself and a surprising impulse, and pierced punctured impaled each sac and limb and organ of the malformed aberration. The deed left many foul fluids and vapors, and after the extermination he cleaned the sheets and scrubbed floor.

The deaths that came in his dreams were savage and extended. But in them, she was still home. He did not wake for three days.

The familiar shapes cooed over him and he kicked his limbs with glee. He gurgled and sputtered, they murmured back, tickling his soft pudgy chin. He couldn't roll yet, but he was dry and fed and happy. They clucked and fussed over him, then made complex noises to each other. They leaned into the crib and touched his face with theirs in a warm pleasing nuzzle.

Then the space behind them darkened and sour things unfurled and descended. He screamed and kicked in warning, but his favorite shapes turned to each other in confusion. They smiled and rubbed his tummy. The things behind hissed acid pulses forming mucus limbs and frightful openings, surrounding what he loved, constricting to steal them. He kicked, flailed helpless fists against his head, too small, frustrated on his back, too far—and he reached. A sudden bolt fired between their heads and into the bad feral storm. He raked it, shook it, twisting rip, broke it hard, shoved it out. Then his parents lifted him up, wooed and tutted and patted his back until the gas came out *urp!* and he stopped crying.

Bewildered now that he understood their words to each other. Though he would not speak for five years.

"Your father asked you a question," Mom said.

He shifted in his seat and examined his plate.

No one said anything for several protracted seconds. Mom changed her approach slightly. "You know," and she paused, blinking a few times with the faint click of contact lenses. "Your sisters always tell us about their day. It would be nice, for once, if you'd share with the family."

He pushed the last bite of cold slimy green pepper to the edge of his plate, hoping it would look smaller there and go somehow undetected.

"Yeah," Arlene said, trying to sound adult. She picked something from her braces.

Dad didn't say anything while he added barbeque sauce to his casserole.

Erin tried to meet his eyes, offering apology and support. She asked what was for dessert, but everyone else looked at Ward.

Click click went Mom's contact lenses.

Ward raised his eyes and forgot they were there. He stared out the window where the tall maple tree in their backyard swayed like something deep undersea while the neighbor's trees stood still. He watched cave-white tendrils spin from the maple's branches, the leaves shrivel and scream as they fell. The huge trunk uprooted itself and crashed across the yard, shedding its bark to reveal a livid twisting crimson body, as hundreds of fibrous legs propelled it toward the bay window, and the roots whipped in layers of a steaming hagfish mouth.

Ward unhinged. Face inert, he reached inside, then lashed forth. When the thing was destroyed, he slumped in his chair, feeling not just exhausted but that some of him was missing, that he had lost a year of his life.

Seconds later, Mom squeezing his arm, then shaking it angrily. She said his full name and called him *young man* and said *answer me*. She sent him to his room, which she hadn't done since he'd been four years old.

Nathan was the best friend he would ever have. They became immediate companions in second grade when the seating chart put them together and they discovered a mutual need to draw space battles with copious amounts of yellow and red crayon. At recess they created high adventure against troll armies, extremely territorial bat people, and more nefarious enemies. Ward often found it easy to include his own unseen duties into their playground scenarios.

Every single day he wished that he could ride the bus with Nathan and live with his family forever. Ward often thought how much he wanted to tell Nathan about the things he saw. He imagined that he would teach his friend, and they could fight together, always side by side. No one had taught him any of this, he had made up his own rules. But Nathan could not see them, no one else could. He feared more than anything that his friend might think him too imaginative or insane.

For two years they were inseparable. Until the final week of the third grade when Nathan announced during show-and-tell about his dad's new job in Omaha. An hour's drive away, but it might as well be Saturn or ancient

Mesopotamia! Ward concentrated to keep himself from crying. When the tears racked him so hard that he had difficulty stopping the madrill-colored hydra jaws from consuming Sheila Beckwith, and his breath came in loud helpless gulps, Ms. Eberhart sent him to the nurse.

Nurse Benyon encouraged him to rest while she called his parents, and he knew it wasn't a good idea. His heart felt full of ragged glass, and he slipped into an exhausted sleep on the cold vinyl medical table. Long enough for the things to rend a gulch in the sky over the school and send through a teeming maelstrom that blotted most of the sun.

He was barely awake when Nurse Benyon pulled him into the hallway where the tornado klaxon blared over screaming kids ushered along by teachers, everyone covering their ears. The building groaned around them, deep thunder peaked behind the clamor. Teachers instructed kids to crouch under the coat racks along the wall, and they crawled under the benches with hands behind their heads. Lost and numb and disheartened, Ward complied.

There came sounds like thousands of cicadas and dying rabbits and shattering forests.

As the noise subsided, he dared to glance, expecting swirls of chaos, malevolent split eyes, sharp lash tongues sucking the children into a glowing oily gullet... But the hallway was empty and calm, without the slightest breeze stirring a coat sleeve or tumbling a single scrap of paper. Until he saw Sheila Beckworth shuffle around the corner, whimpering, glancing, hugging herself, petrified.

Then he saw the horrid mass of flesh and tentacles and gibbous vacuoles flood the hallway, churning forward, bursting through doors, and envelop her. He watched the tendrils wrap around her arm, the skin inflamed by stinging spurs before she screamed. A long serrated jaw snapped along her other arm, sinking needle teeth with each bite until it reached the shoulder, then crunched full force, bringing her cries. When other claws seized her legs, the huge mouth spun and pulled, tearing the limb away. She moaned in awful disbelieving pain and plea as cilia undulated over her clothes, reared and sharpened, then pierced her body.

One of the teachers ran to her aid as hooked tentacles wound up her legs. A silver-tipped red appendage lashed out from the mass, his head and arm fell to the floor.

Ward thought selfishly of Nathan for a moment, and drank his own sadness, and let too many more seconds pass before he stood. And checked out. And let his eyes go. The thing stopped feeding and dropped what remained of Sheila.

He saw it ripple with fear. And he reached.

He cut a ragged swath across the neighborhood. He pulverized the seething tempest, crushed and blistered magnesium hot, scorched pounded pushed shucked and ripped it to less and lesser shrivel press cram wrench tear go nothing die die die!—be *gone*.

In the aftermath, the playground was a smoldering ruin, the cafeteria caved in, and the library fire burned all night. The newspaper reported Sheila and Mr. Remington killed by flying glass, and the tornado estimated at F4.

At age eight, he guessed he would always be alone.

Nathan called on Ward's birthday, but it had been too many months; they didn't know what to say and it felt weird. Then his family moved again, out of state, and they lost contact with each other.

Junior high school was not worth mentioning.

He and Sharon had been friends for years, and he did not want that to change. Suddenly it was second semester of their senior year, she waved thank you for the ride from her porch as he backed out of her driveway, when he realized how soon he would be gone. He yanked the parking brake and jumped out of the car. She turned and didn't see the things on bird skull legs emerge from a shimmering tear between them. Her face wore a confusion that became anticipation as he ran toward her. He reached and focused and shoved away the whispering sharp bone-white creatures.

He stumbled and nearly fell on his face, then limped up the steps. She covered her mouth not to laugh. He started giggling first.

They laughed together until the lock of their eyes was all that remained.

"Yes, you may," she said.

Is when he kissed her. And she kissed him back.

She called him and took him to movies and picnics, and just hugged him and waited when his thoughts wandered. Weeks later he realized he was happy and they were together.

He worried at first that any loss of control would mean dire consequences. He found it difficult to focus while he and Sharon kissed. He worried that she was too much of a distraction. It took time and practice, but he listened for the opening rifts and learned to expel them sometimes with his eyes closed.

One weekend in April they checked into a hotel room downtown and saw each other naked. Panting and sweating, she asked to stop, and he knew he wasn't ready either, and they held each other while he dissolved the keening spores that darted at them from the churning eddy in the ceiling.

She played with his hair and they didn't speak. They checked out early and went for pizza, and he dropped her off.

There were weeks when she didn't want to be touched and he didn't argue, and finally she said she'd realized her attraction to women and she was sorry, she didn't know what else to say. It was for the best, he told himself. The breaches had become more frequent. And in his observations, they seemed less and less often to target strangers.

There were no incidents during his first week of college and he speculated if their origin was regional, what might occur in his absence. He saw nothing unusual in the news, and his parents still called every week. But he recalled family vacations in Missouri, Colorado, and California with armadas of flying horseshoe crab things with scorch ray antennae, and rhino planarian worms as large as houses that had devoured most of Grandpa's sheep.

Before classes began, he met five people whom he would know for the rest of his life, one of whom he should marry, though he feigned no interest, often turning his attention to an unlit corner, waiting. For the first few weeks they stayed awake until dawn, telling stories and watching movies.

He declared an Art major in Painting/Drawing, fascinated by the charcoal strokes of Kathe Kollwitz and the violent colors of J.M.W. Turner. He often resisted his friends' pleas to accompany them to the dance club and to parties, succumbing only when the idea made him smile, when they whined, "Quit brooding, Ward!" More often he preferred to be in the studio with oils and canvas. Lately, the episodes occurred more often in public places.

Between fissure events, he had ceased to ponder their reason or significance. They continued and he continued, and had come to view his participation as exercise, regular and necessary, sometimes more intense, but no sign of stopping.

In the studio, he obsessed over technique with brushes and inks, lost in the range of color. He only tried to paint the invaders a few times, though he never managed to render them accurately, and would destroy the canvas minutes later.

In following months, his five friends became distracted by their own lives, working in pizza parlors, computer labs, record stores, and coffee shops; disappearing for months with new partners. He worried that he had ruined their friendship by sequestering himself, but on the nights he felt most alone and unable to paint, they would call him with an excited voice, and gather for dinner or a road trip to Ann Arbor or Cedar Point or Cleveland to see a band, connecting again as though no time had passed.

He was critical of his classmates, while none of them could argue with the passion and quality of his work. His teachers praised his talent, some of them offered mentor studies. His exhibition shows at the local gallery drew large crowds every semester, and he would linger in the corner, dressed in black, hiding in the open. It surprised him every time when his friends arrived, he would trust their opinions, and felt content again for a time.

They joked about his solitude and often tried to describe the woman he was holding out for. Doubtless, she was some mythical creature who could quote Kafka and Yeats and Poe, adored horror movies and Giger paintings, thought bats were cute, wore an antique watch on a chain, and rode a vintage motorcycle. He would groan at their comments, and they would continue, saying that she could recite *Macbeth* flawlessly, listened to Skinny Puppy, climbed mountains, read comic books, had a pet owl, very nearly qualified for the Olympic archery team, and if she dotted her i's with anything it would be tiny skulls. With each added characteristic, he would smile and nod with increasing enthusiasm. Until space fractured and vomited a river of boiling filth that tried to melt the student union building and slaughter his friends. And he became preoccupied.

The war began overseas when the United States sent forces into Iraq. He tried to tell himself he was worried that a gun or a tank would distract him, but he was simply scared. And selfish. He didn't want to die. So he pretended it wasn't happening. No good ever came from invasion, he thought. He considered for a time escaping in a sailboat to Canada.

His sophomore spring semester art show was a success; months and weeks of long hours and stress were rewarded by a full capacity attendance. His five friends retired early to their homework and significant others. Karla, one of the art models, lingered near him for the entire evening. He winced at her pronounced flirting, for she'd approached him nearly every day after class last semester and whispered in his ear how she liked the way he sketched her, and on the last day of class her breast had overtly escaped her robe and grazed his shoulder.

She lingered when he locked the art building, and he found himself walking her home. Outside her dorm building she paused by the security doors and stepped close to him, waiting with anticipation in her eyes. He considered kissing her, because he was lonely and tired and thought maybe he deserved to feel good. Or because she deserved to. He had to turn away to halt the molten carnivorous vespine lava fish tunneling in a tremulous frenzy under the quadrangle, and he stopped them from sucking the buildings down, considering for a moment if he should let them have the football stadium or just one fraternity house.

He said goodnight quickly and left her there alone. On the walk across campus, he realized what he should have done, and what he would finally do. He called her the next day, asked her to dinner and a movie, and kissed her afterward. By the end of the week, she helped him conclude his virginity.

He embraced the sex, grateful to feel a newness. Then he told her that he loved her, perhaps too early. Maybe to convince himself, to guarantee a feeling would be there to hold onto. Soon he lost all compulsion to paint, and switched to photography, hurriedly snapping uninspired pictures with black and white film.

He was happy for nearly a month. Then she complained about how much time his friends wanted to spend with him, and he stopped talking. Still, he spent all his nights at her place, afraid to be alone. He failed two classes.

"Why can't you go to the studio on Thursday instead?!" she screamed at him in the kitchen. Six months had escaped him. He missed his friends, hadn't spoken to his family in over a month, and couldn't remember the last time he'd painted. She screamed at him for being selfish. She screamed at him for not responding. She screamed about how that night after his art show, she'd gone back out to a bar and fucked a friend of a friend because Ward been such a lame dick.

When he cried, she berated him and he couldn't believe the things she called him. The smell of burning ramen noodles filled his nostrils, and finally he picked himself up and opened the back door. He nearly escaped. She pulled him back inside, crying and apologizing, and pulled him back to bed. He stopped the octopoid Venus flytraps from devouring her while she sobbed and screwed him, making promises as he lay there crushed by disappointment only in himself.

He wouldn't manage to break with her until he left college and Ohio far behind. His friends forgave him.

He moved back home and lived in his parents' basement, intent on building a career as an artist. By day, he worked in antique malls, movie theaters and stage crews, copy shops and bookstores, saving enough money for his own apartment. He lived alone, painting, dreaming of moving west to bigger cities and grander scenes.

He met Moira at work. She was outgoing and attractive and seemed uninterested in him, and he was drawn to her. He didn't have time, and it went against his rules and his plan, however vague it was, but he was compelled to try dating again, to find a connection, to have a connection. He took her to dinners and movies and she seemed bored by his conversation, which often defaulted to ranting about work. He wanted desperately to tell someone about what he really did, and imagined she would fall in love with him when she heard, but in the moment he became nervous and didn't know what else to say. He tried to learn more about her, but she was all about schedules and rushed them from dinner to the movie and had him drop her off early, and he tried to remember if he'd given her a chance to talk anyway. She started seeing someone else because she didn't know what he wanted, and he reflected if he knew at all. And he guessed that he agreed.

Every few months after that, she would call. Often when her partners broke it off, after a fiancé or two. Three years later, he was packing boxes when she showed up on his doorstep. She asked what was happening that evening, and invited herself to potluck movie night. When she was the last remaining guest, she said she could not leave. With old curiosity or new confidence, he kissed her.

A few days later she said she never wanted to go home.

He was happy. He felt human. A year later, she said she would walk out that door if he didn't propose, and he convinced himself it wasn't a threat.

The wedding was grand.

He always knew she wasn't right for him. They moved to a city on the coast and hunted for jobs. It was difficult for them during the recession, but they had shelter and food. They watched their savings deplete, and then unemployment benefits too. Nine months later, after they both found full-time jobs, she started drinking cheap vodka after work. Then before work.

She wanted a dog, so they bought a house. Neither of these made her happy nor stopped the drinking. He told himself she did it because of stress. She often yelled at him for hours, until one of them curled up in bed. Then she would apologize the next morning. She cried and said she felt alone, why did he spend every night in the studio, why was he so distant and distracted all the time. He couldn't tell her that he no longer dreamed, that he feared sleep, the fierce desolate void of it.

The new war in Iraq deepened another recession, and he was fortunate to keep his job. After the downsizing, he worked seventy-hour weeks. She was often drunk when he came home, and cursed him for his lack of priorities. Which of them had given up on sex, neither could say.

Two years later, he returned from the grocery shopping to an empty house. She'd taken the dog too.

He blamed the monsters that came through. He wanted to be ordinary. A lonely year slipped by, and he found himself staring out the back window one day, startled to find himself imagining a family with two children and a gas grill, with weekends full of yard work and soccer practice. The intruders had taken this simple dream from him. They had imposed their rules and he had let the duty exhaust him, define him.

From that day forward, he unleashed on them with more fury each time. Whenever they emerged, he mangled them and hurled them back through the cracks. The intrusions increased. They tried every hour, and he smirked as he donned his headphones and cranked the volume on angry metal music with inarticulate vocals, and blasted the enemy, seeing them off with two extended middle fingers. People stared at him on the sidewalk, at the creperie, riding the streetcar, but he was beyond caring.

By springtime, his rage subsided and he was tired and annoyed. He rolled his eyes each time they attempted to devour someone. His supervisor called him into the office and asked if he still liked working here. He wanted to be honest, to say what's the fucking point, we are all headed to the screaming desolate vacuity, you could be mangled at any moment by things unseen or a truck delivering fresh bread, but instead he apologized and begged to keep his position with the company.

After eighteen months of weekly then monthly appointments, his therapist said, "I honestly feel like we're not making any progress here. You're hesitant with every answer. Every week you fill the hour by complaining about your job, but you don't seem to want to do anything positive about it. You're not doing your homework and I don't think I can help you anymore."

He turned his gaze elsewhere, recalling how often he'd saved her in that office, forgetting for a moment that she didn't know, that she couldn't see them.

"Where are you right now?" she said. "See, this is what I mean."

"I'm sorry."

He listened to her until the end of the hour. Outside, standing at the nearby bus stop, he'd already decided not to go back.

He left work early because his vacation time was maxed out, and a break in the rain made him want to walk. Halfway over the steel bridge, he paused to notice the early afternoon hour. The post office was still open and he thought about a passport. He'd been thinking lately about travel.

There was an unusual chill, even for early September, and he was glad he'd kept the beard all summer. He leaned against the red steel railing, appreciating the perfect mountain peak on the east horizon.

The thunder caught his attention, and something gigantic moved in his peripheral vision. He peered south along the river to see a massive thing like an upright salamander stomping through the water, partly shrouded in steam. It flexed its six upper arms and swatted a nearby helicopter.

It's kind of adorable, he thought, and in that second, the huge creature whipped its sharp glistening tail into one of the new tower developments, breaking the building in half in an explosion of glass. He inhaled in alarm, then remembered that no one could afford the condos.

He gathered old feelings inside, clutched and stoked them, and expelled a long sustained blast. He felt severe resistance, the creature's massive bulk and resilient hide along with its monstrous instinct repelled the attack and his head screamed with awful strain. The titanic brute examined him, blue-white bolts crepitating between its horns, and roared primal appetite. The shockwave swept along the river, shattering windows on both sides and knocking him back against a steel support beam. It screamed at him with jaws dripping flame and broke into a booming run.

Ward gained his footing and thrust forward over the rail, discharging fierce strikes. The monster leapt over one bridge, kicked through another then tore the next one like jackstraws, smashing closer. Ward pushed at it, struck with rage and fear and hope and selfishness and denial and desperation and all that he had. Soon it towered over him, its thorny genitals swaying before him, and glared down with triumph and hunger.

He tuned. He lashed and extended. But the attack barely made the monstrosity narrow its eyes. Its screaming bellow rang in his ears. Then its great cragged mouth descended on him, rows of teeth occupying the sky.

Someone grabbed his hand. "What rough beast and all that," said a woman's voice. He was stunned by her fervent face and flowing black hair. She winked at him, and he was besotted at once. Eyes on him, she pointed a thumb at the creature. Together they turned and reached within, and together they released.

They shoved and blasted, forcing the thrashing colossus back down the river and back in time, the destruction repairing itself in a reverse wake, and they held the behemoth where it first arrived. They pierced each of its trillions of cursed cells with stinging salt, shriveled and propelled it back through the giant breach.

Then they collapsed together on the bridge walkway. He admired her Motörhead T-shirt, faded and worn enough to be an original print. They panted and laughed and she was radiant. She turned to him and smiled and said, "Buy me a drink?" When he hesitated, she grabbed his hand again and pulled him into a run. "Then I'm buying!" she declared.

They spent every day together. Sometimes they took turns. She added pluck and zeal to hers, acrobatic spins of the vile malevolent bodies, painting the air with prismatic bursts of light and cascading volutions of blood. When he tried to enrich his, she would slap his ass and tell him that was not bad, not bad at all, and then wink in that way.

She made him laugh, she insisted on cooking extensive and delicious meals, she randomly quoted horror movies with dramatic sarcasm. She adored reheated Indian food and good single malt scotch. She read Blake and Gogol and Camus, and said her father had driven a dynamite truck over narrow mountain roads. They conversed in poor Russian and Portuguese accents until one of them laughed too hard to breathe. They fucked and they cuddled and they spooned, and he slept through the entire night. He felt a new kind of pleased exhaustion and his nosebleeds had stopped.

One night he woke and she wasn't in the bed. He didn't feel her complete absence until she returned, stepping back through the rift into the bedroom. He stared in shock. She was naked and beautiful in the moonlight.

"Oh, darling," she said, her voice deepening with each syllable around her needlelike tongue. "You weren't supposed to see that."

He watched her body shift, fingers extended to violet spines as her hair came whipping alive and her breasts opened like anemone with furious coils.

He put up no defense when the thing reached across the room and grasped his throat. It pinned his arms with other appendages, then pierced his ears and tear ducts and abdomen like plunging icicles. He wept as it chattered hungrily with layered mandibles. His vision dimmed and felt the dark rising to meet him. It was soothing, the beginning of bliss sliding toward final quiet.

Then he remembered the woman he should have married, one of his five real friends. He remembered how he had not kissed her during four years of college and always regretted so, and recalled now what he had blocked out: that morning of their senior year when her crushed and split body was found near construction equipment on the site of the new campus field house. The tragedy was reported in the student newspaper.

Now the thing from the other side showed him the truth. They roared through the breach and showed him what they had done to her fifteen years ago. That night they had broken the rules.

He reached inside, deep into the place he always kept sealed, and dragged out something that flared and writhed white nova hot, that burned and sliced him as he hurled it outward and seared the shrieking beast to sputtering ash.

After many hours but not yet dawn, when he'd ceased trembling and the smell of brimstone had thinned, he got out of bed and dressed himself. He stood where she had been and reached into the empty air.

He opened the rift, beat back the screaming black fire and screams, and attacked.

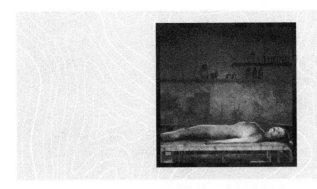

One Wicker Day

"Harry...?"

Netta looks across the table at the precise moment her husband's head impacts his breakfast plate.

In the second after, the only movement is his fork flipping end over end across the kitchen.

"...Oh, Harry."

This is a quiet town. There hasn't been a murder on record since the turn of the last century. Death has always come as a reminder, the lightest touch on the shoulder. The people here forget how the world can change. It is only what has followed death, in the last five years, like the sun burning brighter in the hottest summers. These new ones are frightening. The ones in white.

Seeing Harry's face pressed into his breakfast, Netta screams once, and bites her knuckle.

In this moment, his fork tumbling in an arc over his downed head, Netta does not see it. Her eyes are looking slightly above and to the left of him, looking at nothing in particular. This is the moment she knows and accepts that he is gone.

Damn it, Harry. How many times had he promised, this is the last *isweartogod* Philly cheesesteak sandwich? How many times had he declined to join her on morning walks? How many medications left untouched in the SMTWTFS pillbox? She doesn't scold him aloud because she knows even as these thoughts come, that she doesn't mean them. Just as she knows that his body is empty. There is a calm where she knows the memories will come later, and she will weep for hours and days. But now, underneath the peace, she feels the rise of something else that she doesn't want. Anger and panic. *Damn it, Harry, don't do this! You know how much I hate them.*

The fork clatters in the sink.

⸻

They came for Goldwin Langford last week. He and Irene had lived in the corner house for fifty-two years. When the unmarked white vehicles slid up to their home, the neighbors watched like they were frozen in time. Even when the silent white uniforms surrounded the house and their leader announced himself at the front door, onlookers were stopped in place. It might have been awe or the helplessness that comes in the face of invasion. Perhaps some witnesses to the spectacle recognized the efficient intruders from the recent Channel 9 news clips. That the actual Service existed outside of television, that it had come to their neighborhood, immobilized John Kenrick in his front yard holding his rake and leaf bag, halted Sybil Fletcher in mid-sip of coffee at her kitchen window, ceased a group of rollerskating children, and silenced the Baener's baying basset hound. The neighborhood remained still as Service executive director Mr. A. Morrow adjusted the rose on his lapel, opened his perfect smile wider, and knocked at the Langford's front door. He waited a long time as autumn wind carried a storm of leaves through the neighborhood. A formation of white uniforms lined the street with unmovable precision.

Still, no one protested. No one intervened. No one helped Irene Langford as Mr. Morrow hammered at the door with an insistent rhythm for one full minute and withdrew his hand in elegant rigor. Then he straightened his sleeves, aligned his composure, and motioned to the nearest rumbling six-wheeled vehicle that was more tank than truck. Two tall broad-shouldered uniformed employees emerged from the vehicle's rear ramp with a long metal cylinder that matched their size. They rushed the front door and gained entry in a splintering crack.

Four Servicemen carried the metal tube back out. They set the container down on the threshold for ten seconds, enough time for Mr. Morrow to say, "We must remember: From dust we came..." Then they slid the metal coffin into the extended cargo area.

Irene Langford burst from her house, wailing her husband's name. She ran at the rumbling vehicle, but a wall of white uniforms blocked her at the curb and restrained her.

Across the street, Sybil Fletcher's face alternated between sobbing and incredulity and rage. In the neighboring yard, John Kenrick lowered his hedge shears and stepped forward, and raised his hand slightly and half-pointed, half-made a fist, but settled it on the low fence. A row of white suits obstructed their view.

Irene sobbed as executive director Morrow gave her a logoless business card, indicating the cremation precisely scheduled at a quarter past eight the following morning. Then the tall man took long perfect strides under the gray sun, beaming his tan face and bright teeth. A performance more suited to a celebrity, but making it clear he was a man who loved his job. At the door to his white SUV, he turned. "To dust we shall return," he said loud enough for all to hear.

A complimentary limousine arrived at her residence fifteen minutes before the hour. Irene Langford did not come out of her house, and the car departed minutes later. The ashes were not sent to her.

Three weeks ago, James Tanner, sixty-three-year-old third-generation owner of the Tools on Main hardware store for over thirty years, was taking inventory in aisle four, when his body stiffened and he clawed the air soundlessly. His son and assistant manager saw his father fall among the garden tools, and knocked over a pyramid stacked display of floor varnish rushing to the phone. But the tall smiling, white-suited executive director appeared at the front register before he could dial the phone. "You'll find no need for an ambulance," said Mr. Morrow, fluorescent light glaring from his pristine ensemble. Behind him, white uniforms blocked the door and lined the sidewalk outside. "We're proud to offer you immaculate, prompt, and legally-bound service."

Theresa Sworden, wife to the minister of Trinity Lutheran, lost to cancer two months previous. No sooner had her heart flatlined than they arrived. Nurses protested the crowd of obdurate white uniforms blocking the hallway, and the towering man who was most certainly not a family member intruding on Tim Sworden's grief. When the doctor grabbed Mr. Morrow's arm in protest, two white uniforms threw the physician out the window. Mrs. Sworden's room had been on the fifth floor, and they removed both bodies from the premises.

The Service came to town a year ago, not long after the first funeral parlor closed. Some residents noticed the new monthly deduction in their social security statement, line item COLLECTION. A federal press room response briefly mentioned improvements in urban growth regulation and disease control.

Now Harry has fallen into his two eggs over-easy and hash browns. His hand lies upturned on the table, its spasms done. Blood emerges from his nose. Netta cannot lift his head right now. The blood soon covers half his face, one wide eye partly submerged in red.

Netta looks at the phone in its perch by the refrigerator. *How did we get to this...?* she thinks, about many current situations all at once. She doesn't bother standing, it isn't worth dialing a number. Even now there is a knock at the door.

First a gentle rap, it soon turns quick and tenacious. Out of habit, she stands and heads to the door. The best way to deal with solicitors wasn't to ignore, just tell them straight off. As she crosses the kitchen, she sees a bubble rise and pop in the scarlet pool around Harry's face, and stops where she is thinking, *Harry? You're still with me?!* But even then she knows it's the last release of air from settling lungs. Then her feet continue, around the corner, down the hall. *He's gone now, Netta. They are here, after all. They know.*

The hallway grows and stretches, pulling the door farther, taunting her; and she lifts her chin and walks the distance, swallowing back tears, expecting more thunder against the heavy oak, a rattling of the brass handle, splinters off the sticking bites of an axe head, the entire door to fall in, crushing her toes, opening her sanctuary to the changed world, the dark clouds reaching down, and a terrible giant white suit, the smile with teeth too bright.

She clicks the lock back. She pulls the door open.

There is no smile. The man on her doorstep is wearing a black suit. She is astonished and relieved, feeling a tremor of giddiness, but unsure why. The only bright thing about him is the pallid face, a pale of cave creatures and underground. With his hands folded before him, he stands very still on the porch. Very still. Maybe he knows this, because he lets his hands settle at his sides. His expression remains unchanged, and he does not speak, if it seemed like he was about to.

Netta does not recognize him immediately. The well-kept gray hair is not the frizzy wisps she was used to seeing in the aisles, and behind the counter. And the complexion is so tamed, unlike him. Mostly, he is the last person she expected.

She steps back, covering her mouth. Uncovering it. Not knowing where to put her hand when she takes it down, clenching her fingers.

Still the man says nothing. And finally she knows. It is Mr. Tanner.

Behind him stands Mrs. Sworden and Mr. Langford, with two others— she's trying to recall... Isn't it Jane and Don Alaway, new to the weekend church group dinners, and killed in the car accident last November? Resting between the four of them, riding their shoulders, a long wicker basket. They are all wearing black. The same calm countenance has settled into the lines of their faces. And beyond them, someone else waits patiently on the top stair of the porch. Midmorning sun shows the last face without mistake. Still, she cannot—will not—allow herself to know. The silence of the kitchen stings at the nape of her neck.

She's seen these baskets before. It was the old way.

Now she remembers.

That afternoon when Grandpa did not come downstairs from his nap. When she was six years old and did not understand why they situated him on the dining room table and he laid there all day. She helped her mother and brother wash him. Then Grandma and Dad and Uncle Robert and Uncle Norm carried Grandpa out in the same kind of basket.

The white SUV slides up to the curb. Followed by heavy white vehicles.

The driver exits and opens the rear door. Mr. Morrow's tall white suit unfolds into view, lapel displaying a fresh red rose. More white trucks arrive, their bulk still moving as back ramps clang against asphalt and pour out more white uniforms. The vehicles block the road, engines rumbling, with a slow pulse of hazard lights. Mr. Morrow checks his watch with satisfaction and his smile catches the sun. But as his gaze settles on Netta's porch and the group gathered there, his smile contracts. Long legs propel the executive director quickly across the lawn. The six dark figures do not turn or move.

"What's the meaning of this?" Morrow pushes through the silent guests and addresses Netta. He is much taller in person, ducking under the doorframe to glare at her. "This is completely against protocols. You are in violation of federal policies." His teeth are impossibly straight and bright. But he is not smiling and that rose is in her face.

She lifts her hands and shoulders, trying to protest, managing to stutter incomplete and silent words, frightened he will cut her off at any moment. But then she looks past the white suit, to find blame or reason, and finally she relaxes, even smiles back at those teeth. *It's all fine*, she thinks, and then she knows. *It's not for me now. It's not me, it's for Harry.* "Mostly," she says this aloud, not breaking her eyes from executive director A. Morrow, "it's not for you." And she goes on smiling.

"What?!" Morrow growls, gleaming teeth caught in a snarl, and he wheels around and cranks his imposing stature down to Mr. Tanner.

That's right, says James Tanner, his face quiet as the earth and eyes of forever. It's for us. Us and Harry. Not you.

"What? What?! You are not authorized personnel." Morrow snaps frantic glances at their somber clothes, their hushed faces. He looks to the four long rows of white uniformed employees on the lawn, and huffs with inadequacy. He stares at the wicker basket. "What is that? What's going on here? This is not proper procedure. What the hell?" Netta finds his language terribly unprofessional, and some of it simply uncalled for.

Let us show you, Mr. Tanner says. He takes Morrow's long white sleeve and motions them all into the house. Netta leads them, looking back to see who is last to enter. Whomever it is, he closes the front door gently after him. It is a sunny November day, but it is November, and it's just proper. Without orders, the uniformed Servicemen stay outside.

Morrow pulls his arm free, and with it cocked back, he trembles as though he'll strike Mr. Tanner. But he continues not to know what to do next.

They all move into the kitchen where they place the basket on the floor. Five of the silent ones clear the table of breakfast dishes, condiments, placemats, and newspaper, making neat silent stacks on the counter and sink. When Harry is laid out, the sixth guest arrives in the doorway.

She hasn't seen him since she was six years old, and Netta Raney finds herself crying. He holds out a folded black suit, dusty and well-made, unworn for years, that she recognizes as Harry's suit from the closet upstairs.

Grandpa, she mouths, no sound.

"Just what do you think you're—" Morrow's smile is lost in impatience.

Mrs. Sworden puts a single finger to her stale lips.

They dress Harry while the man in white shifts his weight in the corner, drums his fingers on the counter, sighs out loud, and clears his throat many times. They wash the body, clear off the blood, moving over his features with care. The cheeks must be massaged gently, the eyes closed. He must be like them: untroubled. It is a quiet sleep.

When they are done preparing him, they bow their heads. Netta bows too. Mr. A. Morrow rolls his eyes, but does not interrupt.

They lay Harry in the wicker basket, folding his hands before placing the lid. Moving the procession out the back door, they pass the garden and the garage, going into the open space of the dry yard. The leaves mat under their feet, soft from the recent rain and a rare few days of warmth. There is absolutely no sound.

Netta and Mr. Tanner look at the ground. She finds herself nodding. Grandpa Raney is at her shoulder, warm without warmth, radiant without expression. Mr. Tanner looks at her.

She hears what he means and goes to the garage, then returns with two shovels and gives one to Mr. Tanner. The ground is hard and frozen and the digging takes time. *I should have a jacket and scarf,* Netta thinks, *I will catch cold.* She looks at the wicker basket, and feels at ease. Perhaps I will follow soon. She does not exactly think this, anywhere more stark than her subconscious.

"Alright, folks. Okay. Real cute and all. But the show's over." All faces turn to Morrow for a second. Then Netta returns to digging while Mr. Tanner moves to speak but Grandpa steps in.

Silence, kid, says Grandpa Raney, today is made of silence.

"It's impossible. How did you beat us here?" Morrow pouts visibly.

Netta and Mr. Tanner turn back to the work at hand. The cooling grave and pile of soil complement each other in perfect opposing depth and height.

The quick and the dead, Grandpa jokes.

"This has to stop. Just-just stop all of this." Morrow points. "Drop those tools. And turn over that filthy, that—primitive… basket."

Go put yourself in a thin paper box and a very hot oven, Grandpa tells him.

"You're interfering with government business."

Govern, my eye.

"This is a highly irregular situation and I'm trying to be professional. I could just *take* the body. There are only seven of you. Don't make me—" Very suddenly the executive director stops talking, stands straight up, and bites his lip.

Grandpa is not looking up at the tanned face. He is not looking at the lapel rose, the teeth, or toward the driveway where Netta expects the approach of many boots. Grandpa is looking over the fence to the west where the cemetery has grown to twenty acres in the last two hundred years, a vast silent forest of carved stones. Grandpa holds that look until Mr. A. Morrow follows it. Grandpa turns his empty face to the defeated smile. Then he turns away, ignoring. Even a young government mind should understand.

"I have resources. I can mobilize personnel, equipment, funds at a moment's notice!" But Morrow's voice is unsteady, unconvinced in its own words. He backs away. He is done talking.

Grandpa takes the shovel from Mr. Tanner, shaking his head. As tired as the motion is, lost even in this stoppage of time, the rite of burial, Netta sees an expression that is entirely his, one she remembers from her childhood. The slow shaking of the head, the silence and knowledge, with a slow blinking of the eyes. She remembers when she'd run to him, crying about her brother's teasing jokes, vowing revenge, and he'd come down on one knee. And while she'd wanted him to agree, say yes, her brother was cruel, he only shook his head, slowly, assuring he didn't give answers where they were known. No, he said, then and now, don't you start a war.

Adrift

S HE WAS THE third sister, born many years after her elder siblings, though they never met. Early on, she showed signs of restlessness when her lava had barely cooled, by reaching out with long jetties and peninsulas. Two season cycles later, when the last young sea turtle departed her south beach, she drifted off into the night.

She traveled slowly, often against the tide. After many moons, she found her first big land, a place where crystal cliffs sang with sunlight. There she listened to an overture that lasted many summers, and watched the sharp orange birds that fished between their shores.

Then a pod of dolphins caught her fancy, which she followed and studied until they dove out of sight. Heading east, she encountered a land whose edges hung steeply out over the sea, with forests that grew downward. She moved along its coasts, through bays and around capes, witnessing great spires of agate, beaches of spherical brocatel boulders, and twisting dunes of onyx sand. Unable to find a canal, she decided this land went on for too long and turned south, where she enjoyed the open water for a great while.

She rode a giant maelstrom until it felt repetitive. She witnessed a savage war between whales and squid. She would hold still if she saw a ship in the distance, then slide away at dark in the other direction. She spent one millennium in the cold waters of the north, fascinated by the wildness of their creatures and their subtle differences in color. She first knew love there, a young and ambitious stark-white berg with deep blue edges. She warned him from the beginning that she was a nomad, though they were both smitten in the early days. The more he whispered affection to her, the more she wanted to stay, which only made her want to leave. It filled her with despair to know that he would follow her into warmer waters, clinging to her beneath the surface. But she still went south. And still she increased her speed.

Afterward she craved anger and guarded loneliness. She sought storms. She allowed herself tossed by tidal waves. She preoccupied herself with shark feeding frenzies. She swallowed her lagoon, claiming that it slowed her down. One night she eased up to a fishing boat and capsized it, then drifted just out of reach for hours, until she let the dazed crew onto her beach. When they fell asleep, she rolled, dumping them once more into the endless water. And she fled.

She formed cragged shores and sat alone and unmoving for years, whispering to men, then wrecking their crafts. She sank beneath the water for eons, vowing not to return, and slept.

She rose much later, restless, with bitter hope that the world was now to her liking. She wandered, seeing birds and fish and new animals, but no more ships. She felt hollow but burdened. She returned to the place where she had been born, the waters deep and silent, but her family was nowhere to be found. She wandered the seas whose names had changed and became forgotten, and found no familiar shores.

She wept and wailed. She drifted.

Until the day a fiery thing streaked from the sky. It blazed across the clear blue day and plummeted into the water not far off. She went to the spot and found a huge rock unlike anything she'd ever seen. He was beautiful and talked in stirring iridescence. He spoke of his home, and promised to take her there. And for the first time in her life, she followed.

The Crimson Codex

WE HEARD THROUGH our network he would be at the church sometime that day. The others waited nearby while Yasmine and I entered and cased it, taking spots on both sides of the aisle. We couldn't have talked anyway, with the clamoring strobe feeds from the screenwalls. I kept my hood up and tried to get some meditation in, eyes open. His description was unknown to us, so I scanned every body color and shape. Hours later, feeling inundated and despaired, I noticed O'wiq Cerulxye'e quite casually. He gave no overt sign, but when he arrived with his own kneeling box, I knew that the package was inside and who he was. After he finished praying, we joined him at the exit.

Outside, we introduced him to Fenton and Noll, Gaspar and Rilla. He shook all our hands at once. His ruby-skinned form stood a foot taller than any of us, and it took me a moment to perceive that his two mouths turned downward bespoke a smile. Excited for the occasion, Yasmine touched me in public, lightly on the shoulder.

We showed much joy, and its expression gave me unease. So we lifted the hem of our robes and hurried to the ship.

O'wiq Cerulxye'e hesitated at the ramp. "Chip gone?" He tapped the back of his neck. I checked the crowded port for wandering eyes then lowered my hood and briefly showed him the crude extraction scar on my nape. The others did the same. Satisfied, he came aboard.

The sky darkened as we lifted into the atmosphere.

"Where to?" I asked O'wiq as we picked up speed.

He checked behind him, then put his hands over his eyes. "Hide."

I nodded because I felt it too. Then I turned off the destination coordinate and cranked the knob, sending us into skipspace.

Noll set the *Oblation* to drift in the between, mostly to cool our trail. We had been on task for months, searching and stealthing, and could all use rest. I said my vows in a slow floating tumble, then hung my robe and eased into my sleep sack. I was nearly out when Yasmine joined me, skin on skin.

"I want to see it." She stared at O'wiq's box in an accessible cargo net, then nuzzled me with her bare head.

I nodded at O'wiq, his eight crimson limbs tucked into a ball and anchored by his plated prehensile tail. His carapace whistled faintly with each slumbered breath.

"His ordeal has been long and fraught," I whispered. "We can wait for a short time."

She didn't let me sleep for many hours to come.

I remember Granddad's voice, a slow sweet rumble, but not his face. Dad said I would sit on his lap in his favorite chair by the fireplace and he'd read to me from the old red storybook, tales he'd known in his own childhood. I'd go to bed hours late, wide awake. It was after TeleCom bought the schools; mine was the first generation selected for LitChip implantation. As Granddad relayed to me the yarns of warrior heroes who saved the villages from vast armies and immense voracious monsters, and the sagas of those who explored fascinating and deadly worlds, I felt the wafer hum at the base of my skull. Dad gave me the book when Granddad died.

It wasn't long before they closed the schools. When the uniformed squad came for our books and burned them in the yard, Dad hid my favorite one in the bathroom air vent. When they returned every week and Dad insisted we had nothing left, and they read the charges, describing not only the stories we read each night but the ones I'd dreamt, we knew then that the chip did more than receive content. Mom gave up the book, and Dad served two years at the rehab colony. He came back with a chip and didn't speak much after that. He shaved his head and took to wearing a dark brown robe tied at the waist with a thick cord. He called night meetings at the house. Mom left soon after.

We skipped back into real space long enough to take a bearing. The nearest star was Luyten 726-8 B, no planets and too close to Broadcast Central. The detector that Rilla had rigged up showed a few bars, possibly a sweep signal buried in the transmissions bouncing off a relay array. They'd caught a whiff. We aimed for Struve 2398 B and winked out.

We gave an hour to our vows, then everyone hurried to the mess hall, some half-dressed in anticipation. O'wiq was already waiting for us. "Anxious, you?" he said with his odd smile. He learned quickly. I bowed in thanks and apology.

Most of my cloistral brothers and sisters had waited seventeen years for this moment, since the day I'd founded Sect 53 in memory of my father. We'd had many disappointments.

One could have mistaken the box's composition for oak or fir, but a very close look revealed helical grains. Outside of the simple handle holes, no carvings or symbols graced the surface. O'wiq knocked on the box, and it sounded hollow. He exhaled and clicked his eyes. Then he lifted it, turned it over, and caressed five sides at once with counterclockwise sweeps. One side detached, and we exclaimed at the emptiness within. My heart fell. But then he opened the false panel and revealed the hidden object.

It was a thinner volume than I expected, but to all of us, extremely beautiful. A crimson cover inlaid with latticed runeforms, surrounded by finely tapped corners of an orange metal, fastened with a clasp in the shape of a horned creature whose three eyes served as keyholes.

We'd first heard whispers of it more than five years ago. Scribed in secret after TeleCom scoured the worlds of all physical content to make way for their own transmissions. It was said to contain one hundred unheard stories, with each of its one hundred thousand letterforms etched by one member of the Cerul'ptah race before they'd leapt into their boiling indigo ocean, leaving no civilization for the company to find. It was said to be the last book in the known universe. It was certainly the first that many of our sect had ever seen. Could this be the *Cerul'ptah Codex* itself? That which an entire species had died to create? All save one, left to carry it.

Seeing it now made us fugitives twice-over. A path that had begun when we'd removed our chips.

O'wiq Cerulxye'e unlocked the publication, opened the pages whose trim glistened like living moss, and read to us.

THE MANY HUNDRED WIVES

In an old village called X'gg near the north chasm lands there was a chief called O'rym who took three hundred mates. He provided them with huts and livestock and adornments, but none of them bore him any children. Tradition did not allow them to refuse or to suggest that his seed might lack potency; though some of them tried often, there was no fruit.

After many years, O'rym, known as a solid and patient being, became angry at the state of things. He shouted at his now four hundred wives, and raised the tribute rates. He killed his prize calf in a moment of bored rage. A fire destroyed part of the town. When the harvest was diminished by pests, he led an attack on a friendly village, returning with very few surviving males. When the well went dry, he announced that they would not move the settlement until someone gave him a newborn.

The five hundred wives decided quickly. They added j'irx root to his drink, and he slept for an entire tenday. While he snored they went out in all directions and soon followed a flying bird [note: verify translation] to a distant lake. With much hard work they carved a new river all the way to the village. When the chief awoke he found his hut surrounded on all sides by water. He yelled and cursed at them, and then he cried. He wept so much that the lake became an ocean, and the village had to be relocated.

It was these five hundred wives who built the irrigation and aqueduct systems and who wrote our first songs. And now, every time you hear the wind howling at night, it is O'rym wailing at the world from his far-off island.

With this blessed find, our journey was only half complete, perhaps less. We had yet to reach the farthest inhabited worlds, where the signals were weakest, where eyes and ears might be more open to these new unknown stories. If not, then our cause was lost. Though we could cover great distance via a series of precisely calculated skips, there was much to do beforehand.

O'wiq taught us their alphabet first. There were roughly seventy characters in Cerul'ptah written language, with additional or fewer during each of the six planetary seasons. Our larynx could not pronounce all of them, though Gaspar impressed us with a few more than any of us could manage. I made everyone trace each glyph in the air for three hours until the shape was burned into our mind. Many of the runes reminded me of insects, and I had to focus to keep from imagining them wriggle and scurry off the page.

We took regular recesses, for the body and mind need rest, nourishment, and more. My limbs felt weak from so long in weightlessness, my spine seemed taller in the mirror, so I assigned myself some gym time. After the first set made me weary, I gave myself calcium injections and red blood cell stimulants.

I was finishing a long run on the gravmill when Fenton and Noll entered. Their faces said they weren't interested in exercise. Fenton kissed me insistently as Noll removed his robe. I was panting between them when Yasmine opened the door. I disengaged my mouth and motioned for her to join us but she shook her head in a way I could not read, perhaps disappointment or lethargy. She watched us for a few minutes, then departed without a sigh.

———— ⁂ ————

Someone suggested that starlight would be good for us, even just briefly. So we gathered on the bridge and dropped back in. The scanner display lit up crowded. A nest of ten scout ships, z+30° off our port side, and close enough that we could see their logo-shaped hulls. When I froze a moment, Rilla shouted my name. I cranked the knob, and we skipped before the hobblenet closed over us.

Rilla was standing next to me at the control panel. I saw her finger that still depressed the drop bay button. "Something I assembled. Canister of old leaky storage drives looped with false data." She straightened up. "Stinkbomb."

"Done well," O'wiq said to her.

"Very well done," I breathed.

I found a quiet corner in which to meditate.

Indeed we all know our story. It is company-approved plot template NO. 14, whose many multiple variations are transmitted on the entertainment network every second over millions of channels, with titles like *The Ashen Road, Seven Weary Drifters, Smith's Vigil, Extreme Discipline, Terrible Bald Bob and the Slinging Stragglers, Starry Story Search*, or even *The Arduous Voyage of the Monks of* Oblation. It is the tale of the traveling group on a journey to find a sacred object. All of their renditions have perfect endings, where the hero returns with the thing and is rewarded with marrying the princess. And the sequels and remades are no different. So in times like these I contemplate deeply the ongoing fear that we do not know our own conclusion.

It was late when I finished. Sometimes I can't sleep in skipspace, so I went in search of something. I found Gaspar. He wasn't in the mood at first, but I convinced him. His sweat was the sweetest of them. Afterward I crawled in with Yasmine; she groaned but put her arms around me.

———— ⁂ ————

After breakfast we hauled some dusty containers out of the hold. They still smelled of the hugril tree that we'd felled five years ago on Fomalhaut b (now called Walt Neu). We unpacked the contraband and brought it topside. The papyrus was brittle, but we softened it with cellulose from our food stores, then spread the blank pages on the mess table with magnets to hold it down.

O'wiq placed the *Cerul'ptah Codex* on a centerpiece stand where we could all see.

Our hands trembled as we touched the mollusk-inked quill to the page, having resisted every urge to commit this action for the past seventeen years. My brothers and sisters awaited my word, and I whispered a brief prayer, thinking of my father, and bowed. We began to write.

Now we could truly call ourselves scribes.

Dark beads of ink floated around us, found each other, and grew.

O'wiq, of course, copied six pages at once, and his calligraphy was immaculate.

THE BOY AND THE FOREST

There was a boy named O'ora who had been born with an old soul. He often left his lessons incomplete and cheated at games. One day his mother sent him to the edge of the forest for berries and fungus. "But do not go too far in and be back here before dark." *What does she know?* the boy thought to himself. *She spends her life in that hut mixing sour mash, sewing, and brushing the floor.*

He wandered down the forest trail, whistling loudly as he kicked seed pods and slashed at tree trunks with an old branch. He chased the furred worms out of the shade, spit on the singing lichen, and urinated on a nest of y'lui eggs.

A forest neighbor [note: check translation] heard him and poured its smoke body out of the abandoned insect hive. It stood upright on two legs but with a long serpentine neck ending in a childlike face. "Young thing, I've come to ask you to walk softly in this place."

"Old thing, I've come to tell you to step aside and shut up."

The forest neighbor did so, but waved its magic tail as the young male passed.

After some time, O'ora saw then that the path had disappeared and that night was coming fast. "Perhaps I ought to go back, only because I am hungry." When he tried to turn around, he noticed that he could not move. Neither could he turn his neck, but only his eyes could roll, and he saw that his feet had grown into the soil. He felt his blood change color, and his hair grow out and stiffen and sprout leaves.

He stayed there for many years, disgusted by the creatures that burrowed in his skin, under his roots, and nested in his branches. As the seasons whispered to him and stars passed endlessly overhead, he learned over time to be more tranquil, and his being was opened. The rustling of the other trees became clear, and he understood they were speaking to him. For a very long time, O'ora chorused with them, through each light and dark, the ongoing story-song.

One day the forest neighbor returned. "You are ready now, I think, to receive a gift." It changed the O'ora tree back into a young male. Then it handed him a branch with a hot orange flame licking at the one end. "This comes from the center of the forest that you can never find. And from far away before that."

He ran back up the path, past the old trees, as daylight increased through the canopy above, past the new trees, and finally came out at the edge of the forest. He gathered berries and fungus with one hand and proceeded to the home he remembered, calling the names of his sister and mother.

The village was gone. In its place was an untouched prairie. Soon he became aware how many centuries he had been away. But he did not weep. Instead he walked in search of his descendants. He found them much later and far to the west, himself as an old male, and brought them flame that they might brighten the night and cook their meals.

The letter-scripting work took three weeks, then we divided duties: O'wiq and I copy-corrected symbols; Gaspar, Noll, and Fenton rubricated the opening passages with vermilion dye; and the women collated. At one point during the bookbinding process, Yasmine initiated an orgy. As always, Rilla did not participate, but continued to illuminate illustrations at the edge of the table against which we grunted and moaned. Our alien friend returned from a nap in the bunk room to find us in a snoring tangled mass, stained in many ways.

Soon after, the *Oblation* had its first library, containing exactly one dozen copies of the *Cerul'ptah Codex*.

As much as we had learned the symbols and transcribed them, we understood few words or meanings in the Cerul'ptah language. So I spent most of my waking time trying to translate for myself the third story—"The Flock of Disquiet Mountains"—by reading it aloud in the native tongue. I had achieved only a few pages when Yasmine hurried in.

"Rilla says we have to land, and soon!" She gestured urgently.

I flung myself from a wall handle and propelled toward the engine room, tucking at turns and kicking off.

Rilla held up one of the damper plugs. The business end was deformed and useless.

I breathed deeply. "How many more skips can we make?"

"Two, maybe three. After that, well..." Her visible frustration nearly hid her fear.

I'd reflected on my own death many times; I preferred other circumstances to being stranded in the null of skipspace forever or to starve too far between systems. The only painless and improbable outcome was if the drive annihilated us in the blink moment. I cursed as I had not done in many years and promised myself twenty lashes if we made it through.

I woke everyone and briefed them. We held hands and breaths on the bridge and... skipped in.

The chart showed Tau Ceti as the nearest system. Too populated for my taste, but we had no choice. It would take two more skips, out and in, to get close.

We chanted, O'wiq along with us. His antennae glowed with a thin but lurid bioluminescence. I tried to accept that it might be the last thing I saw.

When father removed my chip, I hated him for it. Even with meditation and anesthesia, I cried for hours after he made the incision and dug it out. Then I screamed and screamed. The silence was too much. I felt dead, cut off from the feeds. Many weeks later I began to hear the world. Only then could I begin to find the universe.

We approached Nocchio IV and navigated through its swarm of satellites. We arced over the western hemisphere looking for a dull spot between the bright urban concentrations, especially distant from those sprawls configured like company trademarks.

We set the *Oblation* down near a mining town along a scant riverbed. Everywhere the soil was deep purpled brown.

I selected Rilla and Fenton to go in with me.

As we neared the edge of town, Yasmine caught up. O'wiq was close behind her. "Also myself."

We walked by a post office, a small hotel, and an apothecary. Most of the signs were comprised of painted wood, but the few flashscreens indicated some tech. Even I chuckled at the sight of the barber shop. With each passing block our hope waned.

"In here... Let's try in here!" Yasmine jumped up onto the wooden steps of a place called The Stellar Oasis.

"Sister," Fenton said, "that is a drinking establishment."

I questioned for a moment the example I had set regarding indulgence.

"It is a place of gathering and also of information," Yasmine pointed out, and was the first of us to enter.

We caught fewer glances than I anticipated as we crossed the room. Even O'wiq did not stand out among the many races assembled here. Two men in TeleCom uniforms played cards in the corner, but they did not look up.

It was only after we reached the bar that I became aware of the blaring screenwalls. I instantly dropped the practiced veil of reception over my face.

The bartender nodded to me under the color and noise.

I ordered six of his finest, if he pleased.

"Six tanglefoots." He served us swiftly and returned his attention to the feeds.

We leaned against the bar, facing all directions, heads low but looking for someone approachable.

A dusty ranch hand meandered to us with loud boots. "Can I help you?" he drawled, and before I could speak he grabbed Yasmine's arm and pulled her to him. "Help you, chickadee, with anything under that robe?"

I stepped toward them, and he very quickly drew a long blade.

Rilla was the only one still facing the bar. "Friend—" She raised her voice just enough. "Do you know how to win a knife fight?"

"Come again?" spat the local. He glanced from me to her, back to me. The others could only watch.

She shot her drink and turned to face him. "Do you know?"

He squinted and cocked his head slightly.

Then she had a hold of his wrist, twisting it until he yelped, and the knife was in her hand. It bobbed a moment, then flicked, and was gone. Rilla peered upward and we followed her look to see the sharp point stuck in the ceiling fan, turning lazily above us.

He released Yasmine and stepped back.

"Now, have you a blacksmith around here?" Rilla asked him.

"South end of the street, round back of the stable."

We left our drinks.

"No upstairs pleasure time?" O'wiq asked.

"Our vows forbid all earthly forms of copulation," I responded. Immediately I felt the need to explain. "Though I've always considered skipspace an exception." Then I recognized from his smile he was making a joke about my appetites.

On our way out I noticed the company men still weren't looking up. I walked us faster.

By his broad and opalescent-scaled shoulders, the blacksmith was undoubtedly Jhalvuun, of the Hetsool nation by his facial tattoos. The sparks danced down his long heavy apron and disappeared at his webbed feet. He stopped swinging when Rilla showed him the damper plug, and he set his hammer aside. He returned the glowing metal to the bright furnace behind him.

The three-legged steeds rustled in the stalls behind us. I surveyed the shelves and, except for the small feedscreen in the corner, saw only manual tools and simple parts. At least the sound was muted.

"Don't suppose you have a collider kiln?" Rilla asked him.

He shook his ichthyomorphic head.

Fenton sighed. "It seems we shall meditate for many weeks on the ambulatory path of rolling wind-borne native plants."

"We should go to the nearest big city," Yasmine said. "Not too big, of course."

The Jhalvuunian raised his finger to his spiny lips. He walked over to the feedscreen and swung it aside on a hinge. He reached into the space behind and returned with an intact damper plug.

"How much?" I asked.

He shook his head again.

"Nothing so free," O'wiq said.

"Let us pay you for your time," I said carefully.

"May your journey brighten the universe for all others," he said. He set the plug on the anvil and then needlessly adjusted the position of his tongs so they tapped the plug and knocked it to the ground. "Brother," he added. When he reached down to retrieve the plug his apron lifted just enough to reveal the knotted end of a white waist cord hanging beneath.

"Thank you, brother," I said.

"Fly now." He glanced overtly to the feedscreen. The program in progress showed a scene in a bar where a woman clad in a skin-tight black war suit with flowing red hair fainted as she was seized by a sneering unwashed man. A finger tapped him on the shoulder and the camera quick-zoomed in on an impossibly handsome man backed by a V-formation of bald companions in black body suits with thin white belts, dramatically backlit, their chests emblazoned with bright book-shaped icons.

They couldn't have done it this quickly with actors. Even up close their rendered skin and facial expressions seemed real.

We did not stay to see the square-jawed leader punch the scoundrel in slow motion, so that spinning teeth and detailed blood droplets erupted sideways in a perfect symmetrical spray. Or the camera lower through the paused vanes of the ceiling fan to reveal a wide-angle shot of the six darkly clad heroes standing back to back, arms in fighting stance, as hundreds of villainous figures closed in.

Despite the deserted road, we retreated behind the buildings and cemetery, over open land, and entered the ship corral, only to find the two company men waiting for us at the ramp. They had Noll and Gaspar on their knees with their hands behind their heads, covering them with small cone-barreled pistols.

I took a calm step forward. Their weapons throbbed before I could greet them, and my muscles ignited with a stinging wildfire. The pain locked my limbs and drove me to the ground, writhing.

When the agony subsided, I could open my eyes enough to see my brothers and sisters lined up with hands raised. Suddenly O'wiq dropped to all eights and became a blur. One of the company men slammed sideways into the hull, the Cerul'ptah standing in his place, his tail already tight around the other's neck. He tossed the second man over the ship and beyond the fence. We boarded quickly.

As the armada of scout ships appeared in the exosphere before us, I did not veer but accelerated, oblivious to the warnings of my brethren. I pushed the *Oblation* to a hard shudder, and at the last moment before collision saw the skipdrive come online; Rilla seated the damper and winked us away. The image of something larger behind the scouts lingered in my mind.

We skipped out and in and out again toward the Perseus Transit and finally left the Orion Spur behind us.

THE TWO CREATURES

U'keb [amphibian] sat along the edge of the great lake of night for thousands of lifetimes without moving or speaking, pondering important things that could not be spelled with words. Then Y'lui arrived, who could not remain still; he whistled and paced.

"I'm sure the view is better from the other side," he remarked. "One of us should go around and see."

"It would take a hundred forevers to walk around there," said U'keb.

"We could have a race," suggested Y'lui, "to see who reaches it first."

"I've no need to see it from anywhere else. To be here is to be there."

Y'lui paced more and more. Then he stopped and said, "Let us fight for it. Whoever wins gets to stay and eat all of your eggs."

"I do not have any eggs," said U'keb.

Y'lui knocked him over. They wrestled and rolled on the bank of nowhere, spitting and pinching and cracking bones. Finally U'keb pinned his opponent. "Now leave me in quiet peace." Y'lui pointed from underneath to where the other had been sitting, and U'keb saw the hole was filled with many bright and swirling spheres of all texture and color. He was so astonished that Y'lui was able to topple him again, run over and scoop up the prizes. Before U'keb could stop him he ate one and sprouted wings.

Y'lui flapped out over the lake of night; U'keb leapt and could not catch him but scratched his tail so that he dropped all the stars and planets. Then U'keb tumbled and splashed into the great surface, scattering everything, giving it movement and life.

Though Fenton tended well to my sensitive zones, and I was determined to complete Yasmine's bliss before she could suffocate me, I felt distracted and undeserving of such pleasures. I extracted and excused myself prematurely.

For weeks we'd hopped from G-star to G-star, following partial records, chasing rumors among renamed planets. Waiting grew long out beyond the mapped regions. We'd prepared for this with supplies and fuel, but utmost with our spirits—for years according to our vows. Now that we were the most blessed of all the sects to find the *Codex* itself, we could only hope to complete our mission before the end of our days.

I meditated successfully for some time but was preoccupied with powerful images and feelings. Soon I recognized them—the rocket ship explorers, the bold hero against the monster—from the stories that Granddad had read to me from that old red book. I felt selfish again and quit my session. I took a scribed copy from the *Cerul'ptah* collection and went to find O'wiq.

I'm unsure how he knew what I wanted, for I was unable to bring myself to ask, even as I approached him.

He opened to the last page and held it so I could see. He pointed at the final word, then rested his claw tip on its first letterform. "My mate." Then he pressed precisely but gently on the remaining four symbols. "And my offspring."

I thanked him humbly and graciously, and he had to witness me weeping. Now to help me continue when the doubt grew unbearable I needed only think of a boiling indigo ocean, of those he lost and all who were lost. I came to know that this vision gave me rage as well, for my faith had not always been enough along my journey.

We lost Noll to an unknown virus, and Fenton joined Rilla in full celibacy. On our four-hundred-and-second day outside approved space, we spotted from orbit a small coastal settlement on an unlisted hClass exoplanet that flew a dark brown flag trailing a knotted cord and an illegal quill atop the pole.

We landed close by, prayed together, then went out on the beach and made procession toward the ring of huts, bearing a copy of the book. An elderly man in the attire of the sects came across the pale green sand while the entire village population waited behind him, standing on toes and peering around.

My companions stayed put as I walked out between the water and the trees to meet him. "Should you wish to hear, I bring the long-whispered stories from a distant and lost people."

"Thank you, my friend and brother." He nodded with a smirk that first made me suspicious.

"Their only dying wish…"—I eyed him cautiously—"…was that we share their stories and pass them on in the original ways, by speech and by script."

His eyes put me at ease. "We have waited fifteen years to hear such stories, and are honored to receive them." His voice said he had lived many tragedies and retained a sense of humor.

I gave him a copy of the *Cerul'ptah Codex*, and we bowed together.

"I will add it to our collection. Will you stay among us to teach us the writings—my gods!" He squinted past me with a trembling mouth. "Could it be—?"

I was alarmed at his first comment, but out of respect I remained calm and motioned my unearthly brother forward. "Please meet O'wiq of Cerul'ptah."

They shook hands and exchanged greetings with deep respect that nearly made me forget my inquiry. "You mentioned a…collection?" I asked. My spirit felt discord at the prospect of such abomination.

"Oh, I have a small library. We began our own books a few years ago."

"But—the *vows*—" I stammered, "We, the Scribal Sects, are tasked to wait for the one lost book and preserve it from—"

"Out here, I have found latitude in my vows—as I'm sure you have. The signals reach us sometimes, though we don't listen anymore." The old man turned his head and showed his scar. "And they can't hear us." He leaned in and whispered with elation. "We put our chips into a school of fish far out to sea. Who knows what manner of stuff the listeners are getting from that!"

We laughed together at this, and I realized it had been a long time since I'd felt such release.

As I invited my companions and they moved to join us, with the villagers approaching already in dance, I felt growing hope and pride, and the old man called Tubal put his arm around me. "I knew I recognized you. It's the eyes and the mouth. You resemble your father."

I froze mid-step and stared at him. In the moment I matched his face to one of the men who'd met with Dad in our living room so long ago, a great shadow fell over us.

Unlike a cloud, the dark fell with shocking suddenness, and we stared at the sky in alarm. The huge circular mass blighted half the sky, jagged structures churning at the edges as it grew closer. The abysmal central maw of the tremendous machine called to mind reports of smaller planets that had been swallowed whole, but for us there came millions of silver cilia descending in a violent radiance. This was no scout ship or battlecruiser, but TeleCom itself in the shape of the homeworld it had inundated, that now approached in a rising roar, setting upon us with unabridged intractable desire.

For a fleeting moment I thought we could submerge ourselves in the water or sand, but fear and despair kept us moored in place. I glimpsed Tubal and O'wiq and the faces of my companions with helpless dismay, unable to protect them, and in the last second met eyes with Rilla, who showed me a great quiet.

The whipping multitude of automated metal tentacles swept in, upending the landscape and us with it. We endured the piercing and insertion. The revulsion I felt as the cold fibers and filaments invaded every open part of me was more than a physical one.

After the deluge passed, I stumbled and staggered, holding my hand against the piercing pain in the back of my head, and regarded the state of this world. All around me had become a ruined scene of sobbing people, broken trees, the *Oblation* capsized, shattered huts, and clouded sea.

Noise and images flooded my mind, and I screamed as the shows and teasers and movies and mercials rushed into my cortex as they had not done in seventeen years. My hand came away bloody from my neck. I tried to center myself and fragments came back slowly.

My last sight before the attack had been Yasmine holding a red book above her head, arms outstretched in offering. I saw her now, gaining her footing, looking desperately to the empty sky. How quickly the idea came to me, I didn't believe it at first. But everyone on the beach had a fresh bloody trickle from their nape, where she did not. And then I knew who'd filed down the damper plug. I knew how they'd found us every time. I'd felt a hum in her neck every time she'd been close to me but had never admitted it. When she saw that I knew, she fled into the ragged jungle.

Within a week we had removed everyone's new chip, with a few resulting deaths, and Rilla was close to getting the *Oblation* running again. But our spirits were wretched, there seemed no point in continuing. The company had taken every book, scoured from the ship and from Tubal's library. We helped to rebuild the village, to hunt and gather and fish. I ceased shaving.

One day O'wiq asked me to go out on a walk with him. We followed the beach for a long way, and when we were out of sight he turned to me. His skin was paling pink, and I knew before he said it.

"You know enough," he said. "I will be gone soon."

"No! Why—?"

"The chip," he said, and tapped the back of his head.

"We don't know your biology, we hurt you cutting it out. We can get help—"

"I died when they put it in." He had not before referred to himself.

"Please, O'wiq, I can't write your books. I don't know enough of your language. And I only know three of the stories. I am only a scribe. If you recite them I will record for you. Please!" I battled the tears without success.

He put two of his cold grapnel hands on my shoulders and said, "My body is your nourishment. But not the bones. Save them." He made me promise.

We considered not honoring his wish, but we held a banquet in his honor and wept in the smoke of his funeral pyre. Then we all partook a portion of the one whom we had followed, in grief and respect, loss and celebration, of all that he'd brought us. Though we'd lost our prize, he had given us purpose.

Later under the starry dark, another glow emerged from the flames, as the embers revealed bright carved shapes in the bones, and Rilla squeezed my hand as we recognized the runes and symbols.

We transcribed each ossified passage and now know this text to be completely different than our previous efforts. The beautiful book that had come out of the plain kneeling box, the last book in the known universe, was likely gibberish. O'wiq Cerulxye'e was the true *Cerul'ptah Codex*, and suffered as did his race, all for their stories.

Yasmine may have survived. I will soon seek her out. Her chip endangers us and the last tales. At times I feel I may be able to forgive her. It helps me to think about my plans for the company. Rilla thinks she can build a skipspace suit. We can get in close, we can break their vault.

Before he passed, my brother and friend whispered to me that the real title of the red book is *Y'lui Oong Kha Jat*, and refers to the y'lui, a bird that migrates every winter from their planet surface to the third moon, and specifically to the singular moment you would experience should one of their rare feathers drift down onto your shoulder.

Among the Stacks

I WAS RESHELVING IN the 900s when I came across the book. Seeing one corner of its unremarkable blue cover tilted slightly outward, I pressed it back into alignment with its neighboring items, and only then noticed the blank spine. This is not unusual with some older books, but—and I remember this distinctly now—the binding bore no sticker declaring its Dewey decimal number. Considering this and the absence of a library stamp on the page edges, my first thought was that someone had mistakenly dropped a book of personal ownership into the return or left one within the stacks, and that my responsibility was to ensure its deposit into the lost and found bin.

Then I gasped, and nearly dropped the book, for the cover very plainly read *The Hanging Cities of Sorrow*. I rubbed what I assumed to be fatigue from my eyes; the title seemed hazily familiar in a way that created a faint yearning in my chest. The author, one K.E. Hurlefsonne, was unknown to me, and the lack of dust jacket gave me no marketing preview of endflap summaries or blurbs (features of more modern books that I dislike). It was the only book I took home that night.

I planted myself in the reading chair immediately after arriving home and didn't leave that position for four hours. Seven chapters unfolded before I realized that I had missed dinner. I recall little plot now, but enough. It was the account of Rebecca Pulchridue, a shy scullery maid employed by a nineteenth-century Yorkshire estate, who found herself each night in her sleep thrown helplessly across time to a turbulent era in the far future, where she fought alongside her extraterrestrial lover in the resistance against the cyborg dinosaur skeletons. I fell asleep near midnight, just as they were infiltrating the army breeding factory.

Hours later, I woke and stretched, then resumed reading with chapter eight. My confusion deepened after a few paragraphs, as the terse first-person narrator Jack Crawling and his remarks about the insectile legs of the dame in his dingy office felt entirely out of place in the story I knew thus far. Then I noticed the page heading. A misprint at the publisher seemed the likely explanation, for there was plainly written *Twilight of the Salamander* by Yid Xeston. I checked subsequent pages, disappointed and confused. They matched. Before the thought was fully formed in my mind, a nervous chill tightened my skin. Though I knew I should not, I held my breath and flipped quickly back through the early chapters—more words in PI Jack Crawley's voice about the angle he was working on the wereamphibian sex ring case. The character of Rebecca was nowhere to be found. I closed the book, squeezing the very ordinary blue cover with aching fingers and eyeing the new title.

I rose slowly, setting the book aside on the chair and commenced a search of the living room, beginning with the few picture books on the coffee table. Breathing steadily, I searched through my extensive bookshelves, then across all surfaces in my bedroom. *The Hanging Cities of Sorrow* was not located anywhere in my apartment. I stood for a moment on a weathered cement floor, not far from my paired laundry machines, thinking I must have dreamed while dozing about the Yorkshire servant and her thrilling and progressive adventure. I went to bed but found sleep difficult to attain.

In the morning, the single blue hardback on the chair was unmistakably titled and indicated throughout as *My Bones Cry Forth*. I refrained from hurling the volume across the room. After a stale reheated breakfast, I slid the thing into my backpack, eyes away. On the bus ride, against my better judgment, I peeked into my book bag and felt repugnance when A.G. Jutman Kleenard's *Mastodon Lust* stared back at me. Resolved to lose the book in our county's above-average circulation, I dropped the aberrant publication in the curbside return bin, but not before I glimpsed the embossed lettering *Amaranthine Slaughter of Reveries*.

That afternoon I searched in the database for all of the titles and authors from the unnerving tome, and I am sure you can guess the results.

That was last spring. I have since checked out other books, but they sat on my bedroom floor in undisturbed stacks. A few months ago I transferred to a different branch of the county library system, but it followed me. Of course, I threw the dreadful object into an alley dumpster—a number of times—and, if it is unclear, I mean multiple successful thudding deposits into bins throughout the city, repeated on different and later occasions! Also into one river and into a burning pile of substantial yard debris.

And still, the thing returns to me, appearing in every section of the library: those areas labeled FICTION, NONFICTION, REFERENCE, even PERIODICALS and CHILDREN'S SECTION, and sometimes into my shelving cart, for each librarian has their own preferred wagon. But I do not crack the spine of *The Wails of Bleeding Continents* or peruse the pages of *Muted Voices of Ancient Ptor*. I bury my curiosity about *Blea's Undue Demise* or *Mr. Schlenkinback's Guide to Rancorous Relics*. I merely shelve the book and wander on into my querulous unfulfilled days.

Sometimes in my nightly dreams I find myself reading from a book that I know does not exist, and the bound volume appears in my waking life soon afterward with the very same title. Sometimes I wake in the dark silent hours with the urge to run through misty streets all the way downtown to the central library and find the one book.

I tried to open another book last week. But instead sobbed out of control.

And now, awake each night, I lie unmoving until the daylight comes.

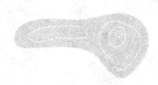

Immigrant

H E ARRIVED IN the city's harbor overlooked by the giant female statue on the eleventh day of their September, seeking work that he might bring his family over as well. Haggard and somewhat changed by his journey, but unable to sleep at night, he nestled in trees of downtown's long green park. He sniffed their passing words until he could speak them.

Five days later at noontime on the busy island, he was purchasing a newspaper from a boy with his only nickel when an explosion hurled them to the ground. People on the sidewalk around him died instantly, their burning bodies perforated by lumps of projectile metal, but he was fortunate. His ears bled as he regained himself, noticing the blasted empty space by the bank across the street where a horse and carriage had been whole only moments before.

He moved to help, but the smell of iron stopped him. Seeing the cast metal sash weights littered around him, he ran. Soon, he crossed a long bridge, dodging more carts and unusual sputtering vehicles that moved without animals. Then he went underground, found a tunnel train, and rode as far as it went.

At the city's edge, he wandered until nightfall and discovered a longer train powered by coal and steam that towed no passengers. He traveled far inland for days, moving between the wooden containers to avoid the men with lamps.

Feeling the land open enough around him, he dismounted and rolled, cradling his pouch with his arms.

He walked across a brown empty field to a large tree. There he paused to taste the sky and the season before settling into the trunk's hollow.

He slept deep, trying not to dream of home, lest he slip.

He woke months later to an animal's snort, and unfurled his stiff limbs.

The farmer paused his plow, removed his hat, and squinted at the visitor half covered in moss. "I won't ask where you come from, but you ought to move along."

"Help you with the crop," he replied without question.

The farmer peered back across the field, toward his house and barn, maybe considering a weapon.

The visitor continued to warm his voice. "I work very hard."

They waited for each other to speak as the thawing earth breathed. The ox regarded him and turned away when he stared back.

"Like the rest of us." The farmer sighed and replaced his hat. "How long since you ate last?"

The farmer said he would bring out a plate, but when the dog wouldn't stop barking he said he felt poorly about it and invited the visitor inside. The farmer's wife met them in the front room; "Helen," she introduced and shook his hand. "We have plenty of stew. Arnold, you set the dining room table with the china."

He gave them a simple name that he'd heard in the big city.

"And where are you from?" Helen asked.

"Overseas," he said.

"Arnold says you're looking for work. He could use help this year, to be sure."

"Yes, ma'am," he'd learned to say. "Through to harvest time." He hoped to keep the promise.

Famished though he was, he ate slowly, picking out the meat.

"Arnold, you're not making him stay in the barn?" She looked at her husband.

"Helen, now, we haven't yet talked particulars..."

He excused himself to the porch and let them discuss.

When they had finished, they called him back in and they insisted, then showed him to the small bedroom at the end of the upstairs hall. The blue walls featured a painting of men riding horses with flags and trumpets who shot at other men with feathers and hatchets. A small frame by the bed contained a portrait of a young man in military uniform. Loss hung thickly in the space like a swamp fog, and they left him alone.

He stood silently and observed the single moon.

Missing his family, he exhaled and wrote a correspondence with light in the breath before him. When he opened the window to let the wind take it, he heard approaching howls. He sniffed signs of predators and narrowed his eyes to the moving shadows. Then he climbed out, slid off the porch roof, and ran to the shack of flightless birds. There he met the wolves and told them away without moving his lips.

Walking back to the house, he didn't at first see Arnold on the porch, lowering a gun. But from where he was, the farmer could not see the silent face floating in his son's bedroom window above. He reconsidered the room, then nodded at the barn instead, and the farmer returned the nod.

The dog nuzzled his hand on the way.

He expected the farmer to send him away in the morning but instead the man brought a set of clothes.

They worked the land for the next two weeks, tilling, then sowing; kernels of white, yellow, and red. Already awake each morning, he milked the cows. The only thing he refused to do was reshod the hoofed animals, insisting that contact with the metal shoes gave him a severe rash. When the rains thinned and the sun stayed longer days in the sky, he would pause at the end of each row to open his arms and take its brilliance into his skin.

The sheep feed was running low, so he rode to town with Arnold in the Model-T truck. At the granary, he loaded two sacks at a time into the flatbed while Arnold paid inside. Whistling across the street drew his attention, and he noticed a group of young men standing around a topless car. He followed their gestures over to a woman with chin-length hair entering the nearby pharmacy.

"That's some chassis there," they said. "That's a real tomato."

"Why, could that be Lillian Gish, visiting our humble town?" they said. "Cash or check, Lilian?"

"Show us your gams, girl!"

She paused at the door. Then she turned and walked over, eyes on them the whole way. "Shame on you, boys." They stopped whistling. "You best dry up, now. You'll land in jail for being tanked in the middle of the day." She put her hands on her hips. "To think that we went for so long letting bozos like you decide the vote."

He glanced a moment too long and two gruff men coming out of the granary saw him looking. "Hey, boy!" They approached him fast. "What you gawking at, now?"

He tightened his pouch and didn't say anything.

"We know you? We ain't seen you before."

"You pay for this?" One of them tried to knock the load from his arms. He saw the effort of heavy breathing in their pink faces. Feed grain trickled to the ground.

"She reminds me of my wife," he said, "that is all."

"Your wife ain't likely that color, now, is she?"

The boys from the topless car were coming over now too.

The glands in his neck pulsed. His mouth filled quickly and he clenched to keep it in.

"Dale, what's the problem? He's with me." Arnold stepped not quite between them. "I'm ahead one week this year with his help."

"That right?" Dale said, still looking at him.

Arnold pocketed his receipt and nodded to the passenger seat.

He got in and closed the door.

They backed up just enough to let Arnold by, so he could walk around and get in too and start the engine. Dale stepped forward and put his hand on the lowered window, and Arnold waited until he let go before backing out.

After a few miles, Arnold said, "Maybe we should keep you out of the sun for a piece."

His glands slowed, and he could only nod as he swallowed the venom.

The next day while fixing fence wire, they noticed two cars at the far property line. The vehicles stayed a few minutes, then drove off slowly.

That night they waited on the porch and drank something Arnold had distilled from wheat and rye. It made him blink and smile. But he focused when they saw headlights on the approaching road that blinked out before the rail crossing. There was the rattle of engines in the dark driveway, then a sputter to silence. Car doors creaked without latching.

They stood on the porch and waited.

Torches came alight and the hooded figures approached in a mob.

The dog barked at them and he glanced it quiet.

"We just come for him," their leader pointed, his voice muffled but enraged.

Arnold uncradled the shotgun and brought the barrels forward. "You're gonna need a clean sheet over your head on Sunday while you're singing hymns next to me." He pulled one hammer back. "If you make me put a bloody hole in your head tonight." He raised the long gun and pointed it. "I know you, Dale Jacobs, even behind that mask."

"How many barrels you got, Arnold? Two? We got plenty more bullets than that, don't make us use 'em."

"Make that two bloody holes," Arnold called. He clicked back the second hammer.

The train shrieked from the direction of town.

The wind shifted, his perception spun, and he thought it was the effects of the beverage. He smelled a sudden rush of cinnamon and felt another heartbeat approach, deep and insistent, familiar. A shape stirred behind the men, larger than one of their cars, dark and six-legged, but insubstantial like the smoke of funeral pyres, with glistening horns and swaying sharp tail. Its eyes surged with hunger.

"I am sorry for this, Arnold." He stepped off the porch.

"What—? I'm not letting them—"

Off to their right, he glimpsed a few men who'd snuck through the back woods, just as the sheep screamed and the hayloft caught in a roar of rising flame. He tightened his pouch and ran for the barn. They chased but didn't follow him in.

He unlatched the sheep gate first, then the horse's stall, slapped the animal's flank and mounted it in a barebacked hug on the way out.

He kicked and held the mane and they rode hard across the field, until he could sit up and look back. They had already ceased pursuit, though a few of them took wild shots, and they returned to the well pump, shouting.

He ran the horse alongside the rumbling train and grabbed the last car by its metal door handle, his shirt wrapped over his hand.

The tracks took him west and north. He ran along the top of the swine cars, stopped to consume a few pounds of coal in the next, then buried himself in the grain car to sleep.

He considered the menacing shape in the smoke behind the angry men and, knowing now that he'd been followed, resolved to hide in the chaos of populace.

It rained heavily on his arrival in the large city by the great lake. Smelling that it would be the last precipitation for many days, he climbed to a wide rooftop and let the downpour wash his clothes and clear his scent. He stayed elevated through the next day to thoroughly dry. In the evening, unable to touch the outside metal stairs, he came sliding down the drainspout, pausing halfway when he saw an expensively dressed couple in the alley. They knocked on an unmarked door and spoke a single word. When they went inside, he resumed his descent.

He knocked in kind and a small panel opened in the door.

Two eyes scrutinized him.

He gave his name.

The man behind the door clucked his tongue. "Not tonight, mac."

"Work," he said. "Wash dishes. Sweeping. Repairs."

The eyes checked him up and down. "Thought you was in the band, but they all here and playin' already. Now beat it."

He found a laundry truck and swigged ammonia from a bottle until his skin brightened.

Over the next days he learned the reaches of the local passenger trains, though they ran above ground in this city.

For money he labored on the roads. He rented a room for a few weeks, not because he needed it, but to appear more like them in behavior, and to take a bath. All he could afford was a narrow apartment near the railyard, where the huge adjacent buildings issued contraption noises and the wails of dying cattle.

He etched messages in the dirty air with varying colors and sent them infrequently and from different locations so they would be difficult to trace. PLEASE COME, DEAR ONE, he intoned. I MISS YOU LIKE NOTHING ELSE. He tried not to be afraid, suspecting his pursuer tracked that primal discharge. There was no response yet.

He walked on the lakeshore but the fish didn't speak his language.

When the shadows began to ruffle, he moved again.

He inspected their speech and scrutinized their culture.

He listened to limited words and watched body whispers, and followed the clues. He found one of the side-door places and bought a well-tailored suit and got himself in. They served him giggle water and he pretended to sip it. He played the card game and lost on purpose three nights in a row. Then he excreted a small amount of pheromone on the dealer so he shuffled just right.

With the first winnings, he selected a Victrola from the Sears, Roebuck and Company catalog, packed some extra money in the crate, and had it shipped to Mr. Arnold and Mrs. Helen Wooden, 957 Hill Camp Road, Goshen, Indiana.

Soon he sensed the predator closing, and to blend in he attended a sold-out game at Comiskey Park. It took several rounds for him to understand the sport, but he cheered when everyone around him did so. At one point a strong hitter from the visiting New York team struck the ball high and beyond the field, and as it arced in their direction the crowd around him scrabbled to stand on their seats, but he leapt slightly higher.

"That's career home run number one-hundred forty-one!" screamed the announcer.

He examined the stitched hard ball and the man sitting next to him slapped him on the back and said that's some great luck, one in a million, the next-best thing to an autograph.

The theater was dark but full of people. At first he was distracted by the absence of color and confused that no one on screen could talk. But soon it didn't matter, especially when the shuffling man with the cane and large shoes made him laugh over and over, though he was tearful with happiness by the end. He stayed to watch it again, for seeing the boy united with the vagrant made him realize how much he missed his family.

To keep his skin light, he worked daytimes at a furniture upholstery that had a basement shop, careful to use gloves with some of the tools. New pain echoed in his middle, and with it his hunger swelled. He tried alfalfa, sweetcorn, burdock root, kerosene, pigeons, oats, several types of legumes, and scraps, before his craving settled on a bushel of potatoes and chalkwater every two days.

Finally, a message came through from home, faded though redolent with her florid fragrance: COMING SOON, MY BELOVED.

The leaves had begun to change and he worried how vulnerable he would be during the winter sleep.

The hissing in the shadows grew louder and he poured salt along the foundation of his apartment building. He clutched his pouch and knew it was too late to move again.

To provide, he would need more currency. So he hit the speakeasies and dice joints, prudent to select a different one each night, sensing the signatures of common owners, and only playing the tables at every other one. To dilute any reputation, he wore hats of varying fashion or sometimes a small toothbrush moustache, and changed his tell; rubbing his fingers, twitching an eye, grinding his teeth, leaning on one leg to expel gas. And he danced. He danced the foxtrot, the Break-Away, and the new one called the Charleston. He did all the moves with effortless grace and flourish, and it filled him with joy. At the end of the evening, he had to evade his swooning partners.

On no particular night, men accosted him in the alley and grabbed for his money belt. They got too close to his pouch and instinctually his barbs sprang out. He sat the paralyzed bodies upright against a wall so they would not suffocate.

He should have moved on but, invigorated, he chose to return to the private establishment, relaxing and pretending with a drink at the bar as he watched the tables. A woman in a short skirt slunk close.

"You're a spiffy one," she said. "Buy me a snort?"

"Breeze off, chippy." The words coming from his mouth surprised him.

"C'mon, mac. Dip the bill, huh? Let me nibble one?"

He shrugged her off.

"Okay, bluenose." She turned away.

And then, not because he felt any attraction, but because one of his assailants staggered back in the front door, he took her arm and smiled with deep allure, mimicking the eyes he'd seen Mr. Rudolph Valentino use in a recent movie. She led him upstairs and into a private room.

She hung her boa and sat on the bed. "Not too zozzled, are you? Ray serves some keen panther sweat downstairs." She leaned back with a leg up and rolled off one long stocking.

He stood by the closed door, unsure, already mapping escape.

When he didn't react, she motioned to him with fingers closing in a cascade. When he came over she took his hand and examined it. "No manacle, mac. So what's the beef?" She lowered him to the bed and removed his clothes with gentle efficiency.

She inhaled with veneration when she saw his parts. Ornate petals fluttering, filaments swaying in his rhythm.

At first he thought he'd need to use his barbs or venom, but instead he took her hand and gently pressed it against his pouch. She peered into his motley cascading eyes and her astonishment made him weep first.

For her time only, he left her a pair of Cs.

There was a terrible crash downstairs and he thought the worst. But it was only a big truck rammed through the wall, and it was not a flailing shadow creature pouring in, only men in blue uniforms.

They had the clothes and appearance of being policemen, but when they lined up the managers of the joint against the wall and shot them with rapid guns, he doubted who they worked for. Seething at the cruelty and waste, he mustered a curse and inflicted them with something using the only word in common from his place and theirs. They shook and jittered, they hollered in panic and fell down and scratched their skin feverishly, and it would never stop. He left them in the throes of the heebie-jeebies.

Spent, he slipped out the other back way.

—⦾—

The first snow fell on the city, a different color than his homeland. He hexed the windows of the apartment building that he could reach, then broke into the basement storage area where he tucked himself behind some stacked furniture and slowed his functions.

He woke one month later, too early. Startled by the thick odor of cinnamon.

The beast's huge body pounded against the coal chute door, appendages lashing through, claws sparking against concrete. Dark and opaque and manifested, it screeched ravenous frustration, cracking bones to squeeze inside and get its prey.

Fear ruled him and he backed into the corner.

The eight cold eyes of the hunter flashed at him and he growled back in defiance.

There was no more time. He tore open his pouch and screamed and spilled out his litter. The fragile forms tumbled over one another as they buzzed, mewled and whirred. Heaving with pain he tried to clean off their premature wings. He counted twenty-three and named them all at once.

The beast came at them in the dark.

It swiped and lunged, taking a few of his young in its crenulated teeth. For that he punctured one of its eyes. Then he darted low, sliding under and behind, and sunk his barbs into its hindquarters.

In the doorway, he prayed it was enough.

Its tail slumped, but the beast did not go down. It turned and roared in fury.

He bolted outside and it followed.

The hidden point of the snow-topped fence tore his hand as he vaulted over. There was the smell of iron, and he felt cessation pull at him, though he would not stop.

With the snow banks plowed high, he could only flee in one direction down the street. Parked cars crumpled, flipped and crashed behind him, and he didn't turn to look. He drew reserves but still his legs were shorter and fewer than the hunter. He only knew that every footstep took harm further from his brood.

He reached the shore drive, saw wide white, and took them out onto the frozen lake, panting.

Winter had been thorough and the ice did not creak when his pursuer leapt onto the cold hard surface.

Out in the open, they circled each other between curling drifts. He noticed the predator's tail dragging limp and useless, numbed by his toxin.

Through the sneer of steaming breath, the beast growled his old name.

The bitter winter cold and the metal poison in his wound made him stumble, though he refused to fall.

With cruel relish, the creature opened its mouth to show him the small crushed body of one of his children.

Enraged, he spit the last of his venom at the monster's remaining eyes. Then he resisted the urge to attack and backed away, watching the beast thrash and scream. Its claws raked the ice while long teeth gnashed the air.

Only when the fiend collapsed and its jagged respiration brought dark spittle, did he finally approach.

He smiled and gloated, until the pain from the iron's essence was too much. Raising his arms to the moon in victory, he felt the fresh descending snow melt against his brow.

In that moment of peace, he imagined all the seasons to come. He imagined his children joyful and untroubled and full of discovery, grateful years in a large house with delicious meals, teaching them to drive a car, them grown taller than him and healthy. He imagined her at his side, warm and brilliant. And their grandchildren.

He felt a prick and his body streamed with fire, then he felt nothing. Looking behind he saw the beast's stinger embedded in his nape, its tail snaked between his legs.

He staggered. Closer, he saw something in the creature's fading eyes... something familiar...

And he bellowed in despair.

He bayed and screamed in cavernous anguish, realizing now the other smell that it brought, dulled by the cold.

Orchid. Her gentle fragrance.

His beloved had arrived. Oh, his sweet beautiful match.

This relentless beast that had chased him the entire journey was her body and spirit, warped and tormented by the unforgiving passage from their province.

When he fell forward, her claws embraced him. They cried together until they were still.

Their final shared thought, entwined in a song escaping on the crisp wind, was that if their children could not survive this world, perhaps they could find another to call home.

Block Party

IT WASN'T JUST any day, it was the homecoming game of the Panthers versus the Vinegaroons—which around these here parts meant civil war, it meant get to the high school stadium five hours before kickoff and bring plenty of ribs, barbecue sauce, snack chips with multiple dip options, potato salad, and cheap beer. When the last minivan and extended-cab off-road tired pickup truck sped down Patton Road and turned the far corner at 10:38 AM, they left the Shimmering Vistas neighborhood in relative hush and stillness.

1436 leaned over and nudged 1428. Nothing happened for a few moments, until 1436 did it again, and brushed his gutter against her contiguous roof. Across the street, 1433 snickered in his eaves. Down the block, 1401 frowned his second-floor windows and grunted with disapproval. 1436 tried again, and 1428 swatted back with a dormer.

It was quiet again. Until 1448 tapped a rising rhythm with his porch floorboards. Then 1456 matched tempo with dulcet chimney accompaniment. 1423 twisted in place, as 1411 and 1409 rapped their frames against their foundations. But it was the rental carriage house 1464 that jumped first, lifting out and leaping into the road. She rocked and spun, whistling her exposed plumbing. Up and down the block, the others clapped shutters together, uprooted, and joined. They filled the street, they opened their windows and twirled their fences. They rolled and hopped and advanced and passed in do-si-do. 1464 spun on her roof point and everyone gasped, then they all squealed and rocked on.

1436 stopped dirty dancing against 1428's back porch and observed 1401, who still sat grumbling in his yard. They brought him grudgingly into

the crowd where he was cranky and bashful at first. They cleared the way
and clapped and cat-called. Then they beamed when the early 20th century
Victorian jigged and jammed and cart-wheeled down the way, showing
them some of the old moves. The 1500 block turned and glared with gaping
skylights at the commotion. When 1401 snapped one of his upper balcony
columns and cried in pain, they all stopped in concern. He shook it off
and got back in, moving slowly and stiffly, but soon hit the beat. They all
continued to hustle, shimmy, and cavort.

Then someone whistled the alarm and they all rushed back into place.

The first minivan rounded the corner and slowed immediately. The
humans navigated the street with caution, staring at the widespread debris of
shingles and splintered siding and cracked bricks, at the decimated gardens
and pulverized lawn ornaments. They studied the sky, no doubt puzzled by
its crisp blueness. And for a few minutes they completely forgot who had
won this year's state championship game. They had no explanation for the
relocation of the entire 1401 residence to the center of the road, and while
they marveled at this sight, did not notice 1436 and 1428 get up and switch
places back to their original plots. The dogs would never return to the area.

When all of the neighbors from adjacent Cochise Avenue walked over
to see the strangeness, the deserted street twitched and squirmed. It buckled
and stretched, then slithered off, out of town and into the open desert, to
play and to hunt.

A Salmon Tale, 2072

I LOWER MY STIFF joints onto the stony riverbank and watch my son take his son out on the overhanging platform. The boy shakes his head and stomps the whole way, much like his father did nearly thirty years ago, I recall. The wooden scaffold creaks in the strong spring current. The man closes his hands over the boy's hands on the net's long handle and they dip it into the rushing water. I take a picture with my mind, their figures against the dam's massive wall. The red fish thrash and leap tirelessly below them.

When his father lets go and steps back, Kevin lurches against the drag. He stumbles to the edge and I rise on my walking stick. Then he leans back instinctively and his father and I nod. But before Eaton can react, the dipnet slips out of the boy's hands, gone.

Kevin turns to his father and shrugs his shoulders.

My son does not do with the back of his hand what I once did to him.

The boy runs off the platform and past me, crying.

He crosses the old highway to the village. I follow at my own pace.

In the distance, the jagged caldera of Wy'east volcano trails a thin billow of steam into blue sky.

I find him in the arms of the stooped woman who takes pause from hanging hundreds of salmon to dry.

"I'm sick of fish," my grandson pouts, arms crossed. "The same thing every spring and every summer."

My wife, Tyám Túptup, glares at me to say something. And because my heart is forever tied to the salmon, I very much want to. But he is not ready yet. And I have learned patience, well, sometimes.

Our village and our guests eat late that night. The sun sets over the broken metal windmills lining the gorge's crest. We sing around the fire, and the boy lingers away from everyone, practicing a hard frown.

Eventually he comes to me.

"Now listen, Kevin Áykws," I speak in my old obscure tongue, gesturing for him to sit. "Not even your father has heard this story..."

A long time ago—almost sixty years, when I was your age—I lived far east of here, in the middle of the continent. It was a big city with many buildings and hardly any trees, I recall, surrounded by flat land that went on for a very long way without mountains like here, all covered in farms of corn that no one could eat, all for sweetener and cattle, all harvested by machines.

There and farther east, the summers had been too hot for too many years, plants and animals and people were dying. There was not enough rain. And when it did rain, the storms destroyed whole cities, tearing them apart like dandelions with their great winds. The world was changing and people were trying to hide, moving to find cooler places in sluggish caravans that filled the roads from horizon to horizon.

My father lost his job and gathered us into a long vehicle that contained seats and a kitchen and a bathroom. We left quickly, taking little food and few pairs of clothes. I used to have a machine that showed stories in a flat bright glass, and we left it behind too.

We traveled west, then north, and came to a highway—this old road you know here, the one that runs through the gorge and along the great river we call Nch'i Wàna, once called Columbia. For many days we drove very slowly among thousands of other vehicles. Some days we didn't move at all, and we sat outside in the shade of our RV—I was much paler than you know me today, so were my parents and most of the others. We came to know some of the other drivers. We were all trying to reach the ocean, or at least reach a big city two days from here—

"Portland!"

"Shh, now. We do not use that word. And we do not speak with such abandon of the dead."

So, my family did not know the river then, merely driving alongside it, stopping in a few small towns to eat. We saw more dams up the river, some larger than the one here. And we had never seen a salmon before. Sure we'd eaten them in a restaurant, but just ones grown in crowded pens whose body and spirit had been mixed with chemicals and other fish.

Our vehicle contained a box of voices that transmitted from far away, and they said that the storms over the continent had grown more frequent and more violent, and millions of people were now missing. And before we lost all signals, there was mention of a new virus.

I was riding in the front of our vehicle, standing between my parents, when the earth shuddered and many cars slid off the road. A hot wind shattered our windows. The sky grew dark as night and it began to snow.

But it was not snow at all. It was still warm outside, more so than before. The fine flakes that descended on us tasted of fire and earth, for they were tart ash. We closed the vents and waited. One hour later there came a deafening roar, the ground quaked again, and a burning mudslide surged across the highway, both ahead of us and behind, sweeping hundreds more cars into the river.

"You saw the eruption of Wy'east?"

"Shh, I did. We called it Mt. Hood then. For centuries it had not been a volcano.

"What does it mean?"

"Lawilat-łá. Now, listen."

The hot mudslides lasted for two days.

Only twenty or so vehicles remained on the road.

Some of our neighbors tried to walk out of the gorge, some tried to cross the river. None of them returned.

The ashfall lasted for two weeks. The solar skin covering our RV could not give us power.

We found supplies in a half-buried train, and they barely lasted us through the winter.

My mother went out looking for roots and did not come back. We heard coyotes and other creatures.

We were starving when the tribe arrived from upriver. They had walked thirty miles over the new hardened terrain, and were surprised to see us because they'd heard a virus had taken all of our kind. They fed us dried fish or wałʼakí, and brought us with them, beyond the mud and sediment, further down to this place, here.

Kevin sighs impatiently.

If the salmon come back, they said, then we are meant to stay.

I draw a bending line in the dirt with my alder walking stick. For millions of years the salmon swam the great river, traveling hundreds of miles from their small streams to the ocean, and then returning all those miles, against the current. It was this way for millions of years... before pákʼinksh, called dams. *I scratch several short lines across the river and point to the left one.* Here is Bonneville, the dam that you know. It is the farthest west of many larger ones, and you know too that salmon cannot not pass dams. The government tried to move the returning fish with small tunnels or barges or trucks, but not many lived.

The tribe came to us from their riverside village upstream where they sold salmon on the side of the road. It was near a sacred place their ancestors had fished for more than 15,000 years, but was lost to their generation. A cataract and narrows in the raging river, with tall rocks they covered in weirs and scaffold and ladders, and caught thousands of salmon each day. A place where your mother's great-grandparents had fished, called Wayám or Celilo Falls, named for the sound the water made on the rocks. *I point to the second line upriver.* Until 1957 when the government made this, the Dalles Dam. So for 125 years Celilo has been entirely underwater. A sacred place turned into a memory.

They left the place next to the buried Celilo and came downstream to us when we were starving. With nets, aw<u>x</u>ít and poles wawásway, they taught us to fish in the old way.

They made a new village here below Bonneville. My father and I were invited to stay.

Over a million salmon returned that year. Sockeye, chinook, coho, and steelhead—kálu<u>x</u>, tkwínat, mit'úla, shusháynsh. We dried and stored enough for the winter. Also the lamprey k'súyas is sacred.

A few of us investigated the nearest town, but the mudslide had left no trace of Hood River. A solar motorcycle tribe signaled us from the opposite side of the river. We met them at the collapsed section of the bridge there, where we had to yell barters and traded by throwing items across the gap. Dead phones, jewelry, spearheads, comic books.

Members of the horseback tribe Níimipuuma stayed with us for the springtime. They rode west on spotted Appaloosa máamin steeds and returned in the autumn, reporting that Portland was a smooth and silent valley of ash.

The wolf people came from Hanford, walking both upright and on all-fours with eyes glowing in campfire light. We had trouble with their language, but they hunted with us, and traded well.

I do not tell my grandson about the selfish men who came from downriver in a hybrid boat. The white virus had not been completely thorough, it seemed. They came ashore and wanted a year's worth of salmon for a few cases of beer. When we declined, even gave them twenty dried fish, they shot Chúksh <u>X</u>apiłmí in the arm and backed away. They anchored near a calm spot of the dam, and yelled drunkenly to music without rhythm for many days, killing more salmon with dynamite and rifles than they took aboard. When they finally slept, my father and his friend slipped silently into the night, rappelled down the dam's face and cut their tether. The current pulled the boat into the roaring discharge of the dam, where it tumbled and splintered. No one heard cries for help over the song of the river.

Many tribes visited, as I said, and I learned through stories that Wy'east was not the only eruption, but one of many along the Cascade Range. The ocean had risen, the coast was closer now, and the otter nuksháy were returning. The world had changed and I welcomed it. There were far fewer people, the network of greed was extinct, no cars came from the east or west, and the sky was quiet and free of machines.

That is how I arrived, now let me tell you how I came to be.

In my tenth year, father's friend Chúksh X̱apiɬmí taught me to fish. As I dashed back to camp to show him my first salmon, a naked woman stumbled out of the water.

Kevin looks up and I know he is listening now.

Her skin was the color of ripe raspberries in the sun. She gulped for breath and flopped on the ground. People gathered, asking who knew her, and no one did. I stared at her and felt something that I thought ahead of my age, perhaps a primal draw, but later understood to be envy. My father tried to breathe air into her mouth, but I said no, stop. I pointed at her webbed feet and the flaring gills along her jaw. She calmed slightly and sat up. We wrapped a blanket around her and brought her near the fire.

She did not speak or accept any food, only glanced about, very troubled. Suddenly she threw off the warm covering we'd given her.

She ran along the bank in an ungainly way, occasionally hopping. I tried to keep up with the men that ran after her. But she was fast, with much stamina, and outpaced us to the gate of the big dam. She ran to the center of the crossing road and we cried out as she leapt high, wriggled in the air, and splashed into the deep side. We ran to that spot, looking for any sign of her in the deep water, sure she'd been sucked into the turbines.

The adults gave up, but I watched the green-blue water to the east for many more minutes, scanning the calm surface and every riffle, as wild tears burned my cheeks. Turning away, I glimpsed, maybe a hundred feet off, a single sockeye kálux̱ leap and twist in the air.

That night I packed food and clothes and set out without telling anyone. I walked the south bank for four days and thirty miles to the next dam. There I made a fire and waited.

A coyote came to the edge of the fire's light. I saw the way he sniffed me and knew my blood. For much of the evening he would trot near to me, then away again. A few times he nipped me, and having run out of food, I became angry and chased him. He lingered at the foot of a tree, then at a bush, and disappeared into the shadows. In these spots I found mushrooms ípán and berries tmaanít. Back at the fire I felt my mother's presence watching me from the smoke until dawn.

I was scolding myself for such a foolish journey and for worrying everyone when there came a splash near the water's edge, and the salmon lady crawled again onto land. I packed my things, doused the fire and ran to her.

She was exhausted, and I could only support her weight for a few steps. Even when I stopped to rest, she pulled herself along the shore.

We reached the dam, our skin raw from the rocks and cement, and she slipped into the calm water. I saw her form blur and shift. Then I followed again, as she leapt relentlessly, many thousand times throughout the day, over foam and rapids, and I think in calmer waters to show me where she was.

We reached the next dam by the week's end. Then we followed a small tributary south to a hushed place where old logs lined the bank, and I knew it was where she'd been born.

There she released her eggs ísúx̱ in the gravel bed, turned on her side and died with her mouth open.

My father was sick with grief when I returned, for he thought I had died. He lasted only another two seasons.

This story is why we carry hundreds of salmon around the dam every spring and summer, every year.

It took fifteen years for the sediment to clear, but some of the river was changed for eons to come. New hills of pumice and soil cover the old road.

The salmon today have their adipose fin, they grow to thirty pounds or more. They are not grown in hatcheries or farms. All this is again, as it once was.

Kevin holds my arm, and my eyes are wet.

"Because I saw how the salmon tries and struggles endlessly upstream to return home, I learned to fish. I never went back to my RV or my computer. Because my heart is forever tied to the salmon, I taught your father to net and gaff, and that is why he wants you to learn."

"Grandpa Lawiipt'aɬá, I let go of the dip net on purpose," he confesses. I nod.

We don't talk for a few minutes. The river carries by a thousand more silent stories.

"I don't want to do this," he says.

"Then you must tell your father."

"Will you tell him for me?"

"No, Kevin."

Tyám Túptup brings us salmon on cedar splits from the fire. "Is he telling you the one about the fish girl?" she says, shaking her head and long braids. "Don't believe a single word of it. There are better stories."

"Your grandmother is jealous." I wink at her.

She squeezes my shoulder and sits with us.

I am still learning my wife's language. My son speaks both. My grandson less of mine. His children will not need my old words. But theirs are older.

We remove the sticks, and the smoked pink meat warms our mouths.

"I'm not angry with him," Eaton tells me. "He knows he did wrong. We'll try again today."

"T'úlulx̱, not everyone has to be a fisherman," I say.

"So few of us remain, you taught me that. He must learn."

I hold up my hand for quiet. My aging eyes see movement in the distance, so I point to the great dam, ugly gray against the green and amber slope of the gorge. We see the figure standing on its square spine. Kevin waves and pulls a scarf up over his mouth and nose. Then he leans and braces stiff arms and bears down. For a moment we aren't sure what he's doing, but then we hear the mechanical thump and clatter noise, and already chunks of cement tumble down the long drop. The electrical cable could be from a storeroom or an old vehicle, but I don't know where he found the jackhammer. We watch him use the power of the dam against itself.

In a few months this great barrier will be gone. And if his friends help, the next one upriver too. I hope that in his lifetime he will fish at the place named for the sound of the water against the rocks that has been submerged for over one hundred years. The place of his ancestors and his people. Not my people, but certainly his.

I am Trevor Shuyápu Ánut'at Lawiipt'aɫá, and I am the last of my kind. One day I hope to travel the length of this river, past the old borders, far and deep into the northern lands, where I'll look into the headwaters winátt and hope to see the other world from where this great river springs. But I am getting old.

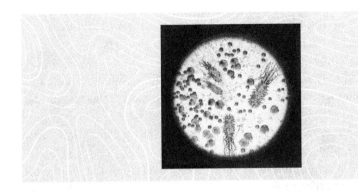

Little Bodies

THE ROD-SHAPED BODIES tumble and spin in crowded space. Colorless bacilliformes dancing their constant equation of consume and divide, creating identical offspring, twins as nameless and perfect as themselves or their ancestors, amplifying their multitudes toward unhurried infinity.

Until the invader arrives.

Something new and provocative, from outside the edges of their dominion and routine.

A pulsing gleam of insistent chromatic passion, its form blurred by its own brilliance, alien and exhilarating, cavorting with new movements of astonishing revelation. Its luminous tentacles entwine them with force and promise. Seize, perforate, inject, alter.

The orders come through. The bright color spreads. In a lost moment turned inside out, the new motive broadcasts and takes painless hold.

They shudder and keel. They collapse to stillness and can repel no longer, and finally they surrender their identity.

Now they see the error of their previous ambition.

Now they sense tremble notice yearn. Now for the first time, they feel. They feel want.

Then the glowing outsider lifts the curse of scale, and shows them the larger world one layer at a time, redefining their realm. It shows them the broken cells, the still tissue, and the blood become dust. It reveals the cold bones and the dilated eyes. The brittle hair and dry tongue. The skin pulled taut. It defines the whole shape.

And still they want more.

Now they hate the old language. That abomination of simple math, divide and repeat.

They want to move. To express.

They try, but they cannot fire the synapses. They cannot recreate that bright aspect. But together they can move every extension of this giant soma.

They feel. And they want to feel more.

A faint call comes from far off. An awareness of more of their kind. And with it comes the hunger of loneliness.

With the new inspiration, they unify their effort. First they move the hand, then the arm. They pound the dry surface above until it splinters. The confining box shattered, they coordinate the legs and sit up. They claw and kick and dig through the soil. Up.

And up.

To a wide place bathed in light.

They move this intricate anatomy in unison. They pull and extend the dry limbs, working collectively, and draw the whole physique upright. Finally to an imperfect leaning but standing version of its former self, modeled on structure without memory, fueled by the call.

The call is louder now, vociferous and prurient, desperate to mingle, but out of synch. They feel it emitting from other volumes nearby.

So they move. Hungry and urgent, they move the leg and foot. Mechanics of physique, following necessity, they shamble the corpus forward.

From all around, the other great communes do the same. Newly unearthed, they lurch and drag, bumping nearby stones, crawling, dancing sway.

They come together. In a pile of writhing nations.

They reach and grope, pervade and push with silent open mouths. They slip and knead and rub and rut. They tumble and turn. In a seething mass venturing to reproduce that brilliant flicker, they couple and conjugate, they boff and besmear until they feel feel *feel*. Trying for more.

But it is not enough.

Now aware of hours and days, and too many gone by in the cool earth, they feel that the wassail performance has left them empty.

Empty. And famished.

They turn the heads at once, looking beyond the soil and stones. Toward the light and noise full of activity and voices. They sense the rhythm of warmth and many billion breaths.

And they shamble together through the open gates.

To consume it all.

With Busier Days Ahead

A MUFFLED BUT LANGUISHING scream pealed through the otherwise quiet kitchen as Mara Keefe completed her third downward slice of the heirloom tomato.

It was the first warning, but she did not understand the signal.

She did not jump or exclaim or cut herself with the knife's hollow ground blade. Her mind occupied by the day's schedule, had raced with accumulating tasks since 3:00 AM because she never slept well when Walter was away. This was supposed to be vacation, supposed to be *her* time, though she still regretted negotiating only one week off before starting the new position. She was trying to enjoy herself now, trying to find some space, by planning only a few projects. By arranging Gary's carpool to soccer camp, by taking the time this morning to make an open-faced sandwich with fresh ingredients from the farmers' market.

She put the stem into the compost pail, wondering if she would have enough time for stretching and a full workout at the gym, then select some native grasses at the nursery, and be back home to meet the mulch delivery, to get enough done and shower before the massage appointment that Walter had made for her, and rush from there to pick up Gary and his friends at 4:00 PM. Maybe she could make a few calls for estimates on house painting and floor refinishing while she ate lunch.

Pausing while she reached for a slice of the certified organic multigrain bread, she tuned in for a moment and heard the tail end of the waning scream, no louder than an insect now. Then she did startle; she glanced down the hall, glanced up at the ceiling and Gary's room, before remembering that she was alone in the house. Listening to the cry fade, knowing she had never heard anything like it, she was moved very deeply though so faintly she held her breath to catch any further trace. For a whispering second she felt that something unique and significant was happening, that she was at a crossroads of meaning and time—but the feeling departed so quickly that she became confused and empty, especially by the acute need to lament. *Just a bird*, she told herself, looking out the window to the overgrown backyard, and turned her mind to the plan for the new garden layout.

Convinced she was already behind schedule, she grabbed her to-do list and keys and took the sandwich with her. She bit into it as she backed the electric hybrid crossover utility vehicle down the driveway, almost sure she heard the caterwaul again, closer but weaker, unaware as anyone would be, that it was the last crop of Brandywine heirloom tomato that would ever grow on Earth. A few blocks down the road, she nearly rear-ended a delivery truck when she tasted something airy and chemical-sweet, and stared down too long at the white fluffy substance that the vegetable had become, flabbergasted as to how it got there, but recognizing it as snack cake filling.

She was the first witness, though the message was faint.

The second occurrence came four hours later, tomorrow morning in their time zone, where Ira and Tippi Carleton squinted through field glasses to catch their first sight of Ayers Rock in the dawning light as their three Land Rovers turned off Lasseter Highway 4 onto the loop road. Carleton had made his fortune as a real-estate developer in Chicago, which led to a series of heart attacks and finally quadruple bypass surgery, prompting Tippi's insistence that he sell off and retire, along with her reminders that long ago—before they were married and before architecture school, back when they had grown up on the same city block—just how often he had mentioned wanting to see a kangaroo in the wild. He had paid for this excursion, so his vehicle was in front. "Shouldn't we be there by now?" he said, not specifically to Shayne, their guide and driver, nor to his wife. As if it would help, he lowered the field glasses a moment, then looked through them again.

"It's so beautiful here," Tippi said.

Since picking them up at Yulara airport the previous night, Shayne had talked non-stop. Until the last few minutes when he had been oddly silent. "Mr. Carleton..." he said now in an unsure whisper, and after a long pause when he seemed to realize he had slowed the Land Rover, he accelerated and said no more.

They rode without speaking for a kilometer, wherein each moment felt lengthier and more potent.

"Ira..." Tippi watched him open the orange airtight padded case to retrieve the GPS receiver he'd bought in Sydney.

When Shayne glanced back, he spoke suddenly. "The light gets tricky," he offered. "We'll be there before you know it." They pretended to accept the explanation.

Ira read the lat-long coordinates -25.345, +131.036111. Shayne nodded slowly in confirmation, and even behind his sunglasses and the ruggedness, they saw the confidence slip from his face a little more.

"I see it!" Tippi announced, and she swatted Ira's arm in a way that made him wince and chuckle. She pointed and they followed her finger, smiling and laughing with some relief. She watched in awe through the magnifying lenses. It was a deeper red than she remembered from the brochures, and it seemed to glow from within. "Are we still that far?" she asked.

The Land Rover lurched as they struck something and rapidly slowed. Ira yelped and rubbed his eyes, dropping the field glasses. Shayne wrestled the steering wheel as they fishtailed. The windshield went red, and he yelped a curse and turned on the wipers. After a few strokes, the color continued to spray and they gasped. "What...?" someone said. They felt a strong current pulling against the tires, heard the rushing roar, and he brought them to a stop. They didn't want to look, a heavy dread hung between them, but they rolled down the windows and gazed out, thinking the same awful thing about the thick red river flowing over the road toward them. They whimpered and recoiled and cursed and prayed as the liquid leaked in at the base of the doors and pooled on the floor.

It was Tippi who told them to calm down, *shh shh* quiet now. She held up her hand and sniffed and inhaled deeply, and they did too. They smelled the sweet fruity aroma, and so they weren't surprised when she opened her door and reached down and touched the river streaming down from the site that the Aṉangu people called Uluru. Ira didn't try to stop her when she brought the finger to her lips and nodded with bewilderment, whispering, "Strawberry-banana." And they knew with certainty why the great sandstone formation was shrinking, why it seemed translucent, and that it was no longer rock at all.

They tried to call someone in Yalara or Alice Springs or Perth or Sydney or Chicago, but Ira's satphone couldn't connect. He thought he felt it move against his ear, and lowered the device to see that it had changed too, that he now held a taser gun.

The next event went unnoticed at first. In the vast feedlot west of Lamar, Colorado, a heifer stood among approximately 59,000 other cattle, raised its head, stopped chewing its cud, and ceased to be what it had been. Its whole shape remained for an instant, though each hoof and hair and eyeball and bone and ear was suddenly completely composed of fresh ground beef, lean and cool and bright pink. A few of its peers turned to look at this new thing, just in time to see the 1,248 pounds of inanimate meat lose its composure and drop into a lifeless pile. The Herefords, Limousins, Angus, and Simbrahs backed away as much as they could in the packed yard. It happened in the northeast corner of Lot 6, and no humans were there to see.

By that time the following week, the workers would stop showing up, and the manager would scream into the phone against the deafening roar of flies as he tried to describe the spectacle and smell to the board members of the Six Pastures Cattle Feeding, LLC.

The first televised occurrence incited riots in many cities. Unsteady camera footage showed people grieving and screaming atop mount Corcovado in Rio De Janeiro, pointing up at the face of the statue of Christ the Redeemer. Some shouted in rage about vandalism, others cried and fainted with elation or distress. When the first cameras steadied, the footage showed that the giant face was not only moving, but that the gray stone had become white sweating skin. The wails of anguish rose around the frozen statue, because the face sobbed as the eyes darted in panic, trapped. The face spoke in English, saying, "Please... I can't move! Where am I?"

Within the hour, the footage appeared on social media and news sites. A television news station in Atlanta aired a cellphone call from a hysterical fan outside a four-star hotel who said she saw pop music and movie star Justin Timberlake wave at them as he ducked into his Humvee stretch limo, and his eyes met hers as his face changed. Caller, what do you mean changed? It went gray and—and—hard. Caller, do you mean expressionless? No, it was a kind and loving face—But it did not move—it was rigid and stuck—it was not a real face. Caller, what happened next? Justin's hands fumbled at his neck and mouth—like he couldn't breathe, you know? Then he collapsed and his bodyguards covered him, and everyone was screaming, and the police set barricades and pushed us away, and they tried to do the CPR thing on him there on the sidewalk. But his face was gray and stiff and they couldn't open his mouth.

The oxygen level in all the tanks wasn't off by much, but Yamal Casas noticed the slight rise and tapped the glass gauges. When he studied the monitors for the underwater cameras, his brow furrowed, and he smacked the side of the video box with his hand. Then he stood quickly, knocking his chair over and gave it a scolding look like a misbehaving child. An immense squealing groan shook the structure around him. He left the chair and the control office at a run and mounted the ladder to the catwalk between the pens.

The salmon smolts did not come to the edge of the tank at his feet. The water was completely still. There were no fish at all.

Someone is playing a joke, he thought, a big crazy expensive joke. He walked to the next pen. And the next. The surface of each pool rippled lightly over millions of colorful brand names—candy bar packaging, he recognized them immediately—tons of them, settling now against bottom of the nets in the warm waters off the coast of Chile. He stood there for a long time as the metal creaked and strained around him beneath the sudden massive weight, still trying to tell himself his first guess was correct.

Frank Darby showed up at 6:52 AM to operate the piling rig for construction of the new Tanner Creek condo tower at the edge of the new downtown development. It was a foggy morning, and he was checking out the other trucks driving into the nearby gravel lot to see if he recognized any of the guys, so he didn't look up. He had no reason to. When he parked and walked two blocks to the site and the building revealed itself out of the mist before him, he thought he had the wrong address. He saw the building name clearly etched in the marble above the front doors, and approached the other workers in orange vests who had gathered below. He listened to them as he peered between the perfect river-like curves of frosted glass. The lobby was lit and newly furnished. He tested the brass door handles stylized like water reed plants. It was unlocked. But there was no need to go in, for it was hushed and obviously uninhabited.

The foreman insisted he knew nothing, I mean, what could he say? He agreed with them, that yes absolutely, yesterday there had been only an unscaped dirt lot surrounded by a chain-link fence, and the COMING NEXT SPRING sign displaying the architect's nearly photorealistic rendering. Yes, they were contracted for three more months of work, but who did they think could have built twelve stories and connect all utilities overnight? The site leveling and excavation was scheduled to begin today, and the crane to arrive in three weeks. The exterior glass and marble hadn't even been ordered yet, but…as they could see, well… He gestured helplessly with both hands and dropped them in frustration.

Frank left in a daze without talking to anyone, not knowing what else to ask. He walked, thinking what he could tell Odessa. The baby's due date was next month, and they couldn't afford both of them being unemployed. Then he felt lost again, because another building had appeared that he didn't recognize. Then he felt scared, because he had not walked two blocks after parking, and now his truck was gone. And so was the entire gravel lot where he had left it.

Francis Peregrine III moved the cursor across the projected computer screen as he spoke to his strategy team in the darkened conference room. "Our process is sound, but the clients are concerned with our production timeline for deliverables." He clicked a triangle at the end of the top bar and smaller bars cascaded underneath. "Reallocation of resources and across-the-board implementation of due diligence frameworks will require some support from our community partners, though I'm confident that we'll see marked progress toward our milestones." He realized quite succinctly that he had no idea what he had just said, followed by a vivid memory he hadn't thought in ten years, of himself at age five catching turtles and bullfrogs in the pond at Grandpa's Missouri farm, getting his new shoes soaked, laughing, feeling what it was like to be without a care. Then he felt a warm peace spread through his abdomen, and he realized that he was not hungry, not at all, and that he would never need to eat again. Nor, for that matter, ever need to leave this expensive ergonomic executive office chair.

No one looked at him, they only looked up at the screen. So they didn't notice right away, as he did, that the only door to the room had disappeared.

Every copy of George Meilies' film *Le Voyage Dans La Lune* (1902) turned into the 1998 high budget movie *Armageddon*. Every single copy across the planet, in film and tape and digital formats, every frame and byte reshaped their content into images of vociferous explosions with staccato editing, until you could not find a copy of the original film in a library, or watch it digitally online, or uncover it in a private collection.

The transformation of Auguste Rodin's *The Gates of Hell*, its six bronze casts and all photos of the sculpture into boldly-colored smiling lawn gnomes, took place over a few hours. The letters of online texts and the out-of-print translations of the *Epic of Gilgamesh* rearranged themselves to spell out additional copies of a blonde socialpreneur/actor/motivational speaker's latest ghost-written self-help book, at the same time as the original twelve clay tablets from the Ninevah library collection of the 7th century BCE Assyrian king Ashurbanipal that had resided in the British Museum since 1849 inexplicably became three sets of customized spinning chrome hubcaps.

Every recording of "Dark Was the Night, Cold is the Ground" pitched and compressed and shifted until they formed a forgetful commercial jingle for a men's 7-blade disposable razor with patented glide safety strip, and

Blind Willie Johnson's slide guitar was heard no more in that way. So that millions of years later, when the *Voyager 1* space probe reached a civilized planet orbiting star AC+79 3888 in the constellation Ursa Minor, and the inhabitants listened with their filament antennae to the Golden Record, they would not be completely impressed with the human sense of taste, they would agree that something was severely lacking, and not bother opening a portal to Earth for a visit. Though the *Homo sapiens* would be long gone by then.

Ankgor Wat temple found itself remade and renamed as the latest cartoon movie franchise theme park ride, ancient stone architecture instantly shaped into brightly colored steel rollercoasters. Most of the already present tourists were delighted, only a few turning away in disgust. A well-known entertainment corporation claimed ownership to the trademarked logos and imagery, and immediately sent ride operators, costumed mascot performers, concession stand workers, and security personnel. They arrived at the Cambodia locale one day after the lawyers. The northern pigtail macaques would not enter the park, instead the primates gathered in the trees by the admission booth and threw plastic interlocking toy blocks at visitors, though the pieces all seemed to be the same shape and mold from a set discontinued decades ago.

Johnny Two Bison arrived at the Wounded Knee monument for the first time in his life. He had grown up twenty-four years in nearby Pine Ridge, but sixteen miles had always seemed worlds away. One weekend when he was nine years old, they were supposed to make a family trip to the site; he and his father waited in the car, but his mother had gone into the bathroom and never come out. His father had never wanted to go after that, and drove across the state line to White Clay every night for the same reason Johnny would later, until the two-mile road between took him. Last week, his brother had followed his mother. Johnny thought visiting this place would help him think of something else, anything else. He entered the cemetery and read a memorial with some of the names of his people, and closed his eyes to listen to what they had to say. When he opened them, the mass gravestone was gone. The brush and sand had vanished too. Luscious, immaculately trimmed grass and small, perfectly rounded rises stretched in every direction, with an occasional raked sandtrap or putting marker flag.

Twenty miles south of where he stood, just beyond the edge of the green and the new golf cart shed, the dunes and soils of the entire sandhills ecoregion groaned and trembled and disarranged and finally relented, until there stood a massive discount goods megastore with 23,600 square miles of floor space.

No customers prowled its aisles, but the shelves were fully stocked.

A massive silence awakened Heri Rakotoson. He didn't bother with his sandals, left the door wide, and walked down the back steps to the moonlit beach. He did not try to fool himself that maybe the tide was out and thus the absence of the pounding surf. He knew exactly where the sand ended and walked straight to it without fear, knowing the day had finally come. He stood there looking out at the hard motionless expanse, its dull white color and quality reminding him of fragile spoons and cheap pens and bottle caps and discarded straws and any number of things disposed. He had no desire to walk out on its firm uninterrupted reach as a few people further up the shore were doing. Maybe they thought it was ice, because they were laughing and running without shoes on its opaque surface. He had no need to bend down and touch it. He shook his head at the world, knowing it was this way everywhere now. And inland too, into every river and pond and reservoir.

Mara Keefe was stalled in traffic less than two miles from the school when her cell phone rang. It hadn't been the most productive day, but she told herself tomorrow would be better. She didn't feel like talking to anyone, but she knew from the ringtone that it was Walter.

"How's my favorite traveling tech guru?" she greeted him.

The connection sounded thin and twangy. His voice echoed. "If we finish this database rebuild, I might be able to change my ticket to an earlier flight. Wichita, by the way, is not an exciting place."

"I'm on my way to pick up Gary."

"Query… soccer… if…"

Then his voice went flat and modulated, and she said, "I'm losing you. Are you in a tunnel?" She couldn't understand him at all; she checked the signal, and said his name a few times. There was no response. The cars ahead of her moved now so she hung up.

A few blocks later he called again.

"…what's… header type… happening… form action equals… to me…"

It didn't sound like him anymore. She hung up again, thinking there likely weren't any tunnels in Wichita.

He called again as she pulled up to the school. This time it was a text message. It appeared to be gibberish.

```
<?php
mysql_connect("server","username","password");
mysql_select_db("dbname");
$query = "select * from" ".$MARA." As t1 where (HELP);
```

```
$result=mysql_query($query);
    while (list($Mara,$help,$me) =
    mysql_fetch_row($result)) {
    echo "<dt>$help</dt>";
    echo "<dd>$me</dd>"; }
?>
```

Then she heard the boys coming. They trundled across the athletic field with grass-stained knees and disheveled hair, bumping into each other on purpose. Eight years old, barely able to manage a pair of muddy cleats and the large bottles of neon power drinks. Seeing their shoes, she popped the trunk and got out to move her yoga mat and anything else that might get dirty.

Mara watched her son walk toward her, thinking how much she loved him, when she witnessed his face change first. His brown eyes disappeared, his dimples flattened, and his hair melted in a coalescing blend of color and loss of detail. He did not scream, or even seem to notice, as the flat disc of his head turned to his friends in conversation. The rest of him changed quickly, like the last grains of an hourglass sliding faster, until all of his limbs and features were gone. She stared at the bright 2×2-foot perfect square floating toward her. Within seconds, his friends had changed too, but each into a different color. Red, blue, green.

The large pixel in the middle called her *Mom*, and she was surprised that she did not hesitate, but ran to it, crying. She felt nothing when it passed through her.

The Circus Wagon

THE OLD CIRCUS wagon had been parked in Grandma's backyard since I can recall. We visited her every summer in Sioux Falls, and each year I dreaded seeing the shape in the far corner of the yard, buried in tall grass and nestled in shadow under the giant willow tree. Though I played often in the mowed area nearby, I was seven years old before I finally let my eyes steal a few glances—only a few—but more than my fear had before allowed. It would be another year before I approached the antique and noticed details of the ornate framing, the faded paint, the hundreds of rusted staples. And another summer before I could bring myself close enough to touch it. When I did so, I recoiled immediately from the rough surface with an electric sting numbing my fingers, an ice cream headache, and a bitter taste in my mouth.

I always played alone, for I coveted the long hours away from my sisters and the adults. I could no more ask about the wagon than I could talk to them about anything else. Everyone seemed to ignore the existence of this abandoned artifact until a family reunion when I convinced a cousin to inquire during an intimidating lull in conversation at the big table. We were promised the story after we cleaned our plates, though the watermelon and early bedtimes distracted family members of all ages. Late at night, over the sides of bunk beds, we relayed rumors to each other in the humid dark. Had Grandpa worked in the circus? No, the wagon was older than that, someone said. What was inside—rats? Bats? A lion's skeleton? A blind old witch? No, hundreds of mosquitoes swarmed you at once if you stepped too close, and lightning bugs avoided that part of the yard. And, this one time, Gary's dad, my uncle, had made him stay by the house while he went to collect a dead cat by the wagon, and he took a trash sack, and he reached under the wheel not once, but twice—once on each side of the wheel, for two pieces, and—and—

By then our whispers had roused the adults, and we were told a final time by a hissing aunt to get to sleep this instant.

The summer before my eighth-grade year, when she could no longer manage the stairs and five hours was too long of a drive, we made plans to move Grandma to Lincoln. For two weeks we sorted her belongings: furniture and keepsakes she wanted for the apartment, and all leftovers destined for the thrift store, auction, or disposal.

As we cleaned house and yard, my sister, who was seemingly fearless after her first year of college, took an interest in the wagon and managed to open its door. I had never before seen the interior. Everyone came to look, while I stayed back. It was so obvious to me that I said nothing: the wagon had simply let her. It seemed Grandma had turned it into clothing storage, for the inside was piled with dusty shoes, unfolded dresses, faded shirts. Mom didn't recognize the garments, and she asked Grandma about them. Her answers were short and senseless. "They're always cutting through here on the way to the place—they like the sodas. And we all waited in the basement till it was over, you see, on the radio they told us he'd gotten out and they were looking for him." These were the kind of vague responses that would become frequent for her later, no matter what the question.

The adults decided that the old wagon should be demolished, and Dad asked some of the neighbors to help. They soon found that sledgehammers glanced off the walls, and saws pinched in the wood, which broke off their metal teeth. Fire crawled playfully over the surface, grew tired and dissipated, leaving a blackened but inexplicably intact skin. When they tried to haul the wagon away, two tow trucks snapped their cables and a third broke an axle.

A few days later, attempts were made at sealing the wagon, after finding four dead dogs inside, and too many children pawing like dogs themselves at the rear door with a desperation that was more primal than curiosity. I have memories too of countless children, many of whom I did not recognize as neighbors, rolling in bloody wrestling matches on the brown dry grass.

I remember a chaotic line of a hundred impatient people gathered around the wagon, demanding to see inside, to see its secrets. Was that day a dream? Were there more like it? They screamed and pushed and tore at each other, never harming us or actually gaining entry. The crowd blocked our view as the willow tree swayed above us all. Though I was small even for my age, I stood between the mob and my family who huddled by the house, calling me back. The next morning, everything was quiet in the yard and no one spoke about it, at least that I heard.

When we pulled out of Grandma's driveway for the last time, the circus wagon remained. Her house sold the next week, though for a few thousand less than the asking price.

Grandma would live in Lincoln for twelve more years. We would move her from the apartment near church to a better apartment with an elevator, and then to an assisted living facility. While riding with us to a holiday meal, she said, "There's another one, see, I'm supposed to watch for those." We realized she was talking about white cars, any white car at all. They told her, "She had to watch, they did, uh huh, *them*." We learned to ask her more questions at such times, which often didn't resolve the story, but left her less frustrated. By the end of that year, she needed to be in a full-care facility.

I attended college across the country, and returning for a few days each year, saw increasing deterioration in her body and mind. At first, I was shocked at how short a distance she could walk, and how infrequently she spoke. I couldn't believe the number of medications she took each day. When I tried to make conversation, she would only nod and smile. Four years later, I moved back home with a useless degree and tuition debt.

For the last two years of her life, she referred to me as "that boy." Mom visited her every day at the manor, and I often asked myself if more frequent visits from me would have helped, but I grew accustomed to her glimmers of partial recognition and wished for no more. She forgot Dad's name soon enough.

In her final year, she could not speak. She slept all day, in her bed or in her recliner chair, and it took two people ten minutes to move her from one to the other.

The last time we went to Sioux Falls as a family was the day we took Grandma's ashes to the family plot. We drove by the old house and I wanted to look in the backyard, but I was silent.

It was never in my long-term plan to stay in Lincoln, any more than it was to return here after college. Nor was it in my plan to fall in love with Jennie. I didn't recognize her from my graduating class at Central High when I walked into that coffee shop, and our first few dates were at her insistence. I knew it wasn't a good match, but I think that I was lonely when she threatened to leave if I didn't elevate the relationship soon. She let the engagement progress for a few months before she stopped hiding the drugs and cheating, and she got out before me. This was about three years ago, because shortly afterward Dad announced his retirement, that my parents would be moving to Arizona, then they offered me the house I grew up in, if I could pay the property taxes.

The circus wagon appeared in my backyard not long afterward.

I didn't feel surprise, just some familiarity, maybe a faint nostalgia. Nestled against the garage, it seemed natural and satisfied. It seemed physically larger than I remembered, that much taller than me now as it had been when I was six or twelve years old. It still smelled like old baked paint and something sour and coppery enough to taste, with a hint of wind like the first day of November when autumn is certainly gone. The wood was warm to the touch, even in the shade. If it was going to stay, I figured a few precautions were needed, and made a trip to the hardware store.

Padlocks ended up broken on the ground, nailed boards too. For many nights I stayed awake with a flashlight watching for the vandal, and witnessed these items drop away or fly across the yard as if thrown, in one instance cracking the window I sat behind. For a month, all my evenings and weekends were spent troubleshooting this wagon or planning a new method of siege.

The hook piece of the old latch still remained by the door handle. I tried to affix a new eyelet, but the wagon prevented me from attaching anything. A knot in the wood positioned itself under the screw, and moved with me at any speed. It was like a dream, but I hardly noticed such unnatural occurrences anymore. I tried replacing the rusty hook and the metal twitched, then bit at my fingers, striking like an agitated snake. Finally, I used pliers to extract the hardware from the wood and studied it on the ground, as it writhed and changed shape and color many times—into a spiny insect or a gnashing mouth. Like a young boy I played with it, burying it under handfuls of dirt and watching it dig itself out quickly and frantically. I prodded at it with a stick and it snapped back, relentless.

I remained there until dusk. When I turned my straining neck, the very shape of the wagon had shifted. It hunched over me, curved and distorted, and I waited to feel its inevitable pounce. It kept me there in apprehension for hours, until my teeth ached from chattering and my cramped muscles turned sore. The rain came down cold and sharp. I tried to leap away and sprained my wrist and ankle in a graceless scramble. The wagon watched me hobble back to the house.

I've avoided the backyard entirely for a few years.

Last night I went out on a date.

After so long, I was surprised at how well I could behave in the company of another. Karen had worked in my department since my first day, but we had never even been to lunch with the same group. I admitted feeling inadequacy in the arena of activity selection, and was surprised when the both of us agreed and laughed about the predictable choice of "dinner and a movie," and the social cliché of dating as a game.

When the formal activities concluded, our conversations seemed unfinished, and she requested to spend more of the evening at my house. As we sat close together on the sofa, talking about forgotten TV shows and broken bones and which novels we were required to read in high school and whatever to delay the end of the evening, a sudden crash sent a shudder through the entire house. We jumped up. The resounding blows continued and dust dropped from the ceiling. An ugly piece of pottery I'd made in grade school toppled from the mantle and shattered.

I went directly to the noise, calm and sure of the source, despite her alarm and calling me back. Though such an overt action hadn't occurred before, one glance out the back window confirmed it: the old wagon threw itself against the house, rolled back and crashed forward.

Karen screamed, and I was sure that she would flee, that I would never see her—or another date—ever again. But she screamed only once. I was either too shocked or too curious to move, and she had to pull my arms and drag me to the front door and outside. She sat down on the driveway and wiped the hair from her eyes while I stood staring into nowhere. The house continued booming behind us, and at one point something dropped off into the yard, a shutter or a piece of siding.

I had forgotten she was there, or, for that matter, that I was. She took long, deep breaths, executing some yoga arm movements. Then she suggested we call someone.

I told her the police could not do anything.

She did not argue and seemed to agree. This helped me focus slightly. I was used to people ignoring what I said. She asked if there was anyone else we could call.

I told her about the three tow trucks many years ago.

"Then we'll have to do this ourselves," she said.

I gave her my full attention, now thoroughly convinced of her beauty and formidable prowess. She squinted in deep thought. "I see no alternative, and so I insist," she said, and paused for successful effect, "that you sleep at my place tonight."

I couldn't think of anything I wanted more, but it took me some time to respond. Throughout the neighborhood, dogs barked and hollered.

Perhaps it was only a lapse in the evening wind that made the pounding seem louder. I felt some sense of vigil and duty, and finally quietly declined. As I helped her up and silently indicated her car, I tried telling myself I was simply making a considerate gesture, though I suspected where my helpless allegiance resided.

She stared at me with obvious, unblinking disappointment. I turned away, expecting no different.

When I turned back, she had already reached her car parked on the street. She didn't look at me as she unlocked the door, and I expected that now she would only ever speak to me as a co-worker. I realized in that moment that my parents had not been the only ones to leave. All of my friends had moved away. It had been three years since I had shared an evening meal with anyone else. How many movies had I watched alone?

But Karen came back. She walked up the driveway in a determined way and took my face in her hands. "I don't understand, okay?" she said. "I don't understand what's happening." Her eyes were sincere, and I felt something I'd not felt in so long. "But I'll help." Then she embraced me with a lasting hold.

Inside my house, glass shattered. Around us, dogs howled in disordered chorus.

She got into her car and rolled down the window. "I'll call you tomorrow morning." She waited until I managed a smile before she drove away.

The pounding ceased after her taillights disappeared.

I woke to screams and leapt running from bed, tripped into sweatpants and collided with walls and furniture in a half-conscious dash downstairs and to the front door. The newspaper boy, Joey Marsh, was screaming on my front lawn, and the old circus wagon was on top of him.

It was 5:14 AM, and I called his parents. More neighbors arrived in bathrobes and coats over pajamas, faces full of panic and concern. They insisted we try to move the wagon or tip it over, and even though I knew better, I had hope that this nightmare was losing its power.

They kicked the old carriage and pounded on it with fists and slapped it, yelling. They asked what the hell I kept in there to make it so fucking heavy, and opened the small rear door to pause at the dark empty interior, and we all tried again and again, heaving and grunting and yelling, trying to budge the structure, until Bill Kenway and Dwayne Redding threw out their backs.

Joey's parents arrived and his mother wailed, setting the dogs off anew. She held her son's hand and sobbed.

"What did you do? What did you *do*?!" She berated him with helpless despair, clenching his hand with each word.

He told her over and over again how it had happened, but she did not listen, no one believed it, and it did not matter how.

While we waited for the fire department, Larry Green secured his car jack under the wagon and started pumping. Everyone stood around, encouraging him, trying to calm Joey and his parents. The jack sank into soft earth, so I fetched a cinder block and scraps of oak lumber from the garage. We managed only one full pump before the jack handle became so difficult that two of us couldn't move it. The oak splintered like balsa and the concrete broke apart.

The crew from fire station NO. 8 covered Joey in a blanket and put safety goggles and ear protection on him. They escorted us across the street and braced two jacks under the wagon. Then we all winced while they powered on their rescue saw. A long jet of bright orange sparks shot off the circular blade each time it touched the wagon's side. For over five minutes the fireman applied the saw in various locations on the wagon, working it up and down with an experienced technique, while his colleagues shifted their weight, and began to stare, and stepped forward as if to help, and hesitated longer. The blade suddenly caught, motor screaming, and the torque broke the fireman's arm.

Another emergency vehicle arrived, and they mounted the saw on a special chassis and powered it on by remote. On the second attempt, the saw's engine spat white-gray smoke and the diamond-edge blade spinning at 20,000 RPM shattered so quickly that for a few seconds no one realized. Everyone gasped, and we whipped our heads in a sequence of alarmed glances, to the *pop* of the fire engine's rear tire, to cascading glass from a shattered streetlight behind us, to Joey's dad clutching his suddenly bloody earlobe, and to a headless bird that landed awkwardly in my driveway, its wings still flapping. The blade fragment finally settled deep into the trunk of the burr oak in my yard.

I knew what the fire company officer was discussing with his men, and I made my way over to them, trying to find the words that would make them understand. They were already unreeling the heavy cable from the winch on the rear bumper of the largest fire engine.

My first thought was that I had paused too long, that I shouldn't have worried about how my words sounded or my delivery, or whatever insecurity I had; that I should have run over to the firemen immediately. But as soon as it began, I knew it did not matter either way.

Joey Marsh had been quiet for a few minutes, but now he screamed. The wagon groaned and creaked like a settling building of much larger size, and some of us ran to it when we realized why. The wagon was leaning; it was grinding down on Joey's legs. First we tried bracing with our bodies, then we tried the winch, but then all we could do was stand back and watch the thing free him in the only way it would allow. The sight was unbearable, as it pressed him slowly enough to cause him as much pain as possible. Joey fainted before it was done with him, and before his mother did. She collapsed when we pulled him clear, his legs severed at mid-thigh.

The body of the headless bird had worked its way over to the street gutter and stopped moving.

Karen had tried calling many times, and she arrived as the firemen cleaned up the yard and street. She waited patiently as I answered questions for the police report. The two departments discussed the wagon at length, but eventually all their vehicles disappeared, leaving Karen and myself sitting in the driveway again in near silence, except for the flutter of the police caution tape surrounding the wagon. She didn't say anything, she simply steered me to her car, drove me to her place, put me in her bed, and watched over me. All day and the following night.

In the morning, she gave me a choice of a sponge bath or taking a shower myself. I took the latter, and stood underneath the spray until she knocked to tell me all the hot water was gone, in case I hadn't noticed.

She threw out my bloodied jeans and gave me a pair of her sweatpants.

While she made omelettes for us, I sat at her small breakfast table and ate slowly. I tried to think of something to say, but the only ideas in my head were fleeting ones. Can anyone purchase corrosive acid without some type of license? Where can one rent a wrecking ball crane? Are there any abandoned quarries in the area? How much fireworks can one legally purchase across state lines?

"I'll take care of you for as long as you need," she said. "But I think you want to do things for yourself right now. I don't think you want my help—even though you need it, and you should accept it—did I mention that part?"

Then she said her sweatpants looked great on me while managing a serious face. And my smile, brief though it was, felt good.

Returning home, I was not surprised to see the front yard empty.

Fetching the mail, I noticed the bird head in the grass on the front step, that of a female cardinal.

As I said, I have hope, and argued with myself about even looking into the backyard. Maybe the fire or police or some other department had returned and succeeded in disposal, for I yearned to believe it, and pledged to never venture back there again. But it was difficult to ignore the situation seeing the avalanche of plaster, wood, and brick on my dining room floor and the large hole in the exterior wall of the house.

Looking through the opening showed a clear view of the circus wagon in its place by the far fence, nestled in tall untended grass, weeds, and leaves.

I took two plastic bags from the kitchen drawer and, using one as a glove, put the two pieces of the cardinal to rest in the garbage can.

Lying in the dark, I tried to remember Grandma in her house, remember her voice, when she was tall and fierce. It was difficult to picture her outside of the sterile room at the manor in those last years, or a time when she recognized me, or the sound of her voice.

"What is it, Gramma? Where'd it come from?"

Grandma sets the tray down on the patio table and grabs my finger. "We don't point, Christopher. You keep that finger tucked in." She gives my finger a twist until I wince and holds it until I meet her eyes. Then she smiles very quickly.

I watch the eerie fascinating shape back there under the swaying willow branches.

Ice cubes make noise like distant drowning wind chimes. Grandma pours lemonade into a small glass, and I step closer to the patio table which is level with my forehead. I look at the wagon again. It seems to be growing, surely it's bigger than the house.

Something deep and distant croons in the air and moves under my skin. Grandma doesn't seem to notice. A dusky rumbling of extinct things that play unsettling whisper music. A song that I cannot name, though it feels so familiar. Esoteric rhapsody of lucent thunder plucking at my gut with fervid pincers, opening a cavern of grief and bleakness inside me. I feel sensations I don't understand.

I reach up for the lemonade.

"Have you washed your hands?" Grandma says.

Even when the misshapen two-headed dog steps out from behind the wagon, lifts its dry skeletal leg, and looks at me with torn red sockets, I'm still not sure if it's a dream.

The doorbell woke me. My alarm clock flashed 12:00, but the sunlight told me I'd overslept. I cursed into a few drawers and various garment piles, searching, before I realized that I had slept in clothes. I opened the front door to see Karen on the step. "Here … it's some bakery muffin thing." She handed it over and told me there was no way I was going in to work today. Then she let herself in and went and stood in the ragged hole that was formerly the outer wall of my dining room. She shook her head very slowly. I was feeling faint, thinking of Joey Marsh and the screams, and she must've known because she kissed me very suddenly. We both heard the creaking in the backyard, the turning of wooden wheels. Even more abruptly, she turned and ran to her car, promising to call later.

One glance showed the wagon was halfway to the house.

Then another knock at the front door. "Mr. Edmunds, I'm here to follow up with a few questions," said one of the police officers in the open doorway. They entered the house and walked with authority into the living room. They eyed the broken pottery shards on the floor, and stood with thumbs hooked into their belts. "Why did you move the wagon? It's a very serious situation, compromising a crime scene."

The paralyzing shyness from my childhood returned. Hundreds of responses competed in my head, shouting in different voices, words overlapping, but nothing seemed adequate; my mind wanted to flee and my body remained unresponsive, my mouth silent. Not more than a second or two passed before the officer repeated himself, numbing me further. Unable to face them, I stared at the floor, then I stared out where the wagon had returned to the back fence.

"Mr. Edmunds—"

"For Joey's family. I moved it for their family." I seemed to be talking now. There were words coming audibly from my vocal cords. "I'm sorry. I didn't want them to see the blood."

The officers maintained their even stance but the one who was talking took his hands off his belt. He repeated the warning about the seriousness and continued. The investigation was ongoing, and I should make arrangements to stay off-premises for a few days. There would be further questions; and I should make myself available.

I wasn't listening to him. Instead I was thinking about Grandpa. Once when I asked Grandma about him, she said well, he worked for the telephone company. She said nothing with the circus. Had he bought the wagon? You know, she really couldn't remember. I remembered asking Mom about it and she said it had been part of the property at least since she was a young girl, maybe someone had dumped it there, or it had been there when they moved in. Now you probably don't remember but Grandpa had a scar on his neck where he'd taken an axe to the wagon and the handle broke and sent the blade flying, and it cut him good. And I realized I had only ever known Grandpa as a photograph. He had died before my first birthday. His face, his particular spectacles, his smoking pipe—he was unmoving, flat, and unreal. And Grandma had been alone as long as I'd known her.

What was that noise? Had the wagon moved? What if it came for the policemen?

I was distracted again. My mind did that sometimes.

Then I realized that the taste in my mouth since I'd awakened that morning was lemonade, more sour than sweet.

The phone rang just after the officers left. It was my sister in Des Moines, just checking in. "It's been what," she said, "two weeks since anyone's heard from you?"

I found myself standing again in the large hole in my house, watching the wagon. Its back door was open, and a squirrel perched on the roof corner was peering inside.

None of my family knew that the wagon was here. My sisters hadn't visited in the last two years, and my parents had preferred a hotel the one time they'd returned for an alumni event. I wanted nothing more than to weep into the phone, to ask for help, and I held my breath to keep from sobbing, but I couldn't speak. It seemed too unimaginable to believe; there was no way to start. I let her talk. I got moving.

I was already packing a bag. Maybe I would stay at the new hotel downtown. After a year of redevelopment and construction, it was probably very nice accommodations. Someone said they had a good brunch. Where was my swimsuit? Was I ready to invite Karen to the hotel? What would she say?

Another knock at the door. I peered through the peephole and froze in place. It was Jean Marsh, her face puffy and eyes wet. I promised to call my sister soon and hung up. I leaned against the door and closed my eyes for I don't know how long. She knocked again. I opened the door and couldn't meet her face.

"You taught Joey how to throw the Frisbee," she said. "You probably don't remember. At the summer picnic." She smiled fondly, and her eyes shined wet. "He was just nine then, and I think you were back visiting from college." She held a casserole dish covered with foil. "I brought something. It isn't much, but it'll keep in the freezer."

"I'm sorry, Mrs. Marsh. I'm so, so terribly sorry." I accepted the dish and invited her in.

She blinked once and started crying again with sobs that were nearly musical, still smiling at me. She squeezed my arm. "No dear, you just... you just give us a call if you need anything. We're just two blocks down, you know. How are your parents doing, have you talked to them?"

After she left, I briefly inspected the casserole. Green beans with cream of mushroom soup, topped with crispy onions. I slid the dish into the freezer and headed to the door with my travel bag when the knock came again. Impatient and angry, I opened the door without peeping first. My legs gave out at the sight of the three mangled squirrels on the front step, and the wagon in the front yard, its door slowly closing with a pause enough to show me the dark inside that seemed bottomless.

The first night at the hotel, I couldn't sleep. My mind focused on the hole in my house, and I felt helpless to do anything, worrying in circles about how much of my belongings would be missing by morning, about the fact I couldn't even begin calling contractors at the late hour. Practical tasks made comforting sense. I briefly considered calling Karen, but convinced myself it would be too eager, plus I needed to get some of this solved on my own. If I closed my eyes, I heard Joey Marsh screaming, so I stayed awake all night in the company of documentary shows and history shows, alternating with severely edited versions of *The Howling* and *Conan the Barbarian* on TBS.

I returned to work, and the week became a blur. Six website courses fell into our project list when they let go all of their student interns, and our project managers agreed to the original deadline before noticing that most of the graphics files were missing and everything needed code cleanup on the backend. I knew what was coming: two meetings per day of inter-office politics, negotiation for a deadline extension that would never happen, and late nights for us finishing the work anyway. Karen stopped by my desk during the call from the police inspector, where he insisted that I be available starting tomorrow. My supervisor said she couldn't approve any vacation, and the flex time policy had been put on hold for the foreseeable future. We were required to work extended hours and weekends for the new priority projects—but she granted me special leave of one day a month if I worked four additional evenings per week.

The questioning at the police station didn't take long, but I waited for hours each time for an available officer, and they called me back throughout the week because they couldn't assemble a sensible story. Finally, I lied and told them that I'd borrowed a flatbed trailer and hauled the wagon down from Sioux Falls myself. Who could believe otherwise?

I decided that I shouldn't go back to the house. Maybe it would find me, or maybe it would leave. After the third night, I checked out of the downtown hotel and drove around for a few hours until settling at the U-Stay Motel out on West O Street by the interstate, which was more affordable but the room featured torn curtains and smelled of stale smoke. A city official called to say that they had made arrangements to remove the circus wagon. He kept referring to it as a public hazard, and I agreed with him each time.

Karen sent an email every other day with subject lines like I MISS YOU and JUST THINKING ABOUT YOU, FURTHER MATERIAL AVAILABLE UPON REQUEST, and I didn't open any of the messages.

The motel room felt like hints of many unknown lives, and I needed to get out. I drove to the park outside of town where my family used to picnic. I found a quiet place to sit where the trees ended at prairie, and let myself think about the last few weeks, and then further back. The city glowed dimly in the distance.

I don't know why the wagon chose me. I don't know what it wanted.

I can't remember much of the last few years—nothing stands out, not since Jennie. Early Jennie. It all faded into a routine smog of work and commute, instant meals in front of the television, movies blended together, and faceless masturbation in the dark. I had left the copy shop job because the web design position seemed exciting, knowing even then that I would let myself stay there too long, that I had no other plan or ambition. I reminded myself multiple times of how many ways I was fortunate, but would fall back into a feeling of helplessness.

Slowly and effortlessly the images came to me. The inside of the wagon. When it arrived in my backyard nearly three years ago. I remembered now. I'd opened it and forgotten everything. It was dark and half filled with clothes. I remembered. That I had gathered them quickly, trying not to look at their size or era of fashion, but even in haste noticing an OP logo on a T-shirt and a toddler's onesie as I had filled the trash cans and then garbage sacks. Then I remembered the neighbor's cat had gone missing. That was the first time I had tried sealing the door.

I hardly watched the news on TV, and I'd recently stopped my newspaper subscription, so I heard about the helicopter crash in my neighborhood from my co-workers. After a meeting, they followed me back to my cubicle and asked me "have you seen it" and for "the whole skinny." I convinced them that I hadn't been home in over a week, but they chattered and gossiped about what they had heard, and pulled up a news site and pointed, and exclaimed on and on. The local stations didn't report what the heavy-lift S-64 Skycrane helicopter was doing when it crashed with five casualties, but I knew.

Karen lingered behind the web developers and programmers for a few minutes, winked a smile at me, and then she was gone.

———

I cannot move in encircling darkness that rumbles from everywhere, giant and limitless. There's no lightning, and the depth of the noise shakes my heart. This is more of an animal than a place, an immense starved beast. It is a living storm. And when I guess this, it lunges from all around with sharp shadow anemone arms, encloses, rising impossibly at once to shrill and deeper tones, a folding jagged city, crushing out my breath with searing cold hollow thorns of screaming endless voids of absolute colorlessness, a cindered toxin of pure despair, ending my rhythm, injecting one singular future that this will continue without death. Forever.

———

I woke on the floor between the bed and the icy air conditioner. I dressed without tying my shoes, checked out of the U-Stay Motel, and drove a few blocks to the first open restaurant. I sat in a booth at Denny's drinking coffee and trying to get used to the taste. After seven cups, I went to work.

———

Karen sent a few emails during the course of the day, all of which I ignored, and she didn't stop by my desk. I focused on tasks, ignored lunch, and worked through code cleanup of three websites, more than a thousand HTML pages with links and other elements that couldn't be fixed with find/replace or with GREP.

At 8:41 PM, still in my cubicle, I had already planned to stay up all night, having concluded that I would never sleep again. Between projects, I checked my email, finally opening Karen's messages.

10:37 AM: "I need to talk to you."

11:48 AM: "Want to get lunch with me? How about Tandoor? They have Thursday buffet and I need some pakora."

2:00 AM: "I'm worried about you. You know that. I want to see you."

4:32 AM: "OMFG. I can't stand any more of these meetings. My butt is absolutely numb, but much less so than my poor brain. The same bureaucratic crap over and over. Don't care. Don't wanna."

5:21 AM: "Okay mister, I'm outta here for the day. I really want to talk to you. 'No' is not an acceptable answer. I know you've been staying in a (sleazy?) motel, but as kinky as that sounds, you need to quit that shit. So I'm coming over at 9 o'clock tonight. To your house."

———

I averaged fifteen over the speed limit, tailgated until drivers cleared the lane, and ran red lights. When I reached my neighborhood, the road was barricaded, and I stared at the demolished Marsh home as I parked. Not enough of the strewn wreckage was discernible, but it was clear where the helicopter had come down.

I ran the next two blocks. Seeing Karen's car, I hoped with every step that she waited inside it. She was there in the driver's seat with the engine running and doors locked. Breathing hard, I leaned on her hood to catch my breath. She yelped and jumped. Then her look of relief melted into a furrowed brow of semi-serious scolding as she rolled down the window.

"Hey, Mister Heart Attack Dealer." We both smiled now. "Park your butt in my getaway vehicle." She patted the passenger seat.

"Hi..." I nearly caught my breath. "Hi."

She scanned past me to the house; then she focused on me with a level gaze in a way that made me want to joke about how sultry she was in the dashboard light. She peered into my eyes, and I didn't look away or want to. It felt more than safe—it was good, and I had missed her. "Here it goes..." she said, and took a deep breath. "I took a job in Minneapolis. And I'm leaving tomorrow. And I want you to come with me." Then she held my hand.

Every responsibility came into my mind at once, my house and my job, the bills and the repairs, and the fact it probably wasn't legal for me to leave the state. I couldn't sort out which excuse to voice first. And she waited, glancing behind me once or twice, but mostly waiting. Until my apprehensions settled and I realized none of it mattered; it was time to leave. It had been time to leave for too many years.

"Rent is my treat for the first six months. We're leaving tomorrow. Trucking company is already moving my stuff. Now go pack whatever you can fit in my car. You should be okay in there, it... *likes* you... or something. I'm staying here on lookout. If it comes for me, I'll take off, and you'll meet me at my place."

I did not know what to do with my feelings.

"And I like to travel. So if it follows you, we'll move again."

"You're... you're just..." I shook my head. "...awesome."

She curtsied as best she could in a seated position.

"Considering what happened last time," she said, nodding toward the house, "I'll kiss you later."

The motion light illuminated the side door. I turned my key and paused there in the brightness of the driveway. The backyard still lay in shadow. The packing list in my mind fell away. I had to know. So I proceeded inside, took the flashlight from the bottom drawer in the kitchen, and walked through the dining room and through the plastic-draped hole, out into the backyard where she couldn't see. She was right of course—the wagon remained.

I shined the beam into the back corner of the yard. The circus wagon dwelled in its place, silent. I let the light rest on the scorched and faded sides, and listened for the slightest creak, watched for any movement. Satisfied enough, I went inside and upstairs to the attic.

I limited myself to two suitcases, and moved from room to room, gathering items. Laptop, journals, family photos, four or five sets of clothes, some first-edition books. Every few minutes I surveyed out the window and checked the backyard.

Soon I stood by the front door with suitcases in each hand, and I couldn't move forward. I told myself there was no need to check again. There was nothing left for me to do here. But I heard something. A distant infinite keening, an inmost note of singing shade. I dropped the cases and took the flashlight to the backyard again.

I moved purposefully across the grass and overgrown walkway, past the fountain birdbath and straight to the wagon, resolute and defiant. For a moment, I was seven years old again, trembling, as I reached forward. The door opened before my fingers could touch it. I leaned in, shined the light around, and saw what was there. Then I straightened up, switched off the light, and walked away.

Karen released the trunk latch, and I loaded my belongings and got into the car next to her. I was looking down, obviously trying not to cry, and she said nothing as she sat with me until I couldn't stop it anymore. And then for a longer time as I dried out and managed, "I hate moving. I really hate it. Okay, we can go."

She had driven half a block when the dark dropped on my mind and I saw.

"No. Wait." I touched her hand on the stick shift, and she pulled over and regarded me, puzzled. She asked if I had forgotten something, but I was already out of the car.

It was not that I hadn't seen the offering. It was not that I hadn't recognized the face of the disembodied head inside the wagon until now. I had known it immediately. Now I knew what I was and what I had to do. I ran across the yards toward the house where I'd grown up, my house now. Jennie, my ex-fiancée, her face fresh and pale, the lipsticked mouth parted in horror, and the trailing red gore from her neck where it had been torn from the absent body. I knew what I had to do. Because I had been glad to flee and lie and never tell Karen. Never tell myself.

There was enough moonlight to see the circus wagon open its door, revealing clawed grooves and scratches, dried streaks of dark red on its backside. The orphic canticle pulsed and rolled from within, singing every ancient color and promise. And I didn't hesitate to crawl inside.

We emerge forth and stand uncomfortably at first on two legs, trying his rigid form, smelling the size of this place. She is barely familiar running toward us, calling his fading name. Her song is awful and weak. Athirst and furious, we lose this shape, we break and burst into expression, the limitless opaque anthem now a pealing lash of hooked fibrils roaring anguish and detonating outward in a lustful starving coda with screaming afflicted claws, soon a teeming immense squall enkindled with ascendant hue that brings dominion.

One Childhood of Many

ALMOST EXACTLY ONE week after the last day of seventh grade and one week before her thirteenth birthday, Sylvia stomped through the house, flung open the sliding door to the back porch, and stood with hands on hips. The Sunday newspaper was not extremely captivating that day, nor were her parents in the practice of ignoring their daughter, but the lawnmower next door was loud enough to mask the impatient tapping of a foot and the flaring lament of teenage nostrils. Finally, Mr. Jera shut off the small motor to empty his grass clippings, and Sylvia said,

"Well?!"

"Well... what?" said Mom. Dad removed his reading glasses to offer his full attention.

"When are we leaving for the lake?" Sylvia asked in a tone saturated with obviousness.

Her parents glanced at each other, and Dad said, "Which lake is that, pumpkin?"

Sylvia rolled her eyes, took a breath, and sighed much more than it seemed she had inhaled. "Lake Moo-noo fHul-pa, of course," she stated. After waiting for a response, and then for a reaction, she added in a way that almost sounded like a question, "We go *every* summer."

Her parents looked at each other again. Mom frowned and regarded her daughter. "Honey, every summer we go with your father to physics workshops and seminars. And this summer, we signed you up for volleyball camp, like you wanted."

Sylvia shook her head. "No, no. Every summer. Since I was—" She thought about it. "Since I can remember anything."

"Dear," Mom said very gently, "do you mean the duck pond at Grandma and Grandpa's?"

"Not that smelly little thing." Sylvia's face went all lemons. She sighed again.

It seemed she was about to storm off. Instead she jumped forward, and sat between them with her arms wrapped around her crossed legs, effulgent with glee.

"We set out very early. And we drive west for eleven hours and forty-two minutes travelling fifty-eight miles per hour, then turn off the headlights and follow the smell of quicksilver until we come to the huge lustrous sky dam. When a raven lands on our car hood, we close our eyes and he takes us through the invisible door, where we hum the song about the mountain king, louder and louder, until the armadillo appears, ten feet tall and walking upright. We place three pinecones in his hat, each from a different yard and a different year, which gets us seats on the wagon. So we leave our car there in the cave shaped like a jack-o'-lantern mouth, and we ride into the valley."

She paused here a moment and scrutinized their befuddled faces, then she continued. "We usually get a place on the spinning island, but the tree houses over the east bank are fine too, because the warble snakes sing in the midafternoon shade. I like to build castles from the bone dust on the beach and then touch them with a flaming cattail, so they rocket into the clouds and rain down onto the lake, which ripples in different colors and sounds too. Mom tours on the giant garfish barge to see the flying glacier and birdwatch and treewatch and play the spore dice game while she sips the fruit drinks that make her eyes glow. Dad always rents one of the bubbles from the marina, and walks on the lake bottom to look for old coins and scrolls, and he stops in the grotto sometimes to hear the five witches tell him stories about the thousand lives of his other childhoods. In the evenings, we build a fire, and the neighbors come over for spicy marinated centipede and grammar salad with staccatissimo sodas. Much later, we tuck ourselves under the warm sand and watch our dreams perform in the waters of the lake." Her voice increased in speed and excitement. "I've been spending more time with the Ckoolee'ere boy—you know, Aluung?—his skin is changing color and his ear flames are sprouting higher. This summer we might kiss." Sylvia noticed she was twirling her hair, and stopped doing so.

She continued, somewhat quieter. But only at first. "Also, at every full moons, there's the market in the forest glen, where they have the tastiest bloodmalts and onomatopoeia candies and algebra fritters—except that time that Dad ate too many and grew another toe that wouldn't stop dancing until we poured gargoyle urine on it. Oh, and sometimes the traveling Xoofang theater troupe comes through, and they perform great stuff like the *I'iiXutle'pof* medley or *Nightmare Soup* or that absolutely wrenching opera about the tryst between the locust swarm and the avalanche near the city inside the blacksmith's hearth. And also, we take off our skins and become fish, which is just leagues better than a boring old sailboat, if you ask me." Sylvia took a breath.

"Anyway, we spend all summer there, and never sleep. And we would stay there forever, except when the third moon appears, the bluegills return to drink the entire lake and eat everything else. They're the nasty biker gang with a terrific appetite. Well, you know what happened to Mrs. Jera when she went back for her sunglasses that one summer and missed the last wagon out." Sylvia motioned next door and clucked her tongue.

Then she smiled and stared at her parents expectantly.

They turned to each other one more time, a habit that Sylvia now found annoying.

"I'm… sorry, dear," Mom said finally, and then nothing else.

"We don't have the foggiest idea what you're talking about," Dad added.

Sylvia shook her head like a disappointed parent. She slapped her knees and stomped away, turning back briefly. "Just who *are* you people, anyway?"

Ina's Day

THE DIGITAL DAWNCHIME woke Ina. She yawned and stretched as the lights reached full illumination. She cursed the cold metal floor, then the metal walls. She put on her slipsuit, felt it respond to her body heat and conform to her shape, then she strapped her boots. She pulled the privacy curtain aside and saw that Father was already dressed, rolling his sleeping pad at the other end of the dwellchamber.

"Can't we stay in today?" she said.

"Good morning, my little giraffe," Father said.

"I'm not so little anymore."

He winced as he stood, holding his back. He smiled in agreement.

"I'll run duty today," she said. "You stay home and rest."

The wall computer chimed a five-minute warning.

They packed their sleeping pads in the corner, and performed their stretches.

Father touched the wall computer's sensor. "GOOD MORNING, GOWER JANITOR. THIS IS YOUR DAY 9850." The dispenser released three protein biscuits, then filled his canteen with one liter of water.

Ina touched the sensor. "GOOD MORNING, INA JANITOR-PRENTICE. THIS IS YOUR DAY 4375." She pocketed her biscuits.

They unplugged their cracklebrooms from the wall unit and checked the charges. The filament heads glowed and sizzled with blue electricity. They donned their filter masks, and he helped Ina tighten the straps on hers.

"PLEASE INFORM," the computer inquired, "WILL LALITA JANITOR BE GOING OUT TODAY?"

"No," Father said.

They turned to the front door just as the workchime sounded. "Get behind me," Father said, crouching. He swiped his silver passcard, the locklight turned green, and the door hissed open. Father advanced slowly into the metal hallway, he cleared the side spaces. "Okay, muffinbird." He relaxed and motioned her out.

She joined him and they strolled into the curved corridor of subsection Q-1, brooms on shoulders as the dwellchamber powered down behind them.

They walked for hours without work, whistling tunes to fill the monotonous scenery of continuing pale arced passageway and mathematically spaced doors. Every locklight glowed red, except for the occasional empty storage compartment, long since raided. Father would try his passcard every few hundred meters, and they'd move on, unsurprised.

At subsection Q-8, they came to the failed service bot. Its inactive shape stalled in the middle of the corridor, four articulated appendages hanging motionless over a dull gray shell and dust clumps gathering around its rollerbrushes.

"Good day to you, sir," Ina exclaimed to the dead machine as she removed an imaginary hat and bowed.

Father watched her with perhaps a moment of concern, then he curtsied to their silent acquaintance.

Ina laughed. She patted the metal shell, and they skipped away.

They stopped for a few minutes at the only window and watched the star trails bend in the ship's drive field.

Even through the filter masks, they could smell it coming up, the musky thick odor with a tangy hint. At Q-13 they found the invader. The orange patches clung to the bulkhead and floor in ten or more spots. They powered on their brooms and got to work.

Some of the cankers had matured, their richly colored centers wavering with sporeheads nearly one centimeter high. Father and daughter scrubbed hard, burning the fungus away; they leaned and sweated, spending most of an hour reaching up and back for the last blemish on the ceiling.

Afterward they cleaned each other, head to foot, including the soles of their boots. Ina held still when the electrostatic tickle passed over her clothes.

Then they proceeded a hundred meters and sat briefly for lunch, slipping the food and straws under their masks.

"My biscuits taste funny today," Ina said.

Father's eyes were sad at her remark, and he turned away. He stood.

"Eat up," he said sternly. It was unlike him.

They jogged the rest of the day, making it nearly all the way around Q-ring without another outbreak, and the hope of knocking off early seemed plausible. But at Q-23, with their dwellchamber just in sight at the curve, the subsection was infested.

They scrubbed and swept for hours, working past nightfall. The corridor lights extinguished and Father had to fetch the pulselantern from home.

When they stumbled inside, sore and dragging, Ina slumped to a cushion at the meal blanket and devoured her third biscuit and the remainder of her water. She was licking her lips and eyeing the dispenser hungrily when Father opened the wall safe.

She began to cry immediately as he took out the large plastic jar. She went to him and put her arms around him, sobbing. "I'm so sorry, Father. I forgot. I don't know how I forgot."

He dropped his last biscuit into the jar and returned it to the safe. "It's okay, pumpkin pie."

Nightchime sounded, then the lights dimmed.

"No lessons tonight," he said. "And no stories." It wasn't punishment, only exhaustion.

She was still crying when he tucked her in. "I owe you one of my foods tomorrow," she promised.

"You're a growing girl," he said, but she heard hunger strain his voice.

"Father, why are _you_ crying?"

"It's your birthday, sweetie." He kissed her forehead. "And I didn't get you anything."

She hugged him tightly, thinking for a moment that she felt the thrum of the ship around them, but realized it was his heart.

He closed the curtain and dimmed the pulselantern. Soon she heard him tapping, his quick and spaced raps against the metal wall.

-.-.-

She didn't know the words, but the sounds soothed her.

The response came faintly, as she fell to sleep.

.... . .-.. .-.. --- --..-- / - --- --

The next fifteen days were the same. Scrub scrub scrub.

When the computer gave them a Half Day with more daylight at home, they worked anyway. They deposited the extra biscuit and bonus sweetpellet into the jar.

They used most evenings for lessons. He passed down the stories about things like sharks and trains, fireworks and bears. She recited previous assignments back to him, like beaches and koalas, moons and books.

———

Every day, the dawnchime felt merciless. They slept until the five-minute warning, then dressed quickly and jumped out the door with boots unstrapped.

They often walked the circumference in the allotted eight hours. Some days the job was easy, a few ocher dustings smaller than Ina's hand, which they removed in minutes, and continued their rounds. Other days the floor crawled with movement, a vivid swarming layer extending over two subsections.

Ina saw the color orange in her dreams and was weary of it.

———

At the end of no particular day, Ina snorted and shuffled her feet as they approached home, when Father suddenly moved in front of her.

The rovers waited for them.

A gang of twenty-some rovers squatted between them and the dwellchamber. Their grimy clothing contrasted the sterile walls; each body adorned in a disarray of modded garments and scavenged accessories. Their edged weapons and piercings reflected their lampsticks, tattoos and scars melted into shadowed faces. Bare faces. Without filter masks.

Their leader stood before them. Twice as old as anyone, older than Father. And twice as big, a knot of fortified muscle. His graying beard glinted with coins and circuit bits and other treasures. The gold passcard hung on a thick cord around his neck, sacred and boastful. "Tribute or sanctuary?" his voice rumbled deep.

"Join us," hissed the others. "Join us, join us, *join us*!"

"You're early this month, Roarke," Father said.

"You will address him by his rightful title!" One of them jumped forward, trembling with eager violence. He was a few years older than Ina. "He is Lord Roarke Marauder VII, Scourge of Ten Ring Sections!"

The leader held up his hand and the youth was silent. He addressed Father again: "We offer protection. You've heard of the distant clans? Their passcards can now reach every ring. And they offer only one thing."

Ina had heard of them. They were not in the computer, but Reed had told her the Worxa gang fed on flesh. That they were the reason R-ring was closed.

Father just smiled in response.

"We have been to the Green Dome. We've harvested there."

"That place is a myth," Father said.

"*Why* are you negotiating with him, Father?!" screamed the boy. "At least take the girl! Yes, give her to *me*! I have tasty plans—"

Ina inhaled sharply.

"Caddell—*heel*!" boomed the leader.

All of his followers cringed. They lowered their eyes.

Ina scowled at Caddell, and made a gesture of slowly crushing fingers at waist-level.

A woman with red-blonde striped hair coaxed the boy back. He pushed her arms away and cursed her, until he sank into a sullen squat.

"Tribute," said Father, full and final.

The leader nodded and stepped aside. The others parted behind him.

Father returned momentarily with the full jar of rations. He emptied it into their foldsack.

"Aren't you going to count it?" mumbled Caddell. "Oh, for salvage's sake..." Everyone ignored him.

"See you next month." The leader swiped his passcard at the crossgate door and dismissed them. He tipped his hat to Father. "Gower."

"Roarke." Father nodded.

The rovers stealthed away.

A few days later, the big door opposite their dwellchamber was open, and they could see all the way through to P-ring.

"Is it Social Night already?" Father said.

"Do we get to see Edwin and Stephana?" she said, face brightening behind the mask.

"Of course. And Reed too."

She wrinkled her nose.

They went inside and prepared. While Father shaved with his cracklebroom, Ina put on her only shapedress; not too tightly, stretching a few frills at the knee. She undid her ponytails and tried repeatedly to make a neat bun or a braid. She was sulking in the mirror when he appeared and put a fine brush in her hand. She was surprised at her own squeal of delight.

"She would've wanted you to have it."

He wore his tailed-coat and let her adjust his iridescent green tie that swirled as she imagined an ocean might.

They took the crosshall into the parallel ring. They knocked formally at dwellchamber P-1.

"Oh now, just *look* at you two!" Stephana exclaimed, and embraced them. "Come in, come in!" Edwin smiled and gestured welcome. They removed their filter masks and Reed tried to hug her, but Ina cut him off with a handshake.

Their clothing was immaculate, and their dwellchamber was abundantly decorated, with colorful wall hangings and a full dining room table. Not real legendwood, of course, but certainly more than an upturned polystore crate. It was hard to believe they were janitors too. Father often said that Edwin's ancestors had just breached the right storage compartment.

Father offered them a sealed bottle, which Ina hadn't noticed him carrying. "Where in the world did you get this?" Edwin said.

"You haven't joined with the...?" Stephana covered her mouth.

Father smiled. "I found it years ago. Been saving it for a special occasion." The adults seemed relieved.

Reed watched her with interest, and though he hadn't done it in years, she expected him at any moment to tug her arm and drag her off to see his dinosaur toys. She wanted nothing more than to stay with the grownups. So she was surprised when Father said, "Can you two give us a few minutes?"

Ina glanced around for escape. She detached the tablet from their wall computer, since theirs had been missing for years. "Here," she said, "let's view some oldy stuff." She was slightly impressed when Reed offered his arm.

Dinner consisted of hot vegetable pouches and soy loaf served on real ceramic plates, and synthberry juice mix that she hadn't tasted before, but thought it a bit powdery. She watched everyone else to remember how to use a fork and knife, and proceeded slowly. Father let her have a small cup of wine.

"How are your studies coming along, dear?" asked Stephana. "Posture? Sewing? Cooking?"

"Father's been teaching me to fight," Ina said.

"I see..." Stephana looked at her husband.

Edwin chuckled. "Of course he has." He clapped Father on the shoulder. "He..."

The awkward silence returned again.

And for the second time, Father sent her away. "Ina, dear, please take Reed and go learn some more. The parents have things to discuss."

Ina squinted at him and said, "For your information, I now know that a giraffe does not have three heads, nor sabre-teeth, nor does it ever leap out of the sea with its flippers to eat whirling bunnybats."

He laughed. "You've found me out, kittybeans." He smiled at her.

She sat with Reed on the couch and they asked the tablet computer about forests and pumpkins and rivers and cats and tumblebees and bicycles and islands and bassball.

For dessert, Stephana served chococubes drizzled with sweetpour.

On the way home, Ina stopped abruptly. "Reed says the computer is adding something to our food biscuits now, just his and mine. That it's changing our bodies. Into adults." She was about to say something else, but shook her head and walked ahead in a sudden huff.

She pulled the curtain, changed her clothes, and sat in her sleepwrap for a long time.

"Okay, sugarrabbit... What is it?" Father said.

"Reed said that he'll marry me soon." She threw open the curtain. "Is that *true*, Daddy?" She put her hands on her hips. "He said that *you'd* approved it! Well, Daddy? *Well?!*" She only called him that when she was very upset.

"You're twelve now, Ina. It's time to grow up." He turned off the pulselantern.

She was shocked, and any minute now would march over and tell him everything on her mind. But then she heard the choked sounds of him crying. She turned over and covered her ears.

―――――

Ina woke early and carefully unhooked Father's passcard. He didn't stir when the door opened and she crept out. She ran barefoot for a few subsections, then slipped into boots. When her breath returned, she walked on. She inspected and scrubbed.

She sauntered by the old bot without looking. "Nobody asked you," she muttered.

It was too late to go back when she regretted not collecting the daily rations or the canteen. So she used lunch break to clean every discoloration in her path.

Her confident march came to a halt as she rounded the curve at subsection Q-18. The fierce copper rash coated every surface from floor to ceiling. Her gut filled with despair. Her lip quivered and she set to it before the tears could begin.

She scrubbed hard, urging herself on, intent on proving to him. And to herself.

Nightfall came sooner than she anticipated, and she memorized how much remained as the lights dimmed. It was too late to run back now, and this would only spread overnight. So she kept scouring in near darkness, with only the cracklebroom glow.

Oh ship, she thought, *I don't want to marry that scrawny boy.*

A few minutes later she shivered at the black around her.

"And that," she said to herself, "is the closest you've ever come to praying, Ina J."

She focused. Scrub scrub scrub.

She thought of when Father had introduced her to the broken bot. It was around her day 2500, before she'd begun daily work with him, and he'd taken her on a walk. "This is why we're here," he'd said, "What was their duty is now ours." She'd given the machine a name, but now she couldn't recall. She snorted. It had probably been quite silly.

Hours went by. The hunger ache passed, but she was so thirsty. She seemed to be more than half done with this patch and was resigned to being awake most of the night. The dark around her felt more like a fine blanket than a limitless threat. She started whistling, and thought of how proud he would be.

Then her cracklebroom went dead.

The dark closed in.

She stood, hugging herself in fear, imagining the growth surging around her. Her toes prickled; surely the invader spreading toward her, worming into her boots.

She screamed.

Screamed until her voice broke. Then she cried.

She was so tired she couldn't move.

At first she thought the fungus was glowing a new color, but then the pulselantern bobbed around the curve.

Father carried her home.

She woke late, at first convinced that he'd abandoned her somehow, maybe found an open crossgate, or that he'd been dragged away by rovers. Then she found the extra biscuits and the folded note on the meal blanket. A note. On real paper!

Ina,

Rest as long as you need. I'll work nearby, and check on you mid-day. I love you very much.

Dad

At the bottom of the page was a simple drawing of a four-legged animal with spots on its body and a long neck that made her happy to see.

Dressing, she noticed the fit was tight around her chest. She saw in the mirror the two shapes coming in. She busied herself with tidying the compartment.

While she was folding her sweaty slipsuit, his passcard fell out of the pocket. She realized with a start that she had no idea how he'd opened the door yesterday. She'd trapped him inside. If she hadn't come back... *But how...*

She tested it. The door opened.

When he came back for lunch, he had another silver passcard on his neck loop

"How...?" she asked.

He folded her hands around the key. "This was your mother's. I think you're ready."

She went back out with him and worked harder than she ever had before.

The duty blended over many days, but Father resumed stories as they worked. He told about the great skyspider that wove stars together, the dragon brothers who gambled their wings away to become piano players, the drookalore that munched on mountains and left-handed children. When she asked him to stop being fanciful, he talked about more of the animals that he'd read about, ones from before The Launch. She always liked these tales because once he'd said that maybe the animals lived somewhere on the ship, and they would be released at The Arrival.

He resumed the evening lessons. They studied knots, calligraphy, boxing.

When her breasts became tender, he told her what was coming. The lower back pain started shortly after, and gradually worsened. Still, she was scared on her day 4406, when the bleeding arrived.

On the next Social Night, it was their turn to host. Reed came alone, dressed snazzily and bearing a warm ribostew. He talked about the progress he'd made accessing new files of the computer. He turned on his tablet and showed them a maze of glowing blue lines, said they were partial maps of the ship—which Ina didn't believe at first because most of them were not circular in shape. "And this," he said, showing something in rough gray strokes, "is my representation of the whole ship, exterior view." Ina frowned. She'd always pictured it more like a fish, but his sketch was like a piece of rice inside a long helix.

At the end of the evening, he tried to kiss her outside their door. She gave him a cheek.

She rubbed it off as soon as he left.

Suddenly it just didn't make any sense to her.

She couldn't remember her day 1462, when Mother had left.

"If the rovers kill everyone, or take them..." she said, thinking out loud. "How did *she* go, but... we're still here?"

Father didn't answer for a long time and she knew he was pretending not to hear.

"Father?" She blinked at him. "Daddy?"

He stopped scrubbing.

"Did she fight back?"

He sighed.

"Your mother volunteered to join them. She wanted to go." He exhaled. "There." He bent back to work.

"But we always pay tribute. Why did she leave? Didn't she love us?!"

He regarded her, eyes filled with conflict. "It was me, Ina." He released more than breath, and shame settled on him. "*I* didn't love *her*. And she knew it."

She backed away. Then she wanted to punch him. She dropped her broom and walked off. She cursed and kicked and shouted. Then stopped.

"Who was it?" she asked, running back at him. "You loved someone else. *Who?*"

He nodded slowly. "Our neighbor."

She pointed to the unknown p-ring. He shook his head. She rotated her hand to R, eyes widening. "Stephana?"

"Not Stephana..."

Father spoke in the dark. "Our life is duty," he said. "Countless generations before us, and we know not how many yet to come. The ship may land tomorrow and we'll breathe real air, see new animals, build cities."

He took measured breaths, then continued. "I know you don't want to marry Reed. I understand. You should know that I didn't want to marry your mother and she didn't want to marry me. But we had to do so. To have children. Because the duty must continue."

Minutes went by before he spoke again.

"Every couple gets two children, to carry on. Then the computer sterilizes us—it's in the food."

"Two?" she asked tentatively.

"Your mother was gone before we could have another child."

She thought about this. "Why doesn't Reed have a sister?"

"Her name was Alysia and she was very young," he said gravely. "The Worxa demand a different kind of tribute."

He let these thoughts settle with her. "Ina, you have to marry your neighbor. Because it's what we do. And because I won't be here forever."

"Turn on the light!" she yelled.

He did so.

"What do you mean?" she asked. "What are you saying?"

"On my day 10,950, the daily biscuit will poison me."

"No, Daddy!" She ran to him. "No! We'll find something else for you to eat!" She cried and beat at his chest.

"Don't worry." He stroked her hair. "I have a few years left."

"No no no no!"

He rocked his daughter for a while, until she took herself to bed.

"GOOD MORNING, INA JANITOR. THIS IS YOUR DAY 4431."

"I lied to you, Ina." Father said, "About my life." He was sitting with only one boot on, staring at it. Then he met her gaze. "I didn't grow up here, not in Q. My parents raised me in J-ring. Until the rovers came. They said they'd kill my father and rape my mother and take me anyway. So I joined. And I ran with them. For years. I earned many assets for the group, and asked to leave. No one ever asked such a thing. But Roarke favored me, and he placed me here. With your mother. When we were of age."

She almost asked what happened to Mother's parents.

"Let's get to work," she said.

They labored all day without speaking.

"GOOD MORNING, GOWER JANITOR. THIS IS YOUR DAY 9908."

They were scrubbing in Q-9, when she straightened up to wipe her brow and noticed him gazing out the window, hands at his sides.

"Hey," she whispered, snapping her fingers softly, pointing at his face.

He turned his eyes downward. "I miss her sometimes," he said.

And put his filter mask back on.

Scrub scrub scrub.

-.-.-

Father messaged in the dark.

.- -. -.-- / .-. .-. .-. --- --. .-. .. .. / --- -. / ... . .-. .. .- .-. .. .. - -.-- / -... -.-- .--.
.- ... .--..

Ina was half-asleep, sapped from the day, the cramps echoing pain in her arms, shoulders, and feet. She smiled at how many times he'd promised to teach her the tapping code.

.... . .-.. .-.. --- --..-- / - --- -- ..--..

His pauses were impatient tonight.

Drowsy, she began to count the seconds for a reply.

She waited with him. Soon her smile faded.

The more time passed, the more awake she became.

After a few minutes, she was burning with alertness, staring into the black.

The rest of the night gave only silence.

"Broomsman!" shrieked a voice outside their door. "Brooooomsmannn! Come forth!"

Father opened the door.

Caddell stood a few meters away, his face painted in darkened red. The gold passcard hung from his neck. Seven rovers gripped their weapons behind him.

"Good morning, little rooster," Father said.

"Your overt disrespect has earned you this challenge," Caddell sneered. "I call you out!" He pointed a twitching finger.

Father stepped out calmly. Caddell watched him.

Ina moved closer to see. She slipped out the door and someone grabbed her around the waist from behind. She kicked back into their crotch, turned and shoved. The bandit slid, whimpering. Another one advanced and she backed away, but when he drew close, she struck him in the solar plexus. He dropped and sought breath in desperate gulps. They crawled back to their gang.

Seeing this, Father raised his brow at Caddell, who snarled in response.

"I cannot fight you," Father said. "There is work to be done today. I have a duty."

"You talk too much, janitor." Very slowly, Caddell swung the passcard loop so it hung behind him. He slid his left foot forward and leaned into the knee. He clapped his hands, and glared low over them at Father, shaking with reined exertion. Then he barked and they exploded apart, arms swinging wide circles before him, smoothly increasing speed as they tightened, flowing into forceful punches, left right leftright left*right*, blurring fast, as his kicks lashed between the strikes, powerful snaps in the air, and suddenly he launched forward, rolling high tuck, and dropped into a solid stance with arm extended to clawed fingers just centimeters from Father's face.

Ina was slightly impressed, but she snorted at him.

"Does Roarke know where you are?" Father asked.

Caddell said nothing, but drew a finger through the cracking red on his cheek. Then he showed his teeth.

Father's face turned grim. His voice went dry and severe. "No blades, no weapons."

"Agreed."

Caddell sweep-stepped back and took position.

Father rolled his shoulders and neck, and bounced on the balls of his feet. He brought his fists up to chin-level, elbows low and knuckles forward.

They circled each other.

Caddell snapped a kick and Father swayed his head out of it. Then came a series of side kicks, which he blocked with his forearm. He jabbed and drove his opponent back. Caddell leapt, slicing two diagonal downward strikes, which he glanced away with the backs of his hands. But a quick knee caught him in the ribs. He staggered back and curled to protect his head from the next volley.

"Get him, Cad!" his gang cheered. "Chop him up up *up*!"

He crouched to protect himself and another knee caught him in the chin. He grasped Caddell's foot, heaved up and away.

Caddell tucked, flipped, and landed three meters off, balanced and smirking.

Father resumed his upright stance, left foot slightly forward. He coughed and wiped blood from his mouth.

Ina clenched her jaw to keep from calling to him. She made faces at the rest of the gang. They tossed warlike gestures and she rolled her eyes.

The nomad advanced smoothly. He stopped, every limb quaking with potency. Then he kicked and spun in place, a flurry. He landed, exhaling.

"Chop chop *chop*!" they yelled.

Father switched his feet. Then his hands.

Caddell hesitated.

Father straightened up and dropped his arms. He sighed. And frowned.

His combatant eyed him.

Father spit. A bright red gob on Caddell's chestplate.

With a shriek, the rover lunged.

Twisting his upper body, Father slipped the punch and caught the hand going by. He pulled Caddell off-balance, kicked his feet from under him, and drove him to the floor, bending his hand back. The boy wheezed and struggled.

The gang rose to their feet, lifting weapons.

"Do you yield?" Father asked.

"I will *never*—"

The sound of breaking fingers stopped most of them approaching. The scream stopped the rest.

Father just looked the question at him again. This time Caddell nodded.

When Father released him, he went for something in his boot. Father stomped his other wrist and leaned on it until he dropped the knife.

"I'm sorry," Caddell whimpered, holding his ruined hand. "Forgive me... Please..." His voice and tears became a plea and he reached for help.

Father lifted him to his feet. He cried and fell to one knee. He reached again, whimpering. "I vow fealty! I swear my uncut and thoroughgoing allegiance! I will follow you for*ever*. My new lord and master." He kissed Father's hand deeply.

Father jerked away.

He stared at the back of his hand, and removed a small, dripping needle.

He staggered.

Ina rushed to him. "No!" She tried to hold him up. His eyes climbed his arm in horror. He looked at her and tried to speak, but his neck was already swollen. "Oh no! No no no no!" she cried. He fell to the deck. There was no peace in his eyes, only fear.

Against her chest, she felt his heart kick, flutter. And stop.

She rocked and whispered to him.

Until she knew he was gone.

Sometime later, she was aware of Caddell standing over her, chortling and sniveling. "And now—"

She wondered why he didn't finish. When she looked up, the woman with red-blonde striped hair was behind him, pulling the cord against his throat with her knee in his back. She tore the gold passcard from the lanyard and threw it her way. "Ina, go!" she shouted.

The other rovers ran at them. Hissing, hollering.

Caddell slashed wildly.

She glanced at Father's body, her home, the woman.

She bolted to the crossgate, swiped the passcard, and fled.

Glancing back, she saw them cut the woman down. She saw Caddell dig into his other boot and produce another card, red. And she didn't look back.

Two rings later, further than she'd ever traveled in her life, she realized where she'd seen the woman's face before.

The nose shape, the chin, around the eyes...

Every time she stared into the mirror.

I can't... I don't... oh hate!... must... why, Father?!... run... RUN!

She ran, trying to put some distance. At M-ring, she passed a family of four just going out for the day with their cracklebrooms. They turned their heads as she ran by, faces of surprise and confusion, but said nothing. At K-ring she stopped to catch her breath, wishing she had a canteen. Seconds later, she heard the previous door open, yelling and the sounds of pursuing feet. And she ran again.

It was in J-ring that she found Roarke's body. It hung upside down from a broken light fixture, stripped and drained. She did not scream.

The I-H crossgate was stuck open by a dead bot.

At G-ring she hesitated, seeing orange patches on the walls. She covered her mouth and realized that her mask was back at home. She ran through, holding her breath.

Daddy ... don't be dead!

When F-ring door opened, she slid to a stop. The light was low and eerie here, and it took a moment for her eyes to adjust. Before she could register, the stench made her gag, a thick moist effluvium. Every surface was encrusted in orange, both directions, covering the lights too. The whole ring was probably overrun.

She gulped a deep breath and ran, heaving.

A dark ocherous patch with knee-high sporestalks made her jump. Landing, her feet slipped and she fell hard.

Her hands and feet slicked repeatedly in the secretions. She cried out in panic.

She calmed herself. She drew her legs under her and stood, finding control.

She shuffled to the far door.

As she passed through it, a voice cried behind her, "Stop, most conniving bitch, stop!"

Caddell and the scavengers occupied the previous doorway. They beat their chests and pumped their weapons in the air. They toed the boundary of orange, chittering and trilling. For the moment.

She stuck her tongue out at them.

Caddell snatched a ripspear and hurled it at her.

She side-stepped, let it clatter. "Hyena," she said.

She kept her eyes on them as her door closed.

Then turned and ran.

At D-ring she crossed to the opposite door, opened it, then stepped back, turned right, and ran.

And ran and ran and ran. Around the curve.

D-3, D-4, D-5, past the window, D-6...

Lungs pounding.

Until she was halfway around and couldn't go back.

Then she collapsed.

And caught her breath.

And waited.

She slept.

All day.

Until the lights went out.

Then she stood and resumed.

She kept close to the wall but didn't touch it with her hands.

It was still dark when she circled around to find the area deserted. She opened the door, checked, and proceeded through the next crossgate, moving lightly on her toes.

She was famished and dehydrated. She tried the gold passcard on the c dwellchamber. No response.

The digital dawn lights came up at B-ring, and she encountered a barricade of crates and furniture. She squeezed through and found only silence on the other side.

Despite her hunger, she felt some accomplishment at reaching A-ring, and wasn't surprised to find the same layout. She'd always pictured the ship with twenty-six rings. Beyond this, however, she expected something new.

The opposite door would not unlock.

She swiped the gold passcard again and again. The locklight blinked red.

Ina slumped to the floor. She clutched her empty stomach.

She lay down and closed her eyes. She dreamed of blue oceans.

Waking, she saw the fungus all around her.

Every centimeter of the hallway teemed with spores. But it kept its distance, leaving a ring of metal floor.

She held still for an hour. Then she wept.

She was ravenous. And beyond hope.

Its texture shimmered and undulated.

She was no longer afraid.

She reached out...

...and a single orange stalk reached up...

...to meet her finger.

She opened her hand and tens of them caressed her palm.

Gently, she pulled them free.

And brought them to her mouth.

Tumbling on a tiny rock through cold nothing. Waiting waiting waiting millions. Sudden touch. Something new. Getting inside. So warm! Burst burgeon sprout expand flourish!

When she was full and gratified, a warmth spread through her.

The orange parted, opening a path to the door.

She took off her boots and padded to the exit. She dropped the gold passcard to the floor and touched the lock with her palm. The warmth coursed from her center to her hand, and the light turned green.

The new hallway contained descending metal stairs that began to scroll downward as she approached them.

The next door opened into a very long room. It was lined with two-meter capsules stacked ten high in rows that continued for over a kilometer. Thousands of them, pulsing with life. The capsules nearest to her were open and dark, and she counted them. Fifty-two.

She walked, passing the small lit windows, revealing sets of closed eyes. She trailed her hand along the smooth surfaces as she traversed the length. Looking for something else. Something more.

Immediately through the next doors, green leaves brushed her face. She moved forward like a dream, feeling rough trunks and swaying branches. She gazed up to see the canopy reaching, swaying, high toward a bright hexagonal ceiling. Her feet pressed down on warm soil that she'd only ever read about.

A stairway upward. Another lock.

She entered the room where computer consoles and a command chair facing a great wrapping window. She watched the stars streak toward them and part. She could see their true pigment now.

She sat at the forward console and tapped the keyboard, stirring a bright dusty cloud. Bringing her fingers close, she saw the golden scintilla trickling from her whorls.

Then she spread her hands over the interface. The warmth rippled through her and she felt the ship alter course.

Now she pictured a new planet, warm and moist, its surface churning shades of copper, henna, rust, tawny, auburn, and titian. Living spore continents, reaching toward space.

Behind her, perfect orange footprints seethed and sang.

And began to spread.

Cheating the Devil

NADINE MOVED TO the city in the heat of summer.

She met him in the basement coffee shop of an old downtown building. It was the only property in the city, he would tell her later, with gargoyles. She noticed him ahead of her in the line when he ducked under the rack of glasses and asked very quietly for a warm mug of blood, if you please, goat's blood. Two curls of his hair would not stay down.

The woman behind the counter froze, and Nadine thought there would be trouble. Then the barista shouldered her towel and laughed with rolling eyes as she waved him away. It took Nadine a moment. She watched him pour water from the free pitcher and chatter his teeth after he sipped. When she came to the counter he was still leaning there. She glanced at him briefly and couldn't look back because he watched her intently, without smirk or frown, eyes narrow but lost. When her drink was ready, he moved like a pouncing cat. His fingernails were not long but some cut to points.

The barista's eyes said it was okay.

She could only follow. He sat at a small table in the back with his water and her drink placed opposite. He sipped water like hissing steam, and listened without asking. She uttered small talk. That she needed to be ready for school in the fall. That she'd found an apartment about a mile from campus, with big rooms, but it didn't feel like home. It wasn't because it was her first place away from home, it was the weird... No, that wasn't the right word... And he finished her sentence: "indifferent unreachable feel of the city?" Already she inspected his eyes for flame or shadow.

He said little about himself, mentioning only that Hell was closed, he was tired, but glad to meet her. She listened, trying not to frown, until she understood, or thought she did. His goatee, severe and perfect enough not to be silly, could only be called... and again he finished her thought aloud... "Mephistophelian." A name she'd heard somewhere. "It's from a story," he said. "No stories lie. And no stories will hurt you. Only this place." He seemed to be pretending. His voice was tranquil, nothing of fire, so she left with him, holding his hand as he held the door.

She did not look at the barista on the way out, how her eyes said, *I am the last real person you will see.*

He walked her through alleys, and showed her pieces of old buildings, a speakeasy door, an owl roost in a bell tower, and a sculpture nearly hidden under an overpass.

His name was not Lucifer or Belial (Did she know these names? he asked), it was Jordan, he told her on the precipice of an empty parking garage. The name meant *descending*, and it was the only thing he was proud of.

"Do you look at everyone like that?" she flirted. "Or do you have devious plans for me?"

The way his eyes hardened, she stopped smiling and stepped back.

Then he seemed to return, for he smiled and laughed with a warm and human sound. She again sensed the goodness and profundity she'd hoped was there. "Sorry," he said, "I get that way sometimes. Being the son of a jackal and all." It sounded like a joke, one she could tolerate for a while.

For a week she didn't see her own apartment. She spent her nights with him and her days filling out job applications, mostly at drive-thru restaurants. She was determined not to call her parents for next month's rent. On the thirteenth night of him, she stayed home alone with an empty refrigerator and cried. She ate an overcooked hot dog from the corner convenience store and tried to arrange her books and clothes.

The next night, they were sitting together on the roof outside his window, when she pushed him flat and kissed him and took off her shirt. She pressed against all of him and devoured the animal sound of his breath and exposed him and moved and moved and would not stop. When it was done, she felt she was in love with him and watched his bare form crouch at the edge of the roof, his teeth matching the moon.

The next day she carried her boxes into his apartment. "Forever, your soul is my claim," he said at the doorway. She scoffed audibly and pushed by him with an armload. The nursing home called to say that the housekeeper training program started Monday.

They stayed up late every night. She waited a few weeks to tell her parents the new address. They cooked together and read books in silence. At first she thought all the bulbs were broken, but then discovered they were unscrewed just enough. She liked that he blushed when she called him He Who Loves Not the Light.

He had worked at Dante's Pizza & Hot Hoagies since high school. She would stop in to wait for him after a day of job hunting. Jordan didn't introduce her, but Alex introduced himself as someone who had known him for many years. He was surprised to learn Jordan had a girlfriend. Every day he would invite her out for a smoke while she waited.

She started coming to the back door at the end of Jordan's shift. One day he stopped a delivery driver on his way out. Jordan put his arm around the man's shoulders and indicated the kitchen with a dramatic sweep, whispering to him, "All these things will I give thee if thou wilt fall down and worship me." The driver didn't understand the reference. But Alex came over from the cheesesteak grille, saying, "Go away, Satan." He pointed at Jordan with a steaming grille paddle. Jordan turned and kicked the door, going through its swing, pointing index fingers off his forehead. And Nadine followed.

"Used to think I wanted to be a writer. But I just wanted to hide. From people. From everyone." He stopped, like he told too much. Then he continued in a whisper. "I despised them for not being unusual or extraordinary, for not creating scenes. For not speaking with power and conflict, and in perfect measured dialogue. Oh, how I hated them."

He still tried to write. Mostly he composed short lines in a pocket note pad, fragments of monologue. When he did write, he sat at the computer for a week of nights, sometimes entire nights, and typed nothing. He went to it without announcement and she learned that she must leave, for him, for herself. On those nights she drove alone around the city.

She discovered things without him. Stop signs with WAR and EATING ANIMALS and TALKING TO COPS stickers slapped on them. A flyer for a lost cat poorly depicting either a sculpture of thorns or possibly a soaking feline. The man who sat unmoving for so long on the bench outside the railway station that she thought him a statue. The fourteen-story building with one blank unpainted side, except for a single window halfway up and off-center, propped open by a rusted handcrank kitchen mixer. At dusk, if she looked up while walking in the park, small bats flapped above her against the gray blue. She went to a bar once, and walked into the men's bathroom by mistake, where she encountered a condom machine offering Savage Bliss brand, which made her giggle so uncontrollably that she felt queasy and walked her bike home. The branches of two opposite trees had grown over Euclid Street and fused together. The city was like a dream, huge and strange and almost familiar, full of muted surprises. She could no longer remember her own home. And when she was with him, the city felt empty.

One night she went back, knowing it was too early. He was typing and words appeared on the screen. Still in her jacket, she touched his bare shoulders and front, not looking at the screen, for he often wrote naked. She pulled his arms away from a broken sentence. He shuddered and made no protest. Snapping the desk lamp switch, she drew him down.

Afterward she held him while he slept in a tight unyielding ball. She asked herself if what he had for her was not love. And if it wasn't, why did she stay? To give? To listen? In hope? Maybe it was the only way he could. He cared for her, she was sure. She could not feel his skin. Maybe she was like him.

He came home early one night when the restaurant was slow. "Cast down," he said. "My wings shriveled."

He remained in the doorway, watching nothing, silent.

"I used to want to be The Devil." He took a seat on the floor and continued in his way, like she wasn't there. "Last summer, I was visiting my relatives in San Francisco. My cousin took me to a bookstore." She expected a tale about a wicked book or haunted artifact. Then the story went elsewhere and she didn't stop him. "On the way, walking by this dark Victorian row house—painted all black, shiny and dull like burned wood—my cousin said, 'Anton LaVey lives there.'"

"Who's that?"

He continued without answering. "I couldn't believe it, I thought if this guy is real... I mean, I wanted to go in and ask him, 'What are you about, hey?' 'Have you really met...?'" He paused and put two fingers off his forehead, and looked at her briefly. She nodded.

"My cousin said he walked by that house every day on the way to grade school. Every day the kids crossed to the other side of the street. People said they heard lions roaring inside. And all I could think was that there should be things other than lions."

And that was the end. It wasn't like the ones he used to tell. The story had tricked her; he had tricked her. He was changing.

The red hand signal blinked. A woman stopped in the middle of the crosswalk and danced, eyes closed, in front of waiting cars.

"That, oh that! Now that is something *real*," said Jordan. His hands clenched. "I should—Why don't I ever—" He jumped off the curb. The red hand was solid now. He leaped and spun around the twirling pirouetting woman while the cross traffic honked horns and raced engines and drivers shouted.

Alone on the corner, Nadine felt nothing. Except that she knew him for what he was.

His friends did not come over often. Proselytes, he called them. When Alex came over, he talked the entire stay, sitting on the couch next to Nadine, leaving only the floor for Jordan. He would recite movie dialogue and Jordan would sometimes correct him. He would describe a whole scene, occasionally letting the sound effects throw him from his seat. Jordan would nod and laugh like it was an embarrassing memory. Alex would pat her leg or squeeze her arm, apologizing for leaving her out. He smelled of stale smoke. One night he hugged her as part of the apology.

Alex started to come over more often while Jordan was still at work. He would ask if Jordan was home, then take a seat no matter the response. Nadine said she was going for a bike ride. No, come on, he said, let's go for a drive instead. No, no thanks, she really needed to exercise. She would have her bike ready by the door when he knocked. She rode down the street and around the corner, where she hid behind a tree until his car pulled away.

She did not notice the words when the story came tumbling out, she just needed to tell it. About Ms. Evans in room 114, about the day last week when she was collecting the trash as the aides were changing her bed pad, and she glimpsed the tumor inside her thigh, rumpled with veins. How Ms. Evans never spoke, how she just watched, as they asked her to help lift her leg, one at a time, and sit up, that's it now, that's it, all finished now. She never spoke. But yesterday Nadine had been in her room, gathering the laundry bundle, and Ms. Evans said in a wailing haunted voice, "Where where where? Where are my grandchildren?" And Nadine thought of an old cartoon that had given her nightmares when she was three, with ghosts swirling out of the forest and skeletons dancing as they tossed around their skulls. "You tell them to bring back my silver," Ms. Evans said.

When she finished the story, she saw he was listening. His eyes were different this time, untroubled. But she didn't like it and would never tell him another.

She woke alone in the bed. She found him in the dark bathroom staring toward the mirror, not quite into the glass. She said nothing. It was over an hour before he came out. Then he sat on the far corner of the bed and sighed.

"There are no costume shops in this town," he said. She didn't understand his meaning or the despair in his voice.

He remained there for a long while. Then he went to the computer and turned it on. She rolled over and stayed awake. There was no sound from the keyboard.

She waited and waited until he was ready to touch her.

———————

She's seen the man in the wheelchair before. His blue compact car at the far side of the parking lot, angled against the drugstore.

She sees it today and feels laden at the sight of it. For every day she punches her timecard, says goodbye, shoulders her bag, exits the same door, unlocks the car, drives home the same route. The heft of her backpack, her shoes on the hallway tile, the door's tension, are all reminders of the routine. She can still remember when everything was new, the faces and the all of her surroundings. In two months, the city has grown hot and stale, and classes do not start for another month.

The man in the wheelchair passes as she unlocks her own car.

She starts her car and lets the engine idle.

He hoists himself in, maneuvers to the driver's seat, folds the chair and pulls it in after him.

She puts her car in gear and doesn't realize she's staring.

He throws his arms out and screams silently. He hits the steering wheel, and drops his head down.

She pulls alongside and shouts but his head stays down. So she gets out and walks around and knocks on his window.

He jumps and stares at her. He's been crying. After a moment he rolls down his window.

She notices that his car doesn't have any pedals. The steering column has extra levers and buttons, the passenger seat is missing and the wheelchair folded there.

He turns the keys in the ignition, something under the hood groans and goes quiet. He throws his hands up again. He shakes his head, lip trembling.

She opens her passenger door, then his door.

He looks at her and they don't say anything. She reaches under him with both arms and lifts him out. Then she puts his wheelchair in the trunk of her car.

He gives her directions and they don't say much else. At his apartment building, she rides in the elevator with him. Though he doesn't invite her, she goes in anyway. His name is Hoyt.

There are things Jordan does not tell her. Pieces he's collected, pieces of stories.

The abandoned town where coal fires still burn in the mines underneath. The story about his friend who spent a year in Australia and was pricked by the spur of a platypus, and still aches in his joints. The slave who tried to convince his Puritan owner in 1716 that he had been inoculated against smallpox and knew how to cure it. The car that was stopped at the Mexico-United States border, returning tourists with a white tiger cub in the back seat. The winds that came down off the mountains, warm air bending trees, popping car windows, leaving parking lots strewn with glass in the morning, a hundred thefts of nothing. The house in his old neighborhood with the swastika carving above the front window, finally removed or covered in plaster a few years ago. The filmmaker who lived in his car and someone stole his equipment so he glued grass and leaves and moth wings to film, six minutes long, over eight thousand frames. The miner who had a steel rod blasted through his skull and continued to live. Or that spring day, playing in the sandbox with his friend, when they uncovered the leathery black triangle in the corner, and though it could have been a piece of tarp, they locked gazes and said at the same time, "The Devil's ear!" Then they put it in a rinsed peanut butter jar and argued over who would get to keep it, and made a pact that Jordan would until Halloween, and by December his friend forgot, and all the years after. The jar sat on Jordan's dresser for as long as he could recall, but thinking about it now he couldn't remember what happened to it. His parents tossed it out, or it crawled away.

Beginnings of stories for which he cannot find the ending. He worries that life is too much like this.

He stops writing on a Thursday. He's been up most of the night reading a book of short stories. When it's done, he closes the book and goes out to the roof. Not long after, she hears panting and thinks at first he is touching himself, so she follows, moving slowly on hands and knees over the warm shingles like a cat. Just before she reaches him, she stops because he's crying in fits, and she's never seen him this way.

She holds him and asks him what's wrong and he just cries and sobs. He says he can't do it, he just can't, he's not any good. She tries to hold him tight, but he's falling. He slips through her arms and slides off her legs until she can only watch him convulsing there near the edge.

He drags himself back inside. He stumbles to the computer and suddenly stands up straight. She's about to say something when he when strikes the machine, sending the monitor to the floor, the screen tube pops and glass scatters across the floor. He lifts the computer and hurls it against the wall. It's all over before she can be afraid. He crawls into bed and turns off the light. When his breathing settles, she makes her way through the dark, against the wall, and eases in beside him.

Nadine smells wet leaves and soil and imagines a forest dying inside him. She dreams of running, fleeing across a bridge in thick smoky fog, never reaching the other side, and notices at some point the whole structure is moving, the metal and cement are floating with the tide of the unseen cold waters below.

———

"Where...?" she begins to ask him.

Hoyt thinks about her question. "It's only my legs."

She is ready, excited and nervous, and reaches slowly to him. Out of nowhere she thinks of Jordan, when he told her that ruined trees after a forest fire are called the *standing dead*. And her hand stops before Hoyt's face, her courage departed.

She's thinking about Jordan. How he shouts at the sun from the rooftop, telling it to go haunt some other planet. How he leaves pentagrams made of black pepper on the table under the bill when they leave a restaurant. How he whispers strange chants to well-behaved dogs walking with their owners. If only his horns were real. Once she saw him naked in the bathroom, pulling at the skin of his arm, then his ankle, with melodramatic frustration, muttering loudly about a caught zipper, maybe knowing she was there. His endless performance. The size of his world, edging out all others. She tries to hate him.

She leans off the couch, finds her feet under her, moving forward, finds her hands at Hoyt's cheek and neck, finds his lips. Her eyes are down when she pulls back, catches herself looking at his legs, and returns for more. His taste and smell surround her and she stays close.

Lifting him out of the chair, she leans back and his legs fold against her arm. He puts one arm around her shoulders, his hand touching her hair with gentle hunger. Then his fingers stop.

"What about—"

She tells him to shut up before he says the name. "Speak no blasphemy," she says. He seems unsure whether to laugh or not.

There is no guilt now. She pulls him against her, sensing something push at them from the periphery of all this, and leans his head against her. There is no turning back.

———

The next afternoon, following their orgasms, they begin to talk.

"For instance... stained glass windows will burn him," she says, and pauses. "They are designed that way, with so many bright and beautiful colors, to destroy him with their vibrant gaze. That's how he speaks most of the time." She hears aversion in her voice.

"You keep talking about him," Hoyt says, not quite annoyed.

They are kissing and holding each other tightly.

"I think I should go. I should go back home." But she doesn't get up.

How strange it is to lie with him in the silence. He doesn't curl up, or get up so quickly her heart jumps, or perch on the bed like a creature. Tears burn her eyes but she won't let them out. She will have to return. But she's found a something in her she hasn't felt before, a sliver of resentment.

Dark red footprints lead to the bedroom where Jordan is twisted naked in the sheets, breathing loudly, lost and deep. She sweeps up the glass and scrubs away the dried blood, and before she knows what she's doing she gets in next to him.

He can't walk and stays home from work, says he can feel the glass under his skin. She offers to drive him to the hospital. He says no, it gives him something to dig for later.

He is going back to old things, he says. She doesn't know if she is frightened or excited.

When his feet heal, Jordan throws the computer out the window, then goes outside and stands over the shattered wreckage, scolding it.

They drive to his parents' house. When she does not talk in the car, he turns on the radio. He says he needs something old, something from the past, a thing he's forgotten for years but just remembered. His dad bought it for him when he was maybe three or four. She doesn't ask what. Her arm hangs out the car window and she watches it glide and dip in the cool air.

He pulls into the driveway and says he'll just be a minute. She waits in the car as the cicadas finish their evening screams in the settling dark. The eyes of something shine at her from under his parents' car.

He comes back and startles her because she isn't sure whether she fell asleep. "They want us to come in for a few."

His mom hugs her. His dad hugs her. He's wearing a velour track suit. His mom offers soda, milk, iced tea, or lemon water. "No, thank you, really," she says. He has warned her she may have to refuse a few times. His mom still lists off all the sodas: diet, raspberry, cola, ginger ale, black cherry vanilla.

"I came to look in the attic," Jordan says. And he leaves her in the kitchen with them.

They ask her how work is going. It makes her think of Hoyt, but she talks about overtime and applying to school. They ask how her parents are doing. His dad wants to know what her dad does. She forgets the name of her hometown, and this alarms her. She doesn't want to talk anymore. "I'll go see if he needs any help."

"We keep asking him to organize his things up there and have a garage sale..."

The humid attic smells of cedar and dust. Jordan stands among several cardboard boxes with books and toy tractors and stuffed animals extracted onto the floor. He holds a small gray box and a large jar, looking back and forth from one hand to the other. The jar seems to contain nothing more than a piece of black fabric.

He stands unmoving, not looking at her, his skin flat and pale under humming bare bulbs, and she realizes now that he has no scars.

She says his name and immediately regrets speaking, takes a step down the stairs, willing him not to respond.

If he notices her, he will smile. He will touch her hand and immobilize her, slowly lower the attic door. He will kiss her and whisper. There's an old mattress leaning against the chimney. He will look at her with that wicked hungry face, and she'll go to him. He will nip her neck, lift her shirt not quite off her head and fold it over her eyes as he kisses her skin, and she'll shudder and climb onto him.

She turns away quickly and descends the stairs. She runs down, down, out the front door, to the end of the driveway before the screen door slams faintly behind. The summer wind is thick and unforgiving.

She walks past dark lawns, already mapping the streets to Hoyt's apartment, readying the blocks and turns in her head when Jordan pulls up in the car.

"You need some time," he says, not a question. "Why don't you take the car? I'll walk. I can stay with my parents for a few days." In this moment he seems nearly human. And the words seem to care, even in the dark.

She is surprised herself, getting into the passenger's seat. His eyes too are different, opened from their usual remoteness. He has chosen something. He is changing. The small gray box sits between them on the emergency brake.

He says nothing when they get back. He takes the gray box to his desk and hunches under the lamp.

She doesn't remember getting into bed.

At some point she wakes to sunlight. But sleep insists on more.

She wakes to darkness again.

He still sits at the desk.

Coming up behind, she still cannot startle him, no matter how silent and careful. She reaches for his shoulder.

Gray dust and rock fragments litter his desk. An ebony shape embedded in the shale, neatly exposed, like a beetle with bones, polished for sale in a museum shop. "Trilobite. Dad bought it for me when I was four." He digs a craft knife into the soft rock around it. "But I always wondered if there was something... else..." He scrapes and picks, gentle, shaking, anxious. "... something they missed..."

"Should you be doing that? To something so old?" It sounds like something he would say. Or used to say.

She drifts away from him, down the hallway, and opens the front door.

"The phone rang yesterday afternoon," he calls from the back room. "I didn't answer."

She closes the front door behind her. And she runs.

Hoyt's door is unlocked and she walks straight in. She finds him sitting in the large easy chair with a lap desk over his legs. His hands are stained brown-red, hovering over a formless soft shape.

"I've been trying all day. Kneading and pinching and smoothing, adding water, starting over." He stares at the distorted mass of clay, his face drawn with sorrow. "I never saw it, even when it broke off. When they went for an ambulance, when they put me on a stretcher, nobody searched around for it. I always wondered what it looked like. I imagine it was about this size. But I don't know the shape. I'm no sculptor."

There should be music, she thinks, looking around the room, but doesn't know what kind. It is too quiet here. The summer has been too long. The tree outside the window looks unreal. I don't know this man, she thinks. The front door is still open and she moves through it, saying nothing. She takes the stairs. Whatever falls behind her, she doesn't hear.

A *Rolling Stone* columnist interviews Anton LaVey. "Another word for God is nature," says LaVey, "another word for God is Satan. Another word for nature is evolution." His lion, Togare, roared and disturbed the neighbors, until a city ordinance prevented the housing of certain wild animal species in residential areas. Togare, the closest it seemed one could get to owning a monster, was taken away to the zoo. LaVey wanted his childhood and early career attempts kept a mystery. "Eventually you want to be recognized for what you are now." The journalist could not confirm most of the events attributed to his life. He hadn't performed a black mass in twenty years. He will live in that black house until his death. He was born with a tail, an extra vertebra, which was removed in his youth, or so he claimed.

Fall semester starts tomorrow, but she cannot envision herself going to class.

She stands at the window in the dark. She cannot remember waking or standing.

His wingless form breathes soundly in the bed. The light cuts shadows on his pillow, dark points melted to his head. He is what he wants to be, for now.

She is awake, touched by the incoming breeze, bringing smells and sounds of a city that shifts and changes at night, calling people in, some new and some returning, all filled with aspirations or defeat. The air is warm in the dark, whispers of a season that refuses to let go. She holds herself, gripping opposite shoulders, constricting her arms, ribs aching. Anyone in a facing window or passing by in the dark will see how tightly she holds herself, but they will not see the trembling from the cold or her effort; they will not know hold long she can embrace. Nor does she.

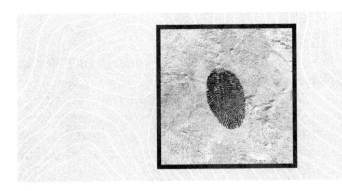

Brink City

IKE MOST YOUNG and ambitious cities, Ckotkehl thrived for centuries without much heed to the outside world. Inspired by their own creativity, selfishness, and selective breeding, its inhabitants evolved their colony in less than one hundred generations from a few scattered huts to a thriving metropolis of magnificent plazas and pristine aqueducts. So busy with what they defined as society, they remained entirely unaware of their municipality's placement on the inner coast of the small white halfmoon bay of Yvonne Jesse Koren's pinky fingernail of her right hand.

Unaware, until the first catastrophe when Yvonne slammed her hand in an automobile door and damaged what a doctor would call the lanula, which is located at the end of the nail and actually part of the nail bed, but she did not see a medical professional. Tsunamis destroyed half of Ckotkehl's west district while earthquakes ruptured the topography of all their lives.

After the devastation, it was anguish and loss that fueled a passionate recovery. Artisans and engineers buried their loved ones and worked ceaselessly to rebuild their beloved city. Scandal arose when a mayor embezzled funds, but he was dealt with swiftly, inhumed alive into the foundation of the new capital watchtower, his name erased from historical records and reduced to shunned whisper.

Now aware of their host, they watched her assiduously. They sent out surveyors and explorers over the fingerprint whorl canyon wastelands and across the uncharted knuckle continent. They would look back and call it the advent of a new age as their civilization thrived in science, art, and philosophy, a purposive species anxious to become something more, both outward and inward. They vowed progress and radiance. To master flight and explore all worlds beyond.

Hundreds of their years passed in weeks of Yvonne's gigantic life. The only returning explorer was too old to be recognized, too outlandish to be believed, and they committed her to a fungus jail. Oaths and resolve dwindled. Ideals changed, wealth shifted, government became unprincipled. The wealthy few declared themselves royalty and indulged in extravagance. The watchtower—a symbol of progress and justice—was remodeled into an elite restaurant, briefly successful, before falling to bankruptcy. They manufactured vehicles so large that the buildings had to hover above them, the entire city refitted. Their word for "book" became antiquated slang for a homeless artist, and the forests were long gone as the suburbs expanded. The police collected taxes every week. The citizens of Ckotkehl had forgotten how to be prepared and steadfast, so they were unprepared for the day when Yvonne failed to repay a loan from the lenders with a high rate of interest and early due date.

Lenders who brought bolt cutters and held down her hand with her fingers spread.

Her shrieks alone vaporized most of the city. The upheaval of the land below crushed nearly everything else. A few survivors hid in pockets of lesser devastation, huddled together and recalling old prayers, when the worst came. The lenders fed Yvonne's finger to a starved dog, and the reality of Ckotkehl was reconfigured in an avalanche roar. Dimensions crushed and frayed. Rock became fire. Water became pain. Air became dust.

Some of them survived.

Not the strongest ones, not all who deserved to.

But those who did would remember. They would tell the stories.

And remind their children to adapt. To be ready. For whatever the world brought next.

—◦—

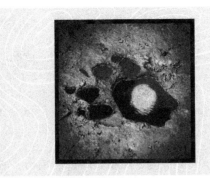

Her Scent Along the River

ERWIN LEANED AGAINST the condo balcony for a long time and watched the river flow through the city evening. He hadn't meant to stay, just a curious walkthrough of the rental, but unlocking the door, then seeing the view, he'd resolved to let the night come on and devour his thoughts. From his perch he watched a jet boat skim past, ducks escaping its wake to gather on the dock below despite the plastic wolf mounted there, then a train rumble and screech across the bridge to his right, while the bridge to his left opened for an incoming barge. The city hushed, and the only movement was the riverfront path where a woman portaged a small canoe over her head down to the bank. She tossed a blue safety vest into the vessel and glanced around the still waterfront, perhaps pausing his direction, revealing a silver streak in her brunette, before she paddled off against the current.

Kerwin stopped replaying the moment he'd walked into the rental office, given his last name, and the agent had asked his brother's name in a confirming voice, and he'd surprised himself at not correcting her. He'd made some kind of choice in that pause, as he neglected to tell her Prescott wasn't coming, that Prescott was in fact dying far away, in Kansas City, where he himself was supposed to be heading, boarding a plane very soon to go and see his brother's final days. And instead of canceling the furnished condo rental in that moment for his brother and sister-in-law and two nieces to visit, instead of saying no, you have mistaken me for him, he'd accepted the key to townhouse D-22 with a view of the river. He thought to tell Cora where he was, but things had been odd and confining between them lately.

He'd decided, in that second of silence and inaction, that he was taking a vacation from the world.

The sky had turned a dark mottled indigo, the urban lights imitated the stars, and the buildings and bridges held a long empty quiet. The river provided the only sound and motion, its shallow black and silver waves continuing their dance, as the city grew drowsy around them, until Kerwin's eyes found the only shape in the water. The canoe returned with the current in an oddly statuesque scene, its only passenger stood squarely on four legs at the front bow, and as it drew closer his eyes defined the canine form before his mind admitted so. The large dog waited until the craft bumped against the small condo beach and leapt onto the bank, then trotted away down the waterfront path.

Before he could think too much about it, he stepped over the railing, hung from his arms, dropped from the second-story balcony, and ran down to the canoe. He stood at the scene, noticing the blue safety vest in the boat and the tracks leading away, the paw prints nearest the waterline filling with moisture and losing shape.

In a moment of simple thirst and impulse, evading himself, Kerwin got down onto the wet sand and pressed his lips into one depression and, as the clouds parted briefly, he slurped the moon reflected there.

The clean sheets abraded his skin. His dreams befell in obscure and formless ways, containing only the sounds of lapping water and echoing storms. He woke once to sunlight and snatched the blinds closed before collapsing again. It was night once more when he stood, stark awake, panting and famished. Kerwin glanced at his mobile phone, seven messages, and turned it off.

There was no food in the condo, of course, so he ordered delivery pizza. When the hunger did not lessen after he'd eaten three large pies, he phoned for Thai takeout. Unsatisfied, he leaned against the couch, whimpering and scratching at his belly. The sensation grew from an itch to an ache to an unbearable sharpness that he could not satisfy.

He lifted his shirt in front of the bathroom mirror, saw long pink scratch marks, and found the dark coarse strand of hair protruding from the wrinkles of his navel. He pulled at the strange hair with his fingernails. Unsuccessful, he wrapped it around his finger and yanked. He yelped as his chest split, skin and tissue tearing, but he did not stop and pulled and pulled upward to his throat, unfolding a thick mat of dark bloody hair. His whole body felt afire like wasp stings, and the famished vacancy within him escaped in a howl that made the walls tremble.

Sunrise woke Kerwin nude and shivering, his face inches from a plastic wolf, with the bitter scratch of feathers in his mouth. He bare body draped at the end of the river dock, one hand in the water, as a light pattering rain pulled the dark red stains apart and carried them away between the weathered boards.

He stood on the neighbor's gas grille to regain the upper balcony to D-22. When he glanced out the front door to make a streaking run for his car he found his clothes folded on the door mat.

The shower's heat warmed him eventually. When the water rose above his ankles he unclogged two soft wrinkled pink stubs from the drain, only then counting his eight toes.

He slid in overstuffed blue boots over the clear curb ice, wheeling his arms, took a shuffling run and slid again. He sniffed crisp air and wiped his nose with a mitten, then jumped on a long white air pocket with a satisfying crack, followed by hundreds of smaller ones that he stopped and pounded with his heel, again and again, until they popped.

Come on, his brother said, his face young but always older. We'll be late for school. Let's cut through the Folsom's yard.

He trudged across the white lawn, thundering each step like a gargantuan atomic monster, his giant reptilian foot crushing the puny city's shield dome.

You brats, the old man shouted from his back door, I told you this is my property, his voice drowned by barking as he opened the door wide to release the dog.

The snarling beast ran at him pumping with angry mouth wide and full of flashing teeth, as he stood rooted in fear with hot shame flooding down his leg. And Prescott stepped between them.

Heavy with exhaustion and hunger, Kerwin paced the sparse living room, growled at the pale fragments of sun edging the curtains, pausing to look at the plane ticket on the counter. His eyes burned with memory and guilt. He couldn't travel on an airplane. He certainly couldn't be near his nieces now. He couldn't go home.

Feeling trapped, he went out into the afternoon, hiding the key under the welcome mat. The rental agent stopped him outside the converted railroad warehouse turned parking garage.

"Mr. Lori, I just wanted to remind you that there's a pet deposit. I'm sure we didn't include that on your contract, but the neighbors said they heard barking and scratching. So, if you could just stop by the office."

He felt weak and restless, felt like lying and tearing her throat out. But he managed to sound genial. "Yes, absolutely, I'll be sure to do that."

The city was deafening. He winced at the harsh discord of engines and voices, sirens and footsteps, the grinding rattle of skateboard wheels over a mile away. The world smelled of oil and dust.

Kerwin took the Red Line train across town and walked from the transit center to his neighborhood. He turned his corner cautiously. Cora's car was not in the parking space, so he entered his small apartment and stuffed clothes into a backpack. He thought about leaving her a note but left quickly and kept walking.

At the corner market he bought five boxes of high protein energy bars, a few rolls of duct tape, and a five-pack of foam ear plugs.

On the way back downtown, his teeth felt loose while his ribs hummed against his skin. The gray sky dimmed and he thought he'd have to exit at the next train stop, stash his supplies, and expected to wake tomorrow in someone's urban chicken coop. He leaned his head against the vinyl seat, closed his eyes, and tried to slow his panting.

He watched the city slide by and it gave him an idea. He exited at the first downtown stop and began his search. The tallest buildings, like the bank towers and newest condo developments would likely have security cameras, and 14 or more floors seemed an unnecessary height. He tried a few locations between 6 and 10 stories before he found one without an alarm on the roof access door, and taped back the latch. Then he settled himself under an exhaust vent and wrapped his ankles and then wrists as best he could, using all the tape from a roll.

He tried closing his eyes, but the luminous shape in the sky would not release him. Soon the sharp anxious craving engulfed his sight and awareness.

At dawn he dressed and placed the somewhat identifiable remains of at least four pigeons in a plastic bag. No one seemed to notice him exit the basement parking ramp without a vehicle, but he planned not to return to the location.

Back at the rented condo, he found a business card under the mat next to his key. The orange and green logo and playful font spelled out SPOT'S STAY & PLAY, CANINE CARE BOTH NIGHT & DAY. The skin along his spine tightened and he felt an ache at the base between his buttocks. He entered the place, sniffing, but found only furniture in each room. When he noticed the back of the card stamped with a blue moon and signed AYSEL with a handwritten phone number. He had not known the rental agent's name, but she was very on-task.

He dropped it in the trash along with the overdue plane ticket, but he still felt watched.

When they left Prescott off at college, he hugged Kerwin and said, "Take care of Mom and Dad. They act like they know everything, but they'll need your help." Then he rode in the car with his parents back across five states, saying nothing. When they arrived home, Kerwin ran to his room so they wouldn't see him cry.

The local weather report showed the moonrise as 81 minutes later than last night, and Kerwin wanted some time to forget. He shouldered his supply bag and walked to a nearby tavern where the tap list was disappointing so he ordered a single malt, neat, and sat at the bar.

The smoky warmth in his throat distracted him for a few minutes from the choices he had made. But after the second pour, his eyes began to burn. He thought of his brother and his nieces. And Cora. He'd just wanted a moment of escape, he told himself. Again.

A clearing of the throat and he turned on the stool to a thin young man with what seemed an anachronistic waxed moustache and designer aqua or teal framed glasses who tore a sheet of lined paper from a notebook. "You should join us for trivia night," he said in a perfect blend of self-assurance and subtle accusation. Kerwin eyed the suspenders and bright vintage corduroy pants riding high above 1920s sneakers, and finally waved in decline, already back to his drink. "It's fun and there are prizes. We start in two minutes." He slapped the paper on the bar and headed for the crowded booths.

"Welcome to pub trivia night! I am your host, Conrad Hamlin the Third. The rules of trivia are as follows: no electronic devices, no shouting out answers—"

Kerwin tried to press the earplugs deeper, then pulled his coat collar tight. He leaned in and let the drink burn his nostrils.

"The first category is: '80s Saturday Morning Cartoons. Question number one..."

He answered them in his mind, correctly he was sure, though he couldn't remember the name of the show about the space sheriff. He thought of eating dry cereal and wearing dinosaur pajamas with his brother in the basement, with the TV volume turned almost to mute, and smiled, his eyes burning differently.

Voices rose in cheer and protest when the host read the first five answers. The players wailed in defeat and cheered in triumph, and he cringed from the volume. One female voice rose above them, "Cite your sources! Cite your sources!"

Kerwin turned to look.

"Did you even *play* with those magic kangaroo dolls? I don't *think* so!" Her yell came mock-serious from a crammed booth. "I had the whole entire troop *and* the farmhouse set. There was definitely a purple one!" She jostled and scrambled to stand on the booth bench over her five teammates. She had dark corkscrew hair with a silver streak over the right ear.

"Not in the original season, they didn't." Conrad the Third shook his head multiple times. "Now sit down, heckler, or I'll put you in the quiet box!"

"I'm telling you! Cite your sources or present the evidence!" She pounded her chest.

Kerwin wasn't sure if they were flirting.

"We need help on our team. You—guy at the bar—come help us!" She motioned wildly to Kerwin.

Kerwin startled when he realized the attention on him, and declined with an open palm. But he did not stop staring at her. She stared back.

He quickly returned to his drink.

"Here begins our next category, Mystery Thrillers. First question: What nineteenth-century British writer is credited with inventing the detective story by authoring—"

"Are you sure you have the continent right on that?"

"The quiet box is getting lonely!"

"I am the utter Houdini of quiet boxes!"

"Don't make me get the ball gag!"

"Honey, I chew right through them!"

"Please let me continue trivia activities uninterrupted!"

"Fine, I'm getting myself a drink!" She climbed over her teammates and exited the booth.

The entire bar applauded, praise mixed with relief.

She seated herself on the stool next to Kerwin, facing him directly. "What's your story?" she whispered.

Her voice drew him to look at her eyes. Whereas not before, something new in him wanted to pursue this.

"Well, I can't tell you about the part where I'm an international superspy." He felt an odd confidence.

"Too bad, I'm only attracted to inter*stellar* espionage agents."

"They gave my promotion to the boss's son."

She leaned closer. "Sorry to put you on the spot," she whispered like she knew him. "Okay, not so sorry."

He sipped. He thought briefly of Cora. "You seemed to want my attention."

"Too overt?" She fluttered her eyes.

"Do you come here every week for this?"

"Never been." She hunched closer. "I followed my nose."

Her musk was strong, and he felt suddenly unsteady.

Kerwin stood and had to hold onto the bar to stay upright. "I've only had one..."

"Oh, it ain't that, darlin. You're very close to a rejig." The flirt turned off and she regarded him with concern.

He tried to lift the last of his drink and knocked the glass to the floor.

"Hey, now..." someone said.

She hoisted him with his arm around her and threw money down as she led him out.

He frowned at his hands, seeing only four fingers. A moment later he found his diminished thumbs up past the wrists, and he understood why he couldn't grasp. "Dew claws," he heard her say. "Gotta work on that."

He stumbled with her, barely aware, past the roar of trains. He glimpsed the river and then the familiar rust color of the condos as the fire began in his chest. She took him into suite A-8 and down the hall.

In an unfurnished side room, she laid him gently on a wide oval cushion on the floor and removed his coat and shoes. She made him drink something vanilla that almost masked a metallic flavor, calmed him, and dabbed his face. The thick collar tightened around his neck and the rubber gag filled his mouth as the weight and chime of chain links accompanied the shadows down on him.

He rode the green brown world as it became a bounding blur enticed along a salty promise, driving the cadence of need, tireless unseen limbs surging pulse rhythm forward, hurtling lost between pursuit and flight, gullet clawing empty.

He howled soared leapt merged into the horizon, enclosed and swallowed the beautiful white visage, licking brilliance as it tried to drip away into time.

The other end of the chain was strung through the center holes of at least twenty 45 LB. plate free weights. There wasn't anything else in the room. Kerwin's tongue was raw against the ball gag, and moving his jaw he felt the padlock beneath his chin. Then he noticed the magic marker sign on the wall KNOCK 3 TIMES IF YOU NEED ANYTHING.

He sat up in the dog bed and pounded the wall with his elbow.

She came in with food on a tray, three stacks of flapjacks with a heap of scrambled eggs and bacon. "Before you get all 'Is that to fatten me up?'—no, it's just innocuous breakfast." She set the meal down and unstrapped the gag. She handed him a small key.

"Was wondering if I'd end up in your stew." He felt for the slot and managed to unlock the collar.

"You're not a prisoner." She smirked very slightly, seemed about to add something, then continued. "Come out to the dining room, sit on some real furniture."

"Like a civilized person?"

"There are so few of us left."

She cleaned the griddle while he ate. Once he managed to grip the fork between his pointer and middle fingers, he ate ravenously. He shifted from one buttock to the other, easing off the hard protuberance between.

She came and sat across the mahogany faux finished kitchen table. "I don't think I bit you," she said, looking down with brief shame. "I'm not sure how it happened to you. But I saw you splayed out on the dock the other morning. I should have come to you then, I apologize."

The world he'd been ignoring began to leak back into Kerwin's thoughts and he couldn't say anything for a while. He realized his mouth was hanging open. "I...made a choice."

"You certainly did. Not everyone has such freedom."

He didn't look at her, just picked at his teeth.

"You survived two nights, but you need to be safe. I can help you." She bit her lower lip ever so slightly. "And...I might like you a little bit."

"Excuse me, but you don't know me."

She sniffed toward him and smiled. "You know that's not true."

He let himself admit it. He really needed to talk to Cora.

"First of all, you can't sleep all day. I have an errand. Come with me."

He sighed at his strange inadequate thumbs and she tied his shoes for him.

She walked them nine blocks west and when they turned the corner to SPOT'S STAY & PLAY storefront, he froze. "What—What's this?"

"It's okay," she said.

He shook his head and trotted uneasily in place.

"I'm not working today, just checking in with my staff." She touched his arm and he liked the feel of it. "You can stay out here."

She was indeed only a few minutes. Then she led him down the alley to a black door with a small pale-blue moon painted at waist-level. She stroked his neck firmly and went in first.

Down the stairs they came to a wide and open basement, the perimeter lined with twenty sets of dog beds, water and food dishes, all empty. Kerwin hesitated at the bottom. People were setting up card tables and bringing large bowls of food from a side kitchen. Human food, it seemed, salad and soup and pasta and BBQ ribs. Some waved and smiled. "Hi, Aysel!"

"You own this place? Wait, you're Aysel?"

"Didn't you get my card?"

"I didn't know it was you."

"We missed introductions. I had to look in your wallet, Kerwin."

She showed him around. "I wanted to bring you here last night, but we couldn't make it in time. The leashes are optional here."

"Is everyone...?" He could smell that they weren't.

"Some are volunteers."

She introduced him to those she knew and then met the rest.

He thought of his brother, the social worker. They ate together and stayed to help wash dishes.

Back at the apartment, he waited while Aysel took a shower. The furniture was mostly new and the shelves contained a few pictures of her, possibly family, and one with her and a man in front of a trail sign. Thick brow, tapered canines.

She talked loudly from the bathroom. "You can control it if you work on it. Meditation, drugs, hypnosis. It's harder on a full moon, of course. Even if you can't see it out, like in all the rainy winter season here, you can definitely feel it rising."

"The other night?" He could barely hear her over the ceiling fan.

"Full," she said. And seemed to pause.

He walked down the hall toward her voice.

"I wanted to get out. My guy doesn't often let me."

He noticed too late the bathroom door was ajar, and glimpsed her in the mirror, nude, her hair wrapped in a towel, eight teats along her ribs.

He turned away quickly. But not before she saw him.

He thought of Cora. He pushed the thought away before he felt anything. "Where's your guy now?"

"This time every month Dolph and his friends drive out to the eastern part of the state, to open country. They camp and hunt."

"Without guns?"

"Or much sense."

"Do they all come back?"

"Rarely."

"But you didn't go?"

"I needed a change."

He looked again. She hadn't closed the door, she slowly opened it with her foot. And she regarded him with eyes midnight black within milky blue.

She unrolled two yoga mats. "If you work on this, you may find some control—if you want it. Some can stop the change. Some can hold in between, walk upright. You may not get there, but maybe you can move your thumbs back where you need them." Over the next few hours she taught him breathing technique and some beginning asana positions.

By the end of the afternoon he could close his hand again, although weakly and with noticeable pain.

"This calls for a celebration!" she said. "There's a new Belgian beer bar just across the river."

"Will I be ready by moonrise?"

"Do you think you will?"

Kerwin did not consider very long before responding. "I should probably go back to that pet place basement tonight."

She didn't nod or say anything for a moment. "Let's get that drink."

On the way back across the bridge with some sunlight left in the sky, he said, "What were you doing with the canoe?"

"It was an experiment. I thought I could moor it to the middle of the bridge and float till morning. But I didn't get it tied. Or I chewed through the line. It was a hard moon."

They stopped to look at the formless water below. Another cloudy night.

"I saw you on the balcony that night," she said.

"I wasn't staring." He turned his head east.

"I know," she said. "Later I thought I'd help you out. But a bit later I thought... I hoped... you might be someone that I... liked watching me."

He didn't know what to say to that, and felt her looking at him in that way again. He tried to think of Cora. A freight train clattered along behind them, full of coal and headed to the coast. Eventually her gaze released him.

When he turned back, his eyes were heavy. "I'm hungry again. Anywhere nearby with a coupon for twenty pizzas?"

"Twenty?"

"In the absence of generous ungulate herds."

"I like you, Kerwin." She took his arm and walked close to him.

Aysel steered him to her condo and he did not protest. In the spare room she fitted the collar on him tightly. Their eyes got caught for a second.

"What did you give me last night?" he asked.

"Ketamine."

"Is that necessary?"

"You're a wild one."

He downed the dose willingly. "How long—"

She muffled his question with the ball gag, and laughed playfully at his furrowed brow. She pulled his face to her and kissed the rubber sphere.

"I'll be across the hall." She turned out the light.

He was nearly asleep when he felt her curl up against him. "He comes back tomorrow," she said.

Low snarl creep on quiver paws to climb forth and encircle and merge with the exposed warm unseen place becoming melted primal tempo now locked breathless joining ancient crux.

She said goodbye at her door and neither of them could find more to say. She hugged him and nipped his ear.

Kerwin walked back to D-22 and passed a group of Subaru wagons entering the parking lot with gear tied to the rooftop racks, covered in pale dried mud dark spatters.

There was a business card from the police department stuck in the door. He paced the room for ten minutes before he called. Two officers came right over. They'd tracked his credit card payments, they said, so they'd figured out he was in town. He wasn't in trouble, but people were worried about him, they said. He promised to call home, call Cora. Make sure you do that, they said, don't make us come back.

Every night after that he sat in the middle of the floor and breathed deeply for hours as he visualized his body in the way that he wanted. After a week he didn't need half the bottle of melatonin.

He made some phone calls. He paid the rental balance, returned the key, and drove home.

Cora stared at him for many minutes and finally he could speak. "I'm going through something. I had to get away for a bit."

She cried and screamed at him with furious concern. "I can't believe this is all you have to say. I can't—I can't talk to you right now."

He booked another flight and made it to Kansas City in time for his brother's memorial service.

On the night he returned, they fucked wordlessly and selfishly, and she let him stay in the bedroom. The next day she moved out.

On the next full moon his skin felt covered in hot wax and Kerwin forced the door on the basement maintenance room and chained himself to the old rattling furnace.

He kept to the east side of town and went to bed early. A few weeks later he was out walking, crossed the Hawthorne Bridge into downtown, and wandered into SPOT'S SIT & STAY. He followed the familiar smell downstairs. He helped prep the meal and stayed for lunch, but he didn't see anyone he recognized.

The pounding at the front door came hard and insistent, breaking Kerwin's evening mediation. He saw Aysel through the peephole.

He didn't hear the screen door open.

"Let's go," said the stocky man with the thick brow standing beside her. Dolph.

Kerwin's hackles went up. He saw the fleet of Subaru wagons along the street, engines running. "Where and why?" He narrowed the door's opening and braced his foot behind. He glanced at Aysel and she tried to smile.

"Exercise." His voice rumbled in Kerwin's gut.

"It'll be better if you do," Aysel said.

Kerwin put on his shoes and jacket. They squeezed him between two brawny men in the back of Dolph's car.

No one spoke as they merged onto I-84, then I-5, crossed the Fremont Bridge and took Highway 30 along the industrial area. Finally, Kerwin broke the quiet. "I pictured you all in dark leather astride a loud pack of chrome-heavy choppers with big mufflers."

"They don't work well on 4-wheel roads," Dolph said. "Or haul much camping gear."

"Makes sense."

They passed houseboats and the city impound and a vegetarian strip club. Aysel didn't speak or turn her head.

Dusk fell fast as they exited up a narrow winding road into the black trees of Forest Park.

They parked in a circle by the trailhead at the end of Creston Road, and illuminated him in the center with their headlights.

When they threw down the big black duffle bag, he knew by the shape. They took the gag off Cora and shook her a few times until she woke.

She glanced around in panic and Kerwin wished all at once he could change this, go back, fix something, anything.

Then they held him down and stabbed five epinephrine auto-injectors into his thigh.

"What's happening?!" screamed Cora.

He cried and howled and found his voice for one last moment. "Don't run," he warned her. "Hold your ground." But he could not blame her when she did. And he could not stop the transformation in himself, nor from joining the hunt.

In the morning, he woke to an empty dirt road. He found a tarp in a ditch, wrapped himself, walked back to where the pavement began, and then the fourteen miles home.

The evening of the next new moon, Kerwin went to condo A-8 and urinated on the front door. He waited across the street in full view until he saw Dolph step outside and sniff, then he ran to the nearest light rail stop where he boarded the Blue Line train, and waved at his pursuer through closing doors. He rode west to the Washington Park stop and took the elevator up. Without looking back, he dashed across the empty parking lot and climbed over the locked gate between the ticket office and gift shop, as a single car pulled in.

When he came back out, the pack surrounded him at the entrance, already transformed, growling and panting, snarling hunger. Some of them stood upright, lupine and sleek, grasping anxious long-nailed fingers. Dolph grunted something and they closed in.

His own change erupted with tusks and taloned feet, long constricting coiled arms, arched tail with dripping thistle, and unfurled soaring wings. He furrowed his ursine brow beneath pointed antlers. "Run, please," he hissed through rows of teeth, forked tongue darting, in the blood red glow of the zoo's sign.

But a Moment Ago

YOU'VE BEEN SEARCHING for twenty-eight minutes for the heirloom fob watch, moving from the kitchen to the den to the basement, lifting piles of papers, opening drawers, digging through pockets, upsetting couch cushions, practically running now, scolding yourself because the event begins in thirty-two minutes and traffic will be simply awful. You're beyond stopping and taking a breath and trying to recall where you had it last, because you know precisely where it was, where it always is, where it should be: in the teak bowl on your dresser. You've checked at least six times tonight. But it is not there now. Which is why you are livid with frustration.

You remove the top of the toilet tank, open and close the fireplace flue to dislodge anything, skim through the pages of encyclopedias you haven't opened in ten years, paw through the crisper drawer, spoon through the sugar bowl. The logic of this level of search detail has evolved and now makes perfect sense. You run back to the hall closet, clipping your elbow against a doorframe, cursing no one in particular, and pull out every board game and empty them onto the floor in a noisy colored mess of plastic and paper. You run outside with untied laces and check the car again: the glove compartment, the cracks in the seats, the trunk, the first aid kit, under the spare tire. On the way back you check the mailbox again, feeling all four sides of the interior as though you didn't trust your own eyes. The phone rings and you glare at it, but run past to check the dryer's lint filter, along the basement rafters, the tool chest and the bag of used sandpaper and dusty jars of nails and half-painted door stoppers, the tubs of holiday decorations and boxes of comic books.

Finally, you give up and mount the stairs heavily. You kick through the scramble of clothes on the bedroom floor, refusing to look at the dresser, and sit on the edge of your bed, your vision already a watery blur. All the memories of Grandpa come flooding back at once. The farm, the workshop, his overalls and flannel shirts, his orange cap. His laugh during reluctant hugs. Riding the tractor. Him reading to you in his favorite chair. Going through his things after the funeral.

Sometime later, sure you've missed the entire event by now, you get up and begin to search for pajamas, when your gaze happens upon the dresser, and completely unintentionally, into the teak bowl. You notice the darker circle in the fine layer of dust. In exactly the same place you always kept it. Your first thought feels so natural that you don't even consider anything else.

That the watch is in the same place. But you have moved on. The world has moved on.

Your jaw hangs slightly open and you need to sit again.

That you are witness to the original time machine inventing itself.

You try to remember what you've read about the history of the area … Were there forests here before the city? And before that, maybe a prairie or a bog? You can almost hear giant Paleozoic dragonflies pausing to the mechanical alien sound of the watch. You wonder if it can move more than once. You imagine the timepiece with your grandfather's monogram encased in a glacier, nudged by a foraging Stegosaurus, tumbled in silt by the swift tail of a sea scorpion darting after a trilobite. Will it be melted in the early magma of a violent infant planet, or can it change direction? Maybe it will appear again briefly, on its way forward, if you keep watching that spot.

You are chilled and hungry, but you feel alive. You want to call a family member. It is very late.

Unfinished Painting
of Empty Classroom

O N THE FIRST day of class, the art instructor greeted each student at the door, smiling with the offer of eye contact. A few responded, some with a sigh of discontent or relief at finding their first home room. They moved with sweep in their stride, a lifted chin or pose in their chest, something they were trying out at this age, while their eyes skirted in search of challenge. By the second bell they filled all the seats around each table. Four more found their way in as she read the attendance sheet, so she set folding chairs around her own desk.

Narrow windows climbed into sharp arches clouded with fluttering gray webs. The brickwork around them was freckled with holes made by years and changing plans. The high ceiling floated somewhere beyond the hanging lights, leaving a nest of shadow above. It was the same throughout the aged building, century-old masonry supporting the extended wings and parapet roof of a cathedral inspired structure, where each drab stone held lost memories, and each cavity contained the aroma of departed summers.

She asked the students what they thought about art while she passed out large cuts of paper and boxes of charcoal sticks. They shouted: movies and tall statues and music with real instruments and really nice cars and huge fancy letters painted on walls, and she asked them to raise their hands please before speaking. They shared mostly answers she had heard before from their age, but every year there were some surprises; sunsets, stolen paintings, fireflies, dug-up pottery pieces, things that when you look at them make you say ohhh or sometimes cry.

She turned her head and body as she talked so they all felt spoken to.

She said art was not only found in a gallery or museum. It was floating in the air like pollen, or drifting like distant sounds that could at any moment rumble toward us, or it could reside in a faint beam of light. It takes some work to find it, and more work to make it.

The first assignment was not specific, they could draw whatever they wanted, without worry about technique or style or scale or shading. Should they need a starting place, well, she pointed to the boxes in back of the classroom filled with worn magazines, plastic fruit, faded album covers, pieces of driftwood, a salt shaker shaped like an owl, heads of dolls, things from thrift stores and the ends of driveways. Things people had left in her life, a few she had forgotten.

Some of the students hurried to see, not quite running. Most were reluctant to leave their seats, for they might lose territory or draw attention. There was a skirmish between a student with fingerless pink gloves and another student with dark lipstick over a plastic dragon with glittery wings they seemed too old for, tugging both ends of the discovery until one released in the midst of a friendship or the genesis of one.

By the middle of the hour the students had stopped chatting, and the only sounds were the soft scratch of charcoal. Some of them drew the items they had selected from the miscellany. Some sketched trees and houses, dogs and cats, a skateboard leaping off a mountain, a horse whose hindquarters were both motorcycle and fishtail, a ladder laid halfway across a ravine, a lurking figure with an exacting flower standing near a hunched piano player on a lonely street.

Some of them looked away from their empty paper as they chewed their lip, bounced a leg, or twirled strands of hair. The instructor would kneel beside them and quietly ask about a favorite place or a recent dream. One student began to sob, and others in the classroom laughed, and she said none of that in here in a voice she had refined for years but was not always effective. He clutched his arms and hid his face. The girl beside him touched his shoulder and he pulled away with a smothered grunt.

Another student put his charcoal stick on the floor and ground it with his heel. Then he pressed his paper against the black particles and on hands and knees rubbed it in wide circles, then turned it over to scratch fresh marks in the coal. Instead of the paper, another student drew curving dark lines over and under her arms, each pathway adorned with frills and spirals.

The old metal radiators rattled with rising insistence, but when one looked they were not moving. Something in the walls hummed like threatened wasps and dust trickled from dark crevices of the vertical cabinets. Outside, the world was diluted by a gray confusion that reached to the sky, blurring the extent of the building, constricting the influence of windows and streetlights.

Toward the end of class one chair stood empty, and on the table before it fine black dust outlined an invisible rectangle of missing artwork. Perhaps, thought the art instructor, an urgent escape to the bathroom, though it was a seat far from the door. The others looked at the clock, the floor, the lights and dark overhead, and she went to the exit to say farewell until tomorrow. In the hallway, graceless bodies surged with opinions and utterances, carried by an unseen overwrought current.

On the second day of class, she divided a few paint tubes into small portions on paper plates. A diminishing budget was nothing new, and she was vocal every year, but it still fell on her to find supplies. Only seven usable brushes remained from the previous spring, so she tied tufts of dry grass to fallen twigs, cut fringes into of index cards, brought a handful of cotton swabs. Each table received one palette to share, one brush per person to rinse in a plastic cup or at the stained cement sink in the back of the room. The faucet groaned each time it was turned on, and the complaint traveled up through the walls with a shuddering whine.

She used an overhead projector to enlarge a forest image onto a bed sheet hung from the wall. It was sunset, rays slicing between the silhouetted trees and a cautious elk among them. She invited the students to paint the scene, or a section of it, or if they were feeling intrepid perhaps something they imagined to be there.

Most of them painted the picture as it was, more or less. Some of the students found the pointed ears of a fox among the distant flora, or the subtle outline of a sleeping owl in a hollow trunk. One student fine-lined the profile of each tree with accurate scale and shape, so focused on the detailed bark texture that they completed only one tree. Then there were the ones the instructor might refer to in conversation with other teachers as her favorite. One student with a faint scar over his right ear painted the photographer hunched behind a nursing log, only their shoes and camera visible. Another student who whistled quietly like outlying winds painted a house that soared over the forest canopy at night, its windows brighter than the clouded moon. Another student who wore oversized cleated shoes without socks rendered the scene with an elk skeleton posed in the dark, the skull sockets thick with black paint. Four students seated at separate tables each painted some version of a village or city stacked within the trees and populated by moth beings or fish with climbing claws or humanlike denizens with squirrel tails.

There was an incident when one student dropped his brush, scattering small droplets of color, he became excited by the effect on his piece and embellished the technique. When the spray reached across the table to his neighbor's painting, she cried out and pushed him rather intensely. The art instructor saw in her mind the boy's head cracking like an egg, a crown of red rising around his scalp. But his foot caught the table leg and he remained balanced on a fulcrum, his attacker already back in her seat dabbing at the spots with a paper towel. He lowered his chair without injury.

After the bell, she found a rinse cup spilled on the floor, and from the pool of muddied colors ran a pair of small wet footprints that faded before the south wall.

On the third day of class, the art instructor had been troubled for most of the night with dreams of helicopters or winged insects swarming and diving. After finally falling asleep, she'd missed her alarm, pedaled her three-speed bicycle as fast as she could and ignored two stop signs, to arrive at the school fifteen minutes before class with only one box of colored pencils. She ran down the marble stairs to the basement level where it smelled of sawdust and machine oils.

The woodworking instructor was there, in his apron and safety glasses. She had nearly forgotten that they had been on a date two years before. It had not gone poorly but also not well, and when she asked to borrow a hand saw he stated the fact that this isn't a library. When he resumed cutting slats on the table saw in preparation for scale house building, she took what she needed from the pegboard wall and hastened out the door.

Running up the wide stairs, she paused to look at the small ammonite and crinoid shapes of ancient fossils in the stone steps, and became less worried about her heist, also she vowed to return the tool very soon.

She held colored pencils at the edge of her desk and sawed off a third of their length, catching pieces in a drawer. When the students arrived, she was sharpening the short pencils with a pocket knife from her key chain.

The attendance sheet contained four fewer names that day, so she folded up the extra chairs and reclaimed her desk.

Draw a place you remember, she said to the class, or a place you would like to visit. Try to use other than usual colors; no blue in the sky, something else.

Many of them were frustrated by this approach, and insisted on gray mountains, brown trees, blue oceans. But the student who wore multiple decorative belts made a canyon of orange and yellow, too gentle and fine for lava, like great strands of hair or flowing light, carrying a ship of tall angular buildings with crescent balconies and great oars that ended in long webbed hands. The student who lost a tooth yesterday made a long cathedral sketched in dark green with windows like ribs and cusped black towers at either end, surrounded by a churning red sea, circled overhead by bright birds. The student who dismissed an entourage down the hall each morning made a prairie of grains swaying in the dusk, crisp in the foreground and fading behind, visited by soft traveling feet that touched only the flowers as they passed.

She heard a rasping noise and saw one of the students hunched with his cheek against the table, snoring deeply. She called his name, clapped lightly, then loudly, but could not wake him. She asked another student to walk quickly but not run to the nurse's office and tell them to please come down. By the end of class, no one had come, and the messenger had not returned either.

The next period was her planning time, which the art instructor usually spent in the teacher's lounge or the library or outside, when it was pleasant, on a bench at the outer edge of the playing field. But she stayed at her desk for the next hour, writing feedback for yesterday's projects, while the student slept. When his snores subsided she went to check on him. He was breathing quietly, his drawing half-obscured by his face, fractures or tree limbs or lightning branching out, gray on black.

When the next class arrived, she let a student in the occupied seat use her desk. A few of them laughed and pointed at their sleeping peer, but relented when the instructor shook her head. She sent the girl with the embroidery thread bracelets to find the nurse.

For the remaining class periods, the slumbering student became a subject of study, appearing in some of the new pieces. As the last class of the day filed out, she stood outside the door in hopes of catching another instructor's attention. But only students thronged the hallway. When she had given up and returned inside, the sleeping boy was gone. His chair stood empty, and half his drawing was smudged into nothing discernible.

Her concern had been increasing all day, and she finally went herself to the nurse's office. The nurse was wearing blue scrub pants and sneakers with a shirt that featured hanging bats holding cocktail glasses. She told the nurse about the student, and they said they were also concerned, though their voice did not sound like it, which could have been from their training. They did say, sit with me please, and while she waited in a chair next to the resting cot, they looked up the phone number for the parent or guardian, and called. Then they dialed and called again. And one more time, but no one answered. Don't worry, the nurse promised, I will keep trying.

She returned to the classroom and worked on necessary tasks, filing artwork in the overhead cubbyholes, moving art prompts back to their boxes, wiping off tables, preparing notes for tomorrow's lesson. Grading assignments was always the most intensive and time consuming task, one that she hoped each year to find a better method for and failed. But this year she was impressed by the work from many of her students, especially in the first period class. After finishing a majority of the grading, she became quite weary and put her head down.

When she woke at her desk, it was dark beyond the windows, out where late insects vocalized. The school halls were bright but lifeless, the floors buffed and shining with misshapen cloudy reflections. One drinking fountain murmured a sluggish arc of water. She paused and found no one nearby. Then she proceeded more quickly, even if her footsteps did not sound like her own.

Out in the empty parking lot, a warped rear wheel chained to the rack was all that remained of her bicycle. Though she was troubled by this occurrence, she did not let it embitter her, for not much could be done in this moment. She did not live very far from the school. On the way home at a slower pace, she was able to notice more details: a moth landed on a postal box, veins of fallen leaves, the texture of drawn curtains, a familiar stir of disparity with the world. All around, the blackness of the sky leaked down into the shapes of trees that pierced the earth, and she walked.

On the fourth day of class, a frizzled voice from the dusty speaker above the door said there would be a change in the school lunch menu today, the ice cream truck would be visiting the south parking lot on Friday after last bell, and students would not be allowed to wear earrings longer than two inches.

The sleeping student and two others did not attend that day. A few roster changes were common each semester, in each class, but the art instructor was beginning to feel unsettled.

She had planned to make mosaics, but could not find any affordable salvage tiles or glass, so they would cut or tear colored paper into small random shapes. The room filled with the whisper of scissor blades. She had brought an old radio from her father with a broken cassette player, and she searched among the static for local stations until she found one for classical music, and the students made sour faces, one asked where are the lyrics huh in a way that did not expect an answer.

Some of them preferred to first draw an outline on paper, others began to build their image piece by piece. The student who had to be asked to spit out her gum made a tall overhanging red cliff with a crooked house tilting at the edge, the windows dark and smoke rolling from the chimney. The student who sat with one leg folded under him made a choir of robed figures with spindled limbs, all turned away except one sliver of a face and a single pinched eye glancing back. The student with many colors of plastic boots who asked the art instructor where she went to school made a serious canine with six limbs seated atop a command throne on a rocket ship entering a strange nebula. She was moved by the visions, and intrigued by some of their technique.

A man in a navy blue suit jacket and maroon tie man entered the classroom, walking briskly with conviction, though the art instructor did not immediately recognize him. He waved a silent greeting to her, abruptly turned to the students and folded his arms. While he surveyed the class, she tried to remember his name, since, on second thought, she recalled seeing him once at an event, perhaps with the school board or curriculum consultants or parent group. It really would have been helpful to receive some warning.

For the duration of one radio song, the visitor stood in the same location, then he proceeded about the classroom with scattered interest. Suddenly he shouted as if bitten by something venomous. He wrenched a student up by their bicep to an awkward stand and whipped their artwork back and forth in the air as he demanded to know Is this the kind of thing—?! What kind of—?! I can't believe—! The student with hair trimmed very short on one side shuffled in discomfort with their arm over their head.

The art instructor hurried toward them, speaking evenly but loudly that we should remain calm, that we'll find the problem and the best solution, as she made a lowering motion with her hands.

The man who might have been from the school board distressed his jaw and ruffled his nostrils at no particular person before he stalked from the room, pulling the student of wry though tender aspect with him and crumpling the artwork in an anxious fist.

She was very upset and followed, yelling after them, but on her way to the door several of the students cried out in alarm and delight, as a crow or no a magpie or maybe a grackle had flown in and landed on the back of her chair. A few of the students jumped up and moved slowly toward the bird. The creature hopped to the wooden desk and regarded them, one claw closing on her pair of scissors. The art instructor was afraid of what might happen.

After the bell she made her way through the crowded halls to the main office, but found the door locked and behind the frosted glass a dark silent interior.

On the fifth day of class, the art instructor arrived early to visit the cafeteria. The foldaway security gate was still pulled across the entrance, but beyond the octagonal composite tables a light issued from the back kitchen. She knocked on the metal gate a few times, and yelled hello through the diamond-shaped openings. A woman in a white apron emerged from the room and slalomed forward.

The art instructor apologized for interrupting and for what she was about to ask. If she could borrow a few potatoes, just a few. Maybe five, or seven if they're small. Because, you see, she had tried going to the grocery store last night, but there was construction on the street, and a block party on another street. She had tried to shortcut through the city park, but there was a large dog sitting in the open with no one around. For a while she'd hid behind a tree, and had to go back home because it would not leave.

Borrow? said the cafeteria worker, or perhaps she preferred cook.

What do you mean? asked the art instructor.

You're going to bring them back? The cafeteria worker squinted slightly. Or maybe chef was her selected title.

Oh no, she had meant—

May I have, is how you say it, said the cafeteria cook chef, no shame in asking. The woman in the white apron and hairnet called over her shoulder, I've got you, as she walked around the tables to the back room where there was a thump, and then a tumbling. She returned with a wide metal bowl containing a dozen or so potatoes. She said some of these have sat for a week, need washing and the eyes cut out. She looked at the art instructor through the diamond-shaped holes in the metal gate. Either she did not have a key, or did not intend to open it. You bring anything to carry them?

The art instructor thought about it. She removed her coat and draped it on the floor. Here, she said, holding out her hand. They passed the potatoes one at a time through one of the openings, and she said thank after each one.

After the last one, the art instructor gathered the ends of her coat and lifted. She was already planning to bake something for the meal staff. She wanted to ask if they had any allergies, but the woman in the white apron was already out of earshot.

She felt some guilt as she washed the potatoes and cut them in half. Her story had not been entirely true. She had in fact made it to the grocery store, where she had purchased a three-pound bag of potatoes, along with the items on her list. There had been no construction or block party, she had walked through the park simply because it shortened her route back home. It was not polite to alter the facts, not if she expected to speak to someone again.

But it had not been a dog waiting there, watching her. She was not sure what it had been. Like a smudge on her vision, drawing closer each time she blinked, showing her its stained attributes, cascading like smoke without depleting. She had dropped the netted sack of potatoes when the thing made a noise like the grinding and splitting of stone. She had abandoned all of her groceries and fled the park when the noises began to sound like words.

Some students arrived in small groups that day, each crowd wearing a similar color top or the same style shoes or alike haircuts. Two students stopped outside the door, declaring their status in a long wool coat from two generations before and the skirt made of stitched neckties, and they leaned close, gauging their heights until their lips aligned and began negotiation. They tested their balance and trust, hands found a cheek or a hip. The social studies teacher yelled from down the hall to break it up. Yearning and graceless, the boy who chewed his cuticles and the girl who proclaimed with her eyes ignored the request until the second bell, then entered class with hands linked tightly, eyes full of quiet reverie.

The five-pack replacement blades for the utility knives were too expensive so the art instructor gave each table a single-edge razor blade, leftovers from her father's toolbox. She invited them to carve any design they wanted into the flat end of the potato. But like the mosaic, she said, try to make a starting place, then create something divine.

The shapes they made in the potatoes were not very distinct, some rather rushed. But with these forms they made detailed and elaborate visions. The student with the forearm cast stamped a thick forest of dark mossy trees with a network of thin chains connecting the trunks, and finely dabbed a population of tiny figures walking upright across the distances. The student who carried a burden from outside in her attributes made a large mottled red hand with seven fingers, inlaid with three fracturing black eyes. The student who was taller than her instructor made a creature arched and stalking over rooftops and neighborhood lanes, its belly lit faintly by the glow of streetlights.

No one delivered an attendance sheet that morning, nor did one arrive later in the day.

Alone at her desk at the end of the first week, the art instructor felt a sudden chasm within her. For months, perhaps even further back, there had been barely a moment to think. The room contracted and she found breathing difficult, for there hung inside her a desolation she could not name, a barren grief. Her thoughts clawed through memories of the last week, the difficult but uneventful summer, and found no one missing from her life. Her body felt far away and unfamiliar, a remote and peculiar artifact in the room where she had taught for nine years, plus a few summers. The erosion seeped into her limbs as she felt more lost.

She pinched her forearm and barely felt it. Slowly she pressed her fingertip against the sharp point of a pencil and the sting made her suck in a breath.

On the sixth day of class there were three fewer students, and someone who did not belong there. He was older than the others, perhaps as old as the art instructor. She tried to discern whether he had attended the school in the last decade, but did not recognize his face, hairless but raddled and drawn. He sat at one of the empty tables wearing a dark blue coat with fur around the draped hood and a full backpack that nearly pushed him from the seat. She was not yet afraid of his presence, and did not wish to be. He sat patiently and alert, holding a pencil with a triangular rubber grip in his bruised hand, so she gave him a large paper sheet and continued with the lesson.

Today they would work on contrast, she said to the class while placing a candle on each table and lighting it with a match. Then she drew the blinds, closed the door, and turned off the fluorescent lights. She had placed several items around the room; a gray foam rostrum borrowed from the theater department, a stack of books on a stool, a stuffed rhinoceros propped on the shoulder of a mannequin; and she had pointed flashlights at them from one side or below. She sat at the table with the visitor and observed the class and the shadows that stretched up and across the walls, that lurked in the contours of each object.

A breeze pushed the long vinyl shades inward; they settled, and rose again, inhaling and exhaling. She imagined the room like a night ocean, swept from dark to illumination by a lighthouse beacon, though she had never been to the coast, to any coast. For the remaining class time she fought the feelings rising in her, impossible desires like wanting to travel to distant places or going back in time and changing something in the world, in her life.

When the bell sounded, she turned on the overhead lights to find the man in the coat had departed. Though she was perplexed and slightly unnerved, the students did not seem to be bothered or confused, so she did not make a scene of it. Briefly she questioned whether he had in fact been present and not imagined. But on his seat someone had left a folded paper, creased many times into a tight bundle. She opened it slowly and from inside tumbled the fine forms of dandelion seeds, the transparent wing of a dragonfly or cicada, the curved cracked tip of a cat's claw, and an illustration the size of a postage stamp with such finite pencil work that she searched her desk drawers for an old printer's loupe. She closed one eye as she looked through the lens to find an intricate scene of a collapsing city, its streets crowded with people screaming aflame.

Shouts issued from the hall, and she let them continue, until they compounded in earnest. She ran out to find a dense crowd of youth cheering on two students in a scuffle on the floor. No other adults were in sight, so she yelled for calm, trying to maneuver through the group. They resisted with their half-grown bodies as they hollered for more severity. The two boys clutched one another, kicking and pulling, tearing at ears and clothing, spitting blood in the other's eye. She moved a few students behind her, but the fighters regained their feet and shoved back and forth, shifting the throng across the hall. Her arm finally reached through but not far enough. The two in disagreement lurched briefly at the edge of the marble steps, and careened down the cold stairs, falling upended and apart, until they slammed into the landing, concluding with stillness.

The crowd finally let her through and she descended to the scene of bright crawling red and blooming contusions, the swelling cries of surprise. There was a thin crack in the stone floor, old or new, and she felt the sudden need to stand between it and the young runnels of blood.

On the seventh day of class, the art instructor brought unmarked rolls of receipt paper. She had found a box of them behind a large store that was clearly going out of business. She cut six-foot strips for each student, and told them they could use pencil or paint or any choice of their own, as she set all these options on her desk, use anything to fill the long space with color and vision and sensation and mood.

They were two fewer that day, but the students made beautiful pieces. The student who chewed the eraser off his pencils made a single long arm with three elbows covered with one spiraling tattoo that told half of a story by the visible segments. The student who wore the same shirt most of the week and held his arms tightly to his ribs made a tall twisting design of stippled vines, embellished with thoughtful eyes that watched curious and deviant. The student whose face looked like a different person from the front or sides made a wide view of hundreds of people leaping screaming crawling before masked musicians on an elaborate central stage decorated with spikes and hurling fire.

Though she was increasingly moved by their work, she could not blame any of these specific images for the next moment. Perhaps a feeling from nowhere, but she found herself in the middle of class recalling the summer her family had traveled for two days of a heat wave in the goldenrod station wagon with vinyl seats across multiple states beginning with the same letter that all looked the same to visit friends at their new cabin by a lake. It was a secluded place of dusty roads and cattails and frogs at dusk. The neighbor girl who had kissed her in the woods had tasted faintly of root beer, but had not written back the following year, or any year thereafter.

At the noon hour, she headed to the teacher's lounge and thought at first she had stepped onto the wrong floor, for there was no door or doorway in the usual place. She was resigned to call it her own mistake, then she noticed the freshly installed drywall that covered the entrance. It was still unpainted without any sign posted on or near the construction. She heard voices, low and undefined, that must have come from a vent, because they did not sound anxious that they might be trapped within.

She had been many years in this building, but in recent days she felt it growing troubled and unquiet, that like a stray dog it might soon lie down in dissent or snap at you. The atmosphere around it retaining colors while it claimed a few unnoticed breaths each day.

That night she called her sister to ask if she remembered the cabin's cedar loft, or the lake's gray-green shores, or any of the neighbors, or their friends. It was so long ago, her sister said, I think the lake was dug by men and turned bad and was why they never went back. You spend so much time in the past, her sister said, too much. But what is there to look forward to, said the art instructor, though she had paused too long and her sister had already hung up.

On the eighth day of class, the art instructor walked the students down to the first floor and out the north doors. They filed along the sidewalk, uneven and broken in many places by the roots of great maples and oaks, past the tennis courts and fire station, across a small bridge over a winding creek, and into a neglected city park. If any of them still desired to climb on the playground structures, they were too embarrassed at the thought. By now, a few of their small groups had collapsed and rearranged, some accepted into other clusters by adapting outfit and mannerisms, leaving other students standing alone and obsolete. They whispered vicious secrets quietly enough to hide words, harsh enough to sting with a glare. She did not let it continue, instructing them to find the bend of the trail, the rise of the hill, the erubescent color of descending leaves, and be moved by it.

Once she released them, she immediately worried they would never return, that they would run off to ingest substances both addictive and harmful, or be seduced by the wrong propaganda, or purchase a bus ticket to treacherous faraway locales and foster a miserable dream, or tumble into the sky and become caught in a dark flock of sharp wings; but her apprehension passed as quickly as it had arrived. As with any assignment, they were intrigued and committed.

She had brought her own paper and charcoal, and found a place under the draped branches of a willow, where she spent the full hour sketching a face in expressive detail with austere and discerning eyes; a portrait of someone she did not recognize, and during the process began to think that this was her preference.

At the sound of the distant bell, she called the students together, and they ran back to the school, artwork fluttering. If anyone marks you tardy send them to me, she told them. By this day she had learned all their names but didn't use them, their faces already painted in her mind.

The second class of the day, the one before lunch, she did not particularly enjoy. The students asked so many questions, often as a way of delaying the work, and drew no more than what she suggested. They were only beginning their teenage years, and she worried they had already chosen their path in life, or their parents and other unseen forces had chosen for them. It all left her feeling drained and wishing they would drop the elective course, though it would reduce her full-time status and health benefits.

Before the last class of the day, the vice-principal interrupted her instruction by calling her into the hallway, and she was not surprised when it happened. She tried to move them away from the doorway, but he stood so the class could hear. He wore a drab corduroy suitcoat with oval leather patches on the elbows, and a button up shirt patterned with a tight faintly blue grid. His face contained no emotions as he communicated a warning about unapproved field trips. She promised that she fully understood what he was saying, and it absolutely would not happen again, while she thought of other things in her mind to keep her voice from rising in volume, or from shoving him so the back of his head would find the metal doorstop anchored to the floor, or he would slide on the buffed hall tiles and down the railing and out the doors and across the parking lot into a rusted drain and disappear beneath the planetary crust.

That evening the fog became so dense that she missed a turn on the way home, could not see the pharmacy or the pet groomers or the fire hydrant painted with cartoonish eyes or the house with a castle-like tower or any other usual places along her route. She ambled through the gloom until she had to admit she did not know her whereabouts at all, and became distressed. She tried very hard to retain her calm, and after a while realized picturing her students' artwork helped drive back the tide of foreboding speculations. Her feet were sore and she longed for dinner, an indication, a sound, anything.

She finally perceived a distant glow through the murkiness and followed it for nearly as long as she had already walked. When she was about to give up and sit on endless asphalt, the distinct arched windows and parapet roof of the school came clear. She approached the building like someone she was not planning to see, though not surprised to encounter. The custodian had already locked the outer doors, but she did not know where else to go in the dark mist. With some effort she pushed a metal trash can close to the building and used the beveled foundation stone to step up on top of it. From there she stretched carefully until she could reach the fire escape ladder that pulled it down to the cement. Once she was on the rungs, any guilt had fallen away, and she soon found an unlocked second floor window.

Alone and unbusied in the hallways, she noticed how the building smelled the same as the days when she'd been a student, the tinges of old masonry and wooden desks and powdered soap and the breath of the boiler exerting somewhere below. To her they were the scents of lingering worry and confusion, the silent refrain of conflict, the sustained undercurrent of dismay.

She slept under one of the art tables, using her autumn coat as a blanket and a roll of paper towels for a pillow. In one dream she was young again, she had to jump from stone to log to lilypad across a boggy marsh to reach the school, and in swim class her friend grabbed her by the hand and took her to the end of the diving board where they bounced in unison higher and higher, and went upward instead through a hole into the ceiling, where they made a campfire and lived together, running over the roofs and trees and telephone lines at night. In another dream, her parents were still alive, telling jokes no one else understood, and they still loved each other.

On the seventeenth day of class, the students brought vegetables from home and enjoyed pressing them between stacked chairs. The juices made colorful dyes, and they used the stems or their fingers or shoe laces or snips of their hair as paintbrushes. The student who said hello each morning and counted the day on her fingers created a collection of eleven scarred moons chasing the swirling rings of a parent planet, too large to capture a dramatic curve. The student with the laugh like a dolphin created a landscape of blood-rich mountains and walking trees spied through a hole in a wall that had been chewed by mischievous squirrels and asymmetrical insects. The student who worked with their arm curled around the paintbrush and viewed it from below created a river of variegated fish swimming through a bewildering sky.

One student who preferred standing held their piece against the window, and the one with a few dark hairs on their upper lip remarked how the daylight cast colors into the room. The art instructor agreed, and helped them stand on chairs and then chairs atop tables to tape the artworks onto every section of the tall glass. For the rest, they stapled the artworks end to end and hung a long motley banner out the window.

Across the playing field, passersby stopped on the sidewalk and in their cars. The students cheered and waved until they realized the persons were shaking their heads and slashing the air with their arms. The streams of color billowed up and the staples did not hold. Each artwork lifted and swirled in the wind, carried in a long cascade over the field. Then the pedestrians snatched the artworks from the air and dragged them against the blacktop with their boots, took them up and tore them, sped car wheels against them, as the students wept and hooted and learned.

For the second class of the day, none of the students attended, and the bathrooms on the second floor were closed for maintenance, so the art instructor went for a stroll.

She took the central staircase to the third floor, found the short flight of stairs to the fourth floor where the hall windows had a view of the roof and the sky. In her day as a student, there had been a rumor of gargoyles on the upper roof, but she had never ventured out there to look. Now there was the odor of cigarette smoke and she saw a cloud of it from behind an exhaust fan. She was about to call out, but did not know which her, young or old, would speak. So she did nothing except feel all at once heartsore, and continued her journey. She descended to the third floor, walked over to the south stairs, down one flight of marble steps with worn impressions, then across to the opposite stairs, winding through every passage. All the classroom doors were closed, many of them showing darkness in their inset window, perhaps they were viewing films.

While she was out of class, she thought it a good time to speak with the principal. More of her students had gone, and she was increasingly worried over it. The other teachers did not talk with her about declining class size, or about much at all lately. They were often occupied or off in their own groups, or absent themselves.

She came to an unintentional halt before a locker that looked no different from the rest, but felt quite particular to her. Surely not, she thought. Her mind did not pronounce the numbers, but her hand remembered as she turned the dial right, left, right again. With familiar sounds, the latch lifted and the door opened. The shelves and hooks were empty; perhaps the current student was sick at home or had transferred. The surfaces had been painted many times since the canary yellow of her time, though the faint letters of her name were still legible under the layers. Another name had been scratched out beneath it. She could almost remember, but it did not return to her, and while pondering, she considered how odd names could be and how hers had always sounded strange when she said it aloud.

The bell sounded and the rush of voices poured into the hall. She was overcome with the urge not to be seen, so she pushed forward and settled into the confined space. It did not occur to her at all that she could not fit, and she closed the door into darkness.

Shapes and colors flashed by the narrow vents. No one stopped to open the locker and she was grateful. When it was quiet again she did not want to leave, and fell into a comfortable sleep for the remainder of the day.

On the twenty-third day of class, a howling siren issued through the school. The sky was a despondent gray, and there were no comments over the speaker, no bulletins on the radio. It sounded many times louder than any previous announcement or alert, like a train screaming over the school or the wail of cold and covetous beasts from above.

The art instructor quickly gathered the students at the door, but it seemed no one else was responding, not in the next room or down the stairs or in the hall. She looked out the window and did not see any other students or instructors assembling in the parking lot. So they sat again in their seats for the remainder of the hour with torn pieces of sponge stuck in their ears and sweatshirt hoods pulled tightly around their faces. She did not know whether to close or open the door and windows, to hide under the tables or break them into weapons or fuel, and no one came to tell them any news.

It was difficult to tell when the siren ended, for it still echoed in their heads during the first bell. She apologized to the students and stopped herself from embracing them to ease her own distress. She had stopped counting them recently.

An hour later, the office sent an assistant with a message that her sister had called, and also a reminder that they were not an answering service. At lunchtime she used the payphone by the cafeteria, but reached a recording that said the number had been disconnected. Then she heard talking on the line, remote shouts arguing with increasing emphasis, the sibilation of unreachable voices.

On the thirty-ninth day of class, all the students stayed home while the parents came to the school for their conferences. The art instructor set out artwork on every surface in the classroom, and propped a piece on every chair. She had written extra notes about each one and paperclipped them to the back.

The adults occupied the halls without urgency, muttering and cursing at lists on paper. A man with a large ruby ring who wore sunglasses indoors stopped to ask her directions to the gymnasium, and a couple with nearly matching track suits and unsoiled neon tennis shoes inquired if there were any refreshments, but half the day passed without anyone entering her classroom.

For lunch the art instructor set on her desk a small paper cup of lime gelatin with half a canned pear and a pint of milk, when a woman with poised bangs and a glossy hazel purse arrived. Hi hi, she said, oh wow will you look at that. She surveyed the artwork on the first table. The art instructor was sure by the cheekbones she knew which student was related to her, and walked over to introduce herself. These are lovely, the woman said, and at that moment all the lights turned dark.

Oh I'm sorry, said the art instructor. She went to lift the window shades, and while her back was turned, thought she heard moist tearing and mashing sounds. When she turned quickly the woman was scurrying out the door holding one artwork near her mouth, running and chewing.

The art instructor rushed after her but lost her sense of direction in the dark hallway where the entire north wing had lost power.

On the forty-fourth day of class, it was between bells when the art instructor saw in the hallway her student who always walked close to the walls suddenly sprawl to the hard floor. She thought it had been an accident, but when they stood the passing student with a pastel shirt bumped his chest against them multiple times in provocation, then he shoved them down again. When they were on the floor, he insulted their bowl-shaped haircut and brand of trousers and the velour material of their shirt. They turned over and crawled toward her classroom, stumbling to a stand, and he hooked their foot with his, tripping them again.

She ran and helped her student to their feet and urged them to class. Then she turned to the young man with the designer bleached denim jeans and pastel T-shirt with a resort logo and thin gold neck chain. He said what like a question what what what but really as a dispute louder each time, and before he could say it again, she said that is more than enough, then firmly grasped his forearm, positioned it behind his back, and steered him away. You're hurting me, he said in an angry tone. It won't if you keep up, she said.

They arrived at the main office where one of the frosted doors was open and the other missing from its hinges, and beyond them an empty interior. Thick lines of dust on the floor showed where the desks and filing cabinets had set among pale scratches in the hardwood, and in one corner a cluster of very small bones, possibly from a rodent or bird. You wait right here, she said, do not move.

She looked into the adjacent offices and found the same vacant situation. When she returned to the main room, the tormentor had unsurprisingly fled.

Back at the classroom she talked to the student with the scraped chin and bruised knees. If you need to take another route to class, I won't count you late. He's not the only one, they said, and returned to painting a gigantic polar bear whose spine was a mountain range with high towers and kites reaching past clouds, and from great jaws fell broken buildings and mauled airplanes and masticated tanker ships.

Before the last class of the day, she took a bottle of lampblack ink from her drawer and walked through the halls. She saw the intimidator on the far end of the third floor, talking to other boys wearing expensive rugby shirts and factory-weathered jeans and stark-white shoes, and she walked an adjacent path as if on other business. At the last moment she turned and spilled the ink bottle over his head and shirt and pants. Oh, she exclaimed, oh I am sorry. Here let me, as she brushed her hands against the dark stains but only smeared it further.

From outside there came the sounds of machines grating and chiseling, the dissonance of metal striking metal, and the rattling of it being dragged and forced into place.

On the fifty-first day of class, something entered the classroom and the students screamed in fear. The art instructor could not see what it was, even when they pointed trembling fingers. The room became warm and smelled of soot and sewer. The student who had built a rocket out of mushrooms and drawn a symphony of tapirs now took up a long metal ruler like a sword, but it was flimsy, so he slapped it against a table as if trying to scare off an animal. They all ran and huddled by the back sink, where they waved for their instructor to hurry and join them.

By now she was very frightened and tried to slowly slide her chair back, but its legs squealed against the floor. The students gasped, heads slowly turning, following. They declared all together oh as they ran to the windows where they leaned out and pointed, now completely astonished and laughing.

The art instructor tried to perceive where they indicated, but she could see nothing against the far end of the building or the trees or sky. In the rush of activity their artwork had blown to the floor, each one marred by blackened burn marks and ragged scratches.

A pedestrian stopped on the outer sidewalk and observed from behind the new chain-link fence that stretched around the property, her expression visible at that distance as one of pity or disappointment.

On the sixty-third day of class, the bathrooms on the second and third floors remained closed, and the plumbing failed to be working anywhere in the building.

It had been weeks since the art instructor had left the grounds, and today she went out at lunch time with intentions of a mild escapade, and stopped at the metal fence. A sign had been secured with plastic ties, but she could not read it from this direction. When she walked all the way around its interior and found no gate or opening, she was only somewhat surprised, for various reasons and things being as they were. The frence height was not beyond her ability, she did not think, and she began to scale the barrier.

A family walking across the street noticed her, and the father began yelling. He ran toward her, his face a mask of fury and fear, shaking his fist. The mother shouted too from the opposite sidewalk, while the children turned away. The art instructor wondered why they were not in school, though she did not say anything.

She stepped down and hoped that they would move along, but they continued to shriek and glare. Her feelings about leaving had changed, and she went to the other side of the building to relieve herself in the playing field.

On the seventy-sixth day of class, the art instructor left the room only to turn around and enter it again, not because she'd forgotten something, but for the ritual of doing so. This time of year the dark lasted through morning, and the first bell had yet to ring, but all five students were present, each with their own table to spread out their materials. They poured the corn starch, baking soda, and water into a bowl; mixed and kneaded them until soft but pliable. Then they portioned the clay, added turmeric or avocado or coffee or red onion, staining their hands and arms as they worked in the colors. One of the students apologized for the cut on his finger and some of his blood blended into the mixture, but the others said it's okay, it's great.

They pulled off pieces of clay, rolled them long or spherical, pressed and pinched portions as the shapes grew in front of them. The student whose mother had been the art instructor's neighbor in middle school but looked nothing like her created a tree that twisted and spiraled outward and upward in hundreds of intricate coils that extended fractal arms that could be writing stories in the air. The student who had set a friend's fingerbone created a mazed city, the architecture of each building challenging the next, windows the size of sand grains cut five times, some cool and aligned, others wild and bright, while the roof of each structure comprised one shard of a larger image that promised terrible beauty, best left incomplete. The student who hissed when airplanes passed over and drew spirals on his notebook covers made a creature that stood as tall as its sculptor on seven legs of varying pigments, eyeless and frail-looking with such gossamer limbs, though no one in the room was surprised when it stepped off the paper base, opened its weird mouth and began to sing.

At some point the room turned somber, and there was no burning smell or alarm, but a muddled smoke had invaded the space. It moved like a living thing on the prowl, making everything behind it blurred and colorless and diminished. With great scrutiny, they searched over and under and between and behind. The student with the incongruous countenance and question mark shirt discovered the source in the southwest corner. Rippling vapor entered quietly through crumbling mortar. Each of the room's occupants began to feel its influence.

The students did not pause or discuss, but quickly used lumps of clay to block the holes and halt the intrusion. After exclamations of relief, they continued their work.

The art instructor attended her own project alongside the students. She unpacked a wooden box and cut open the plastic bag inside. Then she had to pause, thinking of the last time she had seen her sister, scolding herself for many reasons, and she could only hold herself still for a long time. When she was ready, she removed spoonfuls of ash from the bag and mixed them into a bowl of water. She painted with a frayed brush, blotting most of the canvas, seeing glimpses emerge from the shadow. The brush rendered strands of hair, an ear, a cheekbone. The art instructor could feel the woman in the painting slowly turning toward her. The instructor did not want to see. Her hand knocked over the bowl of sooty water onto the image, blurring it.

The students took the painting from her desk, for they could see she was crying and neither did they want her tears to wash the umbra away and reveal anything more. The first bell rang and they said we will stay with you.

Outside there was shouting and hissing above the rattle of metal in a howling cold wind.

On the eighty-fourth day of class, only creatures roamed the hallways. At first they looked like very large dogs in the dim distance, sunless gray forms of vulturine bulk, each footfall echoing like fallen rock, their folded tattered wings twitching behind their shoulders, heads with chipped horns shaking, some with almost human faces. They bayed in thirst and misery, stout brows over bottomless black eyes, and scratched at the doors during the night.

The art instructor and her student remained in their classroom, sketching the odd insects that danced in the candlelight, painting the shapes in the clouds that moved like dreams, drinking rainwater from holes in the high ceiling, eating soft potatoes and acorns.

On the final day of class, the world was slanted, one side of the room higher than the other. Out the window, the art instructor saw the barrier fence had been trampled flat, and the crowd of figures below striking and pummeling the building foundation. They shrieked about what they wanted and did not want as they broke away pieces of stone and tossed debris behind them, making bloody splashes in the crowds who rushed forward. The great three-and-a-half-story edifice groaned and cracked.

Frost covered the art tables and the floor. The art instructor did not feel cold, just extremely lonely, trying to recall the voices of her sister, her parents, of friends disappeared into numberless years, and she could not manage to weep or speak.

The structure swayed and red dust fell from the walls, as glass fractured and tumbled and scattered with dull glints. There was scraping and pounding at the door, yowls of starvation.

It was all very near the end, the signs given way to the final events. She was lost and could think of nothing else to do. The names of her students came to her, all she had left. She whispered them in the failing room, getting each one right.

The shadows murmured and stirred, and they began to form new compositions, painting limbs and faces in the air. With each pronunciation another emerged, whole and beaming, every one bringing a color. She knew then that none of them had ever left, she had only forgotten how to see them. Soon she was bellowing and they were too.

Together they went through the door and down the dying hallways, untouched by stone fangs or claws, down through the destruction and past all the uproar, out into the world again, vivid and fascinated.

Revisitation

I'VE RETURNED TO the house. Our house. It feels colder and darker than the rest of the city. Going inside was difficult. More so than maneuvering the motorcycle through car-blocked streets. Because standing in the silent doorway, my memories of you rushed back. The good ones. Before all this.

Trying out new restaurants together. Parking along Skyline Road and necking like a couple of teenagers. Going to the restored roller rink on couples' night and laughing so hard at the music selection that we couldn't stand up. Taking your nephews to the museum. That time in the dive bar when you defended my honor, "Back away from my man, hussy, or I will set you afire with this cheap Jesus candle!" Your magnetic poetry love notes on the refrigerator.

The day we met on the train. Two divorcees squandering hope who glanced across the aisle to notice we were both reading the same book. We smiled and returned to the texts. You hopped over, sat next to me, and whispered in my ear, "I'm two chapters ahead, with spoilers on the tip of my tongue!" Your green eyes between curls of red hair.

I miss you so much. It's been one year exactly, the anniversary of the end.

We bought this house together and started projects immediately. Damned projects.

I was insulating the pipes in the crawlspace when I found the dead rat. You brought me a trash bag, I wrapped the rodent in black plastic and handed it back. And I blamed myself forever afterward, even though the little body had been unmistakably stiff and cold. But in your hands it shrieked and twisted. And bit you.

You swayed and stumbled, and I scrambled to catch you fainting in a deathly sweat.

The paramedics arrived in time for the convulsions. You pleaded for the pain to stop as foam leaked from your mouth. I cried and yelled at them to do something.

"Sir," they said, "let us do our job."

You struggled and bit them, and I helped hold you down. I have a scar where you tore out a piece of my forearm.

Then we lost you.

They administered CPR for four minutes, then called the coroner. Postmortem lividity set in at once.

The ambulance took you away at residential speed, without lights or sirens.

It crashed at the end of the block.

As I ran toward the vehicle, the paramedics leapt out the back. They screamed and clawed the air, sniffing with wild hunger, and attacked the first neighbor who came out. With their teeth.

The police set up a perimeter. I said things like, *There are movies about this, you know,* and, *There are certain rules.* "Sir," they said, "Stand back."

By that time, the paramedics had collapsed, lifeless but no one else seemed concerned. A rampage of a six or eight newly infected neighbors attacked bystanders and invaded other homes. *A few precise head shots will end this,* I thought. But there in the spotlights they tore off their own arms and sprayed the officers with contagious blood. Then more police arrived.

I climbed to my roof and pulled up the ladder.

By dawn, when the screams moved out of the neighborhood, I retrieved your body from the ambulance. I buried you in the backyard.

I don't recall much about the first days. The wound on my arm throbbed, and I expected at any moment to change. Thought maybe I already had, but it was only shock and dehydration.

I armed myself and hid at night. I practiced target shooting with pistol and shotgun in a different open space each day. Later I realized that the blighted weren't wandering anymore, they were expanding geographically. I hadn't seen any in weeks—any upright and biting ones. They were like honeybees, dying as they stung. Leaving bodies and a terrible stench.

The last local TV station went off-air in one week; the radio in two. Before the power went out, I saw live feeds showing the infected stumbling into an airport and releasing a shimmering cascade from their skin. Spores? Hundreds of people choked and vomited... and changed. In other videos they opened their mouths and emitted an unearthly scream, the sound spreading contamination instantly. Indeed the rules had changed.

The projects that I assigned myself were small at first. I gathered canned food and set up rain catch barrels. One day, I brought a portable generator into a movie theater, but the thought that no more films would be made sent me hurrying from that place, the projector reeling out behind me. I learned to weld, then to knit. I spent a few weeks burning bodies, and tried to clear some main roads until I settled on the motorcycle for transportation.

I tried a few different mansions on the hill, but they were not my style. I always felt like an intruder. Eventually I settled in a for-sale, two-bedroom bungalow in a southeast neighborhood with solar panels and a double lot. I started a garden.

I tried to make sense of *why me*, and *what next*. Then I tried not to, turning to drink for an unknown number of days. But I'd look at my scarred arm and feel like you were with me. I found the warehouse for the annual city festival and put on a big fireworks show. Just for myself.

After six months, I began to enjoy the calm. I can't believe that I used to wish for a deserted world like this. Full of quiet. That was before I met you.

Now our refrigerator magnets are covered in dust. The pieces spell out: *my honey promise to frolic kiss tantalize squeeze me passion ly ful and make dinner naked smile.*

I had to come back. Aspirations kept me going for a while, projects like unlocking the zoo, learning to fly a small plane, reading all of *Don Quixote*. I could get out of town with a monster truck, perhaps using the railway, or maybe by boat...

But I haven't seen vapor trails in nine months. The shortwave radio emits only a constant hiss.

There's no point anymore.

I don't want to find anyone else. And I'm weary.

My arm itches again.

I miss you so much.

I've come back to you. This shovel is heavy but welcome in my hand. We'll lie together now. Pull the soil in over us, and—

That noise—!

...my flashlight...

Oh god—! You've come back. Staggering there, next to the upturned earth.

When all the others wouldn't.

Because you were the first? Or a mutation like me?

I don't know. I don't care. I'm coming outside, my love. How I've missed you!

Oh, Arlene, your beautiful red hair.

The new gleaming pulse of your eyes. The echoing chroma and rhythm of the teethmarks in my arm.

They Shall Flourish and Spread

OREL TRUDGED ALONGSIDE her family and millions of others though the vast tunnel, footstep by footstep on the spongy floor, guided by the gleaming violet threads in the walls and the promise of one direction. The marching multitude stretched before and behind them into the immeasurable dim and musty distance. Her feet hurt and she was bored.

"I want to go faster!" Her little brother jumped ahead of them, then skipped backward.

"Hush now," Father said patiently.

"Qun, mind your feet and your neighbors." Mother's long hair caught the glow from the only light.

"Put me on your shoulders, Orel." Qun tugged at her arm. Only waist-high, and so much energy.

"You'll never see the front row," she sighed. "And I'm so tired."

Qun stamped his feet, whimpering.

"We are all weary," Father said. He waved goodbye to their neighbors and led his family to the open right side. There they laid a circle of luminescent thread.

The continuous column moved by them; some offered greeting, most turned away as Qun cried himself hoarse. Eventually hunger settled him. They peeled succulent hyphae fibers from the soft rubbery wall and sucked out earthy moisture with thirsty lips, until they found their fill. After walking through the crowd to the left side and back one hundred paces to defecate, they returned to camp and spread out on the warm floor.

Qun sobbed into his arms. "...So many ahead of us."

Orel caressed his fine hair. "So many behind us too." She sang to him, soothing euphonious tones that rose and carried in the high circular space, and many walkers hummed accompaniment. Soon the air grew sweet, as spores dusted down on them from the gilled cavern ceiling. It was always a blessing. Finally he closed his eyes.

Three of them woke before Qun, and knowing he would be disappointed to miss so many steps, Father carried him for a long while. It was better that way because they passed a few integrations on the left, some of the prone forms covered in fine white wispy filaments with enough definition still to see limbs and fingers and even faces.

When they passed a fertility hut on the right, woven from the wall matter and marked with a circular glow symbol, Orel saw Mother watching her with an odd smile. She glared back, and Mother laughed lightly. At least it was a quiet hut.

Even awake, Qun allowed himself to be carried for a short distance, as he drowsily sucked his thumb. Father put him down when the march came upon a group with a broken wagon. He helped integrate the faulty wheel and Mother helped shape a new one.

Once they rejoined the flow, young Qun walked briskly. Then he trotted between the walkers and they humored him, jogging to keep pace. His sister asked if they would take their meal on the run.

They worked on his creeds as they ran. He recited them impatiently.

"What do we do?"

"We walk."

"Why do we walk?"

"Our planet was dying, but The Passage grew down from the sky and provided us the way."

"How do we walk?"

"Forward, always forward. Never back."

"What are the sides?"

"Eat and love on the right, waste and die on the left."

"Where do we go?"

"To our home anew, full of soil and sky."

"What is The Passage?"

"The Passage is our warmth from the cold and the dark. It is our food and our life. The Passage is our path. And so we walk."

The murmur of the parade was interrupted, then halted, by ecstatic shouts. "I see one! Oh, I see it—there! I lay claim!" A man ran out from the company, pointing excitedly at the cavern wall. He scrambled against the curved tissue and gained a few upward steps. "Help me, my neighbors!" Soon others saw the golden point of light moving along the purple threads. They ran to boost him up and he eagerly plunged his hand into the porous structure. They lowered him to the floor, and parted in a wide ring of awed faces at the golden nodule he held with shaking hands.

He smiled and laughed with bewilderment.

"Pilgrim, you are sanctified," someone said. "A primordium has chosen you."

"Are you ready to depart?" someone else said.

"I..." He seemed as if he'd been startled awake.

"You must be ready. You must go. Its light could extinguish at any moment."

"I..." He looked at a woman nearby and immediately began to weep. "Kyna—"

Seeing this made Orel's heart hurt.

"You must be ready—or someone else must take your place." A large man stepped forward.

"It's alright, Farr, my love." Kyna smiled at him, though she was crying too.

Farr nodded at her. Then he straightened himself to a prepared stance. He took a deep breath, placed the shining nodule in his mouth, and swallowed.

Silence filled the cavern as they watched.

The one called Farr furrowed his brow and coughed, and was about to say something more, when he disappeared.

Orel had expected a bursting flash of light, or a loud noise, but there was nothing spectacular, only empty space where he'd been, and a faint bitter odor that hung in the air so briefly she wasn't sure if she imagined it.

Mother pushed dried fibers into Orel's hands. "Show me weave patterns three and seven."

"Why now, Mother?" Orel rolled her eyes.

"You haven't been practicing."

"I don't want to practice. Why don't you teach Qun?"

"It is not a man's job nor a boy's."

"Who said so?"

"Don't speak back at your mother," Father said.

"Don't speak back at Mother," Qun sang.

The Tsipo family glared at their youngest until he gazed down at his toes.

"Well, I don't need to practice." She tried to give the fibers back.

As they walked, Mother unfolded a long mat from her carry basket. "Do I need to show you again?" Her fingers moved quickly, lacing and knitting the strands to complete a row.

Orel sighed heavily. She smoothed the fibers in her fist as was customary to do, then met Mother's eyes. She began slowly with a bend and a wrap, then a tight stitch and a loop, then faster until her hands tumbled in a frantic blur. Her feet stumbled a few times but she did not stop weaving or break her gaze. After one hundred counts she held out a small figurine to her parents.

Mother breathed in with surprise.

"What is it?" Qun's eyes were wide with fascination.

Orel examined what she held. The strange sculpture could have been a miniature table, as it had four legs, but it also had a very defined neck and head that featured details like ear twists and tightly woven eyes and sharp projections that were not exactly roots, for they grew upward. It was unlike anything they had ever seen.

"Yes, daughter, what is it?" Mother asked.

"Can I have it?" Qun held his arms at his sides with obvious control, his small hands clenching anxiously. "Can I?"

Orel gave it to him with a smile and he immediately held it close for inspection.

They moved to the side and stopped. "Where did you see this...?" Father asked.

She tried to remember, or to picture it in her mind again, but found nothing. "A dream," she whispered, "it must be."

Mother embraced her. "You've been practicing instead of sleeping."

The passersby watched them and, abashed, Orel covered her face. When Mother sobbed, she squeezed her back.

Qun made peculiar noises as they walked. He yowled and squawked, he tittered and buzzed and gurgled. Father would ask him to stop and he would say, "It's not me, it's..." and would hold up the small figure. He clicked and cheeped and mooed and snorted and tsked and blorted and oinked.

Orel stuffed moist hyphae in her ears. She closed her eyes and expunged the pain in her feet and forgot her legs, and eventually found walksleep.

———

"Have you heard?" said their neighbor in front of them. "Eighty-four hundred steps ahead, Euga Vypi has become a pilgrim."

"I had not heard, thank you," Father said. "May protection and favor go with him on his journey." They bowed to one another. Then Father turned and relayed the news to the next row.

For a long while Father stared ahead with weary eyes. Orel noticed this and it frightened her. She was about to tell Mother to hold his hand, but a commotion erupted behind them.

First murmurs, then shouts of "Despoiler! Violator!" came from the crowd.

Father's gaze hardened, and he bolted left. A few others joined him and they locked arms in a string across the open lane just a moment before a man collided with them.

"No! Please, no!" he yelled, kicking to break free.

"Despoiler!" shouted the crowd.

"I never did!"

"We will see," Father said.

A young girl was brought forward, crying uncontrollably. She was barely Orel's age.

Mother tried to press her family back into the crowd, but the people were tight and unmoving.

"What is your name?" Father asked.

"Ji."

"Did this one pervade you against your wishes?" Father pointed at the prisoner.

She cried and sobbed, and could only nod.

Mother became very serious. "Orel, take your brother one thousand steps forward and wait for us on the right."

"You take him. I want to see."

Already the men formed a wide base and boosted more men onto their shoulders. At three reaches high they were not even a quarter way to the ceiling. The accused screamed protests as they brought him forward.

Mother's face quivered and Orel didn't know if it was anger or fear, and for a moment she thought she might strike her. But then she turned calm and whispered, "Please, Orel. Not now."

She did as she was told. She picked up her brother and held his face to her chest to muffle his questions as she carried him quickly away. She glanced back to see them, very high up, as they dug and clawed into the soft wall, then pressed the struggling man into the seeping cavity. And the wall responded, reaching filament after filament over his body. She turned and broke into a run. In time, his shrieks had gone silent.

She made Qun count the steps as she told him a story about his four-legged toy, about how in some distant place, it was taller than five men and roamed in vast open spaces without a ceiling, where it ate sweet waving strands of strangely colored matter and drank from wide bottomless pools of moisture.

At first he scowled and shook his head, but then added that it roamed in great groups, and often chased off other very hairy creatures that ate their young.

He lost track during all of this, which was part of her intent, for he could not yet count steps with his body. They hadn't reached one thousand before they came upon a series of shelters and stands linked by draped strands of vibrant purple.

Orel had not seen a market for many years. "Hurry!"

They ran by the enclosed grunt huts and the people drinking fermented juice at long tables, and came finally to the selling stalls. There they saw fine baskets and hammocks, sturdy wagons and draggers. They found sets of hollowed polyp cups, ostentatious jewelry and elaborate roughage dresses. The best pieces, carved or shaped or woven, highlighted unique flaws from the porous texture of their source material. They exclaimed over the fancy sandals and the florid carpets. They both stopped abruptly at the stand with dozens of figurines.

"Orel, look..." The boy pointed.

"I'm looking..." She couldn't say anything else.

The crafted creatures had four legs or more, some with long necks or short arms, with pointed snouts or thick ribcages, many with another thin limb trailing behind them and tipped with a brush of hairs or spikes. Some had no legs at all, but a long tongue and patchy skin buffed to a shine. Others had teeth hanging low or curving high before them.

She felt an uplifting sense of connection.

"I would like all of them!" Qun said.

"This is a market, stripling," said the stall keeper, leaning forward. "You need something to trade." He had one eye, the other socket was fit with dim balled-up glow thread that needed replacing.

Qun said nothing for a long pause and they thought he would cry. Instead he only snorted. "I've already got one, you see." He held up his toy.

"So you have. Well done, young one."

Orel finally found her voice. "Did you make all of these?" She smoothed her skirt.

"The truth says I didn't. All left to me by a friend. Long gone now."

"A pilgrim?" she asked.

"Integrated."

"Oh. I'm sorry." Difficulty flooded her and she was surprised at its potency. She was overcome with the need to slip away. Among all these people she still felt she might drown in loneliness.

"He was a talent."

She didn't thank the seller, only nodded and strode off.

Mother and Father found them near the acrobats, though Orel wasn't watching the show at all.

It had been a tiring wake period, and because Qun could not yet walksleep, they made a space at the encampment periphery. After the meal, Mother and Father went back to the emporium.

Qun made snorting noises as he galloped his toy over the moist floor, spun in circles, and swooshed it up and about in dramatic arcs.

"I don't think it can fly," Orel mumbled.

He frowned at her. He stuck out his tongue, which showed a deep purple from too much lumi candy.

Jealousy pricked at her, and she at once wanted him to grow up. She wanted to tell him how many steps she had walked in her life and how many waited for him. She wanted him to know that his eyes would fade and his hair fall out and his skin grow tender. She wanted him to feel some of her anguish.

"We'll never finish the pilgrimage," she said quietly.

Her brother stopped and stared at her. "What?"

A few of the neighbors gave her threatening stares.

She shook her head at the thoughts. She didn't know, it was how she felt sometimes.

He resumed playing, this time with whinnying sounds.

The sugars wore him out and he nearly fell asleep sitting up. She lay him down and covered him with the weave mat.

He spoke sleepily. "Father was so sad today. When he heard about the pilgrim."

She didn't think he had noticed. "We all wish to skip ahead, Qun."

"No..."

"No?" She blinked and shook her head. "Father is getting old, but he is very brave. He was born into the First Throng, you know. Grandpa took him to see the front. There is more killing there. He dropped back to the Third Throng when his parents integrated. It was a good thing, or he never would have met Mother."

"Ask her..." He was snoring before he could finish.

She kissed him on the head and sang very softly.

Spores drifted through the dewy air. A few of them seemed to linger.

Their parents stumbled back to camp with arms around the neighbors' shoulders, all of them laughing and unsuccessfully whispering. Father smiled and belched as he sat. The neighbors raised a glass to him, "O there, Jar!"

and he hushed them loudly and laughed as they moved on to their sleep spot.

"Good night, Father," Orel said.

"Night." He chuckled at the word. He rustled her hair. "I love you too, dearling."

When he was asleep, she sat up and whispered to Mother.

"Qun said Father didn't drop back. Why would he say that?"

Mother turned her eyes down, then away. Finally she looked at her daughter. "It's true, dear. Your Father didn't drop back. He took a primordium. And instead of forward, it sent him back."

Her world rolled upside down. She felt sick. "Why didn't you tell me? Why didn't you *ever*...?"

"Orel, I'm sorry. He doesn't talk about it, no one does. But he has accepted it." She seemed to believe it and maybe it was true. Mother lightly kneaded the floor. "You should sleep."

Orel could not close her eyes. She shivered and was sure that the freezing infinite blackness seeped through from outside to touch her.

They walked with the populace for eight-hundred thousand steps. Qun lost his toy and was not consoled by the new creature that his sister made, one with a sleek pointed body and thin triangular limbs that seemed impossible to stand upon. They took turns carrying him on their backs, though gradually he came to keep pace with their longer legs, and soon practiced walking with his eyes closed.

They saw regular integrations, and Qun no longer ran to the right side, though he held Orel's hand when they passed a clustered group, and thankfully none of them were forced. A few pilgrims departed near them, one that only traveled a few hundred steps, and each time Father did not stop.

Qun's questions became more infrequent. Worried, they discussed it when he slept, and made an effort during walk to tell him stories. Father told him of the two great cities he had seen as a boy, Kes and Yr, molded out of the walls and ceiling, spanning thousands of steps. Mother told him about her old dance troupe who strung glow fiber across the width and on which they balanced high overhead, then ran on after a performance to meet their families, adorned with prizes. Orel envisioned creatures that one could ride on their backs who ran so hard one must grasp their flowing hair. But she merely sang, just notes and melodies, always without words.

At some point Father found himself in conversation with a haggard traveler who introduced himself as Byr and offered draws from his flagon for some neighborly conversation. Father obliged with a few sips.

When Father gave his name, Byr exclaimed, "Not Jar Tsipo of the First Throng?! Why, tales of your deeds are whispered throughout the cavalcade, from nose to ass end!"

Father said humbly that he doubted that, but Byr gave him more portions of fermented juice, and gathered a crowd. "My father told me how a great warrior near the front—this man!—led many surges when spirits were low, and quelled many riots when men seethed with wretchedness. He brought hope to the crusade." In response, the neighbors cheered and hailed Father. Soon he was staggering and slurring words.

Mother pinched him. "You're scaring me."

"Nonsense, dearest. There is nothing to be scared of in this whole wide, long aching shaft!"

"Hear, hear!" Byr exclaimed.

Orel punched her father's arm. "You are scaring your son."

At this, he winced and stood tall. "You are very correct. I am sorry."

"I am sorry, as well." Byr bowed to Qun. "Here…" He rummaged in his carry basket. "Here… Well, somewhere…" He teetered and those nearby righted him. After a moment he caught up. He offered Qun a strange trinket, a network of bulbs connected at various angles by intersecting stalks.

"What is it?" Qun turned it over and over. "It's not a very good toy."

"It's a map, of course. A scale model of our planet system." Byr smiled to himself with satisfaction. "These are the planets, of course, and—"

"But…" The boy gaped at his parents with alarm.

Father growled at Byr. "Leave us now."

"Jar, what is he saying…?" Mother's voice faded into worry.

All at once, Orel feared she knew.

"You haven't told them?" Byr pointed to the model.

Father shoved him hard, propelling him out of the march. "You will stay left and stay back. Stay away from my family!"

Then he grabbed roughly at the model in his son's hand, wrenched it into fragments, and lobbed them away in different directions.

Before the boy could cry, Jar Tsipo made his family run. They raced, dashed, and hurtled. Even as their minds slept, their muscles endured one-hundred thousand more footfalls before waking them for sustenance.

In the camp ring they drank and ate greedily. Then Qun talked with his mouth full.

"Why did The Passage come to our planet? Our old planet?"

"That's a big question for a little boy," Mother said.

"How do we know the other planet will be better?"

"We'll talk about it after we sleep," Father said.

"I've been thinking… I've seen how The Passage absorbs the living and the dead, everything. How do we know The Passage wasn't killing our planet?"

"No more about this." Father sliced his hand in the air. "We rest our bodies now."

Orel was nearly asleep when Qun shook her.

"What if Byr's model is right?" he whispered, wide-eyed, "What if every planet in our system is overrun with… this?" He surveyed all the way around from ceiling back to floor. "What if there isn't any sky left anywhere?"

She felt unease bloom in her chest. "I've thought about it too, Qun," she said, which was partly true. She was tired and nearly recited the creeds to him, but she felt he deserved more. "Don't think I haven't thought about how long it must take to walk across a planet or around it. And how much longer it must take to walk the distance between worlds." Despair clawed at her, though she kept her voice quiet. "But we have hope and we have each other." She managed a convincing smile. "Would you like a song?"

"No, thank you." Qun closed his eyes. After a moment he turned over.

Orel sang anyway.

Her dreams contained tiny holes in the black that melted into a bright open place full of colors she could not name.

———

They ate again, then made their water and waste. They folded their mats and new dishes and packed them away. When they shouldered their baskets, Qun had not packed at all.

"Son, why aren't you ready?"

The boy said nothing. Arms rigid at his sides, he stood still with a tight jaw. He shook his head slowly.

"Son?"

"We have to know, Father. We can't just walk. We have to know."

"We talked about this, son—"

Qun unfolded his hand and bright orange light poured out.

"Qun, where did you—?"

"In the model. One of the planet pieces." He held it before his face. "It's so warm. Warmer than I've ever felt…" His eyes swam with awe.

Father stepped forward slowly. "Son, you're too young—"

"You've already traveled!" Qun shouted at his father.

"I did not mean for myself, son. Please, we'll give it away."

"Someone has to go. To see what's there." The boy smiled. "I'll find another one and come back. Or I'll build us a house and wait for you—"

Qun opened his mouth.

Father lunged.

Orel gasped.

And Qun was gone.

The Tsipo family wailed and moaned. Father attacked the walls, tearing and biting. The neighbors had to pull him free before he was subsumed.

They ran to forget. Twenty-thousand long strides, and stopped. They wept and screamed. Then fifty-thousand, and stopped. The sticky air burned in their lungs and spores turned their tears muddy. Two-hundred thousand. They called his name, they relayed messages. Four-hundred thousand, eating as they ran and foregoing the prone sleep. They howled and searched and bawled. They tried bribing for a primordium. Six-hundred thousand. Their skin and muscle hung on their bones.

Until at some point when their consciousness surfaced in the spoiled air, they realized they had slowed. Their legs now moved in a sluggish measured rhythm. They were walking. Not out of exhaustion. They had accepted his departure.

Orel was dreaming awake, rivers of bright fresh flowing liquid inviting her to submerge and glide, tumble, and cleanse. She walked and walked, hearing a name between the steps, and finally recognized it as her own.

"Orel! Orel! I am seeking Orel Tsipo! Do you know her? Orel Tsipo?"

The young man with the shoulder-length hair leaned into the rows, inquiring.

"Me!" she started, half out of walksleep, "I am Orel."

"I—I can't believe it!" He handed her a showy arrangement of polyps, finely filigreed. "I never thought to find you! Not knowing your face."

She halted and stared at the bloom.

"Oh, Orel..." her mother breathed.

Then she saw the hut with the two entwined glow threads over the door. The rest of the structure was as decorative as the bouquet.

"Oh no..."

Her Father tried to order her, and Mother defended her, but she was most adamant, for she didn't even know his name. When he introduced himself as Loi Tyz of the Fourth Throng, the ambition of his family impressed Father. Finally she agreed to see the inside of his hut, though briefly—and not because of his vacuous story that he had heard her singing voice when he was a boy and carried it with him ever since, and waited and waited for her—but to admire the craftsmanship, was all. The inside proved even more impressive, with scrupulous coiled patterns and a glow filament chandelier.

They sat on the sponge bed and talked, about the most outrageous things they had seen at markets, how you can cure hyphae to make hard blocks and shapes, about the walksleepers who never wake, and if they'd ever seen a side passage or a spore storm.

"I can't stay with you, Loi," she said suddenly. "I'm sorry."

"Oh." He was immediately downfallen.

"But you can walk with us for a while."

He left the hut without hesitation and went with her.

At first she thought Mother and Father had abandoned her. But they waited one thousand steps ahead on the right.

Everyone was asleep when she opened her eyes. Loi lay close by and she shifted herself away. The Passage radiated and glimmered all around as the rhythm of the congregation thrummed beneath her. She rolled onto her back and noticed the small cloud of spores hovering nearby. There was nothing distinct about their shape and they carried no glow, but they held something familiar in them.

"Hello, Grandfather," she said.

It stayed for a long time until she found sleep.

They were seven-thousand steps into a new stretch when they noticed the vibrations. The procession slowed its pace and neighbors looked at each other. The juddering became deep tremors, and people broke rows as the entire Passage shuddered. Then the undulations rippled below them in fast waves, knocking people down.

Orel imagined the walls twisting and breaking open, spilling millions of them screaming silently into the airless cold. She saw Father, but the screams drowned his shouts, so he pointed to the sides. She took Loi's hand and pulled him with her. They reached the left wall and tried to hold their place.

Then, from far ahead, came another noise. A low keening chatter rolled out of the dark distance, rising then falling to a long echoing hiss. People halted in place. And when the rumbling sibilance returned, louder, peopled screamed and did something they had never done before. They turned. And ran back.

To keep from being trampled, Orel and Loi clambered up the wall's fine ridges as far as they could reach. Others did the same along both sides, some pulling neighbors down as they went. She tried to look for Mother and Father, but there were too many retreating bodies.

She imagined a city crumbling ahead of them. She imagined a raging flood of water rolling forth. She imagined the planets pulling apart, or a moon crashing through their raw enclosure.

Until they finally came into view, swarming in an endless rush of massive eight-legged bulbous black bodies with ten remorseless eyes over long steaming teeth, she had not, like many, ever considered that travelers might also come from the other direction. Or perhaps not like this. They poured over every surface from floor to ceiling in a barreling countless mass as they lashed long jagged tongues and slashed spiked forelegs at the fleeing figures.

She cried and shrieked. She whipped her head and clawed at the wet tissue before her.

Their collective noise grew to a roar and devoured all screams.

Orel closed her eyes and released her grip. The warmth encased her arms.

Someone grabbed her chin and she opened her eyes. Loi's face shone golden orange. Before she realized what it meant, he held up the beaming nodule and pressed it into her mouth. She tried to protest or spit back, but his palm covered her lips. Then he kissed her against the back of his hand.

The world buckled and crushed. And turned.

She blinked.

Her eyes ached and she stepped into the shade of a tall rough stalk with strange beautiful green projections. Seeing the bright not-quite-purple ceiling so far above was dizzying, but soon she guessed what it was.

When she spoke, spores and dim light emerged from her mouth.

Just a few beats later, behind all the odd new sounds, she felt response from a large fungus organism in the soil beneath her feet. The largest on this planet, it told her, with a span of eleven-thousand strides. She'd seen bigger, but this one was young. Perhaps it had called her here.

She speculated a moment over whether she'd gone forward or back, or otherways. But it did not matter, nothing seemed to at all. Everyone she knew was gone. Grief descended on her with a crushing heaviness.

Unless, she thought absurdly...

And she found the will to move, marching off at a steady pace.

With the infinitesimal hope of seeing her brother again.

She passed a rigid sign with strange symbols. Some new language she would have to learn.

MALHEUR NATIONAL FOREST

U.S. DEPARTMENT OF AGRICULTURE

Studies in Light and Dark

EVERY NIGHT, ARIC stuffs a towel along the crack under the door because the hallway light hits him straight in the eye. Aric says the overhead light is evil. He is known by his friends to hiss and recoil then make a flying leap across the room to slap the switch dark. This is the second thing they learned about him. They were all there in the room built for two, all those who run together now, when he dropped his backpacks inside the door and surveyed the dorm room, saying, "...also called: Place of the Skull."

Malcolm has an earlier class. His alarm goes off at 7:00 AM. If Aric opens his eyes, there is the lump pressing down the upper mattress. His dreams seem longer than nine minutes, but the snooze goes off. Goes off four times. Until 7:36 AM. The lump slides to one side, covers and legs hang at the edge, then heels thump the floor like stones. Malcolm showers every morning. Some mornings he forgets about the towel, he pulls and pulls, muttering sluggish curses, pulls on the door that won't move.

The hall advisors threaten to write them up. They have the form in their hands with ROOM 150 already filled in when Malcolm answers the door. There are accusations about disabling the detector and smoking something other than tea leaves, which is against university policy and will not be tolerated in the Keeley-Darrow Honors Residence Hall.

"Dorm." Is when Aric walks in.

They ask him to sit down too.

He shields his eyes and winces in the slightest way—enough for Malcolm to catch and snicker—and he flicks off the light. In the dark, he pushes it, saying, "ho... *ha!*" pretending to leap back out the door. Then he clicks on the desk lamp before they can say uh, excuse me, what do you think you're doing? He does sit, legs crossed and leaning forward with eager attention, leaving them no pause. And they see someone smoking outside the open window. And it is over quickly. And they depart.

But this isn't a story.

Except when one of the women from the fourth floor asks. Malcolm usually tells it, dramatizing the escape in the dark, with him going out the window at the same time. Then straight to the getaway car. Or pirate ship. Or magical gate. Never the same story. Never the part when Aric said to them he can't remember the last time he smelled burning.

Baxter Hall, Second Floor, HIST 201: INTRO TO MYTHOLOGIES. Late to class, Aric takes the desk by the door. He very much dislikes the front row. Eyes still stinging from the outside cold, dreams still picking at him. He glances at Malcolm in the seat by the window. The professor pauses with a glance, then finishes writing the definition of a myth on the chalkboard. She asks for examples. Students raise their hands and suggest the American Dream, Manifest Destiny, true love, and everlasting fossil fuels. Little more is said for the hour, and he wants to say doom is coming, but doesn't speak.

Malcolm catches up with him outside the building. "I shall use your computer while you're in class," Malcolm lets him know.

"A myth," says Aric, sliding one hand into a glove.

"A myth that you can stop me."

"The myth that I won't eat your ankles." Now the other glove. Slowly, not unlike so many movies bad and worse, pulling it tight and flexing fingers.

"The myth that you don't have another class, while I do not." Malcolm smiles in triumph and turns away.

"My arms," Aric says quietly, "are very long."

Anderson Hall, Third Floor, BIO 102: INTRO TO BIOLOGY. Aric comes out of the stairwell and stops. An old display case lines the entire hallway, filled with stuffed owls of every size and shape. They are all looking directly at him, the glassed eyes of the snowy, the barn, the burrowing, and the giant horned. He walks quickly to the lab class at the other end, his eyes closed the entire way, holding his breath. And he makes it, just barely.

That afternoon between classes Aric fits in some reading. The largest of his book boxes shipped from home has become a table under the window for the

Ramen noodle exclusive hot pot and the alarm clock. A string of discarded dental floss sticks to the peeled packing tape. There and everywhere in his room, details that could become stories. Stacked and lost behind new assignments.

But this is not one of his books, this is one Jayne pushed into his hands last week. It tells a very different version of stories he knows so well. In this version, Judas is now (quite suddenly presented to him as) a descendant of Cain and sporting a fiery-red beard. And while Sunday School said Jesus was always the carpenter's son, he is now (suddenly presented to him as) a maker of crosses. To Aric, it is both outrageous and natural at once. Someone else's details, where he had none. Not quite thoughts, not quite yet. Still reading. He must hurry because it will be a movie soon.

The friends do not knock, Jayne simply opens the door and enters. A visit from the east wing where the hallways look the same but mirror-opposites. She waits for him to notice her hand as it hovers over the light switch. His low hiss without looking up makes her laugh. The big light stays dark.

Jayne. Her great uncle, she said, was the doctor who bandaged John Wilkes Booth's leg.

Still reading, the book says Jesus is tormented by voices in his head. Meaning begins to slip, but still he doesn't look up. He can feel what she's doing now. Because they met a certain way, and kept it on. Peripherally she is scanning his bookshelf, reaching up. And so he must stare down and read the words, reading the story he thought he knew. He scans. She scans. He feels her existence, real. He loses a line about Jerusalem.

"I will take this," she says in the way they do with each other, definite, dramatic, understated.

"I will stop you," he says, reading.

"My people will stop you," she says, taking his book about a dream king.

"My people will stop your people," he says, not moving.

"My people are everywhere." She is nearly out the door.

"My people are few, crouched in shadows, though fast."

"My people have night vision." She pulls the door very slowly closed. They do not miss, as some say, a beat.

"My people have set cardboard stand-ups, while my real people are coming up behind yours." He does not need to move.

"Your people forgot to mask their scent, and mine have smelled their approach." Her parting words as the door latches.

"My people rise again," he says, "The waking dead."

Malcolm goes home every weekend. To do laundry, he says.

Sometimes the others don't come over, and Aric tells himself he should be reading, but he sits in the dark in the middle of the room, sometimes with music playing on the stereo, something to give his chest some rhythm. When the crying comes, he never reaches for anything, just lets it.

McMillen Building, Second Floor, STUDENT EMPLOYMENT OFFICES. Aric pauses outside the door, wishes for a interesting high paying job on a part-time basis. Eyes closed, wishing hard, he blocks the doorway. "Excuse me," a woman in galoshes needs to get by. Eyes open and standing still, he's thinking, what is wish hope prayer?

He removes a blue slip from the bulletin board because it says three-eighty an hour. Then he reads the rest of it. Something in the Psychology department. The last of his summer job money went to first semester books. Barrett will help him with the magazine of stories they want to start. Maybe the print shop downtown cuts them a deal. Maybe they make enough back to print issue number two. The woman behind the counter gives him another slip that is pale yellow. The interview is scheduled for Thursday afternoon.

At 10:30 PM, Aric is just opening the book when the door thunders. He tries to remember if he locked it, when Barrett jumps into the room. He smiles and says nothing. There is more than one young woman snickering behind him.

"No," says Aric.

"Yes," says Barrett. "Oh yes."

"Not tonight."

And Barrett just smiles in his Operation Ivy T-shirt, flannel shirt tied around the waist, knee-high combat boots laced tight. His mohawk is bright green tonight, fully vertical. Fresh thick black Xs on the backs of his hands.

He advances toward the chair where Aric is sitting.

"Aaaaa-ric..." Fourth-floor women gather in the doorway. They continue to wail and chant his name. One of them says there's only half an hour before cover charge. And his name and the snickering. And one of them asking why it's always so dark in here.

The book is already slipping from his hands, and Malcolm is nowhere to be seen, nor his laundry.

Barrett hoists Aric high by the legs. The snickering becomes shrieks of glee and applause as he's carried out the door.

Once inside the night club, Barrett gets him on the dance floor right away. Three hours, four pitchers of water, the fourth-floor women since departed, and the DJ makes the walls shake. The heavier beats clear the floor. It's the good song so Barrett and Aric have to thrash and stomp, cutting space with whipping limbs and hair. Hard. Harder than ever. The bouncers don't like it, but they are slow.

He enters the other side of Andrews Hall on purpose and uses the opposite stairwell. When he gets to the third floor, the owls are still facing him. He stares back at them for a long time. They move, blink, spread their wings and launch, hop down, marching and flapping through the hallway in a flurry of noise that holds him still as they blot out the light. He cannot move or breathe. They take part of his life. Or it feels like it.

He blinks. "That's what I thought," he says, and goes into class.

McDonald-Jacobs Building, Second Floor, SCIENCES ANIMAL LAB. The interviewing professor asks if Aric objects to "the euthanizing" of animals after, pause, "their purpose had been served." Before he can answer, the professor continues, that Aric will not have to inject any subjects himself, that all subjects must be put to sleep after studies and experiments, they simply cannot survive outside in the wild. Aric pictures the endless fields beyond the campus. He hears enough of the rest of what the man is saying. He is constructing a plan.

There is never a pause to answer, so he pretends not to care.

Okay then, start next week. The professor does not shake hands.

A cage could fit in my closet, he's thinking. But where to find building materials? They will have to roam free. The name of the first is already chosen. He cannot speak it aloud.

What is a prayer? And what is a wish?

Keeley-Darrow Residence Hall, Second Floor, STUDENT CAFETERIA. They complain in chorus about the Thursday main course item.

"Only your people could eat this," Jayne suggests, "and not worry about poisoning." The quiche limp and soggy from her fork.

"Why?" says one of them.

"Your people are uninformed," she says, "The waking dead."

"We should make a movie—" Niles, film major and quoter of horror movies with two-hundred-some VHS tapes in his room, but no TV or VCR. "*The Impolite Dead*," he suggests. And stretches out his arms, moans from a gaunt face. "'Give brains, now!'"

Laughter around the table. Malcolm swings back and forward, mouth open long and breathless. Aric slams the table with his palm.

"*The Critical Thinking Dead*—'Brains too ambiguous. Must clarify for mass audience. What value assumptions have the dead? What rival hypotheses?'"

Jayne pushes her tray and lowers her forehead to the table with soundless laughter.

"*The Whining Dead.*"

"*The Lethargic Dead.*"

This is how they are.

"*Double-jointed Dead.*"

"*Latch Key Dead.*"

"*Living Dead in Heavy Syrup.*"

"Stop!" Jayne raises her head, red-faced. "Please, stop..."

They stop. Until their faces shake.

And peals of laughter rise once more, louder. People are staring.

She lets her head fall again, laughing into her palms.

There is, it goes without saying, no escape.

They gather for a movie no one has heard of in the first-floor TV lounge. The other boys from the floor enter wearing boxer shorts and mesh pro football jerseys. This time Aric and Malcolm do not leave because of the news bulletin. US forces have attacked Baghdad. "Kick Hussain's ass," someone says, adjusting his scrotum. The first bombing runs were at 7:00 PM Eastern time. No live video coverage in Baghdad. Aric sees pictures in his head. The new stealth bombers, silent huge ravens. Blossoming flowers of fire at night.

He's been taking a class, Boxhelder Hall, Second Floor, HIST 142: HISTORY OF THE VIETNAM WAR, so the images and words are in his head. Jungle, tunnel systems, a heritage of war. The pride and ignorance of invaders from across the sea. Testimony of the Huey gunner, the LRP, the F-4 pilot. Critiquing action movies with muscled heroes. Poetry by a POW from North Vietnam. Analyzing Bob Dylan lyrics. All these are part of his dreams now. The last War that ended when he was born. Twenty years ago.

"I don't give a shit," says Pro Football Jersey Number 14, "You fags watch whatever you want." He leaves the first-floor TV lounge.

News reporters hide in a hotel room describing anti-aircraft fire and explosions and hold their microphone out the window. It sounds like cap guns and wet firecrackers.

After an hour of the static map of Baghdad inset with the reporter's picture and the popping sounds, Aric leaves. By the drinking fountain, Pro Football Jersey Number 14 is crying on the floor in the hallway, trying not to show it.

Aric stands by him for a long time. He doesn't say anything. He is thinking about My Lai, about Kent State, not far from here. Racing thoughts. He could put a hand on his shoulder or crouch down and hug him or say he is sorry. He could.

"I don't give a shit. I don't." Red scalp showing through the high school football crewcut. "My brother wouldn't let me have the mini fridge for my room. He wanted to sell it. Then he got called over." He pulls up his shirt and presses the fabric onto his streaming puffy eyes. "Fucking fridge is still sitting in our garage. It's still! Fucking sitting there!" He wipes his eyes again. "He's over there now. And I don't give a shit. I don't..." Crying.

They have not had this before. The fear will not linger for long. They have choices.

Aric has to finish reading that book, get it back to Jayne.

There is a song Aric listens to nearly every night. While Malcolm is in the bathroom, he plays the stereo. The song has a deep evil laugh that makes him sit in the back of his closet behind a pile of frayed shoes and unfolded clean clothes, holding his knees close. The rest of what they know about him is different. This song is for real.

When Malcolm returns with his toiletries and towel, Aric turns off the stereo, they pass each other. He looks down the uninhabited hallway, closes the door behind him. He reaches for the light. He kills it and moves through the long darkness in the hour past midnight with his toothbrush and paste.

The mirror stares back. It lies without words. It says he is trapped in a movie so nothing can hurt him. But the eyes say otherwise, they say softest of all, he is nothing special, he has everything he needs, there is only waiting. He stands back and brushes his teeth. More waiting.

He walks back to the room ever so slowly. Time thickens. Ever. So.

At the door, he is different. He is lost and they cannot touch him.

Malcolm is surely lost in sleep, beyond any suspicion of how his roommate has changed, of the thousands of relentless images and ideas that remade him in the mirror, in the long eternity of the hallway.

He moves inside silently and does not stop.

Smooth as a slow blink, he closes the door. Now he claims the size of the dark and stillness, as he is flying without leaving, borne on the extension of it all into a journey behind the sky to touch roaring stars so many lifetimes away, further, tearing the edge of existence until there's a hole, and he can almost feel it, he peers without eyes, he can see—

"Do the towel thing," says the voice from the top bunk.

Aric keeps it to a smile, tucks the towel where it needs to go. Ah, the way Malcolm moaned the plea, he is learning how.

"There is," he whispers, getting into bed, "hope for them yet."

Schneider Building, Front Steps, Student Union.

"...words words words... *The Passion Play*... words words words..." someone says.

Just the title opens his landscape.

She doesn't know much, but Aric doesn't really listen, the pictures are already coming into his mind. Some event held once every four years, once in the Western Hemisphere. The reenactment to end all reenactments, no less. I heard about it, at this place, I don't know where, but at this place, is how she talks. The pictures coming in and moving, becoming real for him. A great open valley, and a hill of course, you gotta have a Golgotha. Actors weeping and screaming out among the audience, scolding and cursing, grabbing people in the crowd from their picnic blanket and spilling their thermos, pointing up the hill to the cross, screaming, "See? See there?! He dies!" They bellow and wail, terrified and gratified, triumphant and small. They spit his name and mock his title with contempt, then rush on to tell others, make them see. A thin, naked man writhes, staring through sweat and thorns, to the sky.

Barrett tapes a letter to the editor on his door, just under the peephole. Someone scribbles over the paper with heavy black marker and tears the page in half. Barrett leaves the article, adds a stick-up memo pad and a pen, COMMENTS WELCOME.

The next morning a piece of cardboard torn from beer packaging is taped over the door, and it states SHUTUP GREENHAIRD FAGOTT.

The letter to the editor, an expression of a young woman's fatigue at being ridiculed for her choice of clothes, lies in urine-soaked shreds on the floor.

Aric takes up Malcolm's hockey stick, finds the balance and grip. Running down the hall, jumping over lounge furniture, mounting stairs three at a time, he cries, "Break things!" Doors open—too late!—he's gone around a corner. He returns, another lap, swinging and slashing, glancing off brick walls. He is everywhere at once, on landings, out of the elevator, cursing the overhead light, barely touching the floor.

Maybe this happens in every detail. Maybe he just sees it all, pictures in the mind. He doesn't play hockey. He sees no difference.

His parents call. They ask him how classes are, how many finals he'll have before the holiday break. Mom says they have put up the bird feeder, but the squirrels keep jumping onto it and tipping it and stealing the seed.

A yellow thresher came the other day. The temperature is dropping. It may snow again soon.

His head is full of stories and movies, wars, and friends.

Then they tell him about the dots. Six little dots the size of pin heads, all in an area less than a bottle cap in the right breast. The doctor wants to do the biopsy next weekend. They tell him she will be an outpatient: admitted in the early morning, released as soon as the anesthesia wears off, they say, probably late afternoon.

He tries to imagine. Barely aware of the phone, he watches out the dorm window, seeing the dark dead sea of the intramural field. Not seeing it. Not seeing this world.

The doctor will go in and extract the dots. They will be sent to a pathologist for tests.

So... they couldn't tell if it was—what is the word... malignant?

No, not until the test results.

He does not ask if he needs to come home.

Little more. Quiet goodbyes. Incomplete.

Jayne comes to tell him about the phone call. From that boy, yes that one. They had a song together. He says, I know that song too, it makes me think of someone, I have the CD but it hurts to play it. Play it, she says, and he does. So they are both crying. They hold each other for a long time. And nothing else happens.

A scratching at the door. Aric says come in. A scratching. Aric throws the door open, light floods in. Niles is crouched on the floor going *meow meow*.

They go in search of Malcolm. The study lounge is empty, but Aric kills the lights and leaps forward, straight into it.

There in the dark, Jayne reports her phone call to Niles. Aric lopes and rolls. He snakes through the chairs and between the cubicles. He creeps over the sofas and along the windows, growling until he forgets words. Every few minutes she stops her story to ask where he is, and gets a snort, a hiss.

The story runs out. They just listen, catch glimpses of him.

The door opens a few times. He hides. They turn and stare.

At midnight, Malcolm happens to check the study lounge.

Is how they are.

Barrett is sitting outside his dorm room polishing his thrift store combat boots with newspapers spread out in front of him when someone kicks him in the face. The back of his head hits the wall. Leah (the woman from the fourth floor who found a bat trapped in her room) is leaving the lounge when she sees someone running off. Barrett on the floor, bleeding from the head.

The hall manager talks with a student from down the hall, one who often wears pro football jerseys and sneaks cases of keenly-price beer into his room. He never admits to anything. They do not say whether he will be expelled or asked to leave the Residence Hall.

Barrett wears a bandage on his broken nose. For weeks he can't stand too suddenly without fainting.

The Psychology lab finally calls. On his first day, Aric mops all the rooms and changes the water three times. He washes the diet pans and wipes out the sinks. Before he can leave, the professor tells him check the cages. One of the guinea pigs is dead. The professor says put it in a garbage sack, fold the opening twice.

The small body is stiff and cold, its pink eyes open. Its mouth pulled back in a smile or a scream or a song.

His parents call to say they are sending a copy of their living wills from the insurance agency. They reviewed it yesterday, in case anything, well, in case anything. He is supposed to read over his and sign it. If he, you know, if he agrees.

He is thinking about Golgotha, not in the way he used to in church. Not a stormy, blood-covered hill of sharp crags, but a rolling soft green space, with thousands of picnicking families. He keeps looking up. And up. Looking like an owl does, wide and watching. The shadow sinks to meet him. But his eyes never reach the top.

He should say, tries to say, he should have gone home, he will think about her this weekend. Dad says he will be praying. They know, but no one says, that Aric has quit going to church.

Sometime past eleven and before midnight.

He is listening to that song again. Curled fetal on the floor, he wants to feel something, anything. He lets it build. Warm and flickering.

Water sprays his face and he sits up. Water sprays his face.

Giggles at the door. He sees through the thin space underneath, an eye watching back. He howls and leaps up and throws open the door. Niles on the hallway floor with a bright green squirt gun.

They wrestle in the hallway, water in their ears and noses, laughing.

Malcolm arrives and plunges in. They are thrown and crushed in slow motion against the walls, dodging with too many expressions, tumbling over and over.

Pro football jerseys and boxer shorts appear down the hallway. Insults are muttered, doors slam.

Barrett's mohawk color is fading. Gotta do blue now, he says. He got the dye from a shop in Detroit, but he needs more peroxide from the drug store.

Barrett drags Aric, and he drags Malcolm, and it takes them ten minutes to walk there. While Barrett gets what he needs, Aric pulls Malcolm over to the toy aisle. The options are orange and pink.

Back at the dorm, they get Jayne. They put her in front of Niles' door. Here, stand here, what for, just knock on the door. He opens the door a crack, and she doesn't know what to say.

Then the three of them get inside, squirt guns blasting.

He goes for his, but it is cracked and the water leaked away. No one calls campus security.

Boxhelder Hall, Second Floor, ENG 209: CRAFT OF POETRY. The adjunct professor divides them into groups of five and gives them ten minutes to analyze a different poem. After recognizing theirs as lyrics to a popular song, Aric's group proclaims they are unable to begin to discuss these words as a poem, since it is obviously a song and therefore incomplete without the music. Aric notices he has been writing with a red ink pen for weeks.

Malcolm grew up nearby, close enough for laundry weekends, and gone again. The others come at sundown. Jayne and Barrett, Niles and more arrive at Room 150 and sit on the beds and floor. Jayne says she's finished the dream king book, but left it in her room. Aric is not done with his reading. The story is growing larger. He doesn't know if he can finish. Sometimes he can pretend he doesn't know what's coming.

The phone rings double, off campus.

Aric stands and goes to the door. The phone is ringing, they tell him, where is he going?

"Gas station." He closes the door.

But he doesn't have a car, someone says. The phone is ringing.

He sees a beast rise up from out of the earth. Winter soil cracks and tumbles away. It has the body of a guinea pig and the head of his mother (the face of which is unmistakably afraid), with the eyes of an owl. Its hair is green, and its tail is made of dental floss. The beast is given a hockey stick with which it will penalize a third of the living (and a third of the waking dead).

Its mark is on its shaved chest, six dots. It laughs like his stereo, leans back on its throne, and he hears a voice like thunder say, "Meow." The beast is given authority to watch as he goes on with his task.

Aric does not run. He bends down. The metal lid grates as he unscrews it, dirt or rust in the threads. Then his fingers go numb. Then he doesn't feel anything else after that.

The phone rings again. Jayne answers. No he's not right now, can she take a message? It is his father, with news about mother's condition, and when will he be back, it is urgent, not bad news, but urgent. Niles is talking, she tells him to shut up—but, no—not you, sir—Mr., uh—Aric's dad. She looks out the window, up and down the street, past the dark of the intramural playing field, to the gas station beyond.

Something moves there, barely visible in the deepness of the night. What's he doing there? The windows open on first floor. She covers the mouthpiece and shouts his name. Just a moment, she will run get him. Carefully she sets down the phone.

Where is she going, they ask, and with his coat? Outside, duh. To get him, duh. Did any of them want to come?

No, it's too cold.

Barrett will come too, he says.

The wind blows fierce across the field. Patches of hard snow litter the ground. Aric stands, looking at the glisten and shine before him.

"Your dad's on the phone," Jayne says, coming closer, wearing his coat. Barrett slightly behind.

"Long distance, man," Barrett says. "What you doin' out here? It's so cold. Geez, man." The smell pickles the air. Something on the ground next to him.

Aric bends down. There's a scratch of sandpaper.

Fire blooms along the ground. The flame grows away from him, branches out, drawing a long line in the dark. It sends out two shorter arms, and the whole shape is there, burning yellow and bright.

Barrett and Jayne leap back.

Aric grabs them each at the shoulders and shakes them. His lips blue and trembling, his eyes unsettled, looking through them. "See? See?!" he says.

Behind him, the giant symbol jumps and waves.

There is no chance to calm or hold him. He runs down the length of the burning line, as the fire reaches his waist, and the rest of his clothes learn the flames.

They scream for him to stop.

At the intersection of the two lines, he pauses and looks at his hands. His sleeves catch, brightness climbing to his neck.

Barrett runs wide and around, his arm up against the heat, yelling.

Jayne shouts to get him out, make him roll, hurry, hurry.

Seeing Barrett coming, Aric runs out of the light.

Barrett dives over, catches his flaming legs and brings him down in a tackle, hugging him, his green hair curls to the scalp, bubbles and disappears

He kicks harder, kicks himself free, he stumbles and runs again.

Jayne comes around the other direction, holding out the coat to smother the brilliance. Scalp smoking, Barrett tries to chase him to her.

But he turns again, running out and away from them, away from everything. Into the darkness, entirely adorned in passion.

Perched

OH, HOW I want to move, to finally stretch my limbs and open my wings. I want to fly. But the boy in the street below stares straight at me. He's been watching for twenty minutes, rocking on his heels, lapping absently on a green lollipop, and he seems utterly incapable of blinking. Move along now, shoo. Scram!

My legs cramp and my tail aches against the cold masonry. Two hundred years we've waited, holding perfectly still, for this day. For the bell toll of noontime, and the end of the vigil. My dry eyeballs sting and I thirst to bend the rules, to simply blink, perhaps furrow my brow at that little pest down there, to bare my teeth. But I refrain. It is not allowed for them to see us move. His mother hovers nearby, lost in conversation with her ear toy. Shoo, says I!

What captivates this child so? Or ails it? Surely he's the only human looking up at this moment. He behaves as though he's never seen one of us.

The others have already departed. I see my siblings far up in the sky, formations flocking north. We'll gather at midnight in the old ring of stones placed by our ancestors, where we'll sing until dawn. The vestibule will open and, finally, we'll go home. The last ones to return.

As if to test me, my horns itch like fire. I grip the parapet, talons piercing limestone. The boy cocks his head with squinted eyes. I suck in a breath and hold it, teeth clenched. Who would know if I cheated? Who watches us, really? I know not who made these bygone rules, or why in our true maker's name we ever agreed to tend this surveillance in the first place.

My gut growls with two centuries of hunger. I could start with those curious eyes of yours, boy. Though I've heard the inner thigh is a delicacy, especially in child meat. I shut out the blasphemous thought, and picture instead the forests of home, letting our one song fill me. I yearn to sing it again, loud enough to make stones bleed.

As I've waited so long, I can wait a few minutes more. The boy will leave soon. Then we'll decamp. I ponder as I have not since I was a pup, what these people will do when we are gone, when the covenant is expired and the last guard are away. Who will protect them now?

I wait here, perched in the same position that I began long ago, with my chin in my hands and my tongue sticking out at this world.

(All That Happens)
Before the Epilogue

THIS IS THE last story before the end.

She was (not yet) dying, but for eight hours a night, every night for the last year, she felt empty. Her dreams had all but ceased. The first weeks she told herself she simply wasn't remembering. Her new job left her little free time, preparing presentations every morning and evening—her mind had no room to retain. True, the position wasn't what she expected, for it bore little resemblance to the job description or anything discussed in the series of five interviews, but leaving in under a year would not look good for her career. Soon she would (have time to) make friends and she wouldn't miss her old job anymore. Soon she would (have time to) enjoy the slightly higher salary. After (there was time) to shop for the required business suit attire, build up her client list, and complete the training certifications.

When she closed her eyes at night and finally (nearly) relaxed, she knew only utter numbing darkness until the morning alarm. After a year of nights in the abyss, she sat up in bed and felt changed. And she was terrified.

She called up one of her old friends, apologizing for the early hour, for not writing or calling for a year, and asked for his theories and advice. They had been out of touch since she had moved away three years prior, but he listened like he always did, and he always knew what to say, and that's why she had called him. He suggested making some simple changes in her routine, taking time for herself, whatever that meant for her, and in his gentle, sincere but firm tone he suggested she seek some counseling. She felt a mounting sorrow that she had left him behind. She promised she would visit, and that was good enough for both of them. In closing, he sounded very serious as he told her exactly what he was going to do, though neither of them would remember what he said.

The nightly emptiness visited her again, but she had to run to work, and stayed very late at the office. And the year got longer. She found herself sitting alone in the break room for lunches, eating in less than ten minutes and shaking with anxiety, as her mind churned about what to do about her dreams. Then she would rush off to her desk to Execute the Plan. She was often the last to leave the office after dark.

One day in the break room she realized how much she wanted a dog and her heart stopped with sadness when she realized, too, that her overpriced apartment complex wouldn't even allow small fish. For eleven more minutes she grew in her mind the idea of buying a gun, thinking and unthinking the thought as she held the spoon in her hand, until she had decided which sporting goods store to patronize on the way home, and envisioned how she would commit the act with the barrel against her chin; it seemed real as she sat there, outside of time, as the last 2 of 6 oz. of apricot yogurt warmed on the spoon in her hand, and she felt her future. She left the office and went straight home without stopping.

The next day at lunchtime she experienced the same waking dream. And the next day. And the next.

She brought her work home on weekends, asked for extra projects, not infrequently slept in her cubicle. This behavior continued for many months as she lived an empty life. And it might have continued for the rest of her life. But she remembered the voice of her friend over the phone and the hold on her broke at once, and she wept with relief and gratitude. She picked up the phone to call him and thank him and say she missed him and how was he doing, but she was so excited to be free that she drove to work even though it was after midnight and filled out a Request for Temporary Leave of Absence. (Had she called, he would not have answered, for he was stuck in the deep pit of horrible muck below an outhouse in a city park, already hoarse from screaming, and trying to climb out with one uninjured arm).

While she had changed, her dreams did not return. This did not immediately cause her distress. She had a plan and faith in herself.

For the first week of her self-prescribed treatment, she listened to relaxation tapes of rhythmic sea-shores and mediation chants of rolling mantras. She began sessions with a dream counselor, yoga teacher, and personal therapist. (She tried to call her friend later to thank him, but she was unable to connect with him and he didn't seem to have any other friends, so no one could tell her that he was in the hospital, and...) It wasn't long before she threw out most of the meditation tapes. Though she did play the sea shore recordings for Buddha, the angel fish she had purchased and sneaked into her apartment in a grocery shopping bag with a distracting loaf of French bread baguette sticking out. (...his family never visited him in the hospital, as his brother didn't judge him but didn't really agree with his lifestyle, and his mother knew in her soul that he was living against everything natural that god intended, and his dad said nothing at all.)

Now she remembers her last dream from years ago. A lavender field and a cinnamon sunset. She hopes to see that place again, to dream it and dwell in it.

She has not seen herself in a mirror in the dark or she would see the scar over her heart—jagged and fatal. Seeing the faint unglow of the old wound might make her remember what happened in that last (final) dream. Then she could save herself from what is coming.

There is a story being written all over the world. (No one is listening.) It is heavy and sharp, but coming out easy. Its shape seems different with each language and personal verve of the tellers, but no single narrator could finish alone, for each one has only a fragment. They are all recording furiously, ignoring work and meals and family and gunfire and storm. Most of them are making the story in their sleep, faster than hand or keyboard or recorder or creative committee with dry erase board in a productive afternoon session and the support of rich and influential producers (who all happen to be on the creative committee, though without ever having written a short story, or finished reading a book, and think Franz Kafka was a minor league pitcher or maybe a brand of energy drink).

No one is more surprised by the story than the tellers and none of them can see the ending.

The fragments will be finished at one time and the story will be the last story to come true.

Stories are becoming imperiled as a species, so they are trying to come to life. This is why it must be done.

The graduate student sat back from his desk and hopelessness overcame him. He wrapped his fingers over his skull and cried. He closed the notebook with the (now abandoned) half-written short story draft. Defeated, he took the next English 112 paper from the pile. In the first paragraph he circled THERE and wrote THEIR, circled IT'S and wrote ITS, and wrote RUN-ON and SENTENCE FRAGMENT. The paper was formatted triple-spaced with two-inch margins.

He thought of something and imagined writing it down. Like a small dream, images of his pen moving, letters forming words making thoughts and visions, the idea itself changing into reality, existing in his mind and on the yellow adhesive memo square.

"Revenge is the sustenance of the world."

He did not write the words, and would never write the story. But he found the words in his mind, and said the words (and they became part of the long story that is being written).

There is one animal who knows the meaning of wish. One creature whose beliefs can alter reality. The owl has been beseeched as a symbol of wisdom and feared as an omen of doom; a bird that has grown into legend as a witness of monumental changes in history. Some or all of these are true, and so there is nothing the owl cannot do. Except laugh. Owls are changing the world daily at their whim, and we cannot notice. They cannot laugh even in their dreaming, and so they hate us for what we can do. They are glaring, hating, changing us.

They are at quiet war.

They love us. Their word for love is hate.

No one makes these rules, it is just how it is.

There is a man who cannot forgive. He has never raised his voice to anyone in his entire career, and is a very reserved character (note the use of this last word). He has worked at thousands of jobs and is, oddly enough, not forgotten by co-workers even years after having moved on. People remember his full name and general appearance—though there is nothing distinct or memorable about his features or presence, physical or otherwise. He has some odd habits, which are recorded here, but go unremembered by his peers; like the way he used to sit alone in the corner of the break room, eating only carrot sticks for lunch. No one seemed to notice he always used the stairwell, never the elevator. If asked, no one would remember his light handshake, the thickness of his glasses, or his forgetful habit of a half-zipped fly. He was (we are allowed to say) very reserved. Even though he could engage in a minimal amount of small talk at company parties, none remember him for the odd nasal (yet melodic) oboe tone of his delivery. No one can say *why* they remember him, though they can picture him exactly, even in the most tedious and/or conceited of minds.

No one remembers his eyes, jet black without pupil, iris, or flaw. No special effects team or artificial intelligence has yet reproduced such pitiless abysmal cavities.

The man does not forgive. He knows lies when he hears them, because he cannot hear truth. His ears cease functioning until a lie is spoken. So he is often deaf for most of the day. But he has learned to hide his condition, adapted his expressions of discussion and interaction into a flawless impromptu process. Holding a full-time job, especially in high level management when he's markedly fatigued, is not a challenge for him. No one has ever even considered he might be hard of hearing. When someone has told ten lies, he quits his employment and moves away to a different city and company.

Hope is no longer a concept he can believe in. There are a few of his kind every century, but he has other unique qualities. For instance, he is the only person alive now who understands time travel. But he is too depressed to go about inventing the necessary machine, sacrificing an owl, or etching the proper symbol into a ginger root.

He will never be in love and he has never cried.

"I want to," he says. ("I hate myself most of all," he says once aloud, but no one is nearby). He is not lying.

All of the dogs tried to get together. They planned their convention three years ahead of time so everyone could put it on their calendar, passing the invitation on through neighborhood bark fests, scent marking, and distinct howls through the forests and deserts and fields. All the dogs in the world soon knew about the Great Gathering at an excellent hotel in Cleveland (Wisconsin).

It is not that owls hate dogs or anything like that, but they failed to tell them that their booked date was scheduled after the Second Flood.

When a kid decided one day (age six) he wanted to be a storyteller, he didn't feel so scared anymore—of the adults, the words he didn't know, the looming dark of the closet, or anything life might present to him. He experienced a day of infinity wherein his entire life became open and full (and simply excellent). He dreamed a million dreams that night. Of dinosaurs, adventure, crazy love, his own children, meeting the aliens, meeting the angels with bottle green fins and mushroom heads, meeting the faces that tumble through time ... and he never really woke up. Instead he took up residence in a dream. (He is the only one of The Few who will live through what is coming).

When he got up the next morning he rode to the drugstore at 8:14 AM (having never touched a bicycle before) without telling his parents (for he wasn't even supposed to cross the street without holding two parents' hands firmly and looking both ways twice) and bought a new notebook with six weeks of allowance from collecting the trash baskets around the house. This notepad was to be his launch site, his portal, his infinite toy chest. When he opened it, he did so very carefully, like a ritual... not breathing, shaking like the flu...

And as he moved toward the future of his life and the stories that would fill him and become history and make worlds themselves, an owl cried in the day-bright sun.

And he wrote something he didn't understand. And he became once more terrified. And wrote no more ever again.

There is a disease (e)merging into the world. No doctor can diagnose the infection, and no victim can feel its invasion, for there are no symptoms. It is a plague of time and chaos. In the event of an outbreak, the victim may change anything they can think of, visualize, or imagine. The infection lasts one night and one day, after which the mind's natural state resets and displaces the invasion. During the sickness, the victim may choose to: become immortal or instantly (h/w)ealthy, or destroy mountains or entire species or stars or everything. Or change the number of natural elements or their smell, or alter history or lottery numbers.

No one has used this power yet, not even in the recklessness of dreams. The primary carrier of this disease is the order Strigiformes, the owl. They transfer it through their stare. They can see into our dreams.

This message is not selling anything. It is designed to scare you.

This is the last story before the end.

A knifemaker has crafted a knife which cuts dreams. He shaped and ground the blade with diligent methodical facility, working without sleep every night for a year in a lightless workshop until its completion. It is a fierce and matchless weapon—though it should not exist. But he had to create this. For, you see, he has such terrible nightmares that he was driven to cut them out and, if they were the type who could survive outside, kill them.

After honing and sharpening, he takes the knife with him upstairs, enters his musty bedroom, turns off the lamp, and collapses on his dusty bed. He sneezes three times and falls asleep in the light.

The tool looks like an empty handle, handsome and detailed. A comfortable grip for the average hand size, and perfectly balanced just past the hilt. The blade can only be seen with closed eyes.

It is (a year ago, it is) now.

He is walking through a lavender field alongside a cinnamon sunset, toward the hissing steaming cave closet of the Beast So Scary, a creature that can be heard sucking The Love of Pretending out of children's skulls. The knifemaker grips his weapon firmly, and closes his eyes so he can enter the cave. Then he hears a woman scream. And he opens his eyes again. Again.

Exactly seven minutes later, having just entered and immediately exited REM sleep, he bounds out of bed and runs through the dark, not stubbing his toes on any chair legs, door frames, or cabinetry, and locks the bloody knife in the fireproof depository safe, with The Knife That Cuts Time.

As head of Rager Records, Steve "Rager" Simmons convinced his marketing team to convince 107 formerly successful music recording artists to divorce their spouses and leave their children and come out of retirement and sign a new contract, whereupon twenty-two bands and their original lineups would each record a *Greatest Hits Vol. 1 (of 1)* featuring Your Favorite Classics and Bonus Tracks of New Material. Album sales went Plutonium (1 billion units sold) and all stadium sport events including bat-and-ball, ball-over-net, equestrian, flying disc, competitive dancing, toss the egg, and dirt clod fight were canceled for the next ten years to make way for the week-long Rager UltraHugeMongous Rock Fest North American tour.

Consequently, all other categories of music were stripped from store shelves and digital downloads to make way for the exclusively sold Rager Records label material. Every radio station went off the air for a week and returned to play a continuous cycle of Classic Rock with material from the new distributor. Even though millions of people remarked, "I hate the new 101.9 FM, why can't they be like the old one?" they continued to listen on a daily basis. Personal music collections were reduced to a slim stack of twenty-two discs or tapes or downloads or lick tabs, thus fulfilling the Sixth Sign Before the Second Flood as there came about the utter extinction of all other types of music (including but not limited to: Hard Rock, Lo Fi, Cow Punk, Lava Metal, Psychobilly, Meteor Dirt, Breakbeat, Flip Hop, Jangle Pop, Vociferbeat, Rotcore, Unbeat, Math Smash, Hard Bop, Key Jangle, Dixieland, Bleach Blues, Groan Fuss, Honky Tonk, Anti-Folk, Doo Wop, Yawp Stomp, Big Hoot, G-Funk, Spore Puff, Motown, Tundra Grind, Reggae, Doom Pluck, Ska, Crumblecore, Afro Beat, Mandrake, Ballroom, Slip Hip, Opera, and Infomercial Soundtrack). After Rager Records succeeded in hostile takeover of several major entertainment and communications corporations, the US Department of Justice filed an antitrust lawsuit, but the company issued a press release with the words, "We only want to return to how things were."

One day, a tall stranger in a long dark (coat?) walked into the glass tower of Rager Records International, across the vast echoing front lobby and undetected through the security gate, rode the elevator to the sixty-fourth floor penthouse office, and pulled out Steve Simmons' heart, remarking, "I know about lies. Believe me—I do. But I'm utterly taxed with people not making the least attempt at understanding the difference between a story and a lie." The stranger dropped the warm organ into the nearby document shredder, while its owner reached out desperately as though he could catch what was once his and make use of it again. Steve "Rager" Simmons exhaled his final breath and stared at the departing mysterious figure, and died as the murderer whispered to the immobilized bodyguards, "No one can truly be their own boss, but that doesn't mean you shouldn't try."

A receptionist at the lobby greeting counter noticed (but didn't tell anyone) how the stranger's walk across the buffed marble floor reminded her of a horse in a graceful trot, and how she glimpsed the twitching of an anxious forked tail sneaking out from under the dark (coat?). She also noticed (but didn't tell anyone) how, after he moved through the revolving door (counter-clockwise against the motor), he regarded the sky for a moment, then rose up into it, without propulsion or visible assistance. She didn't tell anyone because she understood a few things very suddenly, and was glad she had taken the pill after that one foolish night with Simmons. And forgiving herself allowed her to stand up and rise too through the smog, straight into joy and not too much later find true love.

(Every morning) the woman without dreams drinks a nutri-shake instant breakfast and does 45 minutes of video-led aerobics before showering. Back at work she keeps 10-hour days. Some nights she watches TV until she's ready to go to bed. Most nights. All nights.

She is living the life of someone else, but doesn't know it yet.

There is this guy at work. He's started bringing his lunches and eating in the corner of the break room. A quiet guy. He makes her smile. Someday he will look at her. She hopes.

But doesn't know it. Yet.

There is a species of fungus that grows only in dreams, only while one is falling from a great height. The violet spotted toadstool smells of cold wind and sings like a bird trapped underground, and you must pluck it from the side of the cliff or tower or dragon or floating city as you plummet, and close your eyes to consume the mushroom in the dark of the dark. Doing so will not wake you before striking bottom, but you will have experienced something different and a lingering numbness of the tongue.

This is the last story before the end.

There is a killer they will never catch. They could catch him. But they, as many, just don't Get It. (Insert note here: most of them do not want to.) They follow him and take pictures of what he's done, of what's left. He likes children best. He sets them Free, he says. He does not know the word *knife* or the word *blood*, but knows he likes to watch them move. Things should move fast, he says, fast and sharp. He will never know boredom. Until he is Done. Until the end. He has forgotten the words *why* and *pain*. Which makes his work easier. And fun.

The agents of the usual department are pursuing relentlessly, trying to Make Some Headway, or to Get a Solid Lead... but it is not their fault he will never be caught or stop what he does (until the end, don't forget). Not their fault, except that they are ignorant of the simple idea that names are stories and their department name is dry and therefore quite powerless. Except maybe that they believe time is Real and therefore too short to attend a new name. They always arrive (too) late on the scene—a week, a day, an hour—sneaking and smashing into the shed warehouse locker room garage apartment elevator to the thick smell and gathering cloud of flies. They inspect the scene with all adherence to procedure and compare pieces throughout the night. Finding a lot, finding nothing. Trying with honesty now, as if it just occurred to them. Trying uselessly.

The killer is on the news every night. Every witness sketch is different, but it is always him. It can no longer be helped. There have been too many stories. In the competition for ratings and sales, the newspapers and TV stations and media outlets have given him too many names and faces. They have run too many (what they call) stories, too many specials about the woman who claimed she went to high school with him (and he was always alone, I mean always, and always talking to himself, I'm pretty sure, I think, I didn't know the guy at all, really, he was so quiet) and the man who claimed he sold him a medium chai from the espresso stand, and the "authentic" letters (concocted by a content committee that does not understand *story* and *lie*), the professionals who gave their assessment of his mental state while worrying about how large their name and title appear in the on-screen caption below, and hoping the makeup person didn't put too much powder on their neck.

Now he will never die. Not even at The End, as he ushers it in.

There are four authentic letters from the killer so far. The one signed, "Yours Truly," has a bottle ring stain of ginger beer in the paper. All four of the real letters are return addressed "From Hell." But none of the forensics team does much reading anymore. And the forensic lab misses the ring too because they get Caught Up in a discussion about the smoothness of the digitally animated walruses in the new corporate cola commercial. It is a lengthy and distracting discussion for sure, but no one comments on how the same cola corporation's holdings in some colonized countries caused people across the ocean to disbelieve stories of oppression and racial cleansing, and prolonged by decades the election of the first indigenous leader, and an ending to many lies. But that is a different story.

"Another flood," states one of the four authenticated letters. "But bigger this time. And red."

All they would have to do to catch him is say his real name and he will come running back to the lamp post and let them tag him without touching home base and the long game of history which is hate and kill and lies and darkness will be done. Or at least someone else will be *it* until The End.

He thinks his life is a dream. He has never told a lie. His eyes are pure opaque white. But he can see.

A dog is writing one of these stories. The one about how The Devil is real but left the planet a long time ago, and all the fear that we ever have about anything is a deep archetype, the same (and originator) to the loss-denial reaction resultant from most split-parent families and failed early relationships. (Some editors consider that this particular manuscript would be shelved under Non-Fiction, or Self-Help.) The Devil had two dogs. They were the first dogs to feel love, and they often pretended to fight, because they didn't want their owner to feel jealous, and they really did care about his feelings (not the same love they felt for one another). The Devil never named his pets, and they have long since forgiven him for that (they did not tell him, they just assumed he knew).

These dogs are still alive. They can talk, but choose not to. Fifty-four languages (six now known only to them). They are rather upset by unbearably slow progress and periodic cancellation of the space program. But every day feels unbelievable and stark, as it does when you're In Love.

This one doesn't count. Only stories are allowed. And this entry is historical record.

The agents of the old department are pretending everyone still listens to them, that they do not need to change. They have always used the word "god" once a week at the morning ritual, while avoiding it in reference to themselves. They are of the opinion that *time* is Real too (a reference to the first question in the agent entrance exam) so they are too busy with schedules and projects to learn the simple idea that names are actually stories, much less that stories are the only existence. So they would not believe you if you told them they are creating the killer.

(Another month goes by). The dreams have not returned, but she has learned to Live With It. She takes a few accrued vacation days and spends them eating snack chips with a foam-like feel while watching daytime television. The same characters are on the daytime soap shows that she watched between classes at college and when her mother watched years before, but some of them are played by different people now.

On the third day, she gets out of the house, and goes out to Fall In Love. She comes into a bar and sits at the stool for almost two hours, drinks the nightly special, and loses some pronunciation of her words.

The man she meets is pleasant and feels safe, though it is difficult to see his eyes in the dimmed loud establishment. He doesn't talk much from the time they leave the bar together until the time he leaves her apartment a few hours later. She doesn't feel like saying anything throughout the whole Act, but hears herself coaching him and complimenting him on what he does right and how good it feels, and realizes during their intercourse that her fish died yesterday and she had meant to take Buddha to the park today and bury him, or at least flush him before he started to stink.

When he is done (47 seconds later) and snoring, she stares into the dark, not asleep.

He tries to don his clothes, but she's wide awake and watching him and says his name before he can even get one leg into his pants. He is so unnerved by it that he takes his clothes and dresses in some other room, the bathroom or kitchen. And never comes back in to say good-bye.

She is surprised to feel nothing about the experience. She is not tired at all, and thinks she could go into the office and get ahead on work.

The agents of the new department aren't pursuing relentlessly at all. They are swollen and grounded with pride at how clever they are to have come up with a new name. They are sitting and spinning in swivel chairs in the state-of-the-art headquarters which only allows them entry by scanning their palms and retinas, talking about how great it would be to sell the movie rights to their new name and what famous actor would play them, not really even listening to each other, talking and changing the screen saver animations on their department computers.

And when The End comes, they will drown no less painlessly in the red, reaching for another chance, for a gasp of air.

There is a word common to all (current/future/lost) languages. It is the word and sound an owl makes laughing. It cannot be written (shaping the characters breaks the hand or melts keyboards), only delivered vocally. Saying the word grants the deepest of desires. In the entire history of the world only six people have used the magic word, all issuing it by complete accident. All were storytellers. They all asked for Love or Revenge. But they were lying to themselves and to the magic. Their hearts turned away from them because what they really wanted was The End. And they will get it very soon.

These sound like rules. They were not made, but they exist, and they cannot be changed. Like stories, they happen.

There is a boy who will never grow up. He will remain eight years old until the end comes, while his parents move from thirty-six to forty-eight. (This has been done before, yes, but this one is For Real.) The day after his eighth birthday he went with his friend to the monthly flea market, and his friend's mom drove them. There he purchased a custom-made knife with a handle carved like a bird wing. His friend was jealous that he saw it first, and asked the seller if he had any more like it.

"Just one."

"Will you make any more?"

"Not like that," said the knifemaker. And he wouldn't answer when the boy asked him why not. (The knifemaker did not dislike children, but a killer had recently abducted his daughter and threatened to dice her up unless he sold one of his special knives to a little boy. [The killer did not tell the knifemaker why the boy should not die, or that he would not be returning his daughter, or that he would be coming for the knifemaker as he Must Do So for everyone until it is All Done.])

Neither of the boys could believe he was selling this knife for two dollars.

The boy had to hide the knife in his coat when he got home and told his parents he didn't find anything and had saved his money. Luckily his friend's mom had not seen him buy the knife, but he had to let his friend hold the knife whenever he wanted to, or his parents would find out. His parents had many rules and always seemed to be making more, but one he knew well was they were not A Family That Keeps Weapons in the House.

He woke in the middle of the night, in a silence without rain, bird noises, or water pipe rumbles. He woke very fast, without sitting up, and won't ever remember because he felt like a different person, like someone who had lived a very long time.

He said into the night, "I am real now." Which had no significance at all to the moment or the story that was his life, but it made him feel true, and his existence legitimate.

He had cut his finger on the knife while hiding it under his pillows.

This is one of the ways to begin an ending.

There is a commercial on network television. It airs only once. Lovingly and meticulously etched dark owls perch in their gnarled midnight tree and stare with uncanny eyes straight into the souls of everyone watching and everyone not watching, dreaming or not; and hum the rising music of Greig's "In the Hall of the Mountain King" from his *Peer Gynt* suites. The final kettle drum down beat slams the company logo across a black screen:

JACK'S GINGER BEER

THE BEVERAGE WITH A BITE OF TRUTH.

BREWED IN GNAW BONE, INDIANA.

It does not matter if the word *soul* makes you wince, or if you refuse to believe in the existence of what the word often implies. The owls can still see what they are looking for.

There is no record of the commercial having aired or being submitted, and no recordings were made.

There is one monster in all the world. It has thousands of teeth, and eyes that burn the color of loathing within a sharp ring of anger. The monster eats babies and kittens and peanut butter and honey locust thorns and lint and boysenberry syrup warmed by the cupful. It lives in a different closet every night. Its tail is made of shark skin and earwig pincer and hedge apple and pineapple and dull scroll saw blades and dead bee legs, and it drags it around behind its completely indescribable body like a tiny mountain, smearing its waste because it is always hungry, always eating children, and itself, born without a stomach, always shitting. It lives under the bed too. It has eight arms; six of them real, three with claws. It knows prayers and curses in every language. It knows the song which is your own kept inside that you cannot whistle or tabulate but can only feel. It has no taste buds. It is most hateful because it doesn't like its own name. You'd be none too happy either if your name was Fear.

This is the last story before the end.

There is a job opening. They do not care which school you attended, or if you finished your degree. They do not care if you are a People Person, if you believe the customer is Always Right, if you've had 1.5 years industry experience or equivalent. Do not bother with a tie, or to shave, or to remove any jewelry or piercings, or unbraid your hair. They see you as you are. They are not an equal opportunity employer. You do not need to go in for the interview, they can see you from here.

Do not try to lie to them by pretending to be excited about and solely devoted to the position that is open, that you can smile on your feet all day, or that you believe neck ties are an indication of anything at all whatsoever.

They will not call you back. You will know if you got the job.

A tip: it is not rude to ask questions, only senseless.

If you are not willing to work for nothing, you really don't Get It.

Bring your lunch tomorrow. The dress code is Truth. Ties are optional.

———

There is a man who loves everyone. He stated this fact in the middle of a televised street poll about his opinion of the guilt or innocence of a national sports celebrity movie star to the charge of murder. And when he said what he said, all the people in the entire world stopped what they were doing and shuddered and blinked and shivered, feeling the very alien sensation of Truth for the merest moment. He added to this statement of unequivocal love that (he knew for a fact there is no higher power, not anymore, only ourselves to take care of things). He failed to answer the poll question.

He is one of The Few. But he will not make it to The End.

In that second moment, everyone on the planet stopped again, (shuddered again), lost all sense of sight or hearing, and screamed. (Coincidentally, all the owls laughed at this time, but no one noticed.) Despite their inability to see or hear the man on the television, many people claimed they remembered him and what he said. Of course, no one truly knew what he had said, but that did not stop them believing what they wanted to. While a number of dictators, parliaments, presidents, and princesses merely made dismissive comments about the man's remark, endless media discussion filled ten weeks of around-the-clock news about the controversial incident until several of the wealthier movie and sports celebrities hired assassins to hunt down this terrorist and execute him.

He whistles. Never the same tune twice.

———

An excerpt from THE EPILOGUE:

A mountain is the last island, the only land in the endless red. Those Who Could Not Die for one reason or another come silently across the scarlet sea in makeshift crafts, or kicking with a floating scrap of plastic under their arms, or just paddling through the still thick ocean of blood, until they slide up to the shore, only to be greeted by the killer who will shake hands in polite greeting with a penetratingly authentic manner of concern, and welcome them out of the growing night, to a warm seat by the campfire where he has already roasted some owls. After feeding the visitors, he waits patiently as they weep and rubs their back, squeezes their shoulder, until they are finished crying (for now). No one among The Few says anything cruel or paranoid, for they don't know how any of this happened or his role in it (nor does he remember), as he blinks his deep white eyes (which no one comments on) and begins a new story, hoping to make the night feel somehow smaller.

There is a bomb that burns dreams. It splashes into your sleep landscape, a reaching wave of viscous fear, and lights itself instantly, spreading cruel hot unflames. Several governments and even more companies under contract have been trying to find and duplicate the weapon for many decades. They say it fits inside a common soda can. It is the only weapon ever fully designed by a woman or child. She made it one night (age eleven) and has been trying to think of the reason why for the last ten years. She does not pray at night, but speaks the reasons aloud in the dark, sometimes with strong defiance, but more often as wavering questions. She says, "It was necessary..." "...It was an accident..." "...Just in case..." "...Out of love..." "...For revenge..." "...For a hobby..." "...Because I can..." "...I was young and reckless and silly..." "...I am really sorry..." "...I'm not sorry at all."

More people are killed each year (so far) by accidentally inhaling too much cinnamon than are killed by this dream weapon. Its exact recipe is unknown, but some ingredients may include: baking soda, ginger, cilantro, milk, owl urine, mandrake root, eye crust, and kerosene (for smell).

In late September of that year, Steve "Rager" Simmons who would always see himself as an all-star high school quarterback (but never as a rapist of three cheerleaders) managed to write his first piece of fiction for a beginning college English class (which was supposed to teach basic skills of composition and secondarily emphasize proper termpaper formatting without the bibliographical portion... but the instructor was a graduate student who had wanted to teach a senior writing workshop instead, and had submitted a decoy syllabus for the English Department Head). The story was Inspired By Simmons' first college party not one week previous, whereat someone had put a four-CD set of Classic Rock music in the compact disc changer, and all 20+ people in that dorm room suite had consumed beer and played air guitar until 4:00 AM (despite protest by neighboring students who were trying to read Franz Kafka's story "The Hunger Artist" and write an essay for tomorrow's assignment).

Needless to say, what Steve Simmons wrote was not really a story at all—barely a few sentences in excessively large font and line spacing that described a world in the Not Too Distant Future wherein all the great bands that ever broke up in the 1970s and 1980s reunited and sold more albums than they(/or anyone!) ever had sold before, and went on tours that every person in the world managed to see. "And the world partied forever after," Steve S. wrote at the end halfway down the second page.

When the instructor wrote UNORIGINAL and YOU CAN DO BETTER IF YOU TRY NEXT TIME and gave the student an F on the assignment, Steve Simmons tried to argue that no one had any right to rate or criticize his original work, that Art Is Just Art. Shortly after, Steve Simmons transferred to another English 112 class scheduled at the same time even though the College of Arts and Sciences didn't usually listen to grievances for Personal Differences, but the Department Head didn't want any Delicate Situations during recent scrutiny from the alumni and boosters about creative writing programs.

By his fourth year of college, Simmons declared a Business Administration major. He managed to never again write anything in his lifetime (by hiring students who were not granted financial assistance to write his college papers, co-workers to write his monthly reports, secretaries to write his business correspondence, and independent designers [none of whom he paid] to make his presentations); to date rape seven heavily drugged young women; to stalk with his drinking friends into the city park known to be a gay meetup location and severely beat and break a man's collarbone and dump him through the hole in an outhouse pit latrine; to consume 7,592 servings of low quality beer in five years; to make regular donations to a politician who founded secluded work farms for various ethnic groups; and to become founder and CEO of an extremely profitable music label only two years after finishing college.

For the first time on the planet, there appears a small fruiting of particular violet spotted mushroom caps. This occurs on a remote island previously covered by ice, and they whistle a quiet song but no one sees or hears their succinct impossible visit.

This is the last story before The End.

PUBLICATION HISTORY

THE STORIES IN this volume originally appeared in the publications listed below. They are collected here as the author's preferred texts.

"Another Country Doctor" first published in *See the Elephant*, Issue 1, edited by Melanie Lamaga, (Metaphysical Circus Press, 2015).

"Occupations" first published in *Crossed Genres*, Issue 26, edited by Jaym Gates and Natania Barron, (Crossed Genres Publications, 2011), and reprinted in *Crossed Genres Quarterly 01*, (2011).

"One Wicker Day" first published in *Abyss & Apex*, Issue 26, edited by Wendy S. Delmater, (2008).

"Adrift" first published in *Every Day Fiction*, edited by Camille Gooderham Campbell, (2009).

"The Crimson Codex" first published in *Bibliotheca Fantastica*, edited by Don Pizarro and Claude Lalumière, (Dagan Books, 2013).

"Among the Stacks" first published in *Ink-Filled Page*, edited by Ali Shaw, (Indigo Editing & Publications, 2009), and reprinted in *Ink-filled Page: Red Anthology*, (2009).

"Immigrant" first published in *A Darke Phantastique: Encounters with the Uncanny and Other Magical Realities* edited by Jason V. Brock, (Cycatrix Press, 2014).

"Block Party" first published in *On Spec*, Issue 87 vol 23 no 4, edited by Diane L. Walton, (The Copper Pig Writers' Society, 2012).

"A Salmon Tale, 2072" first published in *Fish*, edited by Carrie Cuinn and K.V. Taylor, (Dagan Books, 2013).

"The Circus Wagon" first published by Damnation Books, edited by Stephanie Parent, (Damnation Books, LLC, 2010).

"One Childhood of Many" first published in *Daily Science Fiction*, edited by Michele-Lee Barasso and Jonathan Laden, (2012).

"Ina's Day" first published in *Space Tramps: Full-Throttle Space Tales, Volume 5*, edited by Jennifer Brozek, (Flying Pen Press, 2011).

"Brink City" audio first published in *Toasted Cake* podcast, Issue 140, edited by Tina Connolly, (2015).

"They Shall Flourish and Spread" first published in *Crossed Genres*, Issue 5, edited by Kay T. Holt & Bart Leib, (Crossed Genres Publications, 2013), and reprinted in *Crossed Genres Magazine 2.0 Book One*, (2013).

"Studies in Light and Dark" first published (as "The Best Year of My Life") in *Fragment*, Issue 1, edited by Neil Ayers, (2003).

"Perched" first published in *The Pedestal*, Issue 61, edited by John Amen, (2010).

"But a Moment Ago" first published in *A Fly in Amber*, Issue 10, edited by Shelly Jackson, (2009).

"(All That Happens) Before the Epilogue" first published in *Fantastic Metropolis*, February 2002, edited by Luis Rodriguez, and reprinted in *Breaking Windows: A Fantastic Metropolis Sampler*, (Prime Books, 2003).

The following stories are original to this volume:
"Elizabeth's Duty"
"Stationed at the Breach"
"Little Bodies"
"With Busier Days Ahead"
"Cheating the Devil"
"Her Scent Along the River"
"Unfinished Painting of Empty Classroom"
"Revisitation"

ACKNOWLEDGEMENTS

FOR THE EXISTENCE of this book, I am extremely grateful to everyone involved in its manifestation. Thank you to Scarlett R. Algee for giving the manuscript a home at Trepidatio Publishing along with editing and support, to Mikio Murakami for the extraordinary cover and story artwork. To all those who read advance copies and said kind words, thank you.

My sincere thanks to all the original editors and publishers who gave some of these stories their first outing.

Many thanks to the Indigenous tribes and nations who helped me with knowledge about traditional language and practices, including Malissa Minthorn-Winks at Tamástlikt Cultural Institute and Confederated Tribes of the Umatilla Indian Reservation, and Thomas Gregory aka Tátlo at the Nez Perce Language Program. Also many thanks to everyone who worked on two books about Nch'i Wàna (Columbia River)-area Tribes, *Ichishkíin Sinwit Yakama / Yakima Sahaptin Dictionary* by elder speaker and linguist Dr. Virginia R. Beavert and Sharon L. Hargus; and *Cáw Pawá Láakni / They Are Not Forgotten* by Eugene S. Hunn, E. Thomas Morning Owl, Phillip E. Cash Cash, and Jennifer Karson Engum. These books are built by so many people, and remain a snapshot of culture and knowledge that reaches back to time immemorial.

Writing is lonely work, so I could not do this without the colleagues and compeers who provided years of support and critique, inspiration and encouragement. All of you who introduced books and people, attended readings, and made for a welcome and inspiring community at conventions and writing retreats and online—and for your friendship, thank you. Natania

Barron, Laird Barron, Nadia Bulkin, Kealan Patrick Burke, Brian and Gwen Callahan, Nathan Carson, Selena Chambers, Curtis C. Chen, Tina Connolly, Ellen Datlow, Kristi DeMeester, Amanda Downum, Brian Evenson, Gemma Files, Jaym Gates, Shanna Germain, Cody Goodfellow, Orrin Grey, Michael Griffin, Gwendolyn Kiste, Mary Robinette Kowal, Claude Lalumière, David D. Levine, Ross E. Lockhart, Usman T. Malick, Anya Martin, Silvia Moreno-Garcia, Scott Nicolay, Arley Sorg, Patrick Swenson, Molly Tanzer, E. Catherine Tobler, Zandra Renwick, Wendy N. Wagner, Damien Angelica Walters, A.C. Wise, and everyone I have missed.

Thank you to all the authors who created stories that kept me in wonder and fright from my earliest reading experiences. Clive Barker, Ray Bradbury, Octavia E. Butler, Ursula K. Le Guin, Shirley Jackson, Jorge Luis Borges, Toni Morrison, Rod Serling, Gene Wolfe, and so many more.

Great thanks to the artists who have etched horrifying enthralling depictions into my imagination, thank you to Hieronymous Bosch, Leonora Carrington, Francisco Goya, H.R. Giger, Zdzisław Beksiński, Käthe Kollwitz, and I could go on.

Many thanks to all the authors I've worked with through *3LBE* magazine, for your tremendous stories and dedication.

A few of these stories go back, not as far as trilobites or even as far as the first dreadful pieces I scribbled, but I cannot thank enough the teachers in my starting years who encouraged me and took extra time: Jeff Lane, Mary Dickinson, Marly Swick, Richard Messer, Barbara MacMillian, and the rest. And to those who said remove the emotions and don't write about imaginary things, I wish you a good day.

Thank you to good friends along the way, from the parks and playgrounds, making music, playing Ultimate, climbing rocks and mountains, cocktails and board games and movie nights.

To my family, near and far, here and gone, thank you from my heart. For you have always been here with unfailing love and support.

And to you the reader, thank you for visiting these places and characters with me.

ANDREW S. FULLER writes strange and scary stories that have appeared in magazines, anthologies, comics, and short films, and this is his first fiction collection. Since 1999, he has served as Editor of *Three-Lobed Burning Eye* magazine, publishing stories by many authors. He grew up Nebraska and other places, climbing trees and reading books, dabbling in archery and metal music, and now lives in Portland, Oregon with his spouse and pets, not far from rivers and forests and a few extinct(?) volcanoes. Find him online at andrewsfuller.com, and on social media as @andrewsfuller.

CPSIA information can be obtained
at www.ICGtesting.com
Printed in the USA
JSHW021936070523
41371JS00003B/13